REBEL TOUCH

"I am not one of your Scotland ladies who would swoon at your slightest touch. I am a frontier woman who must fend for herself and can't afford such silliness." Krista pulled her blanket tighter around her, as if to thwart the tinglings of anticipation that burst within her at the very mention of Gavin kissing her.

Tender fingers traced the line of her quivering jaw. Krista's heart nearly tumbled over within her chest.

"You're nae afraid of me, are ye, lassie?"

"I fear no man. Life has taught me right good about that." So why was her blood leaping and spiraling through her veins? "I can fight and shoot and ride as well as any of you."

Laying his rifle aside, Gavin reached for Krista and pulled her gently into his arms. She would have moved away, resisted, but for the smoldering gaze that held her transfixed. "Ye've my respect as a guide and frontiersman, Krista Lindstrom. But ye've much to learn about bein' a woman, much I long to teach ye."

"You have much to learn about—"

Gavin's lips grazed Krista's, gently coaxing. "We'll teach each other." He eased the rifle out of her hand, letting it fall to the ground. "Ye see, we've nay place to go now, but together."

GW00492911

LINDA COVINGTON

LIBERTY'S FLAME

ZEBRA BOOKS
KENSINGTON PUBLISHING CORP.

ZEBRA BOOKS are published by

Kensington Publishing Corp.
850 Third Avenue
New York, NY 10022

Zebra and the Z logo Reg. U.S. Pat. & TM Off. The Love-
gram logo is a trademark of Kensington Publishing Corp.

First Printing: September, 1994

Printed in the United States of America

Part One

There is na' past to beckon me
To Scotland's bonnie shores
Nay bridges than can span the sea
For love that burns na' more

For darkness seeks to still my heart
And lost I seem to be
In savage wilds where thunder sparks
The flames of liberty.

—Linda Covington

Chapter One

Pennsylvania Frontier 1778

Gavin Duncan staggered through the dense forest that covered the wild terrain of the west Alleghany banks. At least the Alleghany was the river the tall Scot sought. His training as a surveyor told him that there he might get his bearings. His sense of survival told him he must.

Taking a fresh breath to fortify himself for the next climb, he clasped his wounded side and threw his six-foot-two frame forward. Tree branches, stiffening for the winter that was rapidly approaching, raked through his reddish brown hair and scratched his bearded face without mercy. Briars lashed out at the sinewy length of leg exposed by the filthy tartan of his clan, some burying into its coarsely woven cloth to assail him later.

Ordinarily, such things would only prove a petty nuisance to a seasoned highland hunter such as himself, but today was different. Aside from the seeping wound in his side, dealt him by the Tory captain he had been assigned to serve with, he was in a foreign land where even the hills themselves seemed bent on driving him out. God in heaven, it was a heathen place that made his beloved highlands look tame in comparison!

Yet, there was something about it that had made him agree to leave Detroit with Captain Messick after his commission as lieutenant in His Majesty's army had expired. Something that had gotten into his blood and urged him along, knowing full well that a surveyor and mapmaker was little more than a showpiece for the odd assembly of Loyalists bent on taking the Pennsylvania frontier back from those traitors who had driven them out. The host of Indians who accompanied their regiment could find their way through hell blindfolded, as far as Gavin was concerned. And hell was exactly where they'd taken him.

The smoke from the bloodbath he'd narrowly escaped still permeated his clothing. But it was the stench of death and burning flesh that still made his stomach queasy. That and weakness from loss of blood. Cold-blooded murder, that's what it had been. That little settlement had been manned, if one could call it that, mostly by old men, women and children. Messick, however, planned the attack with the Iroquois chief as if it had contained a full regiment of trained fighting men and, when the blockhouse fell after an admirable show of courage, turned the savages loose to do their will.

The Indians had, thank God, made quick work of the women and children. Their hacked and mutilated bodies lay scattered about unseeing while the surviving men had been stripped naked and bound to a tree that had also been stripped down to serve as a stake. Marked for death with black painted faces, the victims had been forced to endure unspeakable torment while a fire, laid to burn slowly, flamed at their feet.

Their manhood was to be the prize, explained one of the militia men who seemed to take a feral delight in the activity. That was why the Indians had left a scalplock of hair on their shaven heads, for the convenience of the one who took them in battle. Convinced that no human being should bear such degradation—the burning coals tossed at their bare flesh, the smoldering sticks poked into their bodies—Gavin put a quick end to their misery with his pistols and musket, stilling the hellish frenzy to a deadly silence.

He should have been frightened out of his wits at the demonic eyes that swung his way in disbelief and rapidly flashed into outrage. His certainty that his "civilized" companions would come to his aid faltered as he heard the man at his side cry out in indignation.

"Fool, you've denied them their prize!"

Gavin turned in time to see Messick's pistol smoke and feel the tearing fire that ripped into his side.

" 'E's done you a favor, sir, an' no doubt about it!" another voice echoed somewhere behind him as he reeled backward, crashing to the damp ground.

There was no chance to reply, no opportunity to curse the bloody lot of them, for suddenly, the trees around the entire clearing erupted with explosion after powder-burning explosion and his consciousness began to fog. All he could remember was running, running for his life as he had never run before, and leaving Messick and his men to whatever hostile force, be it more heathens or colonials, that had materialized from nowhere.

Now he was a fugitive, a man without a friend in a hostile land. Whether Messick and his men considered him a traitor or deserter was of little consequence. Death was the penalty. His means of making a living, his guns, all his belongings were left behind, along with what was left of the embittered life that had led him to enlist in the army and come to the colonies to start with.

Stumbling over an exposed root, Gavin grabbed for a low hanging branch of pine at the top of the incline and broke his fall, somewhat sparing his already bloodied knees as they dug into the prickly fall blanket of multi-colored leaves and needles. Gold, he thought, picking a maple leaf and trying to focus on it. Damn Claire and the golden tresses that tempted his fingers every moment she was about. The leaf tumbled from his hand to land next to another, red like the lips that tasted sweet as God's own nectar and promised heaven with calculating lies. And green, he mused acidly, thumbing the evergreen needles of his crutch. Green as the poison of jealousy spawned from her rejection of his love that even now left a bilious taste in his mouth.

A wave of nausea washed over him and all the colors swirled. He leaned over the branch, uncertain of his balance, and heaved to no avail. His stomach had had no sustenance aside from a few berries since yesterday. Or was it the day before? He wiped his brow with his tartan and inhaled deeply, fighting the unconsciousness that hovered around him like a vulture, waiting for the wound to get the best of him. Part of him wanted to give it its way, but there was another stubborn side that stiffened his legs, raising his body upright again.

Rest, he thought foggily. If only he could rest. Perhaps if he climbed up in the safety of a tree, he might take a few moments respite. A few. Then his mind might clear sufficiently to decide properly if he should continue to try to live or let this untamed wilderness have its way with him. Perhaps the deed of mercy that had brought him to this end might avail him in the same way. The branches rustled as he settled with the grace of a beleagered bear into a more or less comfortable crook. A broken branch poked at his side and he winced ruefully. Mercy? God's teeth, there was nothing merciful about this land!

* * *

At the edge of the isolated creek leading to the main river, Krista Lindstrom froze and glanced sharply at the forested crest that sloped down to the water. Her hands leaving the undone laces of her fringed buckskin shirt, she lifted her rifle from the bank and took cover behind a rock. Sharp blue eyes scanned the treeline from under the flat brim of her beaver hat, noting the gentle swaying treetops against the clear and equally blue sky. It could have been a dead branch falling, she supposed uneasily. Sometimes the lower limbs cushioned its descent, rustling as they did so.

Cautious by nature, Krista leaned back against the rock and situated herself as comfortably as possible. She would wait a few moments. After all, she didn't have to be back at the tavern until tomorrow and the hunting shack was but half a mile away. Since this was likely the warmest it was going to get before winter fell hard upon them, she was determined to take advantage of the break in the weather and bathe in the river. The black caterpillars promised a harsh cold season and the blackbirds seconded their sign. Snow was coming and soon, warm weather or no.

By now, she would ordinarily be on her way up into the mountains with her partner to trap furs for the winter, but he had broken a leg while repairing his cabin roof and trapping was out for him this year. That meant she'd have to trap along the local rivers and creeks and hunt food for the tavern this winter to make up for the income she normally brought to the family with her skins.

She hadn't done badly already, she thought, glancing at the bundle of fresh skins she had to show for her two weeks away. Properly dried, they'd fetch fair price at Fort Pitt. And with luck, she'd have a deer tomorrow, which meant she'd have to ride back out to the hunting cabin with her horse to fetch it.

It wasn't fair that her stepfather made her leave the horse she had paid for with her own money at the tavern by the ferry downriver. It was as if he thought she'd take it and run away, something she could easily do at any time if she were of a mind to. But then, her stepfather had done little to make her life easy since her mother had married the man ten years prior. Perhaps that was why she could never bring herself to call him Papa as her younger sister Marta did.

Krista looked at her calloused hands with a half smile that tugged at her wind-rouged lips. No one would ever believe they were once soft and well manicured, accustomed to playing the harp and harpsichord. Nor would one believe from her worn buckskins that she had once owned gowns of the finest cloth and frequently entertained guests in their Vienna townhouse with the talent her composer father had declared a gift. She was the adored darling of Joseph Lindstrom's contemporaries as well as the aristocracy which supported the arts.

That was another time, however, before her widowed mother was forced to wed the German merchant from the colonies to provide for her two young daughters. Today, she would have to content herself with the sheer luxury of the bath and wearing clean clothing, something she could only do when she was in the woods at the hunting cabin she sometimes shared with her trapping partner Uncle Kurt and his wife. The rest of the time, she wore her filthy buckskin and dabbed on fish oil to keep her stepfather and men like him away.

Ja, it would be a welcome change, Krista thought wistfully, to a girl who remembered the feel of fine clothes against her skin and once knew a ritual of cleanliness inspired by her Scandinavian grandmother. While she wouldn't call the cornflower lindsey-woolsey dress in her knapsack fine by Vienna standards, it was the only one she had. And it was clean, which was more than she could say for her buckskins.

Convinced that the rustling sound proved no threat and taking another look around to be certain, Krista climbed to her feet and started once again to undress. Gooseflesh pimpled all over as her lithe body was bared to the crisp fall air and her small round breasts drew into taut peaked globes, firm and upthrust. She stepped into the cold water and exhaled heavily in an attempt to cope with the shock.

Winter bathing was something her uncle Kurt, an ex-Finnish soldier, had introduced her to after complaining about the smell of the fish oil, so Krista immediately set about scrubbing with the soap her aunt Eva had made her and attacked the stench of her two weeks in the wilderness, trapping and hunting. The Indian woman had scented it with a pleasing mixture of herbs and spices, not sickeningly sweet like the cheap flowery perfumes Widow Ames wore when she vied for Herr Schuyler's attention.

Krista's movements were hurried, for, although she was accustomed to cold water baths, it didn't mean that she luxuriated in them as she did in the summer. After sudsing the length of hair she'd unbraided and rubbing it vigorously between her hands, she took another deep breath and plunged beneath the water to rinse for the last time. Moments later, having shaken the last of the soap from her squeaky tresses, she bolted upright to her feet and proceeded to quickly wring out the wet golden cape that clung to her neck and back as far down as her waist. Then, eager to reach the shore where she'd left a rough muslin towel to dry herself, she rushed out of the water, emerging from the depths like a nymph gilded by the sun.

Suddenly, as she bent over to snatch up the towel, a terrible crashing sound echoed from the top of the hill, followed by an anguished bellow. Her gaze flew to one of the tall stately pines shaking decidedly out of sync with the gentle wave of its companions and she gasped. Whatever it was was barreling down the steep slope and parting brush at incredible speed.

Fearing a berserk bear, for no Indian would ever launch such an attack, Krista fumbled frantically to secure the towel around her slender form and fell into a defensive position behind the rock. Shivering, she lifted her rifle over the edge and aimed at the fast-moving foliage and brush, her breath all but frozen as she waited for the creature to emerge.

It seemed like an eternity before the angry charge stopped and when it did, Krista could hardly register the sudden silence for the pounding of her heart. Why did it stop? she wondered, moistening her lips as she peered in the thicket of short pine at the base of the hill where the animal had suddenly halted.

Silence. Krista debated whether to call out or wait until the beast made its decision to continue with its attack or go away. She tested the wind. It was a good thing she was on the downward side. She sniffed, bemused. Pine. Pine and what? she pondered thoughtfully. Moving closer to her rifle, she sniffed again. Gunpowder, she decided, and sweat—like that of a two-legged beast in great need of a bath.

One brow arched, etched golden against her brow. Now what was he up to? Never taking her eyes from the thicket, which had yet to betray movement of any sort, she reached for her knapsack, her buckskins too far away to obtain, and drew out her muslin petticoat. If she was to fight some wooly bearded mountaineer, by thunder, she'd not do so stark naked. Taking her hands away from the gun, she tugged the petticoat on and returned them. Still no sign of movement.

How long had the man been there? Some of the blood

that had pounded in her ears invaded her cheeks. Had he watched her bathe and then charged lustfully down the slope to take her, only to trip and fall? Her lips thinned. Right good thing, she mused laconically. Maybe he had knocked himself out. Emboldened by her speculation, she raised up and peered over the edge of her cover. It was as still as the painting of the woods cottage her mother had brought with them from Vienna, the one that reminded Mary Lindstrom Shuyler of her childhood home.

Krista shivered, becoming aware for the first time since she'd heard the noise of just how chilled she was. Cautiously, she pulled her blue dress out of the sack and, keeping watch with one eye, donned it rapidly. Although her skirt was still entangled with her shift, she paid little heed. Instead, she picked up her gun once more and, brushing her wet locks behind her shoulders, eased out of the cover to step into her moccasin boots without lacing them.

Maybe it was one of the big knives, as the Indians had dubbed the frontiersmen, either deserting or on his way to join up with one of the recruiting parties that had been in the area. And maybe the fool had killed himself, she speculated breathlessly. Or perhaps he was lying in wait for her. Parting the low growing branches with the barrel of her rifle, Krista stepped into the thicket cautiously. Whatever or whoever he was, he'd stopped somewhere ahead.

A flash of color caught the corner of her eye. Krista slowly eased her rifle around a clump of birch to see the inanimate object more clearly. As she neared it, her suspicion was confirmed. It was no bear, but a man almost as big as one, judging from the path of broken young trees and brush he'd left behind him. Her bottom lip caught in her teeth and trigger finger ready, she approached him silently but for the rustle of her skirt against drying brush.

"Thor's thunder!" she whispered under her breath, coming to a halt at the foot of the unconscious man sprawled before a jut of rocks that had broken his fall.

A wooly beard in a skirt! True, she had heard some of the Scot Irish in the region speak of wearing skirts, but none of them had the nerve to wear one in the backwoods country. This one appeared to have had the nerve but not the good sense to go with it, Krista observed, her gaze traveling up the long length of exposed legs, bloodied and covered with dirt, to see all that nature had endowed the beast with. Skirt or no, there was no doubt he was all man.

Her neck burning at her inadvertent discovery, she quickly tossed a remnant of the plaid cloth over his loins and fixed her attention on his chest. A large patch of scarlet clung to him, browning on the edge to indicate the wound was not new, but seeping fresh around a dark hole where the bullet had torn through the linen, taking some of the material with it into the wound.

Forgetting her embarrassment and apprehension, Krista dropped beside him and placed sensitive fingers at his neck. He was alive, at least for now, but he wouldn't live long if the bleeding were not staunched. She felt under his back to discover another larger hole, wet with warm blood, where the bullet had exited. At least there was no lead to dig out, she mused. It was clean.

It never crossed her mind not to help the man. White or red, it didn't matter, Uncle Kurt had once told her. A good deed was always rewarded. Some day it could be her or someone she loved in need of a stranger's help. Besides, in his condition, the unlucky traveler was no longer a threat.

After fashioning a travois of sorts from two poles she cut and tied together with a blanket and rope, Krista started to roll the man onto it when he began to stir. She stilled as wild piercing eyes the color of dark whiskey stared up at her and then closed again, as if in relief. His mumblings making no sense, she tugged on his sinewy arms and legs until he was in position and then took up the poles. The travois made moving him easier, but once again Krista wished for her horse and damned Gunter Schuyler.

Nonetheless, her strength was sufficient to make the trek to the cabin and get him inside. Lifting his limp body upon the bed was yet another proposition that left her panting and spent. She'd helped Gunter Schuyler with drunken trappers at the tavern, but swore a bear would have been easier to handle than the man sprawled on the cot. At least she could have skinned and dressed it to lighten the load.

She dragged herself up from the floor where she'd fallen upon heaving the stranger's long legs and hips on the cot and added kindling to the embers she'd banked that morning in the hearth. She'd need hot water to clean the wound and, if she was going to remain in the same cabin with the man, he would have a bath before the rapidly approaching night was out.

As she suspected, the injury was only a flesh wound. Provided fever didn't set in, a man of his strength and size would be up and about in very little time. What he needed more than anything was rest and sustenance. Perhaps after she bathed him, she'd be able to get him to take some of the mush she'd made that morning.

Upon washing the dried blood and dirt off his face, she discovered her patient was much younger than she'd first thought. A few years her senior, she guessed, once the rich color of his russet hair and beard was rid of the dust that had dulled its sheen. Further bathing revealed him to be as good a specimen of man as she had ever seen, not that she had seen many men quite as intimately.

As she moved her soaped cloth over the bristle of his legs as far as she dared, for there were some things he

would have to recover enough to wash himself, she could
not help but admire the long muscled limbs that contrib-
uted to a height equal to her own, if not more. The same
bristle, only longer, grew in a triangular mat on the chest
which she exposed by cutting open the front of his shirt.
It swirled amidst ridges of hard flesh and around the dark
constricted areolas, almost tempting her to toy with it in
idle fancy.

So intrigued was she that Krista failed to see the large
hand that reached out and buried itself in her hair. With
a startled cry, Krista moved to pull away, only to have the
hold tighten firmly, but gently.

"Now what would ye be doin' here, lassie? Dinna tell
me Duncan Brae is'na fine enough for ye now."

Krista stared at the whiskey eyes burning into her face,
cursing herself for her uncharacteristic distraction. Her
gun was by the door, out of reach and of no use. "I am
trying to help you, good sir," she managed, forcing a calm
in her voice she was far from feeling. Unaware that it was
not suspicion but the lilting upswing of her accent, the
way some of her words ended in a beguiling "ingk"
sound, that caused her patient's brow to arch, she mus-
tered her bravado. "I have dressed your wound and
bathed you thus far. If you will let loose my hair, I will
now feed you. You are hungry, ja?" The soft "V" sound
of her W's narrowed the gaze fixed on her face. *"Hungry,*
yes?" Krista repeated, wondering at the confusion that
settled in its simmering depths. The tension on her hair
released and she jumped to her feet and stepped away
quickly before the man changed his mind.

"Where am I?"

Gratefully, the penetrating gaze shifted to look around
the cabin.

"My . . . my home," she stammered.

"Where's your husband?"

"I . . ." Krista caught herself. Better he think she did not live alone. "He is hunting, but I am able to defend myself . . . especially against a man in your weak condition."

The man on the cot closed his eyes and sighed tiredly. "Ye need nae fear the likes of me, lassie, in this condition or otherwise. The truth is, I'm obliged to ye. Ye put me to mind of a guardian angel with hair of . . ."

Krista stepped closer as his words faded away. His lips were slightly parted and his breathing slow and even. Between them was just the slightest glimpse of the white even teeth she'd seen bared in a grimace of pain as she struggled to get him onto the bed. Strong, handsome, wealthy enough to wear a gold broach with his family crest on it . . . and no doubt married.

Startled by the girlish speculation that suddenly invaded her invariably practical nature, she grabbed the washbowl and dirty towels in a flushed dither. One would think she'd never seen a man before, the way she was acting! She had, and plenty of them. It was hard to live in the wilderness and not run across the need to have a bullet dug out or a knife wound stitched. Uncle Kurt had taught her to do both well. Plenty men, she sniffed, indignant for reasons beyond her comprehension.

But none had ever said she resembled a guardian angel, an inner voice ventured. She wavered, glancing back at the bearded stranger, now covered with a blanket to keep off the chill of the night air. She'd let him rest while she warmed over the mush and then, perhaps, she'd discover how he came to be wounded. Finding out who he was and what business he had here was far more important than discovering if he had a wife.

Chapter Two

The first thing that registered in Gavin Duncan's fatigue-dulled mind was that the cabin was much warmer than it had been earlier. Perhaps the woman had returned and built the fire up—the tall lithe creature in cornflower blue with eyes to match who smelled of fresh air and spices. He would have done so himself, but the druglike effects of sleep claimed him in the midst of his considering it.

He wondered if her husband was home, for he smelled cherry tobacco in the room. She had said that she was married, hadn't she? It was hard for him to separate dream from reality. All he knew was that he had passed out in hell and awakened in a warm bed with an angel tending to him—an angel who had shared her bed and warmth with him. Hair raised at the back of his neck as he considered the consequences in relation to the tobacco smoke. When had the husband returned?

He opened his eyes a crack as his senses began to clear. Near the hearth where a tempting roast of venison turned on a rope dangling over the fire, three men sat and conversed in low tones. They were more of the type that accompanied Messick, clad in buckskins and ragged clothing that many of the poorer families on Duncan Brae would turn their nose up at. Their rifles lay within easy reach against the stone end wall of the cabin. More voices drew his attention to where three other men were entering the door, each with a turn of wood. But where was the girl?

"Tarnation, Cap'n, close that there door a'fore ya freeze ma ass through to the bone."

The man in buckskins and epaulletts grinned. "It's gettin' a might brisk at that. Our friend in the skirt stirred yet?"

Gavin closed his eyes and forced his breathing to remain normal as the focus of attention shifted to him. They weren't Messick's men, so they had to be colonials. He was too weak to groan aloud, but his silent misery was just as intense. He'd fallen asleep in the arms of an angel and awakened in enemy hands. Unless he'd dreamed her.

A sharp finger dug into Gavin's rib cage, bringing his eyes open with a start to see the peculiar captain standing over him curiously. He'd moved so quietly across the dirt floor that Gavin had had no inkling he was there. "Well, Scottie boy, think you'll make it?"

Gavin struggled with his senses. "I have so far, thanks to your good wife."

"Wife!" The incredulity in the man's voice gave way to a guffaw of laughter which his friends echoed.

"Your daughter then," Gavin ventured warily.

"You been outta your head, boy. I know I need a hair cut something awful, but I sure as hell don't look like a woman."

The brass buttons on the man's coat strained as he bellowed again and snatched up a jug of liquor from the bench where his comrades sat to help himself. Its odor assaulted Gavin's nose as it spilled out of the corners of the colonial's mouth and down the front of his open animal fur vest. If he could but get his head clear, the whiskey could afford the chance Gavin needed to escape.

"Perhaps I was dreaming, sir."

She'd seemed so real—tall, slender, and fair, a gentle creature with skin like alabaster and hair like gold as she dipped into the cold water of the creek. The very sight of her emerging like a nymph not of this earth, cloaked in the blanket of her wet locks, took away Gavin's breath and cost him his balance. He remembered the pain of falling and then awakening in the cabin to find her dressed in simple homespun and caring for him with gentle concern. She was the first sign of gentility in an otherwise heathen land—an angel who had lifted him temporarily from hell.

"How'd ya get yourself shot?"

The abrupt question interrupted his reverie and struck Gavin across the face with reality. "Stupidity."

Again the room rocked with laughter at his expense, but he never blinked. He should have returned home with his regiment when his commission expired, not volunteered to help a half heathen militia. But what the hell? He had no life to speak of back at Duncan Brae. He was a second son and a second choice in love.

The devil take it all, he swore silently, forcing himself up on his elbow. He was still man and not about to lie still while the likes of these made sport with him. Gavin ignored the pain it cost to continue on up to his feet, but continue he did until he looked down at the stocky back-woodsman squared off in front of him. The tension in the room grew thick as the others took in his swaying towering frame and belligerent countenance. Hands moved within easy reach of a weapon, lest he cut loose the thunder building on it.

"Na doubt, ye'll be askin' me name, so I'll be askin' in return for a drink of that brew ye've spilled down your belly before I oblige ye with another word."

Gavin accepted the jug silently offered him and took a

healthy swallow. The homemade liquor set his insides on fire, scorching its way from his mouth to his gut, but the tightening of his jaw was the only inkling he gave of his distaste. He wiped his lips with the back of his hand and recorked the bottle before handing it back to his wary host.

"'Tis the first sign of hospitality this godforsaken place has shown." A rustle of speculative snickers broke out as he absently brushed his tartan straight and tucked the long reddish hair that had escaped his queue behind his ear. "And I'm scarcely fit to accept it. I thank ye for it and the use of your cabin and the dressing of the wound."

"We got us a gentleman amongst us, complete with skirt and scarf!" the crude captain exclaimed with a wry twist of his lips. He turned his back on the Scot to share his humor with his companions.

Gavin felt the fire of the liquor seep into his blood as he straightened to his full height and, with a dangerously crooked smile, tapped the man on the shoulder. "You're speakin' to Gavin Duncan, second son of Duncan Brae and proud to be wearin' the clan's tartan and kilt. If ye've doubt as to the mettle o' the man beneath this, perhaps this will remove it with all due haste."

The unorthodox military man never saw the fist coming until it crashed into his jaw like an anvil of flesh and bone. His head snapped back with the impact and he could have sworn his feet cleared the dirt floor before its power left him sprawled on it in a daze. He touched his jawbone tentatively as his five companions leaped at the tartan-clad giant with eyes of fury straight from hell.

Like an angry bull, the Scot roared and charged through them, taking them halfway across the room before collapsing on the floor underneath them. He still managed to kick one across the room, sending him crashing into the door, while slinging a second assailant nearly into the hearth fire with a powerful arm before the other three were able to pin him, panting and sweating beneath them.

Rubbing his jaw, Tucker Hardy gave the dangerously pale man glaring up at him thoughtful appraisal. "All muscle, fist, and wind, but amight short 'a mudder wit, ain't he, fellas?"

Gavin grunted as his head was jerked back by its thick locks and a long hunting knife was pressed against his pulsing throat. What sort of game were they playing with him? If they'd intended to kill him, they struck him as the sort that would have made quick work of it.

"Supposin' I tell *you* how you come to be shot, Gavin Duncan."

"I might be able to give ye better attention if your friend would put away his dirk."

"What'd he call me?" A red bearded man almost as tall as Gavin himself declared indignantly.

"That's Scot's lingo for knife, Tull," Hardy explained patiently. "You promise to act civilized if I call off my men?"

"I'll hear nothin' about me kilt. My ancestors have fought and died bravely in the tartan for centuries."

The leader of the group lifted one skeptical brow. "It don't appear to me you're in a position to be makin' demands, Scottie boy, especially since we saw you shoot Ben Kiley and his oldest boy."

Gavin's face grew impassive. "They were sufferin' at the hand o' savages."

"Your savages," the man with the knife sneered, his blade cold against Gavin's throat.

"God strike me now, they were not mine!" A shudder coursed through the Scot's body at the very thought. "And if ye saw me shoot the poor bastards, then ye also ken t'was the Tory militia that did the same to me for puttin' an end to that blackhearted torture."

Captain Hardy squatted down and peered thoughtfully at their prisoner. "I ain't one to speak for a Tory, boy, but if yer cap'n hadn't done it, the Indians would'a demanded you take the captives' place."

"There's none left to tell of it now, save your men, is there?"

"Ye've a keen sense of how it goes, Scottie boy," Hardy replied, confirming Gavin's suspicion.

Gavin couldn't help but glance around him with renewed awe. Six in all had taken twenty-five? What manner of men were they?

"The question is, what was you doin' with 'em? You ain't got the look of a soldier."

"Neither do you."

Those holding Gavin down allowed the corners of their mouths to twitch, admiring the Scot's spunk for all the seriousness of his current plight, but Captain Hardy snorted out loud and pushed himself to his feet. "I'll not argue that, boy, but I'll still hear what you was doin' with Messick and his cutthroats."

Aware that all eyes in the cabin were fixed on him, Gavin exhaled heavily. "Tis a long story, sir, some of which I don't understand meself."

Hardy picked up the jug he'd dropped when the Scot had punched him and placed it on the small stretcher table next to the hearth. "Well, the liquor didn't spill, there's fresh roast venison over the fire and we've got the bounce of the night to hear it." He waved his hand at the men holding the prisoner down. "Let him up men, but for the love of Jesus, don't say nothin' about his skirt!"

Gavin ignored the hand stretched out to assist him to his feet and clenched his jaw to hide the pain ripping at his side as he shoved himself upright and made a show of brushing off the dirt. "You're a fair enough host, sir."

The leader of the group took a swill of liquor and passed the jug to Gavin as he peered up at him through narrowed eyes. "I ain't exactly made up my mind what you are, Scottie boy, but will a'fore the night's out."

And he would know whether or not this was his final dance with death, Gavin mused dourly. Not that he cared any more. He'd courted it boldly since he'd received the letter announcing his brother's marriage to Claire. Leaving Detroit with Messick and his heathens was just the beginning. Now that he'd stood face to face with it for the last couple of days, he found he was no longer intimidated. At least the liquor was passing fair and his prospective parting company an interesting lot.

The inn, which was the destination of Gavin's harddrinking and boisterous companions the following day, stood at the bottom of a gentle slope by the river crossing. It was tidy in appearance, with a well-defined yard and stacks of firewood piled high and neatly near the back door of the attached out-kitchen and the main building. There was a barn in immaculate condition to accommodate the horses of weary travelers, and a sharp pitched roof and the catslide off the back suggested the possibility of an upstairs room.

Hanging between two posts in the front was a sign with a military personage, who had once represented King George on a white horse. Now, however, the scarlet coat had been retouched with blue and buff to represent Colonel Washington. The lettering—Schuyler's Crossing—remained the same, indicating it was only the political affiliation and not the owner that had changed.

The delicious scent of roasting meat wafted through the

air to entice prospective guests, but Gavin Duncan's stomach churned threateningly. The good rum and Scotch whiskey to which he'd been accustomed had never assaulted him with such viciousness as the corn liquor he'd shared with his newfound friends and companions. His head hurt worse than his side and his mouth was so dry, he kept having to dislodge his tongue from sticking to the sides and roof.

"Ah, smells like another feast of venison, Scottie boy! Maybe your appetite will pick up for some good German cookin'!"

Gavin all but stumbled from the hearty blow Captain Hardy gave him and cast him a scathing look. "Have a heart, Captain, I'm a sick man!"

"Humph!" Tull Crockett snorted at Gavin's elbow. "I'd hate like hell to wrestle ya, if'n you was well!"

The rest of the men joined in a general round of amusement that almost brought a smile to Gavin's pale face. Through the course of the night, he'd discovered they were a good lot, for all their rough ways. They liked to laugh, hunt, fight, and wench, not necessarily in that order, and above all they resented being told how to live in a country by people who had never set foot in it.

They weren't cultured or educated in a European sense, but their opinions had made an impression on Gavin. Because they took a stand for what they believed in, they were like Gavin now—without a country. He'd never thought of colonials before as anything but traitors. Now, in the King's eye, so was he—not because he resented the Crown, but because he didn't believe what the Crown sanctioned was right. Although he hadn't realized it, at that split second when he'd put those poor souls out of their misery, he had switched sides.

"Politics be damned, right was right!" he had declared

the prior evening, struggling to remain upright at the table as the others cheered him on.

Just before he passed out, he'd felt the slam of Captain Hardy's rock hard hand against his back and heard the old codger taunt, "We was wonderin' how long it would take for that thick Scot head of yours to reckon you was one of us."

He'd been recruited into Colonel Clark's command. With nothing left to go home to, Gavin saw no reason to object. That morning, they'd shoved coffee at him strong enough to hair over a scalded hog and handed him a familiar leather case with his initials engraved on it containing the surveying tools he'd left behind at Messick's camp.

"That Finn Walters said they was a shorter cut through the mountains to Kaskaskia and we could use a real mapmaker to mark it on paper so's we kin get a good supply route goin'."

"How do you know you can trust me?"

Gavin would never forget the drilling look Captain Hardy gave him with those steel-gray eyes that were almost hidden under his thick bushy brows.

"Because, Scottie boy, right is right, and while you're a might long on reckless and short'a mudder wit, you're no fool."

When they reached the rutted yard in front of the tavern, a tall gangly lad whose face was hidden under the brim of a worn beaver hat took the horses and nodded mutely at Hardy's instructions to see them fed and bedded down in the barn. Gavin was so preoccupied with his throbbing head that he failed to notice the way the lad stared at him, although his companions did not. They smothered their snickers politely, however, and ushered him into the building.

There was one long room inside its wide plank door. At

one end was a shallow fireplace used mostly for heating water and keeping the guests comfortable. Short extensions of stone protruding from its face called hobnobs provided extra seating for those who liked to gather about the fire and spin tales on a cold evening. A small door to one side indicated a narrow passage to the upstairs loft. The fireplace belonging to the larger chimney Gavin had noted outside must be in the back kitchen where the cooking was done, he mused, not the least tempted by the added scent of freshly baked bread. The ride on the back of one of his companions' mules and his liquor-induced misery, combined with his weakness, had made him ready for a bed, no matter how hard or ill-placed.

"What you need, Scottie boy, is a hair a' the dog what bit ya!" the captain announced, slamming Gavin's back again, this time nearly costing the unsteady Scot his balance. "A round of hill brew, if ye've got it, good sir!" he shouted, oblivious to Gavin's groan as he addressed the burly innkeeper eyeing them from behind the raised wooden grate of the tap room.

"You vill be staying the night?"

"If this is a friendly enough place and the liquor's good."

"Then you vill pay two shillinks a man for all you vish to eat, drink, sleep, and stable your horses."

"Nary a break for men devoted to keepin' the Injuns from liftin' your scalp?" Captain Hardy retorted indignantly.

The innkeeper gave a short humorless laugh. "A man has himself and a family to keep until they do. A place in the barn with the horses and one goot meal wit beer is half."

"You sure you ain't one of Georgie's Hessians?"

"I am only a poor innkeeper wit two unmarried daughters to support who vill see your coin or ask you to leave."

The appearance of a blunderbuss at the man's ample waist wiped the good-natured smile off Hardy's face.

"I heard you was a stingy old bastard, Herr Schuyler, and damned if it weren't the truth! Pay 'im, Tull."

Schuyler's eyes took on a greedy glint as he watched the tall backwoodsman approach the taproom counter. "Says who!"

"Says a trapper named Walters!"

This time the the innkeeper's girth shook with genuine amusement. "Waltari, my goot man," he corrected. "My brother-in-law."

"We'll have a round of your best liquor . . ."

"Beer for me," Gavin corrected, uncertain even that would be acceptable to his disrupted state of health.

"You're a mountain man now, Scottie boy, and we all drink alike."

"Marta!"

At the innkeeper's shout, a pretty young woman dashed in from a back room to stand at attention while her father slapped an earthenware jug and a stack of wood noggins on the counter. Her round cheeks were as rosy as her braided hair was flaxen, giving her a cherubic look that was belied by the full figure that filled out her shift and waistcoat.

"By thunder, might be you only need to support one girl from what I see," Hardy shouted, nudging Gavin's side with his elbow. "Now don't think somethin' like that wouldn't ease your mind over that high-class wife of yer brother's."

Gavin opened one eye to see the young woman approaching them, her wide blue gaze fixed on him in curiosity. She was easy to look at and possessed a wholesome look that could stir a man's blood and make him ashamed at the same time, but a woman was the last thing he needed at the moment.

"What we have here is a Scot with more money than good sense. Got him a castle in Scotland he does."

Gavin groaned inwardly as he caught a glimpse of lighting interest in the innkeeper's watchful eye. "The man's given to exaggeration and fancy, but, if I were half what he said, I'd not be good enough for this lovely lassie." He summoned a smile as the girl set down a noggin of corn liquor in front of him. She wasn't the lithesome creature he'd come to believe had only been a dream, but she was fair to look at. "And if you're as kind as ye are lovely, I'd be grateful for a loaf of that bread I smell bakin'."

"Ya, sure!" Marta Schuyler giggled as he took her hand and brushed it with his lips. She finished serving the others, but her laughing blue eyes kept dancing back to him in such a way as to evoke a response the Scot wouldn't have thought possible.

Gavin downed the liquor and winced at its bite. Maybe Hardy was right about the hair of the dog, he mused, his gaze following the tavern maid's retreating figure through the door that led to the kitchen. A bit of bread for strength and he just might feel like a man again, instead of a miserable invalid. He coughed as Hardy elbowed him again and laughed.

"Damned it that ain't the first bit a' life I've seen in our new volunteer this mornin'! Have another, Scottie boy."

The others joined in the amusement and Gavin grinned himself. He did feel alive, although it took a flirtatious tavern wench to make him realize it. He sipped the liquor this time, for already he could feel it racing into his bloodstream and easing the discomfort he'd suffered since being shaken out of the cot at sun up that morning. How long had it been since he'd shared a woman's warmth?

It was the night before his comrades in His Majesty's

Fifth left for home, their commissions expired like his. There had been an officer's party and the camp women had been invited. The rum made them more attractive by the time the night was out and . . .

"Have you a name, sir?"

The lamplit scene vanished at the lilting intrusion of his thought. "Lieu . . ." Gavin caught himself. That was behind him now—his impeccable military record and his life at Duncan Brae. "Duncan, Gavin Duncan, fraulein."

"Your bread, Herr Duncan."

"Thank . . ." Gavin's breath caught as Captain Hardy delivered another punch to his ribs. He smiled at the girl and stomped heavily on Hardy's moccasined foot as he finished with a strained, ". . . you."

"Damn me, Scottie boy, them English boots is hard on a man's foot."

"That blasted elbow of yours is'na doin' me ribs a lot of good, man, and I'll stand no more of it!"

Assuming an injured look, Captain Hardy pulled away from the long stretcher table where he and his men had taken a seat. "Well, I've got business with the good innkeeper, so hold onto your skirts till I get back!" At Gavin's dark look, Hardy slapped him on the back and laughed. "Hell's bells, Scottie boy, even your thick head ought to figure out ye're going to be needin' something with more substance for the journey ahead. A set o' buckskins'll not only save what counts as a man, but spare ye a goodly amount of funnin' and fightin', so just sit tight and enjoy the company till ma dickerin' with Herr Schuyler's done."

With face flushed as deeply as her cheeks, Marta Schuyler burst into the kitchen where the tall buckskin-clad figure who had seen to the men's horses fed the cookfire. It was one thing to have a handsome gentleman at the inn, and in her mind the gallant Gavin Duncan was just that, but for her sister Krista to rush into the house and show interest in him was more than her matchmaking heart could stand. She'd never seen her elder sibling so breathless.

"His name is Gavin Duncan and I think under that beard he is quite handsome! How do you know him?"

Krista Lindstrom continued to stare into the fire, waiting for the sparks to settle before she added more wood. "I didn't say I knew him. I said he looked familiar. I must have been mistaken. The name means nothing."

"I think he caught your eye in the yard and you are curious to know more about him," Marta surmised smugly. "Can it be my big sister has finally met a man to measure up to Uncle Kurt's example?"

Krista's mouth thinned with impatience. If her sister only knew, she thought. When she'd left him in the cabin and gone to discuss her quandary over having spent the night nursing the enemy, she thought that was the end of it. When Uncle Kurt told her that there were big knives from Virginia looking for a guide to Kaskaskia, she'd been elated that he'd suggested her in his place and given the Tory little more thought. Here was the chance she'd been waiting for to get away from Herr Schuyler for the winter months.

Excitement had made it nearly impossible to sleep and in the silence of the cabin her mind was given to wandering. However, the burly Scot intruded. He'd been fevered and mumbled a lot, something about a woman called Claire. He'd caught Krista by surprise and kissed her, although Krista did not think it was an endearing gesture. Whoever the woman was, she'd angered the Scot. And when the man realized his mistake in a fleeting moment of coherency, he'd called her an angel of mercy, sent to deliver him from hell. The way he'd said it, his burning gaze fixed upon her in some sort of sinful worship, still made her shiver, but not with cold. It was with something entirely foreign to her.

"I am not one of your man-crazy friends, Marta. My attention is better applied to more productive things," Krista announced, denying her sister's charge and that nervous flutter warming her insides. Listen to her, she thought in annoyance, trying to ignore her physical reaction. Never did she ever think she'd resort to using the same argument her stepfather had given her when he'd destroyed her harp. At least she had the fire to blame for her burning red face as she rose to look down at the sister, who was a full head shorter. "You've been listening to Herr Schuyler too much."

"You spend so much time with Uncle Kurt and his wife. It's unnatural. You were there last night, weren't you? Wasn't that why you were a day late in coming home?"

Krista loved her little sister dearly, but sometimes Herr Schuyler's influence on Marta made her as difficult to tolerate as their stepfather, who was always accusing Krista of having more than a business relationship with Kurt Waltari. The disgusting things the man suggested were unnatural and now he was dirtying her sister's mind with them!

"He is twenty years my elder! I have told you before that I love and respect Uncle Kurt as our uncle and my business partner. I respect or care for no one more except you, liebchen, and Mama when she was living. But I do not feel toward any man the way you do about Russell Vandercliff."

"If not for Russell, I would feel toward Herr Duncan like a woman should feel for a man."

Krista rolled her eyes heavenward. Marta was pretty and sweet, but lacking in common sense where men were concerned. Matching her to Russell Vandercliff was one of the few things Krista and her stepfather agreed on. The squire could take care of someone like Marta, who would always need a man to look out for her.

"I'm going out to the barn. The hay wagon needs to be unloaded so Mr. Shreeves can take it back with him tomorrow."

"Don't you ever get lonely, Krista?"

Krista paused at the door thoughtfully. "Not often," she replied, adding wistfully, "and if I had a harp, I would never feel alone." Oh, how the instrument had been the last ray of sunshine in a life darkened by her father's death. It was almost as though Herr Lindstrom had been taken from her again, this time by her stepfather.

"You will never forgive Papa, will you?"

Krista's pale blue gaze steeled. "No." Upon seeing the distress that settled on her younger sister's face, she softened it. "But I am grateful to him that he has been kind to you, as if you were his own daughter."

"You could have been treated the same way."

"No, Marta. I am Joseph Lindstrom's daughter and Herr Schuyler's indentured servant."

"Krista!"

The slamming of the door was the only answer Krista gave to her sister's protest. She had spoken the truth. There was no love lost between her and her stepfather. She only did his will because, until Marta was married and out of his grasp, she felt obliged to. She had paid her and her sister's way since their mother's death, working around the inn, trapping with Uncle Kurt. After Marta was gone, however, she would owe him nothing.

The guests spent the rest of the daylight hours eating and drinking, so that when evening fell, Krista could hear their boisterous singing and laughter out in the barn where she'd burrowed a small hole in the newly stacked hay to think. Once, when the noise grew particularly

loud, she glanced out to see a tall figure that could be no
other than the Scot, swinging a giggling Marta around to
the clapping and stomping of his companions. As she had
thought, he had recovered quickly enough.

What was she going to do now? The Tory, and there
was no doubt he was one, considering his ramblings about
his orders, was now traveling with the colonial recruiters
as one of them! To reveal his true political affiliation
would only lead to further questions as to how she came
to know about them. She couldn't risk admitting to helping the enemy, especially in front of her stepfather. Herr
Schuyler would make everyone around him miserable
with his violent temper, for he hated the British.

But to say nothing, she realized, would make her an
accomplice, although a reluctant one, in whatever his
purpose for joining the group was. To think that *this* was
what she'd rushed back from the hills for! Never in her
wildest imaginings did she think the Scot would join the
Big Knives Uncle Kurt had told her about. She'd left him
to fate, although well provisioned in as humanitarian a
fashion as possible. Now fate had tossed him back at her.

"Krista?"

Krista rose effortlessly from her perch in the hay as
Marta, wrapped in a woolen shawl, stepped inside the
dark barn with a lantern. Marta's face brightened when
she made out her sister's tall form against the haystack.

"Papa says that you are to come in and meet our
guests."

Krista nodded somberly. This was it. They were going
to ask her to take them across the mountains and Herr
Schuyler no doubt had eagerly offered her services for a
fat fee. It was the answer to a prayer, but for that blasted
Tory. Maybe she could show him up for what he was on
the way.

Marta wrinkled her nose as they walked side by side to

the house. "Oh, Krista, must you rub on that awful oil?"

"It's good for the skin. Mama always said so."

"If you *take* it, not wear it! At least take off your hat and pull out your braid. You're always hiding your hair."

"They are not interested in me as a woman, Marta," Krista snapped irritably. "They wish me to guide them across the mountains. For that, I look and smell as good as any of them."

Marta stopped short. "How did you know that?"

"Uncle Kurt told me he sent them here."

"So you *did* spend last night at Uncle Kurt's? Good thing Papa knows what he is doing."

The insinuation in her sister's voice brought Krista around sharply, her hand resting on the latch of the door. "You have been around Herr Schuyler too long, Marta. He is poisoning your mind with shameful ideas and I am right shocked that you accept them. Surely you know that I—"

Marta rose on tiptoe and pressed her finger against Krista's lips with an unaffected giggle. "Krista, I only wish what is best for you and so does Papa. You will see."

As infuriating as Marta's first insinuation was, her second, vague and obviously amusing to her, was more unsettling to Krista. But before she could address it, her younger sister had ducked under her arm and inside the firelit tavern.

It was far warmer than the barn, but Krista couldn't feel it. All she could feel were the eyes that swung her way. She was accustomed to curious and ofttimes rude appraisals. Her height alone demanded it. Yet they never lifted the hairs at the nape of her neck as they did now. The sudden crash of a bench overturning made her start as a familiar skirt-clad figure bolted upright with more enthusiasm than his condition should have permitted and lumbered across the room to snatch up Marta in his arms.

"Now where did ye run off to, my fair little fraulein! You've an anxious man eager to try this local custom your father was tellin' me about."

Krista moved her hand to the hilt of her hunting knife instinctively, uncertain as to whether her giggling sister wanted rescue from the drunken giant, who continued to swing her around and around until the taproom counter caught them and prevented their stumbling to the floor. Further reaction, however, was stayed as her stepfather hastened to the unsteady couple and, laughing as though he'd had more than his share of the strong-smelling liquor that assaulted Krista's nostrils, extracted Marta from the Scot's arms.

"No, Herr Duncan. You haf misunderstoodt! Not *this* daughter!" He pointed across the room at Krista. "*That* one!"

Stricken was an understatement for the expression that settled on the Scot's bearded face as he focused on the tall figure standing motionless near the door. The roar of his companions' laughter echoed in Krista's ears, but was not the source of the flush that burned her fair skin the brightest scarlet. It was the incredulous whiskey brown eyes that slowly moved from her moccasin boots, up the length of her buckskin-clad legs and over her fringed shirt to search for a face beneath the shadow of the brim of her hat.

"Ye jest, man! This isn'a woman! 'Tis but a lad of length and bones!"

"Take off your hat, girl, and come closer!"

When Krista failed to move, her stepfather abandoned Marta to shuffle across the room and snatch the beaver hat from her head. As he grabbed Krista's arm and dragged her toward the stunned Scotsman, she felt the painful tug of her braid being pulled out, as if to prove a point.

"See? It is the same as Marta's."

"By thunder, it is female, Scottie boy!" the captain bellowed, "and a sight more than ye bargained for!"

The resulting hilarity pricked at Krista's pride, spurring her out of her shock. "Ja, I am female," she concurred tersely, "but I am as good as any man among you in the mountains. Kurt Waltari said as much!"

"Ain't no doubt as to that, is there, boy?" Hardy grunted, helping the disconcerted Scot to his feet. "Looks like we got us a bargain."

Gavin Duncan shoved at his companion in a manner bespeaking his thunderstruck face. "I'll not be tucked in or bundled up . . . whatever that queer German said, with the likes of that! I'd sooner share a bed with a . . ." He wrinkled his nose in distaste. "A dead fish!"

"I'll make her wash."

"Washin' won't give her what the good Lord's forgotten! I'll have no part o' this!"

"Ain't no tellin' what's under them buckskins, boy," the captain railed at the Scot's elbow.

The satisfaction that her "disguise" was working as she intended did little to offset the sting of the crude speculation, but it was the implications of what was being said that gave rise to the wariness in Krista's tone.

"My competence as a guide is all that should concern you, gentlemen . . . that and the merit of your new volunteer. I should wonder more if a real man lay beneath that skirt."

Whoops of amusement filled the room as the Scot squared off before the tall blonde enigma with snapping eyes. The additional inches of height that allowed him to glance slightly down at her did little to intimidate her. Instead, she lifted her chin in challenge and met his simmering gaze in cool silence.

"Sweet Jesus!" Hardy's oath punctuated the dying

laughter, marking a prolonged silence broken only by the crackling of the fire in the hearth.

"After tonight, ye'll have no doubt of that, hinny."

Krista's calm facade faltered with a confused glance at her stepfather. "What is this big fool talking about, Herr Schuyler?"

"Herr Duncan has agreed to bundling with you, Krista."

Scarlet embarrassment fading from her cheeks, Krista paled with the knee-weakening shock that swept over her. "I'll share a bed with no man, much less one in a skirt!" She wished her voice could regain its forcefulness. She wished the floor would open up and swallow her. She wished . . .

"But I'll nay be wearin' the kilt in the bed, hinny."

Krista stepped back, as if the velvet threat of his voice had physically touched her. Unable to depend on her staggered wit to retort or the floor to offer retreat, she willed her feet into action, brushing past the ungiving tartan-cloaked shoulder of her eerily sober adversary to march into the back kitchen.

Marta was on her heels. "Krista, it could be worse. It could be one of the others!"

Krista wheeled in fury. "How could you? How could you not warn me what Herr Schuyler was about?" Such was her anger that Marta's round contrite face blurred before her.

"Papa wants to see us both properly wedded! It's his duty."

"How much?" Krista seethed. "How much is our concerned stepfather getting for this?"

"Hopefully your happiness. That is all he wishes."

"My happiness? Bah! When has he ever cared for my happiness?" Marta was such a dullwitted creature. Perhaps that's why she got along so well with their stepfather. She didn't think for herself.

"You never gave Papa a chance. You always acted like you hated him! He has made me the happiest girl in the world by arranging my marriage to Russell. I could have picked no better man myself."

"You knew Russell. You wanted to marry him and he wanted you! Thor's thunder, I only want to be free of men telling me what to do! I—"

"You vill do as I say, daughter."

Krista reeled against the wall as the back of her stepfather's thick, knuckled hand slammed against her cheek. She caught herself on the window stool and shook her head, as if to shake off the dizzying clouds that suddenly surrounded it. He was angry. His small eyes always seemed to grow smaller and more piercing when he was that way, just as his chest seemed to puff up, like a hen with ruffled feathers. And when Herr Schuyler was angry and drunk, which the odor that accompanied him into the room indicated, he was unpredictable.

"Papa, what have you done?" Marta wailed, rushing to her sister's aid. "She did not mean it."

"I . . . I did!" Krista slurred defiantly.

"Marta, prepare your room for Herr Duncan and your sister. You vill sleep in the kitchen tonight!" the big German barked, sending the girl scurrying from the room. When the door closed behind her, Herr Schuyler turned back to Krista. "So you vant to be free of men?"

"Like you." Years of bitterness welled in Krista's declaration.

"It is unnatural for a voman to vish such thingks. This Scot, I think, vill be able to handle you." A cynical smile lighted on Schuyler's thick lips. "So both our vishes will be answered. I will have made a suitable match for my daughter as a father's duty insists and you will no longer answer to me, ja?"

"I won't be bundled off like some mindless female to a complete stranger!"

"Vould you find Marta's Russell more appealingk?"

Krista rubbed her cheek tentatively. "Don't be absurd! They love each other."

Although instinct bade her to back away when her stepfather moved in front of her, Krista straightened, so that she looked down at his shorter stature. She couldn't help flinching, however, when he poked his stubby finger against her collarbone painfully.

"I give my vord that Herr Duncan will have vone of my daughters. If you vill not go to him, then I vill send Marta."

Disbelief settled on Krista's wary features. Surely, he was bluffing . . . unless the Scot and his friends were paying a dear sum, dear enough to outweigh Russell Vandercliff's promise as a prosperous son-in-law.

It would serve her sister right, she fumed, still angry at Marta's silly acceptance of this travesty. That would stop those irritating giggles of the happiest girl in the world. Besides, she'd said the Scot was handsome. He wouldn't be nearly as repulsive to Marta as he was to her.

"Then it vill be on your head, your sister's misery, not to mention Russell's."

Even as she brooded over the justice of such a fate for her simple sister, Krista knew her stepfather had won. She had not remained under his thumb for so many years just to let him ruin Marta's life now. Hers was already ruined. Besides, bundling did not necessarily mean that she would have to become intimate with the Scot or that a wedding would be inevitable. It only meant that she would share the same bed for a night.

Satisfied with the acceptance slowly overtaking his

daughter's rebellious expression, the innkeeper expelled a
sigh of relief, a hot alcohol-infested breath that made
Krista turn her head away. "And your bedpartner told
me to tell you that if you do not bathe, he vill scrub you
down himself."

Head snapping up, Krista searched her stepfather's
gaze for some sign that he was merely having fun at her
expense. She saw a hint of satisfaction, but there was little
doubt in her mind that he was indeed passing on the
Scot's demand. Her lips thinned with reluctant acceptance. The lumbering giant with the fiendish eyes was
quite capable of carrying out his threat. It was Herr
Schuyler's parting words, however, that underscored her
conclusion.

"I can already see that I have made you a good
match." The laugh that echoed as the door closed behind
him left Krista feeling cold, in spite of the cozy warmth of
the hearthfire—cold and sick with betrayal and apprehension.

Chapter Three

The upstairs chamber Krista shared with her sister was sparsely heated from the warm stones of the chimney which climbed sturdily between two tiny gable windows. Two narrow dormers on either side afforded cross ventilation in the summer time, but they were now shuttered and curtained to keep out the weather. It had once been her parents' bedroom, but, after Mary Lindstrom's death, Herr Schuyler moved into the smaller half of the loft, where the girls had slept as children, to allow them more room.

Although Marta was touched by her stepfather's thoughtfulness, the older Krista understood his motives. The access to that room was from the outside. A steep narrow staircase rose from the ground to a short door which had been cut out when the inside connecting door to the larger room was closed off. That way the local doxies could visit without risking detection from the travelers sleeping in bedrolls on the tavern floor.

Marta thought the noises coming from the other side of the wall were a result of Herr Schuyler's snoring and grunting, but Krista knew better. She'd watched one of the women steal off into the night after a particularly noisy session of physical romance. To Krista's utter astonishment, for Herr Schuyler publicly showed a marked distaste for white men who showed interest in Indian women, it was one of the halfbreed squaws who wove blankets and baskets for sale at the trading post. The blanket-wrapped figure had shuffled away, as if still sore from being ridden by a man twice her size, clutching her money pouch to her chest like a coveted prize.

Although Krista had never seen humans mate, she'd seen animals and, from the noise that came through the thin walls of her room, men sounded like rutting pigs when they took a woman. The very idea made her nauseous . . . too nauseous to eat the warm bread and slice of venison on the plate Marta had fixed for her supper.

Through the cracks of the floorboards, it was difficult not to overhear the ribald teasing the man called Duncan was receiving. Not only was he taking it in good stride, but encouraging the speculation with a few wry comments of his own, as if he knew Krista could hear and wanted to undermine her confidence.

It was working, she thought grudgingly, taking out her frustration on her white skin. Scrub her down, indeed! The very nerve of the man! Well, she'd be clean, but nothing was said about her choice of clothing. Ignoring the voluminous white nightshift hanging on the peg, Krista stubbornly pulled her buckskin shirt on again.

The Scot kept going on about hoping that she would be ready for him and she was not going to disappoint him. She'd discouraged drunken sots before and he would be no different. Most likely he'd pass out the moment he fell into the thick featherbed.

She checked the long board her sister had placed in the bed, to make certain it was centered before climbing in, soft boots and all. Tossing her braid behind her, she fell against the pillow, only to be engulfed in a perfumed air. Recognizing Marta's handiwork, Krista silently swore at her younger sister. There was enough of the scent on her pillow to overcome the staunchest fellow. A quick check of the other pillow revealed an equal dose. Left with little choice, Krista flipped the down-stuffed pillow over and blew out the flickering chamberstick. At least her sister hadn't doused both sides of the blasted thing.

Her eyes had no more than adjusted to the moonlight filtering in through the tiny gable windows, when the stairwell brightened, harkening the unsteady approach of the intoxicated Scotsman. She could well imagine his difficulty in maneuvering those broad shoulders up the narrow staircase sober, but drunk, it posed an even greater obstacle. Her lips twitched as she heard a sudden scrambling, followed by a heavy thud that no doubt bruised those bristle-covered shins of his.

"For the love of God, woman, have ye left no light for a man to see by?"

Instead of answering, Krista held her tongue. Perhaps if he thought her asleep, he would fall in bed and do the same. After all, he didn't seem overly eager to share her bed earlier. He'd only accepted her father's proposal because she'd wounded his oversized ego.

She could make out his giant figure emerging from the stairwell and started to warn him about standing up, when he straightened in indignation only to strike his head against the sloped ceiling. Apprehensive as she was, Krista could not help the giggle she smothered against the blankets. Perhaps he'd knock himself out before he even reached the bed!

"A damned loft!" he muttered under his breath, crouching low as he felt his way across the room.

The bed jarred when he struck it and Krista's heart stilled at his low satisfied laugh. Her clammy hand eased the hunting knife strapped to her leg out of its sheath.

"Are ye in here, hinny?" His groping hand banged

against the board. "Damnation, but you're a hard woman!" Again Krista fought the urge to laugh, an absurd reaction considering the alarm that ran rampant through her body. "What the devil is this?"

She felt the board sliding along her leg and reached with her free hand to stop it from being removed.

"Ah, so ye are in here!"

His hand clamped over hers and, before she knew it, she was being tugged toward him. The situation no longer amusing in the least, Krista panicked and sunk her teeth into the back of his knuckles. With a startled curse, the Scot let her go and pulled away, only to strike his head again on the ceiling. This time a string of curses erupted, followed by the violent removal of the board.

Flinching as it slammed against the floor, giving rise to loud whoops from below, Krista braced herself for the confrontation which now seemed inevitable. However, instead of returning to the bed as she had first anticipated, the giant shadow seemed to hover nearby. Broken and labored breath brought a disturbing mental picture of nostrils flaring with anger only partially spent. It wasn't until she heard the sound of cloth falling soft against the floor that she realized what he was doing.

"Tis time ye learned not to judge a man by his clothing, hinny." The bed gave with his weight as he threw himself upon it and rolled over on his side. "More than a few women have been pleasured by . . . what the . . ."

Her mouth gone dry, Krista pressed the tip of the knife against the hard body that had moved so close she could sense its male heat. "You will stay on your half of the bed, Herr Duncan, or I promise you that you will pleasure no more women."

After what seemed an interminable silence, Krista was shocked to feel the bed shaking—shaking with the laughter that rumbled in her companion's throat. "Ye can put the knife away, lassie. The jest is well done."

"Jest?" Krista echoed uncertainly.

"Aye! Surely ye dinna think I'd really want the likes of ye and ye nearly a man yourself! Since I could'na strike ye for your insult to me manhood, I thought it best to scare ye witless." He howled again, this time less discreetly. "And witless ye are to think ye need a board or a knife to keep me away. A good night's rest is all I long for." The Scot suddenly turned his back to her and tugged the covers up over his shoulders. "I'd suggest ye do the same. We've a long day tomorrow. If I'm any judge of the good captain, we'll not be stoppin' every mile or so to let ye catch your breath."

"I can hold my own."

Again the bed jarred with a deep-throated chuckle. "Aye, that I believe, lassie."

"And I'll keep the knife at hand."

A long heavy sigh echoed from the other side of the bed. "Ah, you're a woman alright. A mouth full of tongue and always after the last word. Suit yourself, lassie, but for the love of God, leave me rest in silence, if I can without suffocatin' from that godawful perfume of yours. I'm damned if I can figure which way ye were the most bearable, before or after yer bath!"

Krista's mouth sagged with a mixture of incredulity and choking rage. Then, just as quickly, her jaw clamped stubbornly before she gave her arrogant companion the satisfaction of meeting his expectation of her. Never had she met a more insufferable man! Had she had an inkling of his character, she'd have let him rot where he rolled to a stop at the bottom of the hill. Damned blasted Tory, she fumed, rolling on her back to stare wide awake at the ceiling. She'd expose him for what he was, if it was the last thing she did. The colonials would take care of him. All she had to figure out was how.

She was still considering her plight when her eyelids grew heavy. She fought sleep, lest she relax and inadvertently snuggle up against the mountain of muscle sleeping stone still at her side as she was prone to do when she shared the bed with Marta. There was as much distance as she dared put between them already without falling off the bed and adding further to her humiliation.

When thick gray clouds smothered the first light of day, however, prolonging the semi-darkness outside so that she had no clue the rising hour had approached, she had finally given in to the toll of the previous day's work and the anxiety of what had surely been one of the worst nights in her life. Nonetheless, when she felt the mattress moving, her eyes flew open and her hand went straight for the knife she'd kept between her and the man resting on his elbow, staring down at her. The blank expression on her face when it was nowhere to be found brought a wicked grin to his.

"Lassie," he tutted in gentle reprimand, "dinna ye trust me when I say ye've na need for your knife?"

How could she have allowed herself to go to sleep? Krista berated herself sternly. Instead of answering, she tensed, ready to spring from the bed.

"Then I am beholden to you for waking me. I've much work to do this morning to prepare for the journey to Fort Pitt."

No sooner had Krista tossed aside the blankets when a long sinewy leg fell across her abdomen, pinning her to the mattress. The fists she drew in her defense were likewise rendered ineffective in a viselike grasp. Although her own legs were free, their helpless flailing only served to make the bed creak furiously.

From the tavern room below a gristly voice rose cryptically. "I see the lovebirds are awake. Reckon that Scot's grin'll be as wide as he is tall."

"You're only makin' it worse for yourself, lassie, carryin' on so," her assailant chuckled lowly. But as his face hovered over her own, his mild amusement faded abruptly. "How did ye come by such a bruise on your cheek?"

"I . . ." Krista groped for the words, befuddled as much by the overpowering warmth and strength of the naked body pressed against her as this unexpected show of compassion. "I required some persuasion to accept Herr Schuyler's arrangement with you." Compassion and, what was it that briefly flashed dark across his countenance . . . disapproval?

"Well, t'was all for naught. We're definitely souls of different tastes and preferences and I'll respect ye all the same."

Stunned by the Scot's words, Krista began to relax. A smile spawned by a mixture of gratitude and relief turned the corners of her mouth up slightly, leaving her totally unprepared for the devilish lips that suddenly swooped down to claim it. Warm, forceful, yet not bruising—the startling assault robbed her of what little breath his crushing weight afforded her, so that, when he pulled away, she could only gasp raggedly for air.

"Nonetheless, I couldna' allow ye to get away with your knife-prickin' wickedness without some pay."

With a strong bounce, the agile giant sprang away to his feet, oblivious to his nakedness, and reached for his clothes. A cheery tune whistled from the lips that had thrown her thoughts into a quagmire of confusion and gave rise to knowing snickers erupting from the low dialogue of the stirring guests below. Unable to settle on a deserving reaction, Krista flipped over on her side, her back to the man dressing at her bedside.

"Tis a strange custom, this bundlin' of yours. Strange, but agreeable," he said at length, his brisk footsteps hailing his exit on the planked pine floor. The steps creaked as he started his descent and then stopped. "And lassie . . ." He waited until Krista grunted in acknowledgment. "I'll be leavin' your knife here by the steps. Ye may have nae need of it with me, but there are some who are not as discernin' as meself."

With a quick patter of well executed booted steps, the Scot was downstairs. Skin burning with humiliation, Krista covered her head with the pillow, lest she be forced to hear him acknowledge the conquest his companions expected until the odor of Marta's perfume had turned the pounding of the blood in her temples to a painful tempo. Let them think what they will, she mused, bitter at men in general. Their brains were constantly in their breeches where females were concerned. Well, she would soon show them a woman was good for more than bed-warming service—at least this one was.

"The devil ye say! N'a word was said about a weddin'!" Gavin Duncan bellowed, his cup striking the table with a ferocity that sent hot coffee sloshing over the brim.

Until that moment, he rather enjoyed his breakfast of johnnycakes, piled high enough to satisfy the voracious appetite with which he'd awakened. His comrades had speculated, as men will do, concerning his luck in the loft, but he offered neither affirmation nor denial as they'd had their fun with him. Yet, when the woman in question had eventually come down the steps and silenced the group momentarily with a gaze as cold as the frost that glazed the ground outside, he had felt a twinge of guilt for letting them run on so. But not guilty enough to marry her!

"We all heard za board strike za floor, Herr Duncan,"

her stepfather was saying, not the least intimidated by the Scot's fierce outburst.

"Confound it, man, that meant nothing! The truth is, I would'na have the knife-wielding wench for your blasted bundlin', much less for marriage!"

"She pulled a knife on ya, Scottie boy?" Captain Hardy echoed in surprise.

Gavin snorted. "Aye, as big as yours and twice as sharp! I tossed the board to put a fright in her and damn me if she didn't put the blade in its place! Tis a fearsome wench ye've raised, innkeeper, and there's na doubt in my mind she can hold her own with the rest of us on the journey, but t'would be like weddin' a man and I'll have no part of it!"

"Then you vill have no guide."

"Fine!"

"Now hold on there, Scottie boy," Hardy spoke up, stepping between the lean giant and his sturdy, yet no less obstinate, adversary. "Time is vital. We need to find that shortcut the Finn told us of and she is all we have."

"And if you think I vill send my daughter off, unwed, with a group of men into to the wilderness, then you do not know what it is to be a father!"

"Is that so?" Gavin challenged, dropping his voice to a lower level, no less full of thunder. "And who will ye punch and bully when she's gone . . . the little pretty one?"

"Krista needs a strong hand. Her sister knows her lot in life, but my eldest . . ."

"Beggin' your pardon, Herr Schuyler, but I think we might come to some sort of agreement if I might speak to my Scottish friend here . . . private like."

The innkeeper nôdded and started for the kitchen, but upon reaching the door he stopped, as if in afterthought. "Do not think the girl comes without some dowry. You came in without a horse. She comes with both a horse and mule, as well as her gun. Considering your plan, that should make her more attractive. Not that she isn't as handsome as her sister beneath that stench and those men's clothes. She is like a fine racehorse instead of a plump little pony and won't require nearly the care that her sister would."

"Fatherly obligation, my foot!" Gavin sneered, oddly outraged by the detached way the innkeeper spoke of the strange girl. He followed Captain Hardy to the opposite end of the long stretcher table where they could speak in as much seclusion as the room allowed.

"Ya need a horse, boy, and we need her. It ain't like ye'll be stuck with her for the rest of your life."

Last night he'd been drunk and the idea of this bundling was appealing, especially when he'd thought it was Marta who would share his bed; and he had slept in a warm comfortable featherbed, which is more than he could say for his fellow travelers. Now, however, he was dead sober and furious that the consequences of this intriguing custom had been carefully withheld last night.

"Is'na marriage the same in this heathen land either?" he inquired.

"O'course it is, lad, but out here, what with preacher's bein' scarce and all, there ain't a whole lot to it, unless the couple wants to make it so. And where we're going, ya can get rid of the girl whenever ye wish. Them Frenchies would pay handsome fer one like her. Injuns too. Or ya could just go yer sep'rate ways," Hardy added quickly, catching the light of disapproval in the Scot's hard gaze. "Won't be no more'n a piece of paper, if that, since ye have no want of the wench to warm your bedroll . . . though I reckon it would put a burr in the bonnet of that lassie gal what jilted ya and give something bitter for yer back-stabbin' homefolk to chaw on for a while."

Gavin chuckled lowly, his eyes sharpening on the wily colonial's weathered face. He could picture the look on Claire's fair features upon reading about his wedding a backswoods female who nearly matched him in height and could work and fight as well as any man. That, combined with joining the rebels, would send his ever loyal and boot-licking brother into an apoplectic fit. Now that was motivation if ever there was such a thing.

"You're a sly one, Captain, part fox and part bear by the look of ye. Whether ye be friend or foe, I've yet to decipher, but I'll give ye credit for a sharp wit and convincin' way with words."

The officer smiled, knowing he had struck home at last. "And your decision will mark what ya are to us, Gavin Duncan. Say yea, and I'll share some a' this wit with ya, for I suspect you'll be a quick learner."

"And if I still say no?"

"Then ya got less sense than I give ye credit for." Upon seeing Gavin nod and bury his face in his hands in reluctant acceptance, Hardy looked up at the men gathered near the fire, and sitting on the hob nobs. "Quit yer hobnobbin', boys, we're goin' to a weddin'!"

Tired from lack of sleep, Krista put an armload of fodder in the corral where she'd turned out the visitors' horses and picked up the bucket she'd used to fill their trough to return it to the well on her way to the back kitchen. A few drifting flakes of snow confirmed her suspicions earlier that week about the weather taking an abrupt change for the worse. They would have to move diligently toward Fort Pitt and on before the snowfall became a serious hindrance to their progress.

After picking up an armload of wood for the fire, she climbed the single stone slab step to the kitchen and

entered quickly. The room was always an inviting one
with the delicious smell of baking breads and roasting or
stewing meats. This morning was no exception. No doubt
Marta had prepared extra for the trip ahead, as she always did when Krista left for the wilderness with Uncle
Kurt. The sweet scent of molasses cakes verified that some
of the baking was for her. Her sister knew they were
Krista's favorites, sticky with molasses and sprinkled with
nuts.

"If you have made what I think, I will forgive you for
last night," Krista grinned, stacking the wood near the
hearth for Marta's convenience.

Instead of accepting Krista's well intentioned apology,
Marta nodded toward the connecting door to the tavern.
"Papa wishes to see you right away."

"What fee did Herr Schuyler ask?" Krista inquired.
She was certain he hadn't missed the fat purse tied to the
waist of the buffalo-vested leader of the group.

Her sister shrugged, avoiding Krista's clear gaze. "How
should I know? I am not much of a mind for business. I
shall leave that to Russell and concentrate on being a
good wife and mother."

"I'm sure you will, Marta." Krista unlatched the door
and started through when Marta called after her.

"Krista, Herr Duncan was not so bad, was he?"

"There's more to a man than a silver-tongue and a
devilish smile, sister. But this kept him . . ." She was about
to say "in his breeches" as her hand rested on the hilt of
her hunting knife, but realized he had neither worn
breeches nor remained in the strange clothing he had.
"On his side of the bed," she finished lamely, too absorbed in her own confusion to notice her sister's apprehension.

The moment Krista stepped into the tavern, the murmur of the occupants stopped as it had upon her exit. But

this time, instead of concentrating on the food before him, the tartan-clad Scot pushed himself away from the table and strode toward her with a glint in his whiskey-dark eyes that sent a shiver of forboding up her spine. She held his gaze steadily until he came to a stop before her, but when he lifted her work-roughened hand to his lips, her bravado faltered noticeably.

"I told ye last night, that ye had my respect and this morning, I'm provin' it by weddin' ye proper."

"What?" The word was strangled with incredulity.

Gavin Duncan took her by the arm and ushered her over to the hearth where Herr Schuyler stood with an open Bible. "Your good father pointed out, and rightfully so, that an unwed lassie has na business gallavantin' about the countryside with a group of men. So I'm marryin' ye, plain and simple."

Krista tried to yank away from the viselike grip that tightened at her rebellion. "You are crazy if you think that I will marry you!"

"Daughter!"

"But Herr—"

"You vill marry the Scot as I say! I vill worry about your honor if you vill not!"

"I didn't have to marry—"

"Be glad that this man is villing to take you after living in the wilderness as you have with Kurt Waltari."

Although she had not been touched, Krista felt the sting of her stepfather's accusation against her cheeks as all eyes turned on her in open speculation. Herr Schuyler spoke of her honor and yet was the first to offer it to a stranger and then slander it before others. She met his small beady gaze and saw there a mixture of warning and hatred—hatred that had festered between them since he himself had tried to take her. She had fought him successfully with the aid of a pitchfork and swore that she would not only tell her mother but Uncle Kurt as well if he ever tried again.

Krista's thoughts were interrupted by a low whisper intended for her ears only. "I dinna want ye as a wife in every sense of the word, lassie, but as a guide only. 'Tis the only way the man will let ye come with us."

Numbly, she turned her face toward the man beside her, letting his words sink in.

"I'll be as anxious as ye are to have this annulled when we get to where we're goin'. At least ye'll be rid o' the likes of him."

Rid of Herr Schuyler? Annulled? The ideas swam about in the confusion of her mind, gaining consideration. It could work out to be the best thing for her, she reasoned slowly. In a few weeks, Marta would be free of him . . .

"You vill step up here, so I can get on vith the vedding, daughter. I've an inn to run and you'f a long journey ahead."

Obediently, Krista moved forward, unaware of the strong arm that slipped around her waist as if to be certain the panic welling in her eyes did not overtake her and cause her to bolt from the room. Her stepfather read a short passage from the Bible concerning a woman's obligation to man, his legacy to all young brides. Krista had seen him perform this duty several times with the same alacrity as he registered deeds and claims. As an appointed authority of the court, he was able to sign wedding contracts and register them in the record books at Fort Pitt to make the union of couples legal until such time as an ordained minister could perform the religious ceremony.

Gavin signed the contract first, his hand bold and firm. Krista's, however, shook as she added her name to the document, scattering the ink on the parchment. It wasn't until her new husband's warm fingers closed gently over hers that she was able to make a legible mark.

"I want you to have this, Krista. I know that I drew it for my wedding, but I will have time to do another." It was a fracture, a beautifully designed wedding document done in Marta's artistic and loving hand. Hearts, doves, and clinging vines depicting the love and permanence so lacking in the marriage taking place made a brilliantly colored border and on the lines, the ink still fresh, was today's date and the names Gavin Duncan and Krista Lindstrom penned in her sister's delicate script. "I am only sorry that you will miss my wedding."

Krista turned her cheek to Marta as the small girl planted an affectionate kiss there and handed her the fractur. This wedding wasn't Marta's doing, but she could not bring herself to return the gesture. "Thank you, Marta. You, always did such lovely work."

It was true. The neighbors were always asking Marta to do the artwork to document births, family trees, weddings, and funerals. Her sister's was a *productive* art form which her stepfather encouraged. He kept her supplied in inks and paper. He didn't destroy them as he had Krista's harp.

"You are as talented as you are pretty, fraulein," Gavin Duncan complimented as he peered over Krista's shoulder at the document her sister handed her.

Everyone loved Marta, Krista mused bitterly, even, it appeared, the man she had just married. And she loved Marta, but at that moment, Krista felt an uncontrollable urge to slap her beaming cherub face.

"We have to get going," Krista snapped, folding the paper in half.

"Krista, you'll smear the ink!"

Ignoring Marta's protest, Krista bounded up the narrow staircase to their room where she'd piled the things she intended to take on the bed. Her buffalo robe, a pair of short skis Uncle Kurt had made her, her gun, and a pistol, and the pack containing a clean change of clothing to wear under her buckskins. Rolled in the bottom of the trunk that had once been her mother's were the belongings she had not counted on carrying. After all, she had thought to be returning. Now, she would never see Schuyler's Crossing again. Resolutely, she added to the pile on the bed the plain blue dress and linen shift, as well as the nightdress hanging on a peg near the chimney.

That was it, she thought dispassionately. She looked around the room once more and then shook her head, refusing to commit it further to her memory. Mama was gone. Marta would soon be living a new life with Russell Vandercliff. She had waited a long time for this moment—yet, she felt neither happiness nor regret.

Chapter Four

The flurries of snow had stopped by the time the group reached Redstone. Captain Hardy and the Scot left Krista and the others warming by the tavern fire, stepping into the trading post, a separate room in the same log structure, to see about acquiring some warmer dress for the ill-prepared Scot. She still could not believe that her stepfather had sold her horse to the man, leaving her the mule to cross country on. But then, she also had trouble believing that she was actually married to him.

Yet as the day wore on, she felt a tug of pity for the way the wind whipped about him while the snow soaked the blanket he'd wrapped around his shoulders. Oh, he hadn't complained, but she knew he had to have been chilled to the bone with the sudden gusts that swept through wind tunnels between the hills and trees. His comrades seemed to be privately amused each time he'd stoically tuck his tartan around his legs in hopes of blocking the icy blasts from the sturdy thighs she had once bathed in utter fascination.

No stranger to such misery after her years in the mountains in much worse weather, Krista finally offered him some relief out of the same compassion that had once saved his life. To make do until they could find shelter, she'd loaned him her blanket and spare leggings, although the leather thongs barely tied around his thicker, more muscular calves and thighs.

His words of gratitude still haunted her ears. "Ye've a kind heart, lassie, whether ye'd admit it so or not."

And his eyes, the way they'd taken on a warmth that had infected her snow-chafened cheeks. There was a hint of a much tenderer man beneath that braying, belligerent front of his. She'd seen it that morning when he'd shown concern over her bruised cheek. Perhaps under other circumstances, she could even come to like him.

If he weren't the enemy, she reminded herself sternly, quietly sipping a noggin of beer at the edge of the bar and watching the others filling their bellies with stronger brew. They'd been followed. She was certain of it. Riding through the forest in that large a number should have silenced the birds, sent them flying through the treetops in a flutter of panic at the disturbance in their habitat. Yet, there was one pair of wild turkeys that called out to each other from time to time from either side of them.

She hadn't been the only one to notice. She'd seen the captain exchange knowing glances with his companions. Like herself, they kept their guns resting across their saddles and their gazes constantly swept the forested land for any sign of unnatural movement. Although the good-natured banter dwindled to a cautious silence broken only by some fascinated observation made by their tenderfoot recruit, their mounts made too much of a stir in the underbrush and dried leaf-carpeted horsepaths to hear a reckless approach, much less a stealthy one. Perhaps later, she'd have the chance to speak to Hardy privately, for Gavin Duncan's Tory compatriots could well have been the source of the expertly executed bird calls.

They could even be in this room, she thought, peering discreetly out from under the brim of her hat at the strangers who had taken shelter from the relentless wind that still pressed on after the light snow had ceased. In addition to the Virginians and the three Pennsylvanians they'd recruited, there were three other travelers, one of whom the burly man called Tull treated to a bottle of kill-devil, British rum supplied from a recent raid on a Tory camp. At the rate they were drinking it, they would soon fall back on the cheap three-cent whiskey and suffer all the more tomorrow.

Pipes of many varieties filled the air with tobacco smoke, another habit Krista failed to comprehend. It seemed to her the men spent more time lighting them and chewing the stems thoughtfully than actually smoking the tobacco. Like babes with a sugar tit, Uncle Kurt had once observed wryly, before lighting his. Oh, she'd tried it, but found it too distasteful and troublesome. Instead, she preferred Eva's habit of chewing on chips of beechnut bark and selected spices, which were not only tasty but gave her breath a pleasant odor, unlike that of many women far more cultured.

Or whiskey-swilling men, she thought, turning away as one of the strangers closest to her—a big-bellied man with thick arms and the soot-smeared face and smoked odor of a smithy—belched loudly. Oblivious to his offense, he slapped his empty horn on the single plank stretched across two barrels that separated the customers from the rack of beer and liquor kegs, when, as if in answer to her wish for a breath of fresh air, the door to the tavern opened, admitting a cold gust that drew the attention of everyone in the room.

In stone silence, two Indians stepped inside and closed the door behind them. Their robes were drawn tightly about them, the hair side turned inward, a sign the snow had started again. Their stoic faces gleamed in the firelight, oiled with bear grease, as no doubt the rest of their bodies were, for warmth. The sprinkling of snow that had whitened their long hair melted as they ran their hands over it, restoring it to its raven sheen. The room was still until Tull Crockett stepped forward congenially.

"Lenape?"

The Indians nodded in assent, shaking the feathers woven in their simple headdress. "I am Red Deer of the Unâmis and this my Minsi brother, a messenger of peace from the land beyond the mountains. We seek shelter from the coming storm."

"*Monsey!*" the man next to Krista snorted in disgust.

The word reverberated in kind around the room, as if the Indians were not there. Krista could understand the men's mistrust, but the Minsi, or Monsey as the white man had misconstrued the name, was a messenger of peace. No matter how hostile his people were, the Wolf clan of the Leni Lanape was the most warlike of the three clans that made up the Delaware Nation, he was entitled to hospitality and protection by even his worst enemies. His companion from the turkey clan no doubt was accompanying him to insure his safety.

At that moment, the postmaster and innkeeper entered the room. "You and your friend are welcome, Red Deer, but I'll be paid in coin or skins, not wampum."

"I have plenty good skins," the Indian replied calmly, dropping the results of a good hunt on the floor at his feet. "We will also take food."

The innkeeper pointed to the large hearth where a kettle of stew simmered lowly. "Help yourself to all you want. There's room for your things in the opp'site corner there."

"Well I ain't payin' to bed down with no cutthroat Injuns!" the man next to Krista grumbled, stooping to pick up his long fur jacket and shrugging it on. "The stable'll serve me just as well and I like the comp'ny better." Taking the jug he'd been nursing in one hand and his musket in the other, the frontiersman strode straight for the door, brushing between the Indians with a snort of contempt.

"If any you other boys got a sim'lar problem, you kin do the same. I know Red Deer and his uncle. If he says the Monsey is all right, then he's all right. Their skins are as good as your gold."

Krista knew the name Red Deer as well. As the Indian shed his blanket, she recognized the nephew of Cornstalk, the Indian chief who had been mercilessly murdered on a mission of peace. There was much outrage among the Indians, even the peaceful ones because of it. She also knew now who had been following them.

Dropping her tongue against the back of her throat to make a hollow sound, she imitated the call of a wild turkey as the Indians deposited their bedrolls where they were told. The Minsi merely looked at her blankly, but she caught a mild hint of humor in Red Deer's eye, followed by recognition.

"Where is the man Waltari, He Who Glides Over Mountains?" he inquired, using the name she had received after being seen skiing down a mountainside the way her Finnish partner had taught her to do.

"He has a broken leg to mend over the winter months," Krista informed him. "I am taking these men to Kaskaskia for him. If you wished to travel with us, you did not have to do so at a distance, my friend."

Red Deer was about her own age, as far as even he himself was able to discern from the number of winters he'd been told had passed since his birth. It was from his mother that Krista had received her first buckskins. Once he had paid her tribute by offering two horses to Kurt Waltari for her.

"The devil take your tongue, lassie! Have ye lost your wits?"

"What man is this?" Red Deer's impassive dark eyes refused to acknowledge the wary Scot who filled the door to the trading post. His attention remained on Krista.

"I am her husband," Gavin declared, pacing across the floor so that the brave could no longer ignore him.

Nor was he inclined to as he took in the plaid kilt swirling about fringed leather leggings. Unlike the Big Knives, however, the Indian said nothing about the odd dress. Krista expected no less. It would have been impolite to insult the guest of his host. Her new husband, on the other hand, was less predictable.

Fortunately for her, the captain intervened. "Cap'n Tucker Hardy's the name and this is the great warrior who braved the anger of the Iroquois and killed their captives out of mercy, sooner than see the men suffer. The Saggenash shot him, but their English bullets could not down such a warrior. He is as big and sturdy as the Leni Lanape. We call him Duncan."

Until now, little that had been said or done had managed to penetrate the placid depths of the savages' dark gazes, but the fact that Gavin Duncan had stood up to the British and especially their long time nemesis, the Iroquois, kindled an undeniable respect there. Krista herself regarded the Scot with some wonder.

"Hawk Shadow and Red Deer go to the council fire of the Six Nations called by your Big Knife chief."

Captain Hardy gave a hearty laugh and slapped Red Deer on the back. "Well then, grab yourself some grub and warm up by the fire. Ye've as long a journey ahead of ya as us." Krista was startled as the seasoned woodsman glanced over his shoulder at her and winked. "And since ya been trailin' us anyways, ya might as well join up with us. There's safety in numbers and, touchy as folks are about Injuns, I wouldn't want nothing to happen to Hawk Shadow there. Travelin' with us'll speak for ya bein' peaceable."

"What the devil is Hardy doin'?" Gavin Duncan muttered under his breath.

"These are good Indians," Krista explained as the men accompanied Hardy to the cookfire. "At least Red Deer is. As for the messenger, if he was to come to any harm, it would only worsen Colonel Clark's hopes for Indian neutrality or alliance against the British."

A light akin to that which had infected the Indians' gaze, flickered in the whiskey eyes that settled on her face. "Do ye really think the man has a chance? From what I've seen, the rebels barely have enough guns and ammunition for themselves, let alone enough to pay off—" He broke off as Krista finished off the brew in her cup and licked her upper lip clean, her hat tilting back so that she had to catch it with her free hand. "Ye missed some on the tip of your nose," he scolded gently, wiping it away with his finger. "Drinkin' beer is hardly ladylike."

"You've already said I was no lady," she quipped hastily, trying to ignore the flush that heated her neck at the seemingly harmless act. She tugged the brim of her hat snugly down on her head. _"And ye nearly a man,"_ she quoted with as much brogue as her own lilting accent would permit. Feeling suddenly awkward, she changed the subject. "What Hardy said about your getting shot by the English . . ."

"Will ye have another?"

Krista shook her head. "I would hear more of that shooting, Duncan."

A look of pure devilment flashed at her in the form of a crooked grin. "Are ye sorry the blackguard missed?"

"He didn't."

Gavin laughed out loud. "Damnation, but ye've a wit,

lassie! I'll give ye that as well. I wonder what my brother and his Lady Claire would think, were I to take ye home to Duncan Brae as my bride after this war?"

Claire. The name leapt familiarly to the forefront of Krista's memory. Claire was the woman Gavin Duncan had mistaken her for. His brother's wife . . .

"Did you really shoot the captives of the Iroquois?" one of the other guests asked, invading their conversation. A wiry sort, clad in tattered gray lindsey-woolsey, he'd been enjoying the company of his own jug at the opposite end of the bar until now.

Gavin sobered. "Aye, I did. I left Detroit with a Tory patrol to fight rebels, not to murder innocent families or watch a fellow man be burned slowly at the stake after seein' his wife and children murdered and scalped. I'm a British deserter," he admitted boldly, adding with a tilt of his bearded chin, "and a rebel recruit."

"Well . . ." The man took a drink and savored the taste as he ran an assessing gaze up and down Gavin's large frame. "You won't be the first to see the right 'o things. Did your captain promise ya yer pick of four hundred acres for pay?"

"Well no, but—"

"Well, that's why I'm on my way east to join up with General Washington's Continentals. That's what they're promisin' regulars. Why don't ye come with me? Wouldn't surprise me if they didn't make ye some sort of officer. They're right partial to men of trainin'."

"I'm a surveyor, man, not a soldier."

"So was the General."

Gavin shook his head resolutely. "Nay, man, I gave my word to Captain Hardy that I would make him some maps, and I'm a man of my word."

Gavin's decision obviously did not sit well with the man. Screwing up his sharp birdlike features, he cocked

his head impudently. "Did ya give your word when you
agreed to come with the Tories from Detroit?"

Krista had seen the type before—agreeable until
crossed, then nasty as a trapped wolverine. But there was
more to this, she observed, watching as embers of emotion
flared in the burning gaze of the stranger. What was he
about, trying to recruit Gavin Duncan in one breath and
accusing him of being a traitor in the next?

The crash of Gavin's fist on the plank bar interrupted
her thoughts and rattled the cups sitting on it from one
end to the other. The men standing there grabbed their
jug and cups and moved away as the tall Scot straightened
to tower over the stranger.

"That's a serious charge, you're makin', man, and I
don't like the gist of it."

Instead of answering, the stranger turned toward the
group who had taken the Scot in. "What makes you boys
so sure this deserter isn't a spy, sent in by Hamilton?"

"Instinct . . . same thing as what makes us sure we don't
like your implicatins, neighbor," Captain Hardy grunted
as he climbed to his feet.

"I can handle my own quarrels, Captain," Gavin announced, stepping squarely away from the bar. "I'm certain the gentleman would like to reconsider what he was
sayin' and share a taste o' that good rum with—"

Gavin never finished. There was a whirl of flashing
metal as the little man spun around and a long blade was
suddenly pressed cold against his throat. "Then handle
this, you stinkin' Tory turncoat! The men you shot were
my wife's brother and nephew!"

"Are ye mad, man? The savages were burnin' them
alive!"

The light from the tin lantern over the bar added a feral
gleam to the man's gaze as he leaned even closer. From
her vantage, Krista saw Gavin flinch inadvertently as the

sharp blade drew blood. The irrational stranger had been so preoccupied with Gavin that he'd forgotten her. One more step and . . .

"And the woman and girl, Tory, did ye have turn with them yourself before the Injuns scalped 'em or did you wallow in their life's blood?"

Krista was as stricken by the fierce roar that emerged from the Scot's throat as she was by the doubled-over body of the stranger who seemed to lift off the ground and fly into her backward, carrying her to the floor with him on top. Her knuckles scraped against the hard-packed dirt, locked about the hilt of her hunting knife. Filled with one sense of purpose, to subdue the stranger before he harmed anyone, she wrapped her legs around his and pulled the blade tight up under his rough-shaven chin.

"Be still, sir, or it will be your own blood you will worry with."

"Thunderation, gal!" Captain Hardy exclaimed, rushing up with Tull Crockett to seize the mad stranger with large calloused hands. "Another second and you'd have had him, quick as any Injun I ever seen! Ain't no wonder that big Scot kept to his own side of the bed."

Too winded to appreciate the admiration expressed in the backwoodsman's comment, Krista inhaled deeply as the weight of the groaning man was lifted from her and started up, when another large hand appeared, one that grasped her arm with the force of a steel trap and hauled her roughly to her feet. Expecting to see yet another expression of gratitude from the man she'd rescued, not once now, but twice, she raised her gaze only to reel in the fury directed toward her.

"I needed no help from Hardy, lassie, and I sure as the devil didn't need your own meddlin'! Ye might have been killed!"

Krista's jaw tightened with the slap of his sharp reprimand. "So might you."

"How did he prove himself to you?" the stranger shrieked behind them at the two backwoodsmen who tied him up. "What did he do to prove he was for us?"

Gavin swung around and grabbed up the jug of rum from one of his companion's hand. "For one thing, I married a woman who thinks she's a man! God knows, nay man should have to suffer such a fate for any cause!"

"At least I am no braying fool!"

Krista caught her bottom lips in her teeth, hardly able to believe her angry outburst. She was unaccustomed to speaking back. It usually meant retribution of some sort, if not against her, against someone she cared for. But what had she done wrong?

She fought the shudder that ran through her as the tavernkeeper dragged the bound drunken stranger into the other room to sleep it off. She wouldn't let the men watching her know this terrible hurt that welled in her chest, vying with a mixture of anger and frustration. They mustn't know how vulnerable she really was, how easily her feelings were wounded. They must think her as insensitive as they.

"Who will drink with me?" Gavin Duncan bellowed, turning away to tilt the jug above his lips.

"I am turning in," she announced to no one in particular, for Duncan was ignoring her and the other didn't want to get involved in the squabble.

"Strike me blue, this jug has a hollow ring to it. How about another there, Mr. Tavernkeeper."

"The six cent or the three?" the man behind the counter inquired.

"The three!" Captain Hardy called out from the hearth where he'd settled back to speak to the Lenape braves.

"Bad liquor and a troublesome woman!" Duncan

snorted derisively for Krista's benefit. "I'd best try for the last o' the vapors, for 'tis the last hint of decent liquor I'm likely to sample till the end of this infernal war."

She could see the Scot's shadow on the wall as he lifted it and drained what was left from the bottom before bellowing for another. How could she have ever thought for a moment that there was a sensitive man beneath that insufferable, arrogant, and ungrateful manner of his? He called the Indians heathen and yet they had far more respect for their women than this so-called *gentleman* from Scotland.

As Krista wrapped her blanket around her shoulders and staked out a spot near the end of the bar where it butted against the wall, the conversation gradually dwindled to a low murmur. She tried to shut it out, but knew that she was being discussed, not only by the two propective recruits, who had just discovered that she was a she, but by the Indians. She had shown them all her worth, she thought bitterly, wondering why she couldn't just let it go at that. After all, they had expressed a degree of admiration, of acceptance . . .

"Come over by the fire, Scottie boy, and let it take some o' the heat out of that temper of yours. 'Tis likely the only warmth ye'll get tonight aside from what's in the jug."

Although she didn't watch, she could hear the booted thud of her husband's footsteps as he joined the group and easily made out his sarcastic inquiry to the two Indians who had witnessed the scene.

"Are your women as troublesome as that one?"

Krista grated her teeth as Red Deer replied somberly. "Not if he want a man to provide meat and lodging for him."

"Him?"

"They ain't got no word for *she* and *her*," Captain Hardy informed the bewildered Scot.

The Indian called Hawk Shadow spoke to his companion in a flow of staccato syllables.

"Hawk Shadow say your woman have no need of a man. He can provide his own meat and lodging."

"Well, I certainly have no need of her!"

"Then quit him and find another woman. How many horses you give for He Who Glides Over Mountains?"

"*Give?*" Duncan exclaimed incredulous at the suggestion. "I was *paid* to take her! Now I can see why the old German wanted to be rid of her!"

Blood drained from Krista's face, pounding in her ears so that the conversation became muted. Herr Schuyler *paid* Gavin Duncan to marry her? But she had been so certain her stepfather would have taken advantage of the Big Knives' plight and charged top dollar for her guide services. Suddenly her sister's feigned innocence of the fee the innkeeper was asking for made sense. Marta was not as dumb as she sometimes made others believe. She had known and chosen not to tell, not to give away Herr Schuyler's plan for Krista.

The force of her sister's added betrayal constricted her throat around the blade of emotion that had lodged there—cutting and painful. To keep the glaze that threatened her eyes from spilling over, she forced her eyelids open, almost to the point that they hurt, and willed them to ice over sooner than betray her as well.

He had needed a horse, she heard the Scot saying above the roar of her humiliation. Marriage was the only way he could get the innkeeper to let her go with them. Captain Hardy had talked him into it, saying it would prove his devotion to the cause.

"Curse ye, man, dinna ye think of the trouble she'd cause?"

"The gal's not caused nearly as much trouble as that hot temper of yours, Scottie boy."

Gavin ran his hand through his coarse straight hair and stared at the fire. "Ach, I suppose you're right," he sighed tiredly. "Meanin' no offense to you gentlemen, but the thought o' the savages I came down here with sets me blood to boilin', much like that poor devil's in there. I've much to learn about this land, I'll admit, and about the . . . what tribe did ye call yourselves?

"Lenape," Red Deer provided. "You are like the young warrior with fire in his head instead of his heart. It is sensible that you know there is much yet for you to learn."

Gavin glanced back at the still figure in the corner, hat pulled down over her face. He'd had his hand clasped about the dirk strapped to his leg, ready to use it the moment he doubled the man over with a well-placed lift of the knee. Then he'd seen the girl go down with him. At first a moment of panic seized him with the certainty that she'd been injured, but as he moved forward, long slim buckskin-clad legs had wrapped about the man and Krista's knife flashed unerringly at his throat. Aye, there was much for him to learn about the frontier, particularly about its women.

Chapter Five

The snow was an entertaining toy for the brisk remainder of the harsh wind that had howled outside the trading post all night. The soft dry powder was whisked away from the brown winter-burned earth in some places and banked in others. Sometimes, as Krista cut her lone way through its whimsical assault, it managed to penetrate the wool of the scarf pulled over her face and threatened to freeze the cloth to her stinging cheeks, so that when she saw woodsmoke rising from the chimney of the hunting cabin where she'd tended Gavin Duncan's wound only days before, her first reaction was relief.

She patted her weary horse, as if trying to make up for their relentless pace since stealing off from the tavern in the wee hours of the morning. Tired as she was, her heart still pounded with the apprehension of being discovered and stopped before she was away. It was a wonder it did not give out from exhaustion, for she had lain awake most of the night, listening to it hammer in her chest while she waited for the men to settle in and go to sleep.

When nothing further could be said to humiliate her, their conversation switched to the more conventional subject of the war, while her thoughts centered around her plans to abandon them. It was decided that Hawk

Shadow and Red Deer wee going to travel with them to Kaskaskia, which meant they had no further need of the woman who thought herself to be a man and had been the source of their amusement and derision from the moment the journey and ridiculous marriage had been proposed. That her stepfather had not charged them a pence, but paid them to take her, was more than the thick skin born of years of constant ridicule could bear.

Her decision to leave was a logical one, she'd argued when she considered their reaction upon discovering her missing with the good horse that was hers by every right. No man would have stood for such humiliation. Certainly, not the proud Scot, whose words had cut her the most. A man would have flown into a rage and taken them all on.

Krista had more sense than that. She was uncommonly tall and strong for a woman, but that night the Scot had tugged her into the bed, and him weak from loss of blood, she was no match for him. Not to fight was as practical a decision as leaving, since she was no longer needed and such a terrible burden to her new husband.

Gavin Duncan could have the marriage annulled in Fort Pitt and she would return to the hunting cabin which Kurt Waltari had constructed when he first came down the Alleghany from New York, before he married and started a homestead on land better suited for tillage. By the time her stepfather discovered her there, Marta would be married and Krista would have Uncle Kurt's backing to stand up to the man. She'd even considered continuing to hunt and provide the tavern with meat and fowl, this time for her own profit. She owed Herr Schuyler nothing now.

That plan, however, had already gone awry. Her initial relief gave way to wariness as she contemplated the chimney smoke again. Someone else, it seemed, had moved in

. . . for longer than a night, Krista observed, noting for the first time the baskets hanging under the catslide of the roof and the cow closely corralled on the other side of the door by young saplings that had been tied to the support posts of the dirt-floored porch. And it was getting too dark and cold to press on for the half day's journey to the Waltari place.

She shivered beneath her buffalo robe, trying to decide on a course of action, when a familiar sound rose from the cabin—a baby's cry. It was probably some destitute family seeking winter shelter before traveling further west, she mused, taking the reins of her horse into gloved hands and starting down to the clearing from her forest cover.

"Haloo!" she shouted, intending to give the strangers ample warning of her approach, so that they did not think her a marauder. "Haloo there, friend!"

The baby never missed a breath, but continued to cry. However, Krista could see a movement of shadows behind the skin-covered windows. She hesitated long enough to offer a quick prayer that the family would not panic and shoot, but give her a chance to prove she was no threat to them. By the time she reached the catslide, the door had yet to open.

"I am a friend," she called out uneasily. "I mean no harm. You can see my gun is still in its sling on the horse."

She wrapped the reins around one of the posts, ready to duck behind the animal for shelter at the first sign of hostility, when the door opened a crack and two pairs of eyes stared out at her, one at the level of a short adult and the other definitely belonging to a small child.

"May I come in?" Krista asked, stepping clear of the animal so that the light that filtered through the door at their back could further evidence her harmlessness. "It is getting dark and very cold and I have come a long way today."

For a moment, she thought she was going to have to go on to the Waltari cabin after all, for the door remained as frozen and still as those who peered from behind it. However, just as she was about to inform the intruder that it was, after all, her cabin, it opened the rest of the way to allow her entrance.

There was no sign of a man, only a woman clad in blankets and a coarsely spun skirt with a child of about three years of age clinging to it. In her arms was the baby who had ceased to cry and was contentedly nursing within the fold of the blanket.

"Many Husbands!" Krista exclaimed in surprise, recognizing the scar left by an enraged French Canadian trapper who had once lived with the woman. He'd struck her across the face with a hot poker, burning, rather than cutting, an ugly ridged mark across her cheek.

"I was told you leave with new husband."

"I adopted the Indian divorce. I need no man to provide for me." Krista glanced over to where a pan of corn mush sat on the hearth. "But tonight I am tired and hungry. I have traveled all day. I'll pay you back with skins as soon as I can for the food."

The halfbreed's expression remained stonelike, aside from wary eyes that revealed her inner distress at Krista's return. "It was here. I only use because I am told you leave with new husband."

Krista smiled. "It is all right. There is room for all of us. I will sleep on the floor near the fire. You and the child can have the bed." She walked over to the hearth and cut out a square of the solidified mush. "But why did you leave Squaw Row?"

Constructed by women who had no braves to support them or had taken white men as mates for a period of time before being abandoned, the little row of lodges lay on the outskirts of the nearby village, close to the trading post which supported the squaws by purchasing their wares for trade. The women worked together, depended on one another, and it was an accepted fact that many of them, Many Husbands included, subsidized their income by warming the beds of the many traders and trappers who came and went. The reddish brown hair of the child peeping around its mother's skirt with wide brown eyes was evidence of this.

"This good house. Better for my children away from coughing sickness."

Krista nodded. She had heard of whooping cough claiming the lives of old and young alike in the village. She supposed Squaw Row was not immune to it. If anything, the Indians were less resilient to the disease than the white man. "Well, you are welcome to remain here as long as you wish. I will be hunting most of the time."

After satisfying her appetite, Krista saw to her horse, tying it in the shelter of the tall pines surrounding the cabin. Upon returning, the baby had been put in a small wooden cradle and the older child now lay in the bed with its mother, nursing as intently as its younger sibling had done. The fire had been laid for the night, so she stacked the extra wood she had brought in to feed it during the night, if necessary.

Many Husbands was not particularly talkative, nor did Krista feel inclined to start up a conversation. She was tired from the journey. The fact that she had not slept well for the past two nights only compounded her exhaustion, so that, before the last log crumbled into the glowing bed of embers and the charred remains of its support, she had fallen into a deep slumber.

She had no intention of letting the Scot into her dreams. He had cursed her sufficiently in her conscious life without invading her private musings. Yet in he marched, handsome and proud, with that charming grin of his that was boyish enough to set even the staunchest old maid's heart tripping. A guardian angel he called her, bending down, not to wipe the foam of the beer from the tip of her nose, but to kiss it. His fingers wound into her hair, fondling it as if it were of the spun gold to which he compared it. Her pulse fluttered wildly as his lips moved down to her mouth, as if seeking further nectar.

As he drank deeply, tasting and exploring, she shuddered with the racking waves of heat that melted flesh and bone to his rock hard body. The big hands that possessed a strength worthy of such a fine build closed warmly on her shoulders, drawing her even nearer, until the fingers bit into her flesh, penetrating the daze of pleasure with pain, sharp and bruising.

Krista groaned in protest as they yanked her from the warm dream world, bringing her to reality as her head struck the edge of the hearth where she was suddenly dropped.

"Vat are you doingk here?"

Blinking furiously to remove the lingering clouds from her vision and focus on the stout figure standing over her, she felt her shoulders being lifted again. Reaching behind her instinctively, she caught herself as she was thrown back to the floor, leaving her ribs exposed to the buckled shoe that slammed into her side. Somehow Gavin Duncan had turned into her stepfather.

"N'dellemùske!" Many Husbands wailed from the bed, where she held her child against her chest protectively.

"You vill go no vere, woman! This house is yours as I promised. I vill get rid of this one goodt this time!"

Sensing rather than seeing the foot come at her again, Krista rolled to the side and to her feet, her senses clearing as she gained them. Pieces of a puzzle she never suspected fell into place as she calculated the distance to the door where she'd hung her rifle. Many Husbands was her stepfather's concubine, set up in her own house now that Krista was out of the way. No doubt when Marta moved out, the squaw would go to work at the inn. And the little boy, now staring in fright at the man who circled around to capture Krista in his short bearlike arms, was his. The eyes were his mother's, but the hair was the color of what was left of Herr Schuyler's.

Forgetting about the small cradle lying on the floor next to the cot, Krista ducked and made the break for her gun as her stepfather charged her. Trying not to fall on it and injure the startled babe within, she half jumped, half dove onto the floor beyond it. However, as she once again rolled to gain her footing, the burly man, seeing her objective, reached the weapon first.

"So you vould shoot your father?" he taunted, leveling the barrel of the loaded gun at her. "Then it would be a matter of self-defense for me to do the same to you, no?"

"It would be murder. Would you spill blood in front of your own son?" Krista accused, never taking her gaze from the lethal muzzle aimed at her. Had she done so, she might have seen the shock that flashed across her stepfather's face. "Would you have him know his papa is a murderer?"

"Take up the babe, voman!" the man snapped at Many Husbands. "My *daughter* and I have business outside. First, throw that knife at your side down on the hearth . . . slowly."

Krista reluctantly obeyed. The sound of the metal blade striking the brick rang in her ears, announcing the desperation of her predicament. In the corner of her eye she saw Many Husbands obediently grab up the now screeching baby. The squaw woman would be no help to her. She was going to have to talk her way out of this, she thought desperately, catching the scent of cheap whiskey on her captor's breath as they stepped out into the cold darkness . . . if the whiskey hadn't made him too irrational.

"Both children are yours?"

Krista gasped as the barrel of the gun poked into her back, forcing her out into the yard where moonlight shafted through an opening in the treetops. What was there? What could she use to protect herself? she drilled, trying to maintain discipline in the midst of her fear. The wood maul! She seized upon the idea, daring to glance over her shoulder to the woodpile on the side of the house where the splitting maul surely rested in its shadow. If she could only reach it . . .

"Goodt fine sons!" her stepfather boasted proudly. "Not daughters who empty a man's purse and have to be married off before he is rid of them!"

Krista turned slowly. "I thought I was your son, *papa.*" The familiar address nearly choked her with revulsion. "I worked as hard as any boy and learned to provide as well as any man my age. Your ovens and cookfires have been well filled with the game I hunted and your purse made fat with my trapping."

"You!" the man sneered in contempt. "I am not sure vat you are, but you are not son nor daughter to me. You always acted like you were better, like your real papa was better than me with his music and frivolous instruments."

Krista continued to speak, easing her way toward the wood pile. Her gun was well oiled and primed to fire easily. She always kept it ready and close at hand . . . until tonight.

"I did not like you, Herr Schuyler, but I worked for you just the same. You were Mama's husband and I respected that." She dared not look to be certain the maul was where she always kept it. It might give away her plan. "And for that, you paid to get rid of me, married me off to a man who wanted me no more than you did."

"Oh, I vanted you, Krista. I vanted to break that independent spirit in you and teach you to be a voman. Instead, you become more and more like a man until I can not look at you vithout feeling angry or smell you vithout being sick. You have shamed me as a man and now I vill shame you as a voman."

The moment her stepfather moved toward her, Krista leapt at the woodpile, feeling in the dark for the handle of the maul she knew to be there. To her dismay, all she found was the rough splintered edges of the split oak and maple stacked there. Chips of bark dug into her palms unmercifully, but she hardly felt it, for suddenly, there was an explosion of pain against the back of her head. Her mind grew numb which, while easing the anguish to a degree, also countermanded the instinctive command to rise and fight. Her legs gave out as she fell against the woodpile, causing it to avalanche at one end beneath her.

Her head struck a series of scattered logs as she was dragged by the feet over them. Rough hands were cold against the warm flesh of her abdomen as they tugged at the buttoned band of her trousers, her leather leggings already worked loose. Krista grabbed their thick wrists, trying to pry them away, only to receive a knuckled blow across the face. Again, her senses reeled and clambored for reason amidst the shrieks of agony.

"No!" she shouted, emerging once more to protest as her trousers came down, turning inside out and locking about her moccasin boots. She tried to grab a piece of wood, anything with which to fend off the man dragging her, kicking furiously, over the dirt yard. The debris lying around the woodblock assaulted the tender skin of her bared buttocks and back.

"Ach, so you are not a man after all!" Her stepfather chortled gleefully.

What he had in mind was worse than the killing Krista

had first feared. Fingers locking about a piece of kindling, she rose up as the man stopped long enough to loosen the laces of his trousers and swung at him. In her dazed state, however, the wood grazed his trousers. He danced back, nimble for a man of his size and girth. Suddenly his foot struck out and again, lights flared bright and her ears roared with the impact catching her under the chin, jamming her teeth and knocking her senseless once again.

She could only cry out in mumbled protest as her stepfather's heavy body fell on her, bruising the flesh between her thighs with pinching, forceful knees that wedged between her own. His liquored breath was hot and rapid, making a snorting sound through his flaring nostrils as he shoved up the buckskin shirt first and then the linen one beneath it. Her breasts felt as if he were trying to gouge them from her chest. Her anguished cry strangled in her throat with repugnance as she struck out ineffectively to defend herself.

Yet it was not that sound that filled her ears, but another, much more vocal one. It was an ungodly roar, too low pitched to be that of an Indian, yet no less savage. The satisfaction on Herr Schuyler's face turned to shock and then fear as he suddenly seemed to take flight, crashing into the side of the house with a startled grunt. Krista flinched as his assailant leapt over her and grabbed him again, as if playing some bizarre game of toss and fetch. The innkeeper shrieked this time as he was hauled up from the pile of wood and took flight again, this time landing on the splitting stump and rolling off with a thud.

It was a man. At least she thought it was. She tried dizzily to make out the leather-fringed legs that closed the distance between the opponents in two long strides.

"By God, I'll na' stand for a man strikin' a woman, much less the wickedness ye were about, mein herr!" The loud crunch of flesh against bone sent her stepfather sprawling again. Krista, however, was trying to pull her trousers up, stirred into a frenzy of modesty not by that, but by the familiar voice of her Scot.

"I was out of my head!" her stepfather pleaded fervently as the Scot lumbered toward him again and grabbed the front of his shirt. "The drink, it made me—"

Duncan punched him again, this time holding him with his free hand for another. "Don't be blamin' your wickedness on good liquor, man. 'Tis an insult to a man with respect for it!"

"But you didn't want her . . ."

"Well, I changed my mind and just in time, by the look of it. By God, I've a mind to—"

Krista grimaced as the whining man was struck again, but it wasn't her stepfather's pleas that echoed in her mind. It was Gavin Duncan's words. *I changed my mind.* She struggled again with the pants that had lodged over her boots when she heard a fearful wail rise from the open door of the cabin. With a babe at her breast and another at her knee, Many Husbands babbled hysterically in her native language.

"What the devil . . ."

The Scot whirled about, brandishing the pistol in his belt. He'd half expected to see a banshee leaping at him from the depths of hell, but at the sight of the harmless Indian woman, he swung it back around to the groaning innkeeper.

"What's she sayin'?"

"She's begging for his life, for the sake of her and his children," Krista translated loosely. The pants had come up, but the buttons had been ripped off. She struggled to her feet unsteadily, her leggings still around her knees. "If you kill him, she will have to provide for herself again."

"And ye, lassie? What say ye to the matter?"

Krista looked over at Many Husbands. Maybe she

didn't hate Herr Schuyler after all. She'd always felt guilty about it, for her mother taught her it was a sin to hate. Even after what he'd tried to do, she could not pronounce the death sentence her angry Scot was ready to deliver with the easy squeeze of a trigger.

"Let him live."

"Confound it, lassie, has he knocked ye daft? He doesn't deserve to draw another breath for his vile ways."

Krista risked bending over to pick up her rifle, long discarded and forgotten in the fray. "And those two boys don't deserve to be left without a father. His only contempt was for girls . . ." She stopped awkwardly. "Me." Bitterness wedged in her throat, but she swallowed it bravely. "He'll treat them right fair, I think."

"Then get your woman and be gone, man! Your daughter's a fair sight better at forgivin' than me."

"No!" Krista swayed and leaned on her rifle.

"Easy, lassie." The pistol still trained on the silent German, Gavin edged his way over to where Krista stood. "Ye need to get inside where it's warm."

"Would you make the children go out into the night?"

"What are ye suggestin'?"

"All I want to do is leave here." Her head was throbbing, her body aching all over, but all she wanted to do was put as much distance as she could between her stepfather and herself.

"You're as confoundin' a creature as I've ever crossed!"

"That is your pot calling me black," Krista quipped, far more gamely than she felt. "I'll get my horse."

"That's a pot and a kettle, lassie, but I'll admit to my own devilish ways." He stopped her and placed the pistol in her hand. "Ye keep an eye on Herr Schuyler. I'll fetch the horse."

How Krista managed to remain upright and alert evaded her, but she did, nonetheless. Her stepfather sat harmlessly on the splitting stump, not daring to push his turn of fortune. His words of apology hardly registered, for all her concentration was fixed on remaining on her feet.

She could rest in the saddle, she promised herself as she saw Gavin Duncan coming from the pine thicket with her horse. She took the reins from him while he took the added precaution of tying Herr Schuyler to a nearby tree.

"For the love of God, will ye tell that woman we mean no harm to the man?"

"*Sehe! Tschitqùssil!* Hush now. Hold your tongue!" Krista obliged. "We will leave him safe for you."

Many Husbands didn't stop altogether, but the volume of her cries was lessened by Krista's words. The Indian woman remained in the doorway, watching as Gavin Duncan placed Krista's rifle in the saddle sling and relieved her of his pistol so that she could mount.

"You took off your skirt," Krista murmured in wonder as it struck her what was different about the man. He still wore his tartan cloak beneath a thick robe of bearskin, but the skirt was definitely missing.

"I only wear it for formal occasions, as I was led by my companions to believe we were to celebrate the night they let the Indians burn those poor souls. My travelin' clothes were lost along the way after the raid, but the trader at the post fitted me out well enough. Up with ye, now."

Ordinarily, Krista could have sprung into the saddle with little effort, but in her current state, she wound up leaning across it and tugging, embarrassed as her trousers slid down around her hips. As she reached behind her, her rescuer came to her aid once more, tugging them up.

"Is this your way of suggestin' a trade of sorts . . . my kilt for your trousers?"

Her color deepened, burning her cheeks. "I . . . my buttons tore . . ."

To her astonishment, Gavin swung up on the horse behind her and chuckled lowly in her ear. "Speak no more of it, lassie. You're safe with me."

The words were as comforting as the hard chest pressed against her back, making further protest too difficult to muster. He was taking her away and, by his own declaration, had no use for men who abused women. His abuse had been of a different nature, but at the moment, Krista was too shaken and her head ached too much to address that or the questions that surfaced as she leaned upon his strength and gave in to her fatigue.

Chapter Six

The flatboat, or Kentucky boat as locals called it, strained against its lines, ready to be cut loose at the water's edge, just as the general had assured them. The morning fog had lifted just enough to reveal the frost-covered banks sloping down to the landing, although it still clung stubbornly to the hilltops, obscuring them from view. The craft was loaded both under and on top of its shed roof, which covered most of the decking aside from a small corral for the livestock. To Cook's delight, a small pig was already harbored in it. Ten by forty feet in measure, the bulky rectangular craft appeared no less ready than its crew to get underway.

The week at Fort Pitt had been a strain on all of them. Upon Gavin and Krista's arrival, they'd discovered that Hairbuyer Hamilton, as the colonials derisively called the British commander, had left Detroit with an army of northern Indians to stop Colonel Clark from further dissuading the western woodland tribes from taking sides in the war and thereby securing a stronger foothold in the frontier. With more pressure than ever on them to make good time and take the supply of powder to the colonel and his troops, the discussion as to the route they would take became a heated one.

Krista might have favored the shortest route along the trace instead of the river route their Indian companions had chosen. But the fact that Simon Girty, one of the traders at the post and an Indian agent of dubious motivation, kept recommending it made the fine hair at the nape of her neck rise warily. Girty's partner had already been jailed on suspicion of treason and Krista was not so certain Girty would be far behind him.

He was right that the trace was the shortest route, but it was also the most dangerous and susceptible to ambush. She wouldn't put it past him to set up just such an event, not only stopping the messenger of peace from reaching the tribal council, but seizing the badly needed powder as well.

When an attempt was made on Hawk Shadow's life and Gavin nearly took the bullet for the brave, however, the decision was made for them. They would travel with the Lenape and the Minsi peace messenger, for the peace messenger was as important to negotiating with the Indians for a truce as the powder was to fighting Hamilton. The last thing the colonials wanted was to anger the Lenape nation with whom Clark had made great progress, for their rage had barely died out from the brutal murder of Cornstalk, one of the chiefs who supported neutrality.

The expedition party hastened to bring horses aboard. Having traveled by ferry before, the two steeds from Schuyler Crossing gave Krista and Gavin little trouble, but a few of the others had to be blindfolded by their owners to coax them onto the floating barge. While man and beast struggled, Krista made her way to where Red Deer and Hawk Shadow placed their few belongings in a hollowed-out canoe large enough to seat three comfortably to ask if she might scout ahead with them.

During the chaos of the previous night's visit, she'd

been so preoccupied with the attempt on Hawk Shadow's life and the news from the Grenadier Squaw of the British plans that she'd neglected to address that aspect of the journey with their Indian companions. Then there was Gavin's intervention in the incident which had puzzled her. It was all the side of her that wanted to believe in him and his integrity needed to soar. Yet her more practical side kept a rein on her emotions and the battle of the heart, combined with the excitement of finally being on their way, made sleep fitful at best.

A distance away, instead of paying attention to Hardy, who was disdainfully studying the navigation manual the general had obligingly sent along, Gavin Duncan found himself watching the tall fair-haired girl speaking quietly with the savages. That she seemed more at ease with them than himself did even less to improve the humor she'd once again disrupted that morning.

He'd begun to think that he was finally gaining some ground in their relationship. As he saw it, he had come to her rescue and gone out of his way to see to her comfort, including bedding down next to her and holding her, despite that godawful stench that followed her about. That he'd wanted to surprised him as much as it had her, for she'd been decidedly wary at first.

He shook himself mentally, as if his recent discovery had yet to register as real. Who would have believed the girl her father pawned off on him was the fair creature who'd nursed him through the fever, the viking princess he thought he had dreamed? Perhaps he'd guessed it, even before her trail led back to the familiar cabin. There was something about her, a quiet grace of movement that was obvious once one looked past the frontier trappings and smell.

Alone for the first time since their strained wedding night, they had actually talked, enough to establish that no matter what lay ahead, there was no going back for either of them. There was too much pain there. The common bond made for a congenial atmosphere and the girl's icy nature was actually beginning to thaw by the time the earthen and log palisades of the fort came into view, warmed no doubt by that which burned in his loins at the soft brush of her buttocks against him as they shared their horse—fishy stench and all.

No stranger to women and their vexing natures, Gavin sensed her attraction for him. Her nervous looks and that fetching blush of hers didn't make it hard to read. Then one bawdy joke from Captain Hardy and she'd withdrawn again. Damn the colonials and their callousness! Not even the knife he'd purchased from Girty that morning to replace the one she lost had brought her back to him. She'd insisted on paying him and, when he'd declared it a wedding gift, promptly reminded him that their wedding was to be ended in Kaskaskia.

The lass had blood cold as the northern fjords of her ancestors, Gavin thought, unreasonably perturbed at her lack of forgiveness for his past behavior and the cool manner with which she'd accepted his gift. He'd done wrong by her and apologized as best he knew how, but by God, the son of Duncan Brae begged no woman. He'd not written Claire to plead his suit when he'd discovered her engagement to Robert and Claire was twice the lady and beauty the tall gangly girl fraternizing with the heathens was.

Strange as it was, though, he mused, for all her expertise with weapons, Krista seemed, not more delicate, but more vulnerable. There was something about the broken, lost look haunting her blue eyes that struck a protective chord in him, too strong for him to comprehend. He could have broken her stepfather in half with his bare hands for what he'd nearly done.

"Ain't a man worth 'is salt don't know a river big as this don't have trees an' bars to avoid hittin'. It's just plain common sense to look to avoid 'em!" the captain scoffed beside him, staring at the river manual as if it were crawling with vermin. "Lessen you want to read it, Scottie boy. Ya got a way that tells of more book learnin' than most."

"Hmm? Oh . . ." Gavin recovered quickly, reconstructing the words he'd overheard, but not listened to. "I suppose it could help pass the time," he mumbled, taking the manual from the soldier as the disrupting object of his real interest started toward them. "Thanks."

He thumbed through the pages in feigned regard until he heard her voice, sweet and lilting, belying her masculine appearance. The absurd thought occurred to him that it would be pleasant to hear her sing. Claire had had a high birdlike voice which she accompanied on the harpsichord for many evenings' entertainment at Duncan Brae. She once confided, if not for the scandalous life associated with theatre, that she would have preferred a career there, rather than that of a mistress of a titled estate. But then Claire would always choose the most comfortable lot in . . .

"I think it is right good that I go on ahead with Red Deer and Hawk Shadow to scout for a place to bring in the boat for the night."

"The devil ye say!"

Krista met Gavin's incredulous outburst with cool reprisal. "I was engaged as a guide, Herr Duncan. That is what guides do."

"Then I'll go with her, man," he announced to the officer at his side, before retaliating with equal aplomb, "That's what *husbands* do."

To Gavin's chagrin, Hardy agreed with Krista. "Cool yer heels, Scottie boy. The gal's right. I'd feel better with her goin' ahead with the Lenape."

"Then I'll be goin' too, especially if ye do not trust them."

"I can take care of myself, thanks to you. Besides, there is only room for three in the canoe," Krista pointed out logically.

The Scot glanced toward the Indians, watching impassively from a distance. He didn't like it, not at all. What manner of women did they raise in these colonies? "Then, for the love of God, take this," he capitulated, his tone expressing his frustration and something else that shocked Krista as much as the gift.

Krista took the pistol he produced from inside his jacket, along with a small horn containing ball in one side and powder in the other. Was that concern she heard? an eager acceptance leaping to the forefront of her thought. Or was he capable of summoning it to his voice and expressions on demand—acting it out, in the same convincing manner as Herr Schuyler had done when paying court to her widowed mother in Vienna, when all along he'd been a self-serving demon in disguise.

How she wished she hadn't seen him conversing with Simon Girty in the trading post that morning! Things had been relatively pleasant between them until she reminded herself that he'd yet to be cleared in her mind of his political affiliation. Seeing him with a man she not only mistrusted, but detested, had not improved her opinion. Once again conflicting emotions squared off behind the impassive face she presented.

"Do ye know how to use it?"

"My aim is not as good as with the rifle, but I know how it works," she assured him, disconcerted by this unpredictable nature of his. If he were setting them up for an ambush, he wouldn't arm her, her practical nature told her. Yet, there was an intangible something that made her reluctant to accept the obvious. Suspicion or fear, she wondered. Was he dangerous to the mission or only to her? Did she dare expose her fragile and long isolated feelings to him, a stranger and possibly her enemy? "I owe you more, Herr Duncan."

"Ye owe me naught but this, my reluctant wife."

Krista caught her breath, her blue eyes widening as he suddenly grabbed the hand with the pistol in it and brought it to his lips, brushing them warmly across it and leaving a trail that reduced her spine to a gel.

"T'would seem more gainly to have given you flowers, but I feel this will serve you better in this time and place."

Flowers. The sweet words struck her like a splash of cold water, defraying the warmth that had briefly afflicted her good sense. Their music room had been filled with such gifts from Herr Schuyler. Her mother had even put them on her father's beautiful ebony piano.

The Scot's were silvered words from a practiced gallant and smooth-talking devil, Krista told herself sternly, a bitterness from the past coming to the aid of reason. Weak as her knees felt, she'd not give him the satisfaction of swooning.

"I agree, Herr . . ."

"Call me Gavin or I'll swim alongside that blasted hollow tree and bedevil you until you do."

It was there again, that boyish grin of his—challenging, teasing, beguiling. Oh, the anger was still lurking behind his gaze, but he was trying hard to master it. Besides, the mental picture of him carrying out his threat was caution's undoing.

"Gavin, then," she gave in, a poorly smothered giggle raising her voice to an amused pitch she could not help. She could see him swimming beside the canoe. The Indians would surely think him mad . . . and so would she. Perhaps madness explained his incomprehensible behavior, or her own, even.

"We'll save the flowers for the future."

More teasing, Krista mused, spontaneously responding in kind, "And a more obliging season. Good travel, sirs. I will see you this evening."

"Keep an eye on the savages, lassie."

"I have known Red Deer since we were young. Because of that you have nothing to fear from him or his cousin. If for no other reason," she added, "they will not bother me because you saved Hawk Shadow's life. They would refrain from doing me harm out of honor to you for that. Their code of honor is different from ours, but it exists nonetheless." There was little point in explaining that the Indians also thought her a bit touched after seeing her skiing during the hunting season; that to assault her was almost as taboo as assaulting Hawk Shadow.

"We'll see."

And if she continued to bask in that warm gaze of concern, she would be undone, for it promised something wonderfully tempting. Krista tucked the gun in her belt, suddenly awkward under the spell-weaving regard of her companion. *Deliver us from temptation.* The words of the prayer her mother had taught her took on a new meaning. Not since she'd curled in her father's lap to sleep had she felt as safe as she had wrapped in a blanket in front of Gavin Duncan as they'd ridden away from the hunting cabin. She'd fended for herself for so long . . .

Stepping out of his shadow, she squinted in the fog-filtered sunlight at the barge where Captain Hardy was now waiting. "I will be waiting for you and the others on the bank by nightfall."

"Come along, Scottie boy, we're set to go!"

Krista pivoted on her heel to take advantage of Gavin's acknowledging glance at the captain, and took off in an easy lope to where the Lenape waited to shove off. Why did it come so naturally to place her trust in him, when logic warned her against it? Thor's thunder, she'd even found herself staring at his lips, as if expecting him to kiss her goodbye like some witless barn maid. How could her body so blatantly ignore her thoughts?

Assuming a crouched position beside Red Deer, Krista dedicated her full concentration to shoving the canoe into the gently moving water and leapt inside with an agility born of practice. Situated between the two braves, she took up a spare carved paddle and put it to the water. As the canoe shot forward toward the middle of the shining stretch of water, it passed the barge, which moved more slowly. Venturing to search the deck for a towering figure of brawn and buckskin, she spotted Gavin at the steerage where Tull Crockett had taken charge of the long oar. He lifted his hand, verifying he had seen her and spurring Krista to do the same.

He *was* concerned! "Thank you again!" she called out, her voice carrying clearly across the water.

"Until tonight!"

His reply set off a round of snickers that made her instantly regret her spontaneous declaration of gratitude. Why was he always inferring there was something to this marriage? What gain could he possibly expect? She was acting their guide, which had prompted the wedding to start with. Her mind again thrown into a turmoil of questions and contradiction, she purposefully focused ahead on the spanning river which cut through rolling hills woven together by forest and brush. At least she was returning to the wilderness where beauty and danger awaited hand in hand to steal one's breath and demand undivided attention. There she would have peace from Gavin Duncan—at least for a while.

Chapter Seven

An unexpected sizzle on the campfire drew Krista's attention from the dark shrouded river to her more immediate surroundings. There was another and yet another as she lifted her gaze to search the halo of the flames. A few faint specks of white floated down into the campfire's glow. Snow, she thought smugly. She knew it was coming. Yet, as quickly as her satisfaction at being right registered, it turned to dismay. This would surely slow them down, particularly if the river started to ice over.

The day's journey had proceeded well enough, she supposed, but where the devil were the others? She and her Indian companions had made camp early and even had time to scout about, in case they were being followed. Although they'd found nothing, Krista could tell by the way Hawk Shadow and Red Deer acted that they were still not satisfied, nor was she. She'd had the feeling they'd been watched all day long and not by the occupants of the flatboats they passed, Tory sympathizers who had been forced from the rebel-occupied regions further west.

Surely the men had followed the markers, she thought, the idea that they'd struck a snag not sitting well with her. As she and her Indian companions moved ahead, they'd circumvented several clusters of trees midstream. Some were rooted to the bottom, commonly called planters, and others called sawyers were loosely attached and rose and fell with the tide. They'd cut a path around them, determined the depth of the river there, and left fresh blazes in the trees to mark the way for the flatboat to follow.

In spring, during high water, the river would afford a greater channel to passing crafts, but late fall showed watermarks on the trees high above the current river level. If the flatboat followed their fresh markings and cut a wide path to the left, it would pass with no consequence. If it didn't the expedition might well end there.

Surely they hadn't missed them, she told herself again, and all this fretting was doing no good. Her efforts were best spent making the camp more hospitable, for when the flatboat caught up with them, the occupants would be tired, cold, and hungry. Busying herself, she moved the firewood she'd gathered into the shelter of the cave, so that they'd have dry wood throughout the night, and put her belongings even further back inside.

With a long length of green wood she pushed the campfire closer as well so that the overhang partially protected it, and applied new kindling. She had just reestablished the spit with the finished turkeys nearby to keep them warm, when she spied two figures loping gracefully along the riverbank. She reached cautiously for the rifle she kept close at hand, but dropped it upon recognizing Red Deer and Hawk Shadow.

"Your man just beyond the bend with the others," Red Deer shouted. "Boat jammed on underwater tree. Had to shove boat off."

Relief flooded through Krista, easing the turmoil her speculation had set off in her mind. Their lookout must not have seen their marks. Perhaps Captain Hardy might do well after all to have his crew read the navigator manual General Hand had sent. "Well, I imagine they're hungry."

Hungry was hardly the description for the flatboat's crew when they finally tied off at the edge of the campsite. She could hear Tucker Hardy swearing as he stomped up the incline toward the inviting smell of roasted fowl and hot coffee. It wasn't until he helped himself to the brew on the fire that Krista discovered there was more to the delay.

"I'll tell ya, some devil tacked that 'ere board right over Red Deer's blaze to make us take the wrong turn around that cluster of planters. If we didn't have as many men and poles as we did, I reckon we'd 'a had to throw half the cargo over. As it was, we lost six barrels."

"You threw the gunpowder over?" Krista echoed in surprise.

"To lighten the craft so we could shove it off, lassie." Gavin Duncan dropped down across from her and reached for a piece of the freshly roasted fowl. "But we kept a line on them to haul back aboard after we were unfast."

"If Scottie boy here hadn't asked why the faded marks on the tree seemed to indicate the other way around, we'd still be sittin' high, cold and hungry or busted up, wet and dead by now."

"Who do you think did it?" Krista passed him a sack of cold biscuits Cook had added to the fare, leftover from the morning breakfast. No one complained about their blackened bottoms, their irritation having found a new source.

"Somebody that didn't want this gunpowder gettin' to Colonel Clark," Tull Crockett grunted.

"The Lenape and I have been looking around right good and have seen nothing out of the ordinary."

"Unlessen someone was waiting on the banks for us to

bust up and then took off when it didn't happen. Tarnation!" the captain exploded, shaking his fingers and dropping the drumstick he'd pulled off the turkey. "This is one hot bird!"

"But good," Tull Crockett complimented. "Looks like you're gettin' more and more of a woman all the time, Duncan."

"Aye, it does."

Although she'd purposefully taken a seat between Red Deer and Tull Crockett to avoid the disturbing warmth and strength of Gavin Duncan's stalwart presence, Krista could not ignore the steady gaze kindling across the campfire at her, nor the way her heart suddenly clutched at the upward tilt of his mouth. "It means you have a right good guide," she insisted in a stubborn voice.

"Give me your canteens and I'll fill them at the river," she offered, suddenly eager to melt into the oblivion of the forest, away from the unsettling Scot and his crude companions.

They were not like Uncle Kurt. He'd never made suggestions that affected her with uneasiness about her gender. Oh, he'd teased her well enough, but in a good-humored way intended to make her laugh at herself and the folly in which he'd caught her. She had had so much to learn, not being raised in the wilderness, but learn she did. At trading posts, she avoided such familiar speculation by staying in the background, but here she could not. She was the guide and expected to sit in with the rest, female or not. Which was what she wanted, *wasn't it?*

Loaded with an assortment of skins and canteens, Krista left the others to eat, her own appetite satisfied by the nervous picking she had done while waiting for news of them. The woods were quiet except for the hooting of an owl in the distance. The snow that gathered on the barren limbs of the chestnuts and oaks and dusted the evergreen needles that reflected tiny darts of light from the campfire. It was thickening, she thought, glancing back to see the density of the snowflakes between her and the opening of their shelter where the men were gathered as close as the flames would allow.

The cave was a godsend for the night, but the next day's travel was going to be miserable if the sun could not chase off the dark clouds that had brought the inclement weather from the west. Being cold in the sunlight was a far cry more comfortable than enduring the same temperature on a cloudy day, swathed in damp robes and blankets. Krista shivered at the thought and proceeded to fill the canteens at the water's edge, her rifle ever ready at her side.

Gavin would need the buffalo robe she slept in to wrap around his broad shoulders and supplement the warmth of the buckskin jacket he'd acquired at the trading post, she mused quietly, unwittingly protective of the greenhorn. As for herself, her vest, garnered from the same animal she and Uncle Kurt had killed in her sixteenth winter, would do well, worn skin side out, like a slicker, to protect her from the snowfall.

A loud snap brought Krista to her feet, instantly alert. Another drew her attention to the right toward the camp, where the man of her thoughts made his agile way down the slope. Once before she'd thought him a bear coming through the brush. The recollection brought a hint of a smile to her lips, even as she sped up her ministrations to finish them. Her chest began to pound as though he represented a danger as great as the burly predator of the wild, for he was a predator and somehow her heart felt threatened by him.

"There ye are, lassie. Damnation, it's a wonder ye can see to keep from fallin' in!"

"The snow brightens things right good," Krista replied,

recorking one of the militia-issue canteens as Gavin dropped to his haunches beside her.

"Then ye can see this."

Krista squinted to make out the shape of the small dark vial he held in front of her, although her effort was needless. She could tell from the scent that drifted her way that it was her fish ointment. "How dare you go searching through my things!" She grabbed for the bottle only to have it snatched away.

"Oh no! I've discovered your wicked secret and will have no more of it, unless ye can give me good cause to let ye keep it."

"Mama said I should rub it on my skin to . . ." Krista hesitated, her mind refusing to recoup from the shock of Gavin's discovery. "To keep it soft out here in the wilderness. This weather is right hard on a woman's skin."

She reached for it again, but to her dismay, Gavin leapt to his feet and hurled the bottle out into the silvery bed of water. It landed with a small splash a good distance away, far from the possibility of being recovered.

"Now tell me the real reason ye keep that godawful stuff on ye, lassie, for, from personal observation, I canna be convinced such skin needs to be softened any more than it is."

Krista struggled to her feet irritably, canteens swinging from her arms and battering her hips. The man would not forget the least bit of intimacy, forced as it had been, let alone have the decency not to mention it. The mere thought of his gently picking out the splinters from her delicate backside after her stepfather had dragged her about the woodyard seared her cheeks with scarlet. But she'd never have been able to extract them herself.

"Because of the oil," she argued, "which you've now sent to the bottom of the river! A right stupid deed to my thinking!"

"Do you think all men are like your stepfather, Krista?"

The softly delivered question slipped through her front of irritation, delving deeply into her soul with its truthful fingers. "No." She sighed with the release of her frustration. "My real papa was not, but . . . but he died and left Mama and Marta and me."

"Is that why you don't trust me? You think I'll leave you too?"

"I don't trust you because I am not so certain of your loyalties, Gavin Duncan. I have been watching you and will continue to for the sake of the expedition, but what I wish is that you would leave." Krista stepped around the solid brace of his legs to make for the camp, when he seized her arm and swung her into his enveloping embrace.

"I don't think you do, Krista."

Krista turned her head away from the kiss that landed on, instead of her lips, her cold-reddened ear. A dizzying heat spread from the contact, intensified by the slip of a tongue into the hollow behind it, like a match laid to fuse, bursting into sizzling little sparks in her brain and giving rein to an already building panic. "I will scream," she warned haltingly as a second arm snaked its way through canteens and water skins to pull her closer to him. Suddenly it was summer, her body shriveling against the more dominant and muscular one, as if to withdraw and cling at the same time.

"What are ye afraid of, hinny?" The question rumbled against the hollow of her neck which had somehow exposed itself to the plundering, seductive lips. "When have I ever acted like that bastard stepfather of yours? 'Twas me that pulled ye from his wicked intent and me that offered ye comfort, when more might have been easily put upon ye."

"Stop!" Krista gasped, startled by the hand that circled

the swelling beneath the buckskin of her jacket and with searching fingers discovered the hardening peaks within. One armload of canteens slid off to the ground as she summoned a defense against the rock-hard arm pinning her against him. "This is force!"

"Nay, hinny, ye're fightin' confusion, not me. 'Tis all I've known since I first saw you bathin' that day in the river . . ."

Her efforts shocked into stillness by the startling confession, Krista leaned her head against a tree, all too aware of the male arousal pressed hard against her with more devastating effect than all his other seduction had managed.

"Lovely as one of those naked angels ye seen in fountains, and the water, no doubt, just as cold as that they frolic in. I thought 'twas a dream."

Whether it was from the embarrassment of his having watched her bathe that day at the river or from the impassioned tone of the admission itself was beyond Krista's comprehension. All she knew was that not even the snow falling softly around them could mar the human heat that drew their lips together, welding them solidly against the weak defense erected by the desperate warnings of her practical nature. Her reluctant response was no longer of her own making, but one of instinct, female to male, woman to man.

" 'Twould be heaven in itself, hinny, to actually see ye as ye were in last night's dream, dressed as ye were meant to be, in silks and lace, smellin' of lavender perfume."

In his dreams! The words registered in the midst of the heady glow of his kisses. This handsome charming man holding her engulfed in his strong embrace had dreamed of her! The very idea seemed as incredible to the girl as it was intoxicating. That he'd seen her as Mother Nature had brought her into this world and thought of her as an angel, was equally so. It far outweighed any embarrassment she might have felt were she out of range of his inviting masculinity.

Instead of drawing away from the lips which sapped the very strength from her legs, so that Gavin's wide powerful hands were forced to cup her buttocks to keep her from collapsing against the rough bark of a tall straight pine, she moved toward them until she could feel their heat, their touch, their passion.

A sensation akin to lightning flashing through a summer night sky tingled in every nerve ending in her body. It even cracked, loud and echoing above the pounding in her ears, and froze the fingers of the one hand that had wandered up her back to wind the thick locks of braided gold silk through them.

Gavin jerked away, trying to sort his own explosive responses from the rifle report he had heard. Shouts from the mouth of the cave further up the bank managed to shake the last of the consuming inferno from his brain. Gently but firmly, he pushed Krista against the tree for support and snatched up her gun. "For the love of God, lassie, just this once listen and stay here until I call for ye," he ordered, his voice still hoarse with desire.

Krista had no chance to answer, not that she could have. It was as if she'd been transported to a dimension that was loath to let her back to reality. Yet, even as she nodded, dumbfounded, the chaos coming from up the hill snatched her to the present. Tories? she wondered, looking down for the gun she belatedly recalled seeing Gavin run off with. Time not affording her a chance to reprimand herself for her uncharacteristic weakness, she unsheathed the knife Gavin had given her and started off in the running Scot's wake, his plea a part of that other world from which she'd just returned.

"Don't shoot, Scottie! We'll get 'im on the run without

calling half the Iroquois nation and their Tory friends down on us."

Gavin stopped in the cover of a tree, taking in the scene of the broken camp. The question "Who?" was on the tip of his tongue when he heard a loud angry bellow. His mouth gaped open at the sight of a large grizzly charging out of the cave on the heels of Hawk Shadow and Red Deer. He started to raise the gun again, when Krista caught up with him and pushed the barrel down.

"No! There are others in the cave!" she shouted, grasping the situation quickly.

The bear must have charged the men gathered at the opening of his home and they must have run into the cave ahead of him. Red Deer, Hawk Shadow, and Captain Hardy had run off to the side and were now attempting to draw the enraged animal out. She stooped down and picked up a handful of rocks. "Use that only if you have to!" she cautioned over her shoulder as she charged head on at the animal.

She let the first of the rocks fly, striking the bear on the head and diverting him from his charge at Hawk Shadow, who was taking to a tree as quickly as his agile limbs would carry him. "He yaah!" she growled, dodging quickly into the cover of a thicket of trees as the bear turned at her. "Hee yaah!" She let another rock fly, once again striking the bear on the head.

To its left, Red Deer imitated her action. The bear, confused by the sudden barrage of stinging rocks, lumbered at one and then the other, giving Hawk Shadow a chance to rejoin the group which eventually drew the beast away from the mouth of the cave so that the others could escape. All shouting and pitching rocks, making as much noise as possible, they drove the bear off, grumbling and growling in defeated indignation. Krista and the Indians gave him chase for several hundred yards before turning back to the encampment.

"Think he'll be back?" Gavin asked Tucker Hardy, dubiously eyeing the direction in which the animal had disappeared.

"Not tonight, I don't reckon. We backed 'im down and he's a far sight better off out in this weather than we are. In any case, we'll build up the fire so's to make sure. I don't fancy taking on a bear fresh up from a nap. Where the devil did you two get to? I was about to send Tull to look for ya when the varmint decided to come home. Tarnation, boy, this ain't no time for honeymoonin'! He's been sulkin' all day like a wet-eared pup tied to a wagon wheel."

To her own surprise, Krista came gamely to Gavin's defense. "We were on our way back from filling the canteens when we heard the ruckus. Herr Duncan wanted me to remain behind, but I left the canteens and came to help. I thought it was Tories at first." She could feel her cheeks growing pink. "I'll go get them."

"Tull, might as well take the horse and go with 'er! Scottie boy, you 'n me'll take the first watch by the boat. The rest o' you boys bed down and enjoy this fire while ya can. Might be a bit toe bitin' tomorra."

It was already "toe biting," Krista thought later as she trudged back up the incline with the canteens she'd dropped in her fleeting moment of weakness. She handed out the canteens and dried her damp moccasins by the fire as the men told the Indians in detail about how they'd taken the wrong turn in the river. There'd been a sign, charcoal lettering on a scrap of wood, nailed to the tree right over Red Deer's freshly cut blaze, with an arrow pointing to the opposite direction of the safer route. If not for Gavin's sharp eye, they'd have broken up for certain.

As it was, they were able to pole to the side so that just a corner of the raft hung on a submerged tree.

Thinking quickly, the Scot had ordered the load be lightened by six barrels and shifted to the opposite corner to raise the barge out of the water enough to skim off it with some hard poling by the men. Once they were freed, they hauled the barrels, tied in a line, back on board and proceeded to take the other channel.

"He's a pure surprise, e' is," Tull Crockett reflected. "What he don't know, he picks up on fast as a jackrabbit."

"Shame e' ain't as good at courtin' as he is at drinkin', braggin', and fightin'."

The conversation came to an awkward halt, the speaker reminded by a gouge from a sharp elbow that Krista was within earshot.

"If he was," she spoke up, breaking the awkward silence, "then he would be married to an English noblewoman and settled in a comfortable manor in Scotland, not bound by a mock wedding to the likes of me and forced to share his shelter with an irritable bear and a band of rowdy Big Knives in the midst of a godforsaken war. It's a wonder the poor man still isn't in shock."

"By cricket, the gal's gotta point!" one of the others roared. "I guess none o' this is what the feller's use ta."

Sooner or later the men would come to accept her as one of them—as their guide and not the Scot's wife. Krista gathered up her canteen to put it with her bedroll and other belongings and set about making up her bed nearby. She snuggled down under the buffalo robe, her gun close at hand should the bear try again to claim its home, and closed her eyes. Although she could not picture the snowfall, she could still envision it, floating down as if neither time nor destination was of consequence. Even at its current rate, the ground would be covered by morning.

She shivered involuntarily and drew her blankets closer, wondering how Gavin Duncan and Captain Hardy fared at the river's edge where the Kentucky boat and horses had been left. She shook herself mentally, dismissing her concern. She was getting as bad as he was, fretting like a worried wife. It was all nonsense, she scolded herself. He was caught up in some fancy notion over her, likely a soldier homesick for his sweetheart. No matter how wonderful it felt to be in his arms, how blood-warming his kisses were, she'd be a fool if she allowed herself to think it was more than that.

No, she wouldn't make the same mistake her mother had, choosing the wrong man; and the chances of meeting a musician like her father were remote on the frontier. She would lead her own life, independent and free of man's tyranny. While her dreams to play music in Europe were forever dashed, she still had a decent life to anticipate here—hunting and trapping in the wilds she loved. It would be more than possible after the war—after Gavin Duncan had long gone. Now that was clear thinking, Krista assured herself, drifting off to a sleep where thoughts still continued, but remained unacknowledged by consciousness.

Chapter Eight

Morning offered a few rays of promise to end the breath-fogging chill and lay to waste the snow which covered the hills and banks. By noon, however, the sun had lost to overwhelming hordes of clouds. It was not the time to be on the river, Krista knew, though from what she'd heard, the weather was more bitter in Pennsylvania, where the Continentals wintered. Worse, game was scarce and supplies scant.

At least their expedition fared better in that respect. As for the weather, she studied the sky where a flock of wild geese winged their way southward in chevron flight. The signs were not favorable for many more like the first comfortable day they'd spent on the river. What was on their side was that the men were a hardy lot. Aside from Gavin Duncan, they had grown accustomed to adapting to the elements. It was that or die in the wilderness.

"Ah, now don't you smell fresh as the mornin' dew, lassie."

Krista started from her reverie, nearly spilling the hot coffee she'd sipped appreciatively while Cook put out the small campfire.

"But I don't notice that sweet smellin' soap I slipped into your sack. Dinna ye like it?"

"It's very nice, but I can't wear anything like that out here in the dead of winter. Indians and animals would smell me a mile off." Upon seeing disappointment flash in the amber glow of Gavin's gaze, she added sympathetically, "But I do thank you. I really don't expect you to continue giving me gifts. It—it makes things awkward, especially around the men."

"The devil with 'em. They were the ones who started this. Seems they knew best all along."

Krista would have given anything to believe what she was hearing, seeing on his face. His leg brushed against hers, setting off an electric shock, which made her want to pull away and yet would not let her go. He tucked the blanket she'd laid over her lap over his own.

"Herr—"

"Gavin," he reminded her, feigning an exaggerated shiver. "For I'd hate to have to take the water this morning to keep up with your canoe."

Reminded of his threat to swim alongside until she called him by his given name, Krista relented with a smile. *"Gavin* then.

"Men, if ye'll come in a little closer, I got me a proposition to make."

Krista tore her gaze away from Gavin's pensive scrutiny as Captain Hardy took a seat across from them. Tull Crockett, Cook, Hawk Shadow, Red Deer, and two of the three Pennsylvanians settled in a circle around the fire, the third on watch near the river.

"It don't take no genius to figger we're being dogged by either Tories, Injuns, or both. I'd say white men, judging from the trick pulled on us yesterday. Now if word got out from Pitt that we was gonna take the water, they'll be dogging us all the way down the Ohio, waitin' at every bend. My question is, are you boys up to fightin' it out or do we want to try to go across land?"

"Hell, if we's ready for 'em, they ain't gotta chance. I say let's keep to the river and make 'em come out to us," a farmer from Pennsylvania piped up, slapping his gun fondly. "Me n' Emmie makes a tolerable fightin' team, even if she is from Kaintuck. She ain't bad on a hunt neither."

"That's right," another joined in. "I seen Abel take the knot out of a pine board at hard squintin' distance.

"Then we'll keep on as we're doin'. Maybe we can get there afore this snow gets too bad."

Krista knew fully what Captain Hardy meant about the snow, but there was something in the down blanket of crystalline flakes that seemed to add a certain spell to an already magical land. Even the tall pines and evergreens seemed to hold it on their branches like queens wrapped in ermine, coveting it. Animals frolicked about in it like children who always delighted in a good snowfall. For the first time, it looked as if she might just need those short skiis she'd put in her pack. They'd already had a good four inches overnight though now it had slowed to a few scattered flakes drifting down now and then.

Because of the problem their first day out and the existence of *some* enemy following them, the canoe remained within sight of the raft for the next few days. A few more snow flurries reinforced what was already on the ground, forcing them at night to make brush shelters to take the brunt of the wind and weather off them while they slept. Krista insisted on taking her turn at nightwatch. As the journey progressed, she was often paired with Gavin, an unspoken and amiable truce having been established between them, for as he had warned early on, there was little time afforded them in private.

On those nightwatches, she came to know more of this husband of hers. He had been raised in the lap of luxury in Scotland, his father Lord of Duncan Brae. The high society in Edinburough and London and the ancient hills of the rugged highlands had been a playground for the young rake until he met his distant cousin Claire and fell in love with her. Suddenly, his wenching, hunting, and fishing were no longer important. He could not have too much of her feminine company.

But he was a second son, entitled to nothing except to join the armed forces or enter the clergy. The very idea of the drinking, swearing Gavin Duncan as a priest made Krista laugh. "I should fear for the poor man to hear your confessions of love," she teased.

"So you think me quite a Don Juan, do you?"

"I think you have a way with women. You're attractive and have that devilish grin of yours, though I personally would do away with the beard. It reminds me of my father . . . old."

Gavin rubbed his chin thoughtfully. "It also keeps my face warm . . . and plays wicked when brushed across certain sensitive places on the skin, so I've been told."

"By Claire?" Krista asked, pulling a guileless expression.

"Now surely a man of such experience as ye make me out to be would have more than one wench at his beck and call. I think it was Jenny."

"Oh."

"Or it might have been Annalee. Now there's a darlin' with a head full of naught but giggles."

An irrational burst of irritation filled Krista, sharpening her previously game voice. "It looks to me like you have been a right good Don Juan with so many women! No wonder Claire chose your brother. There's likely little enough left of you to go around."

Krista struggled away from the warmth of the broad shoulder against which she'd rested and pulled a blanket around her. She'd wanted to know more about Gavin Duncan, but not that much.

"Well now, I'd be most pleased to show you otherwise, should you reconsider fulfilling your duty as my wife."

"I prefer you as a friend, Herr—"

"Gavin."

"Gavin Duncan," she went on undaunted, stamping her feet to regain some of the circulation that had slowed as she rested. "You see, I am not one of your Scotland ladies who would swoon at your slightest touch. I am a frontier woman who must fend for herself and can't afford such silliness. The only reason you feel this foolish fancy for me is because you do not have one of your delicate lady friends who needs your protection and strength. I do not."

"Not at the cabin?"

"I was caught off guard—asleep."

"And you don't enjoy our kisses, I suppose."

"I . . . no! Again, I am caught off guard and do not have the chance to fight."

"So if I were to kiss you now, with full warning, you would be repulsed."

Krista swallowed hard as the Scot rose in front of her. "I would not enjoy slobbering lips and a wet tongue trying to strangle me and lapping all around my ear like an excited puppy, no." She pulled her blanket tighter around her, as if to thwart the tinglings of anticipation that burst within her veins at the very mention of Gavin kissing her.

"You are just pursuing me because I am the only woman for miles. Do not think that I am so stupid as to believe this sudden obsession of yours means anything more."

"Ah, but I have seen ye as no other has, Krista Lindstrom."

"You saw through the eyes of a fevered, hallucinating man . . . more the reason for your folly."

Tender fingers traced the line of her quivering jaw. Krista's heart nearly tumbled over within her chest.

"You're nae afraid of me, are ye, lassie?"

"I fear no man. Life has taught me right good about that." So why was her blood leaping and spiraling through her veins? "I . . . I can fight and shoot and ride as well as any of you."

"But can ye kiss as well, lassie?"

Laying his rifle aside, Gavin reached for Krista and pulled her gently into his arms. She would have moved away, resisted, but for the smoldering gaze that held her transfixed. She had heard what he was saying, even her own answers. She was holding her own verbally, but her feet were glued to the freezing ground, holding her under a spell that grew stronger and stronger by the second.

"Ye've my respect as a guide and frontiersman, Krista Lindstrom. Faith, I've never seen the like of running off a bear with a hand full of rocks, shoutin' to high heaven all the while. But ye've much to learn about bein' a woman, much I long to teach ye, hinny."

"*You* have right much to learn about—"

Gavin's lips grazed Krista's, gently coaxing. "We'll teach each other, hinny." He eased the rifle out of her hand, letting it fall to the ground, and tugged the long braid out of its haven from the back of her jacket, letting it swing free. "Ye see, we've nay place to go now, but together."

Gavin's words were sent spinning into her mind by the sensuous mouth that sealed them, making certain she accepted them. *Nay place to go now, but together.* Krista's lips parted at the beckoning of his tongue. She met it with her own, yet, what began as a half-hearted defense transformed into a primitive exchange between souls, a mating dance designed to give rise to the primitive fires of the human species.

She grasped for reason, carried by sweet sensation into a limbo that knew none. Her plans had never included a man any more than his included a woman, now that Claire had married his brother. The frantic fingers of logic however ignored the practical and seized upon the natural. She and Gavin were two people who ordinarily would not have given each other a second glance, but for the fickle hand of fate and the wild winds of war. How true his declaration rang! They could help each other rebuild their lives.

Krista knew of nothing at that moment that could be more glorious than to spend the rest of her life embraced in Gavin's strong arms, smothered senseless by his fervent kisses. As if the wildfire had finally consumed her last shred of resistance, she surrendered in his embrace, reaching around his neck with inviting arms to bring him even closer. Returning kiss for kiss, each one failing to satisfy the growing hunger gnawing at her loins, she ground her hips against his, instinctively seeking that which could satiate.

In the midst of all the delicious sensations coiling her passion to the point of explosion, one small voice urged desperately for reason. This was not her plan. She was losing. Worse, she did so wholeheartedly. If Gavin Duncan wanted to teach her how to be a woman, she was ready to become his ardent student. He was the only man to ever reach that part of her, to touch the hidden fires beneath the icy exterior of the life-hardened woman. And now he was drawing his lips away, his breath hot and rapid against her cold red cheeks.

"Now tell me, lassie, that ye dinna like that." he chuckled breathlessly, his forehead pressed to hers. He hugged her closer. "And all those feelin's burstin' in your insides are doin' the same to me, hinny, nae because of some woman in my past, but because of the warm-blooded female in my arms. May the good Lord strike me dead, if I'm lying to you, sweet Krista."

Krista heard the sharp thud that widened Gavin's eyes and caused them to roll upward toward unconsciousness, but was too caught up in the magic of that impassioned declaration to realize the presence of danger until his legs buckled and he crumbled to the ground at her feet. Suddenly, she was tackled to the ground by intruders who emerged from the darkness. Leather bindings bit into her wrists and her mouth stuffed with a cloth before she could expel the horror that rose to her throat.

"Drag them over in the brush and move on up to take the others. There's only eight, counting the Lenape."

Krista watched fearfully as the scene began to take shape before her—Indians dressed in leggings and wearing faded and worn red jackets over their loincloths; Indians carrying guns, muskets of British issue with bayonets. Before she even saw their plucked heads with scalplocks, she had recognized them as members of the Iroquois nation. But who had spoken in English amidst the gutteral mumblings of the braves? She rolled her head to the side in time to see another group forming to the left of the unsuspecting encampment. Soldiers! Not Tory militia, but King's men! Surely not the forerunners of Hamilton's army!

A moan at her side reminded her of her fallen companion. Moving closer, she heard Gavin mutter under his breath. "Light Infantry!" His slurred words were no sooner out, betraying his regained consciousness, than a gag was promptly shoved in his mouth.

Krista fell back against the tree to which she and Gavin had been dragged. What had they done? she anguished in silence. They were supposed to be on lookout, not making love. If he'd only kept his mind on his assignment. . . . One look at Gavin's tortured expression silenced her recrimination before the thought was finished. He was just as contrite as she. Moreover, as his head cleared and they watched helplessly as the sleeping camp was easily taken, he grew angry as well.

There had been only one shot fired, but two men were dead. Ole Emmie took an Indian down and Abel Gunter, was scalped by a retaliating savage. The only thing that saved the others from instant death was the control exercised by the commander of the small detail of infantry. That it was exercised at all meant they wanted more than the gunpowder—they wanted information.

Gavin looked down at the girl watching the proceedings with an impassive face. There was no sign of hysteria at the sight of Abel Gunter's bloody scalp being lifted—no sniffling or sobbing—only silence. As if sensing his scrutiny, Krista turned her blue gaze on him, the long braid he'd freed earlier moving across her chest to catch his attention.

He looked away. God in heaven, the devils would no doubt fight for that length of gold. That would be the kindest thing they'd do to her. Memories of the Tory-Iroquois raid on the farm family made him nauseous with anxiety. He'd kill her himself first . . . if he could. Damn the blasted heathens to hell where they were spawned!

His condemnation was interrupted as four of the savages came back to retrieve them to the campsite where the others were now bound and tied to trees while their belongings were ransacked for any goods of interest and scattered about recklessly. Near the fire, the officer in charge addressed Captain Hardy in what was obviously a one-sided conversation.

"Naturally the Colonel will want to question you all

himself, but the more you say up front, the easier I suspect it will go for you."

Gavin stiffened, his gaze narrowing on the officer as the man turned to acknowledge their arrival. Next to him, Krista felt the hair lift at the nape of her neck, for there was no doubt in her mind of the recognition that registered between the two men.

"Cousin Gavin, is that you beneath those deplorable skins?" The officer motioned for one of the Indians to remove Gavin's gag.

" 'Tis high time one of ye lazy Light men came to see what became of me and my companions! I've stood this damnable frontier long as it can be tolerated!"

The Englishman slung off his plumed helmet and marched across the damp clearing, as if a closer look might make him believe his eyes and ears. "Strike me blue, it *is* you! We thought you were dead, killed with Messick and the rest by the rebels." He gave the large Scot a hearty hug and backed away, confusion taking the place of delight on his face. "But what are you doing my man standing guard for this rebel riffraff?"

Gavin grinned. "If ye'll note, Derrick Duncan, I was'na exactly standin' guard when ye sneaked up on the lady and myself."

"Captain Duncan, if you please, cousin." The officer gave Krista a long careful study before returning his attention to his kinsman. "All that I'll question on that is the issue of whether or not *this* is a lady, but . . ."

" 'Tis a long story of sheer survival, one better told over a cup a rum and a warm fire. That godawful corn liquor is enough to make a man think he's gone to hell and back. 'Tis na wonder they're an uncivilized lot. Ye can see what it's done to me."

"You traitorous highland hootin' sonovabitch!" Tucker Hardy growled, straining at the ropes that bound him to the tree. "We saved your worthless hide and this is the thanks we get for takin' ya into our own like a brother."

Gavin waited until his bonds were cut on the officer's orders before replying graciously, "And for that, sir, I am eternally grateful. As for the bride ye forced me to take to suit your purposes . . . well that rubs a little harsh with me yet."

"Bride!" Captain Duncan sputtered in disbelief. "You married *this?*"

"Can ye think of a better way to find out exactly which way we're goin' and how?"

Gavin's cousin howled. "And next you'll be telling me you were only doing your duty with the lady when we took you down so easily!"

"A man must do anything for the King and his country."

"I cannot wait to hear this, you highland rogue! But first, we'll make camp here for the night."

With that, the British officer began issuing orders which were translated by one of the savages to the others. From the reaction of the Indians, it was not well received. They were to get the horses as their prize, but no more scalps, at least not until the command had had a chance to question the prisoners.

Still reeling from the realization that her original suspicions about Gavin Duncan had been justified, that his sweet velvet seduction had been contrived to win her confidence, not her love, Krista managed to make that much out of the Indians' less familiar dialect. But when one of the braves raised his voice and pointed angrily at the two Lenape, the officer nodded in concession and pointed to Red Deer.

"All right, that one, then."

"No!"

Krista tugged out of the restraining hands of her guards and raced to stand before the Lenape. Her face had gone white and her eyes filled with pleading as she turned them on the Scot. "Gavin Duncan, if you have one decent bone left in that miserable deceitful body of yours, don't let them do this! They'll torture him to death for entertainment!"

"And perhaps, young lady, I might remind you that you are but a command away from the same fate," Derrick Duncan derided, motioning for the guards to secure her to the tree with Captain Hardy. "Be glad that it isn't to be any of you," he addressed the others dispassionately, "so long as you behave."

"*N'petalogàlgun!*"

"That's right!" Krista concurred with Hawk Shadow's warning. "It is taboo to harm a messenger of peace or any of his party!"

"Ah, but you see, my dear, he has chosen to travel with the wrong party."

With a wave of his hand, the officer gave the savages leave to proceed with their grisly entertainment and, slapping Gavin on the back, led him over to the campfire. Krista shrank against the tree, helpless, as a struggling Red Deer was dragged over to a tall pine devoid of lower branches and bound to it face first. The six Indians then stripped off their uniform jackets, revealing tattooed and painted bodies armed with instruments of death, far more gruesome than the bayoneted muskets they put aside.

A wash of weakness swept over Krista as one drew a hatchet and, shrieking loudly, buried it in the tree next to Red Deer's head. It was only to unnerve the captive, but Red Deer hardly flinched. If he was to die, it would be a manly death. His upbringing demanded it. A second Indian lashed out with a knife, slashing the back of the shirt Red Deer had been stripped down to and danced off howling fiendishly. A third, fourth, fifth, and sixth took their turn, each one becoming more and more daring, until the shreds of Red Deer's shirt hung from the waist of his belt and his back was streaked with blood.

Not once did the brave cry out for mercy, which seemed to incense the now shrieking Iroquois. One broke free of the group to scalp him, but the others stopped him, not wanting to chance a quicker death than they anticipated. After arguing amongst themselves, one remained to dance around the captive and taunt him while the others retreated to the fire to heap on additional wood.

"Sweet Jesus, they're goin' ta burn 'im!" Tull Crockett muttered.

Burning was exactly what the devils had in mind, but not at the stake as Krista had first feared. Instead they took green branches and held them over the leaping flames until they glowered with heat. Then they skipped and danced over to Red Deer, poking his back and ribs with them. The sizzle of his flesh caused Krista's stomach to churn in sympathy.

Once again, she sought Gavin Duncan out, hoping against hope that she was not the total fool she now condemned herself to be. It was this very sort of torture that had alienated him from the British, at least according to Captain Hardy and his men, who had witnessed the entire thing. Surely he would stop them, even if he still had English sympathies.

All the vows she'd made about not letting a man make a fool of her like her stepfather had made of her mother, about not losing the sense Mother Nature had blessed her with over a silver-tongued devil with a handsome face, wedged in the back of her throat, impossible to swallow. The very devil at that moment was toasting the British Light officer with a cup of rum, as if nothing was amiss— without the slightest pang of conscience! How could he ignore Red Deer's suffering and enjoy this bizarre family reunion?

Again Krista felt faint, as if her very vitality had been drained from her by the stabbing blow of the increasingly evident betrayal. If she lived, she would personally see Gavin Duncan pay for this. She'd wipe that irascible grin off his handsome face forever, not so much for herself, but for her Indian friend.

More concerned over Red Deer's anguish than her own, Krista closed her eyes, praying fervently for a miracle. Nothing short of a miracle could save Red Deer now. These were not braves of honor, for they ignored the taboo of the Indian nation to take vengeance on their long-time enemy, the Lenape. Her Delaware friend would have no chance to escape the long remainder of the night except by death with honor.

Worse, no matter what the English officer said, Hawk Shadow would have to die too . . . if not now, later. They would leave no witnesses to their blasphemy of Indian law. For that matter, they might all die, she thought morosely. The sight of a small group of the uniformed advance guard studying her intently brought to light yet another threat and Krista's staggered spirit flailed even more.

Chapter Nine

"So it seems our Robert has outdone us both," Derrick Duncan reflected wryly over a travel-battered tin cup of British rum. A bitter smile distorted his thin lips. "I had thought it would be you who would sweep Claire away from us."

" 'Twas a title, cousin, something neither of us had in store."

"Ambitious little twit, isn't she?"

"Claire always knows what she wants and gets it."

"Is that why you didn't return after your commission expired?"

Gavin pretended to ponder the question, which struck too close to the truth. All three cousins had joined the ranks of swains who gathered around Claire Eaton's door. No queen had ever been paid more honor, which, Gavin supposed, was why his sweet cousin changed from the innocent he had been so taken with to the practiced flirt. After having three duels fought over her in no less than seven days, the London elite began to call that first week in October Claire Eaton Week.

Claire was lovely, lovely enough to stir the blood of a stone statue with her crystalline blue eyes and pale flaxen hair. But Gavin had loved the cousin he'd known *before* she was introduced to society at the age of sixteen—the sweet sensitive girl who followed him about moon-eyed, more than a little eager to have him teach her the mysteries of love.

So help him, he had resisted as long as his hot Highland blood would permit, for he seriously intended to make her his bride. That day in the stables, however, when he'd walked her out to see the new stallion he'd purchased for Duncan Brae, was his undoing. The sight of her unlaced bodice, brazenly pulled open to expose exquisitely upturned breasts taut with desire, unraveled the last of his gentlemanly defenses.

He had committed body and soul to her, promising to ask for her hand as soon as he was out of the King's army. He was her first lover and vowed to be her only one. Now she was married to his brother, or more realistically, the title, without so much as the consideration of a jilting letter. But for Robert's missive, he would have returned home before discovering the betrayal.

"I wouldn't give it another thought," Derrick responded. "What she needs is a good strong hand, discipline, something our aunt never gave her. She's Robert's burden now."

Gavin didn't miss the satisfied glint in his cousin's gaze. Even before Claire, there was little love lost between the two very different men. He hadn't even known Derrick, the son of his father's youngest brother, was serious about Claire until after a loose-tongued stablehand had apparently spied on them and nearly ruined Claire's reputation by letting their secret out. Derrick had challenged Gavin to a duel, but the big Scot refused to accept. His shorter adversary, fattened and spoiled by his English mother's doting, had gone into a drunken rage and charged Gavin, who stepped aside at the last moment to expose the thick trunk of the oak behind him and his cousin knocked himself out cold. It appeared Derrick was still bitter.

In the corner of his eye, Gavin saw two of the scalp-locked Indians gathering coals from the fire. Another, more recent recollection leapt to the forefront of his thoughts. Nonetheless, he appeared unconcerned.

"I bear no ill will toward my brother. In fact, I wish him and Claire the best."

He lifted his cup in a toast and then emptied it in an attempt to shut out the savagery taking place near the captives. Red Deer strained every muscle in his body to keep from crying out in pain and dishonoring himself before his enemies.

"So tell me, cousin, how come you to be traveling with these renegades, when you are supposed to be dead along with Messick and his other men?"

Determined not to give Derrick Duncan further cause to exact revenge, for past or present affront, Gavin carefully chose his words. "I was with Messick's party, dressed in the tartan for the celebration over our victorious raid, and discovered their idea of entertainment was to burn two white men alive at the stake. Not familiar with savages and their ways, I drew my pistol and put the men out of their misery."

"Strike me blue, cousin! Did you want to take their bloody place?"

Gavin ignored the incredulous outburst. "And for that merciful deed, the militia captain shot me in the side. Then, before I knew what was happening, all hell broke loose and those backwoodsmen came charging out of the trees, shooting and yelling. I escaped into the woods, uncertain as to just who I was running from. The lady found me unconscious and nursed me back to health."

"*Lady!*" Derrick snorted derisively.

"My *wife*," Gavin flared. The fact that he'd had the

very same reaction the first time he saw Krista attired as she was now, made him no more understanding. If anything, it impressed him with guilt to have sunken to Derrick's hypocritical level. What was it about these wilds and its people that made the life he'd led before seem so shallow? Had such a short exposure to them influenced him that much?

Shocked at his introspective discovery, Gavin quickly recovered to the game. "For better or worse, as the case may be."

The brief but dangerous darkening of the Scot's eyes was enough to make Derrick concede as honor demanded, regardless of his true feelings. "Sorry, I mean no insult. It's just that . . . well, she's a far cry from Claire."

"Maybe that's not so bad."

"Did she save your hide from the Virginians?"

Gavin shook his head. "No, my shooting the prisoners and getting shot by my own commander made them think I was on their side. I've been playing it up until I could get a chance to escape, but if Colonel Hamilton is so near, I'd be better off to go on with them to Kaskaskia and take a look at the enemy's strength."

Derrick Duncan straightened abruptly. "You're not suggesting we turn you loose?"

"No, just let us escape."

"I can't do that, Gavin! Hamilton will want to question them."

"They can't tell you what they don't know, and won't know, until we catch up with Clark. All I know now is that Clark needs powder bad enough for us to take this across country to him."

Derrick was suddenly adamant. "I sure as the devil won't let you take the powder!"

A groan from the other side of the campfire once again drew Gavin's glance to the suffering Indian, his back bloodied by the inhuman tortures inflicted on him by the Iroquois. "I'll blow up the blasted stuff and we'll escape directly across land. The girl knows these hills and mountains. When we arrive, I'll gather as much information as I can and meet you . . ."

"In Vincennes. Hamilton's army is wintering there, now that it's taken." Derrick laughed derisively. "They'd put one colonial in charge and the French were easily enough convinced to surrender! Cowards and fools, what?"

Alarm pricked coldly at Gavin's skin as he listened to his cousin ramble on. Hamilton in Vincennes! The colonials knew the man was coming, but had no idea he was this close!

Gavin decided on a different tack, one certain to gain Derrick's favor of his proposal. He'd court the insatiable vanity of his uniformed relative. Derrick had always been easy to manipulate that way. "No doubt you'll get a promotion from this." Gavin lowered his voice to a conspiratory level. "Now here's what I'll . . ."

He hadn't meant to glance over to where Krista was tied to the tree, but when he did, he was struck silent by the sheer horror on the girl's stricken face. Following her gaze, he saw the Indians cutting pockets of flesh open in the raw muscle of Red Deer's back to stuff them with the hot coals they'd collected from the fire.

The same code that had moved him to shoot the suffering men burning alive at the stake showed no discrimination toward the Lenape. No man, regardless of race or political affiliation, deserved this.

"Tell the bloody bastards to quit right now," Gavin growled ominously, "or I'll stop them myself." Derrick might not agree to his demand, but his cousin wouldn't dare try to stand in his way.

"My, my, Gavin. You don't learn very quickly, do you? They're entitled to their entertainment."

Disgusted, Gavin brushed past the apathetic officer and strode purposefully over to where Red Deer hung, half-conscious, no longer clinging to the tree for support. He shouted as he kicked the plank of hot coals, sending them flying through the air and scattering the startled Iroquois.

"No!"

Recovering the instant the coals landed sizzling on the damp ground, the Indians surrounded him, their blood-stained knives brandished. Gavin stood his ground, un-daunted, which held them at bay.

"The Delaware said the Iroquois are cowardly, but I did not believe them until tonight. Does it take six Iro-quois warriors to fight one white man?" At first, Gavin wasn't certain they understood, but the indignation that inflamed their tone and threatening gestures put his mind to rest on that account. "Or that many of ye to conquer a noble Delaware with his hands tied to a tree?" The outrage heretofore silent, erupted into a vocal protest, reiterated by threatening gestures with the knives.

"Big Knife speaks bold words for one about to die!"

"If I do die, it will take all six of ye Iroquois, for I do not see one capable of killing me by himself." It was a risk, but if this Indian honor Krista spoke of was of any conse-quence, Gavin thought he just might have a chance of saving Red Deer.

"No, *one* warrior!" A single Indian proudly stepped forward out of the group and thumped his arm across his chest.

His earrings and leather-thonged medallions glistened in the firelight. Without so much as a flinch in his stone-like expression, he divested himself of the light supplies he carried on his person, rather than in the bedroll and saddlebag of his white counterparts. There was a beaded shoulder bag serving as a cartridge case, armbands and ornamentation of engraved silver and leather, as well British supplied trinkets, and a powder kit made of hollowed buffalo horn.

Following suit, Gavin pulled off his overjacket and shirt, wondering if he'd lost his mind. He'd never fought an Indian hand to hand, especially one as hostile and fiendish in appearance as this. The paint on his face gave it a hideous, intimidating look that made that disgruntled bear they'd run into earlier on the journey look friendly in comparison. Yet he refused to let his second thoughts show. His success would depend largely on quick wit, rather than brawn, which was equally matched.

"Ye'll leave the lot of them alone if I win?"

The Iroquois waved a lethal tomahawk over his dark scalplock and showed a mouth of yellowed and blackened teeth, the front two of which were missing. "Black Bear will win!"

"You are mad, cousin! This will be no tussle in the great hall of Duncan Brae. This is real. Not even I can stop him if he gains the advantage."

"But ye'll see that the others keep to their word if I send this painted demon home to hell?"

Derrick Duncan nodded, leaving Gavin to suspect his cousin was just as eager to see the match's outcome as the men and savages who gathered around. If he did lose, Gavin was certain Derrick would not grieve. Even as children the sullen English lad—for no clansman would acknowledge a true Scot's blood in the London-pampered son of Andrew Duncan—had not cared overmuch for his highland cousins.

Reaching into his haversack, the Scot drew out his tartan and pinned it over his bared chest with the gold jeweled broach bearing the Duncan crest. Adrenaline alone nulled the cold of the snow on the ground, so that he did not notice it. His mind was on his opponent, who watched him with great interest. In the top of his boot, he replaced the hunting knife Tucker Hardy had given him with the special dirk that was a gift from his father on his thirteenth birthday. Sharpened on both sides, it was as deadly coming and going as the tomahawk Black Bear began to swing around.

If the bloodthirsty devils wanted a show, Gavin brooded darkly, then a show they would have. Lifting his head as if to the ancient forest gods, he began to sing a highland battle song, walking proudly around the campsite so that all might see the warrior prepared. The Indians immediately fell silent at the dissonant wail of old Gaelic, their usually stoic expressions so dumbfounded that Gavin almost wished for bagpipes.

"It's the old battle song Grandfather was always trying to teach us," his cousin whispered, somewhat taken aback himself by the ceremony. "Strike me, cousin, you *are* as crazed as they are."

Gavin stopped long enough to look Derrick squarely in the eye. "I'll have your word, the lassie'll come to nay harm. This is none of her doin', but that of a forceful father. And give her my broach, if the heathen should get lucky. She's a Duncan and has the right to it."

At the officer's stricken assent, Gavin took up the song again and marched, tartan billowing about his broad chest and shoulders, to where Krista and the others were tied. The firelight haunted her eyes, making them appear wild and frightened. Although she spoke not a word, they swam with a storm of emotions he wished he could quell—fear, hurt, suspicion . . .

"Will ye kiss your husband, lest ye never have the chance again, or accuse him falsely, lassie?" he questioned lowly.

Krista was unmoved by his suggestion that this might

be the last she'd have to deal with him. If Gavin Duncan intended to save Red Deer, he had a reason. It seemed the Scot always had some ulterior motive for the endearing charm he practiced so expertly on her, changing insult to kindness and hiding deceit beneath the thin facade of honor. Like the chameleon with its coloring, he changed personalities to suit his surroundings at the time.

She shook her head stubbornly, her gaze taking on the heat of the firelight in contempt. "Your kisses are too costly, Gavin Duncan. You have made us all the fool . . ."

Infuriated by the lips that took her own despite her rebuttal, Krista attempted to curse them, snatching her head to the side when she felt something pressing into her hand. Instinctively, she grasped it as Gavin drew away from her and sighed in disappointment. "Ah, to just one time be treated to a wifely kiss, given from the heart.

A *knife*, Krista realized through her confusion. He was creating a diversion to help them escape! *Who* was the real Gavin Duncan? Friend or foe, she puzzled, even as her heart soared above her bitter disillusionment. Catching herself, she quickly hid her elation with a mask of disdain.

"I hope you win, Gavin Duncan, only because I wish to bury a knife in your black heart with my own hand!"

Careful of the sharp blade, Krista pressed against the tree, covering the blade from view as the Scot turned and walked back to the other side of the fire where space had been cleared for the battle. His resumed chanting ceased as he squared off in front of Black Bear and picked up the tomahawk which had been buried in the ground for him.

Raising it above his head like the ancient battle axes hung on the wall of Duncan Brae's great hall—weapons he and his cousins used to wield upon each other in the hills away from the castle where the adults might discover and stop them, Gavin bellowed at the top of his voice. "In honor of the Duncan and his noble ancestors, let the fight begin!"

The air filled with a roar, the likes of which Krista had never heard—a roar that started low and thunderous and rose to a spine-raking shriek as the large Scot charged, driving his adversary back. He swung the tomahawk back and forth, cutting audibly through the air. In buckskins or plaid, Gavin Duncan was just as imposing a figure as his Iroquois opponent. No hideous tattoos marred his bare arms to intimidate, only bulging and angry unfurling muscle.

The fierce, yet graceful and hypnotic death dance cast a spell that silenced man and nature as well. Not bird nor beast dared cry out, nor a tree shake its branches. Even the wind held its breath. The only noise was that made by the opponents—the deadly swishing of weapons and the furious flare of breath that gave the battle tenuous life, for soon one would die.

Krista had to mentally shake herself to escape the trance and concentrate on cutting through her bonds with the hunting knife Gavin had hidden in the folds of his tartan. The thought came that this too might be a trick, an excuse to shoot them before they could break free of their bonds, but she quickly dismissed the idea.

This fight was real. First blood had already been drawn, a gash across Black Bear's forearm which turned his black eyes from hate-filled to murderous. Gavin was a man to be reckoned with, but he was not used to fighting savages. Each breath he drew could well be his last, just as he had said.

Guilt that she had not given him his kiss freely stung as much as the tip of the knife which bit into her forearm from the awkward sawing motion she applied to the ropes. One broke free, giving her more leeway to work on the others. Sweat broke out on her forehead and she felt as if a large hot weight were being laid upon her chest.

Black Bear lunged forward, catching Gavin's tartan with the blade of his tomahawk and hanging it up. As the brave tugged away to free it, the large Scot seized his wrist and twisted it. Like lightning, the hunting knife in Black Bear's belt came out in his other hand, slashing toward his opponent's side. The clash of metal against wood rang out, the knife blade hitting the thick handle of Gavin's tomahawk. Locked in battle, the two opponents struggled.

Her heart now pounding fearfully in her ears, it was all Krista could do to keep from rushing to her husband's aid when the bonds across her chest finally came free. Tucker Hardy caught and held them up with one hand while tapping her sharply with the other. To move might call attention to them and the others had to be cut loose yet. Reason restored, Krista drew her gaze from the firelit battleground to make certain everyone else was engrossed. Reassured, she quickly pressed the same knife into Tull Crockett's hand and returned to her position to realign the bonds.

Gavin had dropped to his knees, the Indian with him, their hands still welded in a deadlock. Black Bear's knife hovered precariously near the Scot's chest, moving back and forth, closer and farther away, as brawn battled brawn for the advantage. On top, the Indian rose sufficiently to throw his body weight behind the knife, but when he did, Gavin caught him with a powerful kick and sent him sprawling across the campsite. On his feet instantly, the Scot raced to the spot where the hatchet had been knocked from Black Bear's hand and kicked it far out of reach.

The Iroquois, now recovered as well, eyed the one in his opponent's hand warily, his remaining weapon, a hunting knife, lightly balanced and ready. Instead of a boastful smirk, his mouth was now twisted in a snarl that made the black and red paint on his face appear more fearsome. Low animal-like sounds gurgled menacingly in his throat to the breathless and tuneless whistle his circling opponent commenced.

"Now come along, Black Bear," Gavin taunted after what seemed to Krista an eternity of hedging, neither opponent making the first move. "I'm beginnin' to feel like I'm chasin' a squaw instead of a warrior."

For a moment the Indian pondered the Scot's words, but as they sunk in, his snarling noise grew into a growl of outrage. Krista glanced aside to see Tull Crockett and the others nod to her questioning look. They were all free. All they had to do was wait for an appropriate time, hopefully before Gavin was killed.

Gavin sidestepped the angry charge, but not in time to miss the stinging blade that laid open a gash on below his rib cage. Immensely pleased with himself, Black Bear whooped victoriously and quickly dropped into a defensive position for the imminent retaliation. Moving the tartan over the bleeding wound, Gavin kept out of range of the jabbing and swinging blade, circling until he could get a clear view of the prisoners. At Tucker Hardy's barely perceptible acknowledgment, he suddenly threw the tomahawk at Black Bear, driving the warrior back in surprise, and grabbed his unsuspecting cousin. His dirk was at Derrick's throat before any of the onlookers knew what was happening.

"Now tell them to hand over their weapons to our men and we'll treat ye far better than ye've done us."

"Damn your wild Highland blood, Gavin Duncan, I'll have you hung for this!"

"Do as I say or ye'll nae get the chance." Lowering his voice, Gavin added for Derrick's ear only. "Go along with me, cousin. I can't tell Hamilton about Clark's strength if I don't escape with these hoodlums."

The frightened officer needed no further convincing. "Do as he says! Lay down your weapons!"

Gavin heard Derrick gasp in shock upon seeing the rebels walk away from their bonds as if they didn't exist and take up the guns. "Now ye control those savages and get ye back to Hamilton with the gunpowder as soon as we leave."

"Tarnation, boy, I knew ya'd not turncoat on us!" Tucker Hardy cried out gleefully as he gathered up as many of the supplies as he could and packed them on the horses. "The rest of ya tie up these fellers so's we kin git outta here with this powder. Scottie's just funnin' 'bout that."

"'Tis nay jest, Tucker. Forget the powder!"

At Gavin's vehement countermand, Krista looked up from where she and Hawk Shadow were helping the seriously weakened Red Deer on his horse.

"They've destroyed our barge and there's no way we can make a getaway across this rugged country loaded down with pack horses or prisoners," he explained.

"Won't be no hurry or trouble if'n we was to kill this bunch. Who'd know we was here?" Tull Crockett challenged.

"The one who sent them, after our friend Girty at Fort Pitt sent word we were comin'," Gavin answered tersely. "As far as Clark knows, Hamilton is on his way from Detroit. I doubt the good colonel knows that Vincennes is in British hands and if we don't get there with the news, the enemy will be down his throat before we can warn him. In which case," he finished, "the powder won't do any good."

"Still think we ought to kill 'em," one of the others spoke up. "Saves fightin' 'em later."

"For the love of God, Gavin, I'm your blood relative!" Derrick Duncan protested as Gavin handed him over to be bound along with the rest of them.

"There'll be nay killin'."

"As I recall, I'm in charge here," Tucker Hardy intervened crustily. "We appreciate your quick thinkin' and help, Scottie boy, but Tull's right. I ain't much on killin' a fella man, but this is war. Take 'im over with the others and—"

Hardy broke off at the commotion which ensued. As the men and prisoner passed Krista, who held up a torch to provide more light for the examination of Red Deer's wounds, Derrick Duncan broke free. Lifting Amos Cook's pistol from his belt before the man could react, he moved with amazing speed for his portly stature to seize the startled girl. The sound of the hammer being pulled back and the sight of the barrel resting against Krista's temple stilled any attempt further to stop him.

"Two can play at this game, cousin," he panted heavily. "Now drop the torch, girl."

"For honor's sake, Derrick, that's a woman!" Gavin started for his cousin, but Krista's gasp as the gun was shoved against her head halted him.

"I said toss the torch!"

Instead of doing as she was ordered, Krista began to cough spasmodically from the smoke that rose in her face, in spite of the gun pressed threateningly to her head. In the corner of her eye, she spotted Gavin take another step only to be checked by the gun swinging his way. Seizing the moment, Krista pivoted suddenly and hurled the flaming torch onto the canvas-covered powder stacked nearby. The dry tarp with which the men had been covering the barrels when the fight erupted, ignited instantly and the entire camp erupted in chaos.

The Virginia company raced into the woods, throwing

their bodies to the ground a safe distance away while the light company and their Iroquois comrades exited on the opposite side. Running blindly after her companions, expecting either a pistol ball or an explosion to knock her down at any moment, Krista was tackled instead by Gavin's heavy weight and thrown to the ground. At first, she thought it was the force of the explosion, which lit the forest as if it were midday. All around her, tree limbs and brush crashed, causing her to bury her face in her arms. At any moment, she thought to feel it pin her to the ground.

However, all she felt was the hard body already crushing her, protecting her from the shrapnel of the ignited kegs of powder. By the time her hearing recovered from the noise of the explosion, Gavin Duncan was pulling her to her feet and ushering her ahead of him into the woods, behind the forming line of sharpshooters. Gunfire cracked and split the loud hush of the billowing fire that raged where the powder had been, but it only lasted a few moments. Captain Derrick Duncan and his light infantry troop were making a hasty retreat into the darkness of the woods, having lost most of their weapons and all of their horses to the rebels.

Tugged behind a large chestnut sufficient in girth to hide the two of them, Krista found herself enveloped by the tree to her back and her rescuer to her face. "Safe!" he declared breathlessly. "Are ye hurt, lassie?"

Numbed by the lightning speed of their narrow escape, Krista nodded. They *were* safe, thanks to Gavin Duncan.

"Tarnation!" Tull Crockett swore a few yards away, tossing a smoking British rifle with fixed bayonet down in favor of one of the long rifles. "Them damned stabbin' irons makes a good shot pure near impossible!" His next shot did not miss. "Ooh wee, got that brush-topped red bastard!"

All around them, the frontiersmen were whooping and hollering, some breaking the undisciplined rank to give the enemy chase and forcing their comrades to hold their fire. Yet it was only the sweat-dampened, rugged face of the Scot that held Krista's gaze. She reached up and wiped Gavin's brow, as if to erase the furrows of concern raised beneath an unruly lock of reddish brown hair.

"I am sorry I did not trust you. I promise to be a better wife, if that is what you wish." The words seemed to draw them closer, even though their bodies already touched.

A mischievous twinkle surfaced in the gaze Krista found so intoxicating. "Is that so, now?"

She exhaled heavily, as if a weighty burden had suddenly been lifted with her long overdue concession. "Ja, I too am big enough to admit when I have been wrong about someone."

"Now *that* ye are," Gavin chuckled softly, ignoring the tug of responsibility to go help Tucker Hardy and his men. Knowing his cousin, he imagined retreat was one of Derrick's best executed maneuvers; and not even the Indians were fool enough to take on the armed Big Knives without muskets.

Krista smiled shyly, taking the affectionate teasing over her uncommon height as it was intended. He had leaned forward until she could feel his breath warming her lips, yet not making the contact the responding woman within was yearning for.

"But are ye big enough to kiss your husband?"

"Here?" She hadn't counted on him expecting her to kiss *him*. A burst of insecurity backed her as close to the bark of the tree as she could get.

He closed the brief distance she'd put between them, leaving her no escape, no room to act or think beyond his request. What little breath she drew was shallow. She tried to ignore the rapid birdlike flutter of her heart.

Surely he felt it as well, just as she had done once when holding within the palm of her hand a wounded and frightened bird she'd rescued.

The wren hadn't known she meant no harm, but she knew Gavin Duncan would not hurt her. He'd risked his life for her tonight and now all he asked for was a kiss, something her sister Marta could bestow with a light-hearted giggle and no hesitation. As much as she disdained her sister's flirtatious nature, Krista found herself wishing she had inherited a portion of it. The only other kisses she'd been privy to were those the man holding her had given her, or rather, forced upon her.

"Well, Krista?"

Her eyes never wavering from those expectant ones searching her face, she puckered her lips as she'd seen Marta do under the mistletoe and pressed them against Gavin's with such ferocity that only the hands she'd locked behind his head prevented his astonished withdrawal.

"For the love of God, woman!" he exclaimed, moving his tongue tentatively over his lips, checking for blood.

Krista's face flamed in humiliation. Why couldn't he have just kissed her and been done with it?

"It was right good as yours!" she blurted out disconcertedly. "And if you did not like it, that is good with me! Maybe then you will leave me alone!"

An unsuccessfully smothered laugh sneaked through Gavin's consoling, "Krista . . ."

Crossing her arms irritably to keep the distance between them, Krista snatched away to make a hasty retreat before she made an even bigger fool of herself, when she felt a sticky warmth on the front of her jacket. Her gaze dropped to the bare chest where the ugly gash Black Bear had dealt Gavin had clotted, dark against his skin. It had broken open again and new blood seeped slowly out of the wound, soaking into his disarrayed tartan.

A good wife would see to his wound, but after her degrading failure, Krista abandoned any inclination to be any such thing. She had never intended to marry and should have stuck to that plan instead of entertaining the idea of being something she didn't know how to be. Besides, he might have had the decency not to laugh at her. If he'd wanted an experienced woman, he should have taken up with Many Husbands!

"*That* would not have happened if you had enough sense to tend to it, instead of getting some notion of kissing in that crazy head of yours!" she accused hotly. "You are too foolish to be a good husband! I have changed my mind and right good too!"

"Krista . . ."

Krista yanked her arm free of the hand that reached out to restrain her and lashed out at Gavin's face with her drawn fist, taking him by surprise. Her knuckles struck the cheekbone, the impact sending signals of pain up her arm. With a frustrated cry, she drew her bruised fist to her chest as Gavin staggered backward over a piece of fallen deadwood.

"And your head is too hard!" she charged, pivoting sharply to retreat before the moisture in her eyes built to the point of spilling down her burning cheeks.

Part Two

The fiery tempest clears my eyes
To all that waits me here
A flower wild, with sky-blue eyes,
And sun-kissed golden hair

With heart renewed, I'll sing the song
That rings o'er land and sea
And pledge my breath and body strong
To love and liberty

Chapter Ten

The small expedition spent the remainder of the night in the encampment. Aside from Red Deer's injuries and a few raw wrists, their miraculous turn of the tables on their captors had left them unscathed. Certain the British and Indian patrol would not double back on them, they still opted to keep two guards on lookout while the others got a couple of hours of sleep. Even those slumbering kept one ready hand on a loaded rifle and an ear cocked for trouble, for trouble in the wilderness did not necessarily require a war to manifest itself.

Ignoring the bedroll Gavin had put down for her between his and the fire, Krista helped Hawk Shadow see to his Delaware brother. After the remains of the charred coals were washed out of his skin with the rum that had been abandoned, powders carried in his shoulder bag were sifted in. A poultice of herbs was moistened and applied to the suffering man's back. Although she worried about infection, Krista knew enough not to question the Minsi. His brooding hostility was barely suppressed and needed no urging to lash out against anyone, friend or foe.

Besides, if she had had her mind on keeping watch instead of basking in the charms of Gavin Duncan, this might not have happened. A warning shot could have avoided all of this. She longed to say that she was sorry, but sensed an apology would only worsen the tension that thickened the air.

When they had done all they could, Krista settled down with a blanket beside her fitfully sleeping Indian friend, her back to a tree, and closed her eyes. She was tired, hungry, and distraught, not only over Red Deer's condition and her inadvertent contribution to it, but over her inability to do those things that allegedly came naturally to her sex. Instead of showing Gavin that she was willing to act the part of a wife, she'd only further deepened his initial conviction, as well as her own, that she was inadequate as a woman.

Life had not afforded her the opportunity most women had to develop feminine wiles. She hadn't had the luxury of becoming hysterical at the sight of a rat or waiting in a tidy cabin, clad in a stiff white apron, for a man to bring home their supper. She'd had to hunt the food, dress it, and cook it in the mountains. At the inn, she was also the provider. Until now, she thought she'd had the better life than her sister Marta. Until now, she hadn't missed any part of being a woman, particularly if it meant suffering a man's clumsy and no doubt hurtful lovemaking in return.

She could still see her stepfather that day he'd caught her alone in the barn collecting eggs for Mama. He'd cornered her in a stable and proceeded to tear at the last of the day dresses Mama had had made for her in Vienna. It was as if he was ripping away her childhood and all the wonderful memories of a life she'd never see again.

Krista was devastated as she pulled away and tried to piece together her bodice, unaware of the more dangerous prospect awaiting her. Like the vicious destruction of her beloved harp, she thought her stepfather's assault just one of his drunken attempts to eradicate the fond memories of home of which he was not a part.

However, when she looked up from her futile ministrations to see his swollen manhood exposed to her innocent eyes and realized he was not finished with her, she went into a panic. Forgetting her tattered bodice, she tried to climb over the planked partition of the stable, only to be dragged back down and thrown into the hay, her stepfather's unwashed and sweating body on top of her. The hot fetid breath he panted over her face and breasts, smothering and nauseating, threatened to make her faint.

But she didn't. She couldn't. To faint was to give in. Instead, she drew up her leg so that she could reach the small knife strapped in her stocking—a knife Uncle Kurt had given her for Christmas, for helping him skin and dress his hunt. Even as she felt the blunted force of Herr Schuyler's passion pressing against her tender yielding flesh, she brought the knife up to his body and checked his thrust with the tip of the blade against his ample girth. Cursing profusely, her stepfather rolled away from her, clutching the small nick she'd given him in her desperation.

For the first of many times to come, she wished she had driven the knife all the way in, killing him, for at that moment, she was certain he was going to murder her. But instead he drew up his trousers and stormed out of the barn, leaving Krista shocked and dismayed. Could she have killed him? The definitive answer surged in her blood before she had even finished the question. Yes! And she would if he ever tried to do something like that again.

To ensure that he was not tempted, she never wore any of her dresses in his presence and only confided in Uncle Kurt and Aunt Eva, for she'd long given up trying to talk to Mama about Herr Schuyler. The rough-mannered innkeeper had done them a great favor to take in a widow and her two daughters. It was all Mama thought about then, so it was up to twelve-year-old Krista to deal with this on her own, grateful for the support of the Waltaris.

Instead of complaining about her stepfather, Krista had held her tongue to keep from upsetting or hurting the woman who, for whatever reason, loved him. But Krista knew now that Mary Lindstrom Schuyler was afraid of the man. He had intimidated them all—until that moment. From then on, it was only Mama and Marta who cowered under his tirades.

Instead of sunlight filtering in through the tall trees above them in the morning, another gray sky cloaked the dawn. Chilled to the bone, in spite of her winter clothing, Krista savored the last of the hot coffee in her cup and walked over to her newly acquired horse, a British tacky abandoned in the hasty retreat the night before, to finish packing. The extra blankets and supplies were a godsend, for the signs of the weather did not bode well at all. Even now an occasional snowflake could be seen drifting aimlessly through the cold dry air, the forerunner of the storm brewing in the hills.

With as many of the horses as could be gathered in tow, the small entourage set forth toward the high sloping forested hills and plains that lay between them and their destination. Behind was the charred debris of the kegs that had held the gunpowder and the wreckage of the Kentucky boat that would have provided a much smoother journey. Although there were enough horses now to afford fresh mounts every so many miles, the rugged terrain leading to the trace was going to be difficult.

Gavin was unusually quiet, falling back behind Krista and Captain Hardy to ride beside Tull Crockett. Although, as far as she knew, nothing had been said about their negligence on the watch, Krista sensed that her partner in guilt was bearing his equal share, particularly after seeing up close the degree of torture Red Deer had endured. The fact that he'd been instrumental in stopping it and freeing them seemed to have little positive effect on his brooding. In spite of herself, Krista could not help the compassion she felt toward him.

That he had been full of remorse was evident when he'd lifted the wounded Indian onto the travois they'd constructed for him, setting him down as gently as a mother would its babe. Those whiskey-dark eyes had been full of torment and apology which refused to be assuaged by the forgiving nod his suffering burden gave him.

By day they moved with the utmost speed afforded by the burden of the travois and supplies they'd confiscated. By night, men were assigned in pairs to keep watch, lest the retreating light infantry join with reinforcements and give them chase. Aware that it would be impossible to hide their trail in the fresh falling snow, Krista chose the most direct path to the trace instead of trying to travel discreetly through the thick trees. Besides, they were more vulnerable to ambush in the forest.

In that respect, it seemed that fortune was with them. Not one of the seasoned frontiersmen had seen any sign of their being followed. However, the weather did not treat them as fairly. When the snow finally stopped, the wind picked it up and hurled it in their faces. Large banks formed in their path, forcing them to backtrack to find alternate routes through the rocky terrain.

The only one who didn't seem to feel the bite of the first winter storm was Red Deer. Burning fevers made it necessary to pull off some of the blankets and skins piled around him to try to get it down. Everyone took turns riding on the travois with him, feeding him bits of snow to soothe his parched mouth.

"There is a salt lick near here, a little to the north," Krista informed Captain Hardy as they watched Hawk

Shadow trying to control the delirious brave one evening. "The Delaware have a small encampment there. I think we should take him to his own people to be treated. A sweat lodge and medicine man is what will save him, if anything."

"How far outta the way?" Hardy asked grimly.

"Twenty miles . . . maybe less. There's also a French Canadian trading post nearby called Fauxville. It's possible we could rest there and replenish some of the supplies."

"It's also closer to Vincennes," Tull Crockett pointed out. "I ain't got no hankerin' to run into any more British patrols. 'Sides, ain't no guarantee them frog eaters'll be friendly. The Brits buy plenty o' their hides."

"Colonel Clark reported Kaskaskia and its surrounding French-held territory was supporting the colonials," Krista reminded them.

"And if we don't get him somewhere, the man'll die. This weather's nae fit for man nor beast!" Gavin Duncan pulled his buffalo robe tighter around him, as if the futile act could ward off the cold. He reminded Krista of a great black bear, bundled up so. "And if the townfolk are for the good King George, ye men can act like you're under my command. I've a lieutenant's uniform in that sack. Maybe we could find out what Hamilton is up to and—"

A whistling thud cut Gavin off, drawing instant attention to the arrow quivering in the tree only inches from his face. Almost simultaneously one of the guards shouted "Injuns!"

Krista did not need to see the warriors who erupted from the cover of the snow-crested forest to spur her into action. Snatching up her rifle, she took cover behind the nearest tree as the others did the same, scattering to make more difficult targets for the bullets and arrows that now peppered the air. As she lifted her rifle to her shoulder, she caught a glimpse of Hawk Shadow trying to tug the travois with Red Deer on it into a thicket of brush just as a ferociously painted face appeared in her sights. Following the hostile warrior with unerring accuracy, she squeezed the trigger.

His war cry strangled in his throat as he jerked convulsively with the impact of her bullet. Bayoneted gun dropping to the ground, he staggered sideways, then straightened, as if recovering from the deadly shot. But before Krista could close the distance between them, he suddenly folded and pitched forward into the snow. Dropping her own rifle without reloading it, she grabbed the other side of the travois to help Hawk Shadow when Gavin appeared at her side.

"Get Hawk Shadow into cover, lassie. I'll take care of this."

Realizing the importance of Gavin's order, Krista immediately turned the travois over to the Scot, who pulled it into the brush as easily as one of the horses, and started for Hawk Shadow. The messenger of peace, however, outraged at this second affront of the taboo which forbade Indians of all nations to attack him, had seized the fallen Iroquois's rifle and kit and joined in the fray. There would be no holding him back, Krista thought, gathering up her rifle and loading it before attempting to follow him.

Spying the Minsi locked in combat with one of his ancient enemies, she tried to take steady aim at his opponent. The constant movement, however, made a clean shot impossible. Her legs propelling her into motion, Krista ran through the low-hanging branches, knocking the snow that had gathered on them to the ground. Her hand was already on the hunting knife she intended to use, a weapon she could control, when a loud explosion to her left made her hesitate.

She glanced in that direction to see a tomahawk drop

within a breath of her face, to the ground. Just as rapidly, it was covered by the falling body of an Iroquois warrior. With no time to contemplate the closeness of her call, she launched herself at the back of the tall skin-clad Indian forcing Hawk Shadow against a tree and buried her knife low in his back, driving upward with the deadly thrust she'd been taught but, until this day, never had had to execute.

She had felt muscle and bone give beneath the sharp blade before, but it had been that of an animal, not a human being. The very blood coursing through her veins froze at the same time as her victim, weakening her stomach to the point that she felt as though she'd be sick.

The man fell, carrying Krista forward with him as she sought to retrieve her knife. There was no time to consider the scarlet-stained blade that came free, for a bullet whisked by her ear, bringing her out of her stupor with a sheer instinct to survive.

"Hawk Shadow, come with me!"

Grabbing the Indian's arm as he attempted to reload the British rifle, Krista began to drag him into the cluster of trees where Captain Hardy and the others were carefully picking off the targets that had started to thin out and dropping them with the calm of a turkey-shoot contestant. But as she reached the others, the warrior jerked his arm from her grasp. Expecting a struggle, Krista turned and was horrified to see part of Hawk Shadow's forehead blown away. Beyond, boldly holding a smoking rifle in hand, was a buckskin-clad figure, his narrow and angular features oddly familiar.

Simon Girty? she wondered as the white man flashed her an evil grin and ducked back into the darkness, shouting to the Indians in their native tongue. It couldn't be, part of her argued. He was in Fort Pitt.

She hardly felt the wiry hands that grabbed her by the

scruff of her neck and yanked her into the trees. "Load fer us, gal!"

Once again snatched from her shock by the urgency of their situation, Krista picked up the first of the rifles tossed her way and pulled the stopper from the powder horn. She quickly poured a measure of powder down the barrel and followed it with ball and patch. After seating it with the ramrod, she primed the weapon to fire. The frizzon which held the priming powder in place had no sooner been closed, when the weapon was snatched from her hand and she turned her attention to the next one.

Over and over, she repeated the procedure, not stopping to look to see how the battle was going until she noted that the shots had begun to fade. At her side, six rifles lay loaded and ready to fire, but the men who had been using them were out in the clearing now, firing a few parting shots at the retreating war party. Scurrying to her feet, she stumbled out of the cover and over the dead body of Hawk Shadow.

"Whoa, gal, no need ta hurry now. They's hightailed it outta here. You're a helluva hand to have around in a pinch and I'll be the first to say so," Captain Hardy was telling her. "If I was your husband I'd be proud as a peacock."

Her husband? *Gavin!* Krista thought, trying to hold back the tremors that infected her. She looked up to see the tall Scot hauling the travois out of the cover. Six bodies lay scattered about it so that he had to kick some of them aside to get the litter free.

"That Injun alright?"

"He's nae dead," Gavin answered abruptly, "but he's nae well at all. We have to do something. I dinna think his friends will believe us that we didn't kill the peace messenger."

Tucker Hardy continued the thought. "And that would

be all the Delaware would need to get stirred up, now the stink about Cornstalk's death has finally died out. How many horses we got now?" he asked suddenly, turning to Tull Crockett.

"Three so far. We may find more with the daylight."

Krista didn't miss the lack of enthusiasm in the Virginian's voice. It was possible they would find more, but it was highly unlikely. Their attackers would not leave good horseflesh wandering about if it was at all avoidable, even in retreat. Indians considered themselves born to hunt and to plunder the enemy. But this time, Krista knew instinctively that the horses were an afterthought. Girty, or someone like him, had come for one purpose—to kill the messenger of peace and inflame the Lenape against the Continentals.

"To hell with the horses, we's lucky to be alive!" Cook snorted indignantly. "I say let's hightail it straight down to that tradin' post. The Injuns kin come take this feller here and do what they will."

"No, Red Deer must come first!" All attention shifted to her, but Krista's determination was not daunted. It was not only a matter of life and death for her Indian comrade, but a matter of war and peace between the Lenape and the colonials. Without an Indian witness to the events that had happened, they would have no hope of convincing the already wary Delaware to remain impartial in the conflict. Colonel Clark's impressive accomplishments to date in the Illinois territory would be in vain.

"We do not have enough horses and traveling on foot over this terrain will render you worthless to Colonel Clark for days."

"What are ye tryin' to say, hinny?" Gavin asked gently.

A heady warmth spread thrugh her as she tried to reassemble the plan scattered by the serious regard her husband gave her.

"I'm saying, why not let me go to the Indian village and get help and horses? I know the chief. He is Red Deer's uncle and a good friend of Kurt Waltari. We have been entertained by White Owl many winters."

"Ya want to take our horses and leave us here?" Captain Hardy asked skeptically.

Krista shook her head. "No, I will need no horse. We are at the top of the ridge. There is a hunting trail Uncle Kurt and I have cleared through the foothills. It's well marked. Meanwhile, I can make better time going down to the valley on foot."

"On *foot?*" Gavin's initial respect for her opinion gave way to incredulity. "Were ye struck in the head by one of those tommyhawks?"

"You forget, sir, that I have spent the past ten winters here. With a horse, you'll have to take a more circuitous route or risk having it come up lame. We usually worked our traps with a sled and these."

Krista reached down into her bedroll and pulled out the small skis which protruded out both ends of it. "It is how I earned the name, He Who Glides Over Mountains. Finding a path fit for a horse will only slow me down."

"If those savages don't come back and kill ye first."

"The lot of you will draw more attention than me," Krista responded practically. "Besides, I will be careful."

"How long do ya reckon it'll take, gal?"

Krista thought a moment. The snow was not too deep, and in the hills there was likely to be a harder frozen surface beneath. "I will be back by tomorrow with help." She looked over at Red Deer. "Just keep him alive, even if you have to remain here to do it. We'll find you."

"By God, I won't allow it!" All attention shifted to the belligerent Scot standing over them. "For the love of God, Tucker, she's a woman! She has nay business wanderin' about this godforsaken land, visitin' savages alone."

"I can take care of myself, Gavin Duncan." Krista placed a sympathetic hand on his arm. "I have gotten you this far and not led you astray, haven't I?"

"Aye, but we've been plagued by the devil's own. 'Tis nae that I doubt your abilities as a guide. Ye've proved yourself well, lassie. 'Tis all that wildness out there that ye can't control."

"I wouldn't be sending the gal if I didn't think she could do it," Tucker Hardy spoke up on Krista's behalf. "And I've heerd about them sticks there, tho' I ain't seen 'em work. Ain't none of us can keep up with her, if there's a lick o' truth to it."

Gavin felt himself losing ground. "And what if she takes a notion to leave us on our own, like she did before?"

The concern on his face made it impossible for Krista to take offense at the suggestion. There was something akin to panic in the eyes that challenged each and every man assembled there. The big brawny Scot was afraid, Krista realized. Afraid for her.

"There comes a time in a relationship, husband, where one must trust the other on instinct alone. If you put your faith in me, I promise on all that is honorable and sacred to me that I will not fail you."

As Krista listened to her own words, she realized the conviction in them. She wouldn't fail him, not as a guide, nor as a wife. When they were safe and privacy afforded them, she would ask him to teach her how to please him. After all, she had known nothing of hunting and trapping until Uncle Kurt taught her how. But she was a quick learner.

Chapter Eleven

If Gavin had been concerned for Krista when she set out for the Indian village at the salt licks, he was even more so after she'd fetched the help they needed and the entire party became guests of the Lenape. The moment they arrived, she left them to be steamed alive in a sweat lodge while she worked with the tribal medicine women on Red Deer. He'd tried once to see her, only to be run off by two squaws who chattered like magpies and pinched like geese.

He saw that evening at the council fire in the great lodge that his concern had been needless. His resourceful bride was given the seat of honor next to the chief, her every word listened to attentively. No longer shy, she was in her element, speaking as easily in their tongue as she did in English. Grudgingly, he had to admire the way she stood up to the more hostile of the warriors and defended the volunteers, declaring that they had been listening to the singing birds, liars who would turn the Lenape against the Big Knives and cause much bloodshed.

Nor was Gavin the only one who admired the way He Who Glides Over Mountains held her own. His ribs were black and blue on either side from sitting between Tuck Hardy and Tull Crockett and suffering their elbow jabs each time Krista countered the angry accusations thrown at her. But it was White Owl, the chief of the Lenape, who paid her the greatest honor.

In accepting her word as the truth, rather than that of the men who had argued that the Big Knives were fighting to take away the Lenape hunting grounds, he offered her the pipe of peace first.

"May we put this matter between us out of our minds now. The two dark clouds that run toward each other from the north and south are not those of the Lenape and the Big Knives, but those of the Lenape and their ancient enemy, the Iroquois. They must be punished for breaking the Mengwe taboo."

Nonetheless, in spite of Hardy's translation that the Lenape would not give them trouble, Gavin was glad to leave the camp and the recovering Red Deer behind. He'd learned all he wanted to know about the Lenape, at least for the time being, and was anxious to make camp with more familiar comrades, like Colonel Clark's militia. With the wampum White Owl gave them to vouch for their good intentions and to declare their friendship with the Lenape, they had one less enemy to worry about.

Hamilton's foragers and scouts, however, more than made up for the loss, demanding everyone's attention on the overland journey, to the extent that it wasn't until they'd come up on a small French village nestled in the hills that they realized it was Christmas. At the center of the settlement, a church bell filled the air with its joyous ringing. As the weary travelers speculated about the political sentiments of the populace, the sound of voices united in song glorifying Noel met their scarf-wrapped ears.

After a short discussion, it was decided that Gavin and Krista would go into the town and arrange for accommodations at the local tavern if there was no sign of the British occupation they'd witnessed in the last outpost.

After all, Captain Derrick Duncan's word of the French
so quickly switching sides after the show of force Hamilton presented at Vincennes had done no more to put their
minds at ease than the news at Pitt that Clark had won the
French over as allies. No frontiersman worth his salt
would put much store in a lot that was rumored among
many colonials to live on frogs and salads.

When Krista saw the men, women, and children pour-
ing out of the small building with no sign of a uniform
among them, she was overcome with relief. Listening with
half an ear to the fluent French the Scot had surprised
them with earlier, she scanned the cluster of buildings for
a sign advertising room and board. She spied one, just as
Gavin left a particularly obliging couple with a "Merci
beaucoup" and pointed to the same advertisement which
Krista strained to read in the distance.

"There's an inn, right there," he told her. "They call
it Le Renard Rouge. Better yet, a number of their men
have been harassing the British patrols, acquiring quite a
supply for Colonel Clark. Looks like we might make up
for our misfortune after all."

"Ja, good!"

Krista blew hot air into her gloved hands in a futile
attempt to heat them. The harsh winter had come up on
them so abruptly that she'd had no time to acclimate
herself to the change. At least she'd never suffered so from
the cold before, until this trip, not even in the mountains!
She'd even welcomed Gavin's warmth and extra blankets
at night instead of protesting as she had been inclined to
do at first. She glanced up to see her companion grinning
at her.

"Do you think there's a chance we might secure a
private room?"

His question, the drop of his voice, the way the light in
his gaze intensified, so caught her off guard that she

stumbled over her own feet. In a fraction of a moment, she was in Gavin's arms, stammering and flustered beyond her experience.

"What will it be, hinny? We've come this far together." He lifted her chin and brushed the red tip of her nose with his lips. "Shall we let fate have its way?"

"Is . . . is this a proposal?"

Gavin's laughter shook Krista in the cumbersome confines of his embrace. "Nay, hinny. 'Tis married we already are. The matter is, shall we stay that way or nay?"

"I don't know. I . . . I haven't thought much about it."

Her answer started in an admission of truth, but quickly trailed into deception. At night, just before she closed her eyes, it was all that filled her mind. She'd listed the man's good points and bad points until fatigue had muddled her ability to think at all. During the daylight hours, she had to force Gavin Duncan from her mind to remain alert in case of running into the enemy unaware. In spite of it all, she'd made no decision. When she did, it would be well thought out, not one of those impulses of the heart that brought so much heartache to some women.

"Damnation, woman, I've shown more patience than the man Job himself!" Gavin expelled impatiently. His gloved fingers snared the shoulders of her buffalo robe to keep her from backing away. "I'll know before this night is out and I'll know why as well, or the decision will be made according to your father's wishes."

They'd reached the small tavern made of log and stone and stood under its swaying sign with faded red lettering and the likeness of its namesake painted below it. Her companion, however, showed no interest in entering until the matter between them was resolved.

Unaccustomed to the use of feminine wiles, Krista at-

tempted to pull away. "You are making a right good fool
of yourself in front of the entire settlement!"

A battle raged within her, clashing like the heat that
sprang into her blood from his suggestion with the cold of
the bitter air. Her confusion multiplied as she continued
to look up at him, his face handsome and striking, even in
anger. What was it she was afraid of?

Surely, not the man himself. Gavin Duncan had
proven himself worthy of her respect. He practiced a code
of honor which not only rescued her, but held his manly
passion in check longer than most men would have, given
the same opportunity. He'd fought to save Hawk Shadow
and Red Deer at the risk of his own life, though there was
no love lost between them. Before she even knew him,
he'd shown mercy to those tortured dying men and alienated himself from his King as well as his proud heritage.
There would be no place for him at his home, now that
he was a traitor in the eyes of the Crown.

From deep within her chest, an overwhelming acceptance welled, only to be assaulted with doubts born of
years of distrust where men were concerned. The result
glazed her eyes, revealing her torment in spite of her
efforts to hold it in check. Upon seeing it, Gavin dropped
his hands and slammed his fist into the thick post supporting the sign. Shards of thin ice snapped and fell to the
ground.

"Ah, lassie, I dinna wish to cause a single tear in those
bright eyes of yours. I'm not patient by nature and the
journey with ye so close has wearied me to this." He
brushed some of the frozen debris from his arm and
stepped under the catslide of the roof. "We'd best see to
the accommodations and leave the matter until you're of
a mind to discuss it."

"Before the night is out!" Krista bit her bottom lip,
punishing it for allowing her heart to speak. Gavin turned,

a thick eyebrow cocked in surprise. It felt to Krista as if her heart had not only spoken, but had risen to her throat, where it beat so loudly, her ears rang. "We will decide tonight."

One corner of Gavin's mouth turned up wickedly. "Faith, hinny, I've already made up my mind, 'tis yours I'm waitin' on."

"You're *certain?*"

"I may be the fool once, but dinna let it be said that I'll make the same mistake again." The big Scot opened the door for her and stood back, gallantly motioning her in ahead of him. "Enter, milady."

The first thing that managed to penetrate Krista's shock was the darkness of the main room. The windows were covered with hides, which blocked out the little light the gray sky permitted. As her eyes adjusted, she made out two long stretcher-base tables, their tops as worn and battered by the serving of many meals as the chewed and swayed stretchers which bore the wear of many a pair of boots. Turning on a spit in a large fireplace at the stone gable end was a large shoulder of meat, most likely venison, she thought.

However, it was not the tempting roast that held her attention. Beside it, walking patiently on a treadmill, was a white short-haired dog, contained by a rope enclosure. Gears connecting the contraption to the spit kept it turning. As she walked closer to the fire, she noticed the floor was almost black with caked dirt. Herr Schuyler, for all his faults, would never have allowed an animal near the food, much less let his floors become packed with filth to this extent!

"Ah, bonjour, bonjour!" A short wizened woman, with graying hair that had not seen a comb in ages, burst through the door which Krista assumed led to the kitchen.

"I thought that I heard someone come in. Will you men be staying the night or just eating here?"

"My *wife* and I," Gavin corrected smoothly, "as well as half dozen or so more will be staying the night. Have ye room?"

The woman eyed Krista dispassionately and waved her arm. "I have all this. We move the tables against the wall of a night to make room for the travelers. If you have a bedroll, you will have a bed."

Gavin gave Krista a disappointed shrug. "It seems fate is insistent on giving you all the time you need to make up your mind, lassie."

"Where are you from to be out on such a day as this? Surely it is not by choice!"

"Virginia."

"And where are you going?"

"Kaskaskia."

"Ah, to join the Colonel and his brave men. Bon! My nephew is now with them."

"Are you sure you haven't a private room for my wife? The travel has been wearying for her and privacy has been scarce."

The proprietress shook her head in denial. "The only other room I have is the kitchen and the bedroom my husband and I share. That is all!"

"This is fine," Krista spoke up, explaining quickly to her annoyed companion, "We are only a few days to Kaskaskia. I can manage till then." The scowl she earned made it clear the rugged Scot was not as concerned for her benefit as he was for his. "And besides, I have not made up my mind."

"Well, in that case, I'll be takin' your horse back to the others. With six, we can double up for the short distance here. Maybe the lady here has somewhere ye can at least freshen up."

"If I see your money first, monsieur."

"Ach, the folks of this country are as tight as Scots!" Gavin grumbled. He dug into the sack he wore slung over his shoulder and withdrew the jeweled broach bearing his family crest. "Will this do until our captain returns with us?"

The woman's eyes narrowed as she caught the gold broach, but when she turned it toward the firelight, they widened in astonishment. "What grand lord did you steal this from?" As if afraid to trust her eyes, she bit at the edge.

"For the love of God, woman, that broach has been in the Duncan family for more years than you can likely count!" In one stride, Gavin reached her and snatched it from her hands. " 'Tis not to be gnawed upon! Those jewels are as real as you are."

"Then you *are* one of Hamilton's men, a nobleman at that."

"I used to be Gavin Duncan of Duncan Brae in Scotland, youngest son of Laird Robert. Now I'm just Gavin Duncan, surveyor and volunteer in Colonel Clark's militia . . . and you are?"

"Marie DeMotte, proprietess of Le Renard Rouge. Who I used to be is of no interest to anyone." Her gaze, Krista could not tell if it was gray or a pale blue in the dim lighting, showed her curiosity had only been whetted by Gavin's admission. "And this is your lady?"

"Aye and she needs a place to . . ."

"I can manage on my own, *Gavin.*" Krista felt awkward with the name her husband encouraged her to use. "I will get my pack and you can be on your way. I am certain that Mrs. DeMotte and I can manage."

"I'll toss it to ye at the door. There's nay sense in gettin' your feet cold all over when they've just started to thaw."

Krista reached the planked door at the same time as

the Scot and stepped back to let him through, when she
was surprised by the sudden kiss he planted on her lips.

"I'll be back in a while, hinny. Mrs. DeMotte will see
ye well cared for, I'm sure."

Instead of tossing her gear to her, Gavin personally
delivered it and then rode off with her horse in tow to
fetch the others who waited a mile or so on the outskirts
of the little town. Krista, in spite of his consideration for
her, stepped out on the porch to avoid keeping the door
open and losing much valued heat. She watched until he
and the horses were but a singular speck, dark against the
snow-covered ground. Then, gathering up her belongings, she went inside where the proprietess checked the
doneness of the roast.

"You are not from his Scotland, are you?"

Krista propped her rifle against the wall on a crudely
crafted rack for that purpose and hung her kit on a peg
above it. "No, I am from Pennsylvania."

"I thought you looked German."

"I am Viennese" the girl informed her hostess sharply,
not in any way wanting to be associated with the lineage
of Herr Schuyler. "My stepfather was German."

"And what of your father?"

"A musician and composer. He played any instrument
he picked up."

"And I suppose you were too young to learn to play
anything, since you look no older than my nephew."

A part of her that had remained closely guarded and
protected for a long time opened with a dreamy smile. "I
played the harp . . . in Vienna that is." So long ago and
far away, it seemed as if that girl had been someone else,
someone perhaps that Krista had known well.

"Is that so?" Appearing no longer interested in the
subject, Marie DeMotte lifted one of the ropes on the
treadmill and took up a leash, heretofore unseen by

Krista, to lead the dog into the kitchen. "This is Armand! My husband is too stingy to hire me help with the tavern, so I must depend on this dog. How is it that a girl from Pennsylvania is married to a Scottish nobleman?" Her face suddenly brightened. "Are you with child?"

The suggestion was so ludicrous, Krista nearly laughed. Instead, she reached down and petted Armand. "No, I was married for my ability to lead my husband and his men into this territory. I used to trap with my uncle in the Illinois country and the mountains."

"But your man, he is so . . ." Marie searched for the right word. "Attentive."

"You were going to show me a room where I might freshen up before the others arrive."

Realizing that she had learned all she was going to for the moment, Marie De Motte picked up a piece of the trimmings she'd cut to test the venison and fed it to Armand. As the dog began chewing with great appreciation, its tail wagging furiously, she unleashed it. "Go, Armand! To the kitchen and wait for mama."

Still working on the large chunk of fat and gristle, the dog trotted off obediently.

"And now, *Madame* Duncan," the exaggeration leaving doubt that it was meant in a respectful way, "I will show you to the room I share with Jean. It is yours for the remainder of the day, for I shall not see it until all are abed tonight."

A small door off the kitchen, which was no cleaner than the tavern's main room, led into a sparsely furnished bedroom. A chest and a double bed with a mattress in great need of fluffing left the room looking empty, even for its negligible size. Not even a washstand was available for the bath Krista had found herself looking forward to. Lack of privacy and the harsh weather had made the hygiene to which she'd been so meticulously raised next to impossible. Unless there was a bathing room.

The idea was so ridiculous, considering the primitive and unkempt conditions she had seen that Krista dismissed it abruptly. Instead she asked the whereabouts of a bowl and pitcher.

"It's in the back under the porch. There's a rainbarrel full of water, but you'll have to break the ice to get some. I keep a chunk of wood out there for just such a purpose."

"Would you mind if I filled it and brought it inside to wash? I've been traveling in the cold for so long, I'm not certain I haven't taken a chill."

It wasn't that Krista couldn't wash outside. Hadn't she braved the creek water just as winter was closing in? What she wanted to do, however, was remove her clothing and wash thoroughly with that scented soap Gavin had put in her pack after throwing away the fish oil. Stripping outside would not only be uncomfortable, but there was the risk of someone coming up on her.

"I promise I'll put everything back just the way I found it."

Marie DeMotte exhaled heavily, as if making a grand concession. "See that you do, madame."

"And might I warm some water?"

Another grand concession. "I suppose, since there is a fire going for the supper anyway. Just stay out of my way. I am a lonely woman who is worked far beyond her limit."

"What does your husband do?" Although Krista did not particularly like Marie DeMotte, her claim to loneliness piqued her curiosity.

"Since this war, he comes and he goes. He goes and he comes. It is always the same. I never know when or how many he will bring with him."

"He's in the militia with your nephew?"

"Non, non. Jean DeMotte will take orders from no man! He buys and sells the supplies to the army, but for gold, not the worthless dollar the Yankees pay."

"I would think gold would be hard to come by."

"Not if the militias steal it from the British pay wagons!" The older woman laughed humorlessly. "This war, madame, it is a game for the men—men of all ages, both rich and poor and red and white. It is the women who are left to feed themselves and their hungry children."

"You have children?"

"Non!" Madame De Motte's fervent denunciation startled the girl. "For that I have been blessed. It is enough to keep myself and Armand."

Since both dog and mistress were gaunt, Krista could only gather the woman was barely getting along.

"I have too much work to do to stand here chatting with you, madame. You rest and pamper yourself while your man still loves you and there are no children to wear you out when your chores are finished."

What a miserable woman, Krista thought as she deposited her haversack on the bed. In it was a spare shirt and trousers and her only dress and shift. If she wore the dress, which was the only clean garment left her, she could wash out her other clothing and hang them by the fire to dry, provided Madame De Motte did not object. If so, she'd put them outside and let them freeze dry in the seemingly endless wind.

While water was warming on the fire, Krista fetched in additional wood, making the stack by the door waist high. Then, seeing her hostess struggling to take the roast off the spit single-handed, she hurried to her aid and helped put it on a large pewter charger. Her mother had always had Widow Ames to help her. Sometimes, even Herr Schuyler himself would see to the heavier chores, for he was particular about the way his tavern was run. Perhaps

Mrs. DeMotte had good reason for her sour disposition.

The soap Gavin had given her had a pleasant scent, spicy yet possessed of a hint of sweetness. Krista worked it into the rough linen washcloth the proprietess had laid on the bed for her and scrubbed her bare skin until it was pink and hot in the cool air of the sparsely heated room. It felt wonderful to be clean again, to feel the soft wool flannel of her dress on her arms and the linen of her shift drawn between her thighs and tucked in her waistband to serve as makeshift drawers. She felt . . . like a woman, she mused, staring at herself in the mirror.

And she had women's chores to do. To avoid risking another of Madame DeMotte's scowls, Krista set about washing out her clothing in the scented water and hung them out on the porch rail to dry, since her hostess had hung a kettle of hominy to go with the venison on the trammel over the fire. Last, she washed her hair and rinsed it thoroughly with the clean cold water she'd put aside. While it dried naturally around her shoulders, like a golden cloak, she directed her attention to the travel-beaten buckskins that had been airing outside during her earlier ministrations.

Stretching them out on one of the tables, she began to scrape and oil them, working the leather which had been stiffened by the cold wet weather into the softness Red Deer's mother had attained when they were first presented to Krista. She would try to do Gavin's as well, she thought, certain the man had no idea how to care for the leather clothing that had replaced his woolen tartan and kilt.

Gavin, she thought, laying the buckskins over the foot of the bed to reorganize her pack. Buried in the bottom, she discovered her flannel nightgown. Would she wear it for him? Would she say yes to remaining his wife? She tugged the gown out and hugged it to her chest.

She wanted to. All the reasons began to run off in her mind like the petals she'd seen Marta pluck one by one from a daisy to see if some boy truly loved her. He was good to her now. He was honest. He was courageous and smart. And handsome and strong. That was what she'd first noticed about him, once she'd bathed his muscled body and dressed his wound. It had stopped troubling him almost before they left, which made him as resilient as she suspected.

And he wanted her. She hadn't had to chase after him or lure him on with flirtatious smiles and coy glances as she'd seen her sister's friends do around young men. He was doing the courting with his stolen kisses and warm embraces, his tender concern and that reckless grin of his that could send her pulse skipping erratically.

Hadn't he satisfied all her doubts? He'd apologized for his initial treatment and disdain for her. He fetched her back to the expedition and coddled her almost to the point of irritation for one who was not used to such deference. He'd fought side by side with the volunteers against an army to which he had once belonged and rescued them from a relative, risking not only disinheritance and persecution by the Crown, but by his family as well.

It was as Gavin had said when they arrived at Fort Pitt, neither one of them could go back. Forward was their only recourse. Why not together as husband and wife?

Taking advantage of the idle time she had left, Krista fluffed up the flattened featherbed and straightened the linens and quilts piled on it. By the time the dust settled in the little cubicle, she still had not come to a conclusion that gave her any peace. Perhaps it was love that was missing. She climbed on the bed and tugged a blanket over her thoughtfully.

How did one define love? Her logical approach to

discovering the exact nature of an intangible and illogical feeling left her only more confused, until the comfort of a real bed seduced her into slumber where logic had no place at all.

Chapter Twelve

"Ja, my stepfather owns an inn in Pennsylvania," Krista answered the insatiably curious mistress of Le Renard Rouge.

The girl had awakened upon hearing someone in the loft of the building dragging something heavy across the floor. The same confounding thoughts which had hovered in her mind as she had drifted off to sleep would not allow her to return to it, even after the noise had stopped and she heard the innkeeper bustling about the kitchen again. Not one to enjoy idleness, Krista offered to help Marie DeMotte finish preparing a meal for the coming group of men. Her offer was eagerly accepted and, as she sliced the succulent roast thinly, in order, Madame DeMotte said, to keep the men from hacking off large chunks and taking a hog's share, she found herself questioned to the point of irritation.

"But my sister did more of the cooking and cleaning. Since Herr Schuyler had no son and was too stingy to purchase game from the locals, I did the hunting to fill the platters with meat and fowl."

"Your husband should be glad that he has a wife of so many talents. What was that instrument you said you were fond of?"

"The harp," Krista sighed. "I would play it for hours while the other children frolicked outside. It was my pleasure."

Marie stirred the dried apples she'd made into a pie filling to make a Christmas celebration for the travelers who had missed the holiday. The sweet scent made Krista's stomach growl, even though she'd tasted a good share of the venison when the woman wasn't looking.

"A harp. I wonder . . ." Krista looked up to see the French woman watching her closely. "There is an instrument a schoolmaster once traded for a month's bed and board here, not that I could use it," Marie snorted derisively, "but it was all he had to pay for it. It is in the corner in the main room, collecting dust. Perhaps you could make a jovial tune with it for tonight."

Krista's breath froze within her chest and thawed with the doubt that ensued. A harp here in the middle of the wilderness? Surely the woman was mistaken. Besides, she noticed no such thing when she'd scrutinized the dimly lit room earlier. But there was that commotion which had awakened her—the sound of something heavy being dragged across the loft floor. She pushed away from the table.

"I will look," she offered, refusing to allow her excitement to build for a crushing disappointment. The noise could have been anything, a trunk or a simple plank being dragged out of the way.

Wiping her hands on the apron Marie had loaned her, she walked into the main room as if expecting someone to jump at her. In the firclight from the large hearth, she made out a familiar outline—a thick sturdy frame, wide at the front and tapered toward the back to a simple curve carved in painted wood. Her steps quickened as she crossed the room, already wondering if all the strings were intact, for it *was* a harp! It was smaller, and plain in design compared to the ornate one her father had acquired for her, but it was more than she ever dreamed to find in a land so far removed from the musical culture of Vienna.

She ran her callused fingers over the strings and winced as some of them rang pitifully out of tune. One, two, three . . . she counted, relieved to find her touch had not deceived her. They were all there. All it needed was tuning. After an experienced search, she found a small compartment where the tuning key was hidden and set about righting the pitch. Although Madame DeMotte had evidently wiped the main of the dust from it, by the time Krista had eased the strings into harmonious tune, her hands were filthy.

"So what do you think, Madame Duncan? It is a fine instrument, non?"

Well aware that the sudden appearance of the instrument was no coincidence and doubtlessly had to do with the impressive broach Gavin had left as proof of his good intentions, Krista nodded. "It is not as fine as that which I played, but is well made enough to provide an entertaining tune, I suppose."

Yet, when the others arrived a few moments later, she could no longer maintain her indifference for the sake of the shrewd innkeeper. The moment Gavin ducked under the low entrance, Krista flew across the room excitedly, the hair she'd forgotten to braid flying about her shoulders.

"Oh, Gavin, come! You must see this!"

The other men might not appreciate her discovery, but one of his station could. The idea that she had once placed him in the same category as the others, uncouth and crude, never crossed her mind as she grabbed his arm and tugged him in the direction of the harp. She only knew in her heart that she wanted him to share her joy—a joy that was so consuming she hardly noticed the dumbfounded expressions not only on her husband's face, but on those of his companions.

"It cain't be," one of them murmured as Gavin gladly followed the girl in his dreams, the lovely lithe maiden swathed in cornflower blue with dancing eyes that, at that moment, shamed the brightest star the good Lord put out at night.

"Look! A harp, Gavin! Can you believe it?"

"Nay, lassie, 'tis an unexpected find indeed."

He felt ashamed that he only provided lip service to her overflowing enthusiasm, but his was of a far different nature. He'd discovered a wild rose hidden beneath buckskins, its fragrant scent covered with the strong smell of fish oil. She did look like a tall Viking princess, with golden tresses falling wildly from a proudly carried head.

"Just listen!"

Krista laid the harp against her shoulder as she sat on one of the benches she'd dragged from the tables. It was a soft white shoulder that was hinted at by the brief exposure the heavy harp tugging at the material of her dress presented. Flexing fingers that were long and tapered, their blunted nails the only evidence that they did not belong on such an elegant instrument, she began to caress the strings in rapid wavelike patterns that ranged from a low clear resonance to a higher tinkling sound.

"Tarnation, gal, ya look like an angel playin' that thing! Who'd 'a ever guessed it?"

"Sounds like one o' them symp'nies the rich folk's are kind'a fond of," Tull Crockett complimented, the hat Krista had never seen removed from his head respectfully in his hand.

She laughed and Gavin was reminded of the hand bells the acolytes played in the church near Duncan Brae. Her weather-rouged cheeks and pale skin might have been the model for the china dolls he'd seen little girls play with. She was more beautiful than even he remembered.

"But Tull," she chided gently, "these are only octaves, finger exercises. It has been so long since I played that my hands are not as practiced as they once were."

"Hard as we've traveled, ya'd think she'd had enough exercise," Amos Cook grunted, fascinated with the way her fingers rolled over the taut strings exacting melodious music as if there was nothing to it. "May I?" he asked respectfully. At Krista's nod, he imitated the motion, the resulting noise giving way to an outburst of protest.

"Ain't one bit o' angel in you, Cook, so's ya might as well let the gal play!" one of his companions guffawed.

"Aye, go on, lassie. Play us a tune," Gavin encouraged gently.

It wasn't as much his words as it was his tone and the pulse-stirring way he looked at her as he backed away and shed his outer garments that made Krista hesitate. He smiled, as if understanding something unspoken between them, something Krista could feel but could not fathom. All she knew was that if he were to ask her to share the rest of her life with him right then, the answer would be a wholehearted *yes!*

The first number she played, one of her father's pieces, was received by enthusiastic applause, as were the succeeding ones she had learned as a child. Later, however, after a jug of killdevil had made several rounds, requests for more familiar songs were made. Never having played them, but certain of their melodies from living at an inn, Krista put her fingers to the strings and relied on the gifted ear her father had once told her she possessed.

When Madame DeMotte served the succulent supper of venison, wild greens, yams, and dark bread, Krista could not bring herself to part with the instrument. As crudely as it was made, it had a sound that lifted her spirit and filled her heart to overflowing with long denied release of that which she'd kept hidden all those many years in Pennsylvania. Even when Gavin made a place for her next to him at the table, she kept playing, explaining that she'd eaten while helping Madame DeMotte with the meal.

While it didn't sit well with her husband, Krista refused to let his scowl intimidate her. She would explain, she told herself, when she gave him the answer to his proposal. Yes, she would remain married to him. As she pondered his reaction, she realized the reason behind his suddenly dour mood and ended her song. It was as he had said. He had waited longer than most men. She owed that much to him.

"I thought ye said ye were full from carvin' the roast," the Scot accused as she took the empty spot beside him.

"I am, but my fingers are sore and I'm thirsty."

It was true. Unaccustomed to the repetitive stroking of the strings, Krista found her work-hardened calluses were in the wrong place now. Boldly, she took his noggin of killdevil up and sipped it. The fiery alcohol got as far as the back of her throat before her body rebelled and refused it further passage. Half strangled, she began to cough convulsively, the burning liquor finding its way to her eyes as well as her nose.

"Has a bit of a bite, eh, lassie?" Gavin teased. He produced a handkerchief, chuckling along with the others who had witnessed her swaggering attempt to join them as an equal. " 'Tis wine ye need. Madame, fetch a bottle of decent wine for my wife, for only the sweet shall touch the sweet," he finished, catching Krista's gaze with his own before studying the lips he referred to with undeniable interest.

Krista felt the effects of the wine before she even tasted it, warm and heady. Gavin Duncan could do that to her with a look, a touch, a word. Reminded of her purpose in abandoning her harp by the devastating nearness of his manly body, she blurted it out in a rush.

"I have decided to be your wife!" At the startled but satisfied cock of his mouth, she went on. "I am not good at being a woman, let alone a wife, but I will try to please you right much."

Gavin drew her into his lap, his arm slipping about her narrow waist. "The good Lord made ye a woman, Krista, and He makes no mistakes, to my mind."

Krista's ears roared with the cheering and clapping surrounding them as Gavin kissed her, not just a simple brush of the lips, but a long, caressing kiss that left no doubt in her mind that he knew how to release the woman within, if she did not. Then the pounding of her blood, fired by the intimate sealing of the agreement she'd made, deafened her to all but that.

Her long legs tangling with Gavin's as she twisted to receive his attentions more earnestly, Krista caught a glimpse through half-lidded eyes of Madame DeMotte standing primly beside them, the bottle of wine Gavin ordered in her hand.

"Will you be having the wine or not?"

"Just put down the bottle and leave the lovebirds be," Tucker Hardy chided boisterously. "They been strainin' at the bit for this since the weddin'!"

Foreign voices invading the sweet world which had enveloped her, Krista pulled out of Gavin's lap abruptly. Her flushed cheeks burned with embarrassment as her wanton behavior registered. What was it about the man? she wondered, concentrating on uncorking the wine in a fluster. To do such things in front of an assembly of people was horrible. Only animals showed such lack of restraint.

To her dismay, Gavin took the bottle from her and filled the small cup. " 'Tis nay disgrace for a man to kiss his wife, lassie," he whispered as he handed it to her. "I'll warn ye now, I'll kiss ye when and where I please, so ye might as well adjust to it."

Krista gulped down the wine impulsively to avoid responding. Her body was doing enough of that as it was. What she needed was time to restore order to it.

"We got a weddin' to celebrate!" Tucker Hardy announced, lifting his noggin of killdevil in a toast. "Till now it's been black gum against thunder, but by golly, it looks like Scottie boy knew what he was waitin' for. To the newlyweds!"

Gavin refilled Krista's glass, his gaze never leaving her burning face, and handed it to her. "Ye canna lift an empty glass to that, hinny."

Her hand shaking, Krista took the cup and joined in the well-intended toast. She wished she could slip under the table or off into some corner, for being the center of this attention made her miserable. There was, however, a retreat that would satisfy all. "We'll have a dance!" she announced, bolting from the table before Gavin knew what she was about. "We'll see which of you can outjig the other."

Her knowledge that a challenge was as good as her present company could ask for paid off. As Krista hurriedly plucked her way through a familiar country dance tune, Tucker Hardy and Tull Crockett squared off.

The arrival of six more visitors interrupted the little party briefly. Krista was introduced to Monsieur De-Motte, an unimpressive man with rounded shoulders who immediately submitted to his wife. Commanded to help her serve the newcomers, he quietly obeyed while the others encouraged Krista to resume her playing. The French settlers were no less rowdy than the Virginians and joined in the country dancing.

Lacking women, Tull Crockett and one of the newcomers donned tablecloths, tied in apron fashion about their thick waists, and assumed the female role so that partners could be found. Forgetting Gavin's brooding scrutiny from the corner where he spoke to Mrs. DeMotte, Krista lost herself in the lively jigs and country dances, laughing at the men's antics and soothing her increasingly dry throat with the wine Captain Hardy kept in her glass to keep her from having to take a break. It was only after Amos Cook had fallen under a table and the music was stopped long enough to extract him that the midnight chime of the church bell, reminding them of the hour, was even heard.

As the twelfth note struck, Gavin Duncan rose from his corner retreat and announced the end of the festivities. "We've a long day ahead of us tomorrow, laddies, and 'tis time for my lady and I to repair to our room. If ye'll party more, ye'll do it without Mrs. Duncan."

Repair! It sounded as if he were the lord of a castle announcing their retirement, Krista thought in amusement as she watched her husband cross the room, parting the assembly with his purposeful stride. Upon reaching her, he took the harp gently from her shoulder and steadied it in a corner. When he turned, however, and took her hand to his lips in preparation to lead her off, the wine she'd consumed and the absurdity of Gavin's behavior made it impossible for her to stifle the giggle that escaped.

"Stop being so silly! You act as though we have a room, instead of a few feet of space on a filthy floor!"

"We do."

Krista's grin faltered. "But Madame DeMotte said there was only . . ."

"The room she shared with her husband," Gavin finished smugly. "Which I have purchased for the duration of the time we remain here."

"What?" Digging in, Krista held back.

"These good men have just relieved a British supply train of its powder and supplies. Tomorrow Captain Hardy and the boys will take a look at it. He's thinkin' of replacin' what we lost. Now let's say good night."

"With what?" Krista insisted, as he took her by the arm and ushered her toward the kitchen door. "What are we going to buy them with?"

"Goodnight, gentlemen!" Gavin bellowed, giving rise to hoots and shouts of congratulations.

They had no money with which to pay, Krista thought as she was herded gently but firmly into the bedroom. Not even Tucker Hardy's purse contained that much coin. And the room, how had Gavin arranged for that? She looked at him in disbelief. Surely he hadn't paid the woman for it with his broach, the only thing of value he possessed! Why, a piece like that had untold value, not only in a monetary sense, but in a sentimental sense.

"You didn't give her your broach for this shabby room!"

Pleased with himself, Gavin nodded. " 'Tis of nay use to me as a Duncan now. Ye've married an American, not a Scot nobleman, hinny."

"But you could buy the whole place for what it's worth! I have a right good idea you have lost your senses!"

"I have, hinny," Gavin murmured. He reached out to bury his fingers in her hair. "I think I lost them the moment I spied you coming out of that creek, dressed in naught but what nature had provided you. I must have struck my head and knocked them out when I tumbled from the tree and down the hill." Somehow his fingers found the fastenings of her dress. "A picture to behold ye were that day and one I'd see again this night."

His meaning sinking in, Krista grabbed at the open front of her bodice. "I . . . I have a nightgown. I can dress myself."

She wanted to be his wife. She'd said so, but she'd had no idea that it was to be so soon. She thought there would be time between here and Kaskaskia to prepare herself. Yet, even as her mind reeled with shock, her body had begun to warm to the sweet seduction of his softly burred words.

"Please?" She lifted an imploring gaze to his, seeking an understanding of what she herself was at a loss to explain. "I promise I will share your bed and not run."

Yet, even as she spoke, Gavin was uncertain that she would not do exactly that. He was rushing her and it was plain that she was frightened by it. As a man, he knew surrender was but moments away, but his loins threatened to burst with anticipation, so long had they been denied.

"Then put on your nightgown. 'Twill nay doubt be an improvement on what ye last wore to bed."

Krista breathed a sigh of relief as he dropped his confining arms and walked to the other side of the bed to undress, leaving her to her own pace. What was wrong with her? she wondered, swallowing hard to force her heart back into her chest where its frantic beating would not choke her. This was what she wanted, to accept Gavin's ardent attentions and let him carry her beyond the pleasure she'd already experienced from them.

Yet, as she opened her haversack and shook out her wrinkled nightgown, her anxiety was not assuaged. It would not be like the lovemaking between her stepfather and his sluts that she'd heard through the wall, she told herself sternly. A flutter of nausea twinged in her stomach until she resolutely forced those sickening memories from her mind.

Glancing over her shoulder shyly, Krista was grateful that her husband was engaged in untying a knot on his leather leggings. Hurriedly, she dropped her dress and shift off her shoulders and shoved her arms into her night-gown. She knew what he would do and that the first time it would hurt. But not much, she recalled one of Marta's newlywed friends confiding to them in the kitchen during a visit. She shook the voluminous flannel over her day clothing before letting the blue dress and petticoat fall around her ankles.

They struck the floor with a thud that startled her, until she realized it was Gavin's boots that had made the noise. Nervous, Krista picked up the garments and painstak-ingly folded them to repack. As she tucked them in the bag, her fingers struck her hairbrush, reminding her to braid her hair before it became impossibly tangled. Sitting on the edge of the bed, her nightgown fastened to its high neck, Krista began brushing the locks with vigor in an attempt to vent some of her building apprehension.

It wasn't until she felt the bed give under Gavin's weight that she realized her husband was ready for her, even if she was not for him. The heat from the chimney afforded some warmth, but it was too cold to linger out-side the blankets. Nonetheless, Krista mastered an invol-untary shiver and began to divide her locks into three sections for braiding.

"Dinna braid your hair, Krista. I'd have it the way it is, a golden cloak shimmerin' over your shoulders like an angel's very own."

The shock of Gavin's velvet words sent Krista flying from the bed with a gasp. Swinging back to the door, her brush clutched to her bosom, she stared at the naked man, who twisted about to see her. Once she'd admired the magnificent body on display before her, but now, she would only allow her gaze to rest on his.

"I . . . it will tangle." Her voice had reached an un-precedented high pitch.

Gavin got up from the bed and approached her, muscle

blending with muscle, unhampered by the restraint of clothing. Krista's view dropped enough to take in the magnificent spread of his dark furred chest and remained there. "Then I'll help ye with it in the mornin', hinny. 'Tis cold and I'd have ye in bed before we both take a chill."

His foot caught on the haversack Krista had inadvertently dropped, sending it sliding across the plank floor. Krista watched the leather pouch until it stopped against a trunk and returned her attention to the man who continued toward her. Then, and only then, did the sight of his aroused manhood capture her gaze.

It came again, that sickening feeling she'd known when she'd seen Herr Schuyler's thick desire threatening her. She'd been younger then, young enough never to suspect anything like that existed, let alone to be apprised of its use. Although she'd escaped him in time, her innocence had been shattered and the way she looked at men changed forever. Only with Uncle Kurt had she been completely at ease, for he'd never shown that sort of interest in her. Not like Herr Schuyler.

"Krista?"

"No!" Krista wielded the hairbrush at the symbol of her fear like a weapon, driving him back in surprise. Except that it wasn't Gavin, it was her stepfather.

But for his quick reflexes, her aim would have been true. "By the gods, woman, have ye taken leave of your senses?"

The familiar voice made her hesitate in her attack, long enough for Gavin to seize her wrist and twist the brush from her hand. Her head rang with the heavy breathing, the harsh grunting sounds, the threats, louder and louder until she screamed to shut them out. Then all she knew was a smothering hand clamped over her mouth, shutting off her air, making her dizzy and weak—too weak to fight the arms that swept her up into the cold air and deposited her in the warm bed.

And words—sweet, tender words—cajoling her from the fog where she lingered between darkness and the candlelight from the lamp by the bed. "As God is my witness, hinny, I'd nae harm ye for the world. Ye've nay need to fear your husband."

Gavin? Krista wasn't aware she'd whispered his name until he answered.

"Aye, 'tis me. Ye've given me a fright, hinny. Now open up those bonnie blue eyes and see ye've naught to fear. Come along, now." Coaxing lips brushed her eyelids. "I'll not believe a lassie who would fight like a man and chase after a bear with the savages would swoon at the sight of a naked man."

Krista opened her eyes to see Gavin's face a breath away.

"What was it, hinny? What was it ye really saw?"

Her eyes blinked rapidly to clear her mind, to focus on the man she had married, the one whose warm body cradled her, safe from the world. "My stepfather."

Gavin cursed, the rush of his vehemence veiling the words from her ear. Yet the anger she saw on his face did not frighten her in the least. Instead, she sought refuge in it and the force behind it, snuggling even closer until the thin flannel of her gown might well not have been there at all.

"That night you came . . . it was not the first time he tried . . ." An involuntary shiver ran through Krista, but Gavin quelled it with a hug, as if he'd not allow such memories back.

"Ye needn't tell me. I can imagine what a man the likes of him could do."

"I drove him away with a knife. I've carried one ever

since, until the night he caught me asleep and took it from me."

She felt the press of Gavin's lips against the top of her head. "And what about now, hinny? Would ye have a knife, for if so, I'll take my leave and join the others. Ye've been badgered enough by men and I'll nay be part of it."

Krista drew away and tossed her head in an effort to move some stray lengths of hair from her eyes. If any man could make her forget, could teach her how to unleash the woman so long imprisoned within, it was the man lying next to her.

"No, husband. I would have you as I promised."

Gently, she caught herself, as she bent over and pressed her lips to his. When he did not move, she leaned into his body and wrapped her arms behind his neck, her fingers undoing the queue he kept neatly tied there. As he had done to her, she kissed his forehead, his nose, each eye until she had returned to lips that this time responded with equal tenderness.

Suddenly Gavin's arms were about her, rolling her to her back. As their lips were torn apart, he chuckled. "So, there's vixen in ye after all. Do ye nae ken what you're doin' to me, lassie? You're about to ruin my chances of remainin' patient, like that hairbrush of yours nearly finished any hope of me provin' a decent husband this night."

Overwhelmed by guilt, Krista caught his face in her hands. "I am truly sorry, Gavin Duncan. It wasn't you, it was—"

"Hush, lassie." The gentle command vibrated against her lips. She could feel the warmth of his breath, the sincerity of the heart beating against her breasts. "Relax and let me love you, Krista." His beard tickled as he sought out the sensitive skin of her neck where her pulse thundered like tiny drums answering his heart, begging him to do just that.

" 'Tis nae shameful to show your body to me, hinny, for how else can I show ye how worthy ye are of love, nay, worship." Nimble fingers laid waste to the fastens that held her gown tightly at her neck. More and more flesh was exposed as they worked their way down to her waist, yet Gavin did not tug her bodice open to leer at her breasts—breasts that ached for the same tiny kisses he planted in a neat row from the hollow of her neck to the indentation of her navel. Instead, he nuzzled it open an inch at a time until, swollen in all their glory, the firm globes were arched toward him imploringly.

Krista watched as he covered first one with his mouth . . . nibbling, tasting, breathing hotly against it . . . and then switched to the other. The heat swept through her, flooding her loins with such ferocity that she drew up her legs as if to stop the quivering desire in her abdomen. Distracted by the heady torment of her breasts, she was hardly prepared for the searing caress of his hand, moving up the inside of her leg and taking the flannel of her gown with it. Again and again the expert fingers left a smoldering trail toward the wildfire generating within her very being, until her gown was no more than a twisted ring of material hanging about her waist.

When he drew away to remove it, Krista offered no resistance. If the window over the chest were to blow open that very moment and fill the air with the icy blasts of the wind whistling in the eaves, she would not feel it on her naked skin. Entranced was what she was, captivated in a spell of seduction from which there was but one escape. Her gown tossed somewhere over Gavin's broad shoulder, he leaned over her, his body grazing hers, and paused for one last lingering, bone-melting look before blowing out the lamp.

The darkness closed around them, but Krista was only aware of the lean aroused body that nestled between her legs to resume the flesh burning torment. The shaft that prodded her stomach, eager to take her in the same domineering way Gavin's tongue plundered her mouth, no longer posed a threat in any sense of the word, but promised untold rapture. Thoughts of Herr Schuyler had vanished as though they had never existed. Thought itself was no more.

All Krista was aware of was touch, presence, and then, as Gavin drew away from her clinging, pleading arms and maneuvered his throbbing desire over the moist receptive haven of her own want, she knew she would discover even more. She rose up instinctively to meet the driving possession, crying out more in wonder than in pain as it claimed her untouched body and crushed it under the lightning assault.

The stillness that followed was disrupted only by their ragged breath and the echoing of their inflamed hearts and bodies. The bed refused to creak, but seemed to hold its breath as each of the lovers grew accustomed to the intimate union. Filled and yet, unfulfilled, it was Krista who moved first. She sought out Gavin's face with her hands, unable to speak, and when she found it, traced the sensuous lips that had played havoc with her body. Gradually the statuelike posture of her lover thawed, his mouth coming to life to capture her fingers and flay them mercilessly with his tongue. Even when released, Krista kept her hand there, so that her palm and then the inside of her arm tingled with its fierce play.

Unable to lie still, she began to wriggle and churn beneath the pinning weight of Gavin's hips, riveted with sheer pleasure. That, however, was no longer enough. Her inner muscles quivered and clutched at him, goading him to end this torment once and for all.

"Easy, lassie, or I'll not be able to contain myself. 'Tis a harsh temptation ye are, innocent or nay."

"Then don't!"

Krista grasped his hips and ground her own against them in an effort to quell this fiery frustration that would not leave her be. With a groan, Gavin obliged the gnawing hunger that inflamed him beyond endurance. The bed squeaked with the fury of his thrusting, and Krista's body rocked with the impact. Instead of complaint, she raised up against him, her breasts grazing his sweat-dampened chest, and locked her arms and legs around him—her own desire rendering her desperate for release.

Round and round her senses spun, tightening about his body, his virility, like the ropes on the swing she'd had as a child. And when the wanton anticipation would coil no further, she let go with a loud gasp, reveling in the pinnacle of ecstasy. The spiraling finale swept her in a whirlpooling response of heightened senses, faster and faster until her very consciousness was threatened, and then it began to slow—a sweet, lethargic drifting of contentment in the arms of her partner.

Gavin, she thought dreamily. Something like this could only happen with one man in a lifetime, and her no-good stepfather had married her off to that man. Much as she hated the innkeeper who had almost ruined this precious experience for her, she owed him gratitude for that.

This was love. Krista not only knew it in her head, but in her heart and body as well. There was nothing more she could ask for in a man than what she had in Gavin. Smiling sleepily, she went into his arms and rested her head on his shoulder. Almost nothing, she reconsidered, catching the strong scent of horse, leather, male, and too many days without soap.

"Gavin?"

Gavin nestled his face into the back of her head. "Aye, hinny?" he mumbled drowsily.

"You need a bath."

Perhaps if he'd had one ounce of energy left, Gavin might have belly laughed. Instead, he chuckled and drew Krista even closer. His hands roamed the contours of her body as if to be certain he hadn't dreamed the entire episode as he growled lowly, " 'Tis gettin' even, lassie. Just gettin' even."

Chapter Thirteen

The inn was filled with the smell of baking when the men returned from dealing for the stolen powder. Gavin broke away from his companions and circled around to the back. While they warmed themselves by the fire, he intended to seek an entirely different source of warmth.

The very thought of Krista denied the bite of the freezing rain that hammered onto the roof over the back kitchen door as Gavin broke the ice on the top of the rain barrel and dipped out enough to fill half of the wooden bucket next to it. Fingers aching from the dip in the icy water, he fished out a bar of soap from his haversack and proceeded to wash as best he could, within the confines of his outer garments.

Curses of every nature assaulted his mind as he shivered and drew off his jacket and the soiled shirt beneath to exchange it for a clean one, before donning the warm buckskins again. After a few moments to brace himself, he made the same exchange with his leggings and trousers and shoved his discarded clothing in his haversack to seek the warmth of the back kitchen before he was beyond use to his wife at all.

Neither man nor beast should be subjected to that sort of weather, much less the girl who looked up from a tray of hot molasses buns, just from the oven, and beamed brightly. That was why he had to talk to her, he told himself, to tell her what he'd agreed to do that morning. Damnation, it was for her own good and the good of this cause he'd adopted as well. Not many women could be approached by such a proposal, but Krista was practical to a fault. She'd surely understand.

"Gavin, there you are! Look! I have made them just like Mama used to." She pinched off a little piece and met him as he rounded the large work table to take her up in his arms. "Here, taste."

Krista in an apron was another vision he would tuck away for the times when he needed a lift of spirit. Gavin captured not only the treat but the sticky sweet fingers that delivered it. Trapping them with his teeth, he methodically licked each one. "Ummm . . . delicious!" he pronounced mischievously, "but 'tis this sweet that I've had a cravin' for all day."

"Gavin!"

Her lips tasted of the molasses she'd been baking with, betraying the fact that his ever surprising wife was not above the temptation to sneak a sample or two of her own creation. As his arms tightened about her small aproned waist, so did hers do the same to his neck, sweeping off his hat with fingers that raked through his chestnut dark hair. God, she was warm, he thought, soaking in her nearness . . . and soft and beautiful. When Marie DeMotte cleared her throat from the corner of the kitchen where Gavin had failed to see her, he was so caught up in the fervent exchange that her reminder went unnoticed as well.

His wife, however, did extract herself from his arms with an embarrassed, "Ohh!"

"You have paid for my room, monsieur." Blood beginning to flow again through his veins, thawed by his enthusiastic welcome, Gavin was not the least daunted by the remark which only served to heighten his bride's radiant glow. "Right ye are, Madame DeMotte, and that's exactly where I'm headed."

Catching his unsuspecting wife off guard, Gavin swept Krista up in his arms and carried her to the door of the adjoining bedroom. He'd been snatched from her warm bed before dawn to acquire the powder Marie DeMotte's husband had told them about and was anxious to be back in it. The bed was an excellent place for husband and wife to talk, he justified to himself smugly. By the time he reached it, however, her astonishment gave way to ire.

"It is the middle of the day!" she reminded him, scrambling to escape the iron hold of his embrace.

"Aye."

"Everyone will know . . ." Krista drew up her long legs and ducked as her husband carried her through the opening. "Everyone will know what we are doing!" The door slammed behind them at the backward thrust of her husband's foot.

Gavin put her down gently, his lips twisted in a wicked grin. "And just what is that, lassie?"

He didn't think his bride was capable of a deeper shade of scarlet, but she was. Suddenly the wide, indignant eyes were downcast, their fan of golden lashes quivering nervously as she sought the right words to express herself. It could be called coy, but Gavin knew there was not a coy bone in Krista's lovely body. She was as guileless as a child and in a woman, that indeed was a rare find. Which, he thought, feigning a big yawn, made her all the more fun to toy with.

" 'Tis nay shame to takin' a nap. Ye kept me up half the night with your lusty cravin's." He dropped down on the mattress and patted it. "I thought ye might be in need of some rest yourself as well."

The way she futilely struggled to school her disappoint-

ment into a mask of indifference was almost more than
Gavin could stand. "Actually," she began with a guilty
dip of her lashes that sent a tide of desire surging in his
loins, "I slept late this morning." She stepped away and
pretended to scrape an imaginary smear of flour off her
apron.

" 'Tis the privilege of a new bride, I suppose."

Krista straightened primly, her face as innocent as an
angel's. "If you are going to sleep, I will go help Madame
DeMotte in the kitchen."

The moment his new bride moved toward the door,
Gavin reached for her waist and dragged her back to the
bed, where they both landed unceremoniously. He silenced her startled yelp with his mouth before she gave
the mistress of the place confirmation of what she already
knew. Not that he gave a tinker's damn, but the girl
squirming beneath him would.

"Damn you, Gavin Duncan, I ought to punch you
right good!" she blurted out breathlessly when he gave her
reprieve.

Tempted to get lost in the sapphire pools which revealed far less anger than Krista's voice indicated, Gavin
rolled away and stripped off his outer wear instead. "And
that, as I recall, you're capable of doing *right good*," he
mimicked playfully. There it was, that little twinkle of
amusement he'd grown so fond of. "But I would much
rather talk," he went on, more assured of her repaired
humor. "Under the covers." And the talk would give him
time to recover from his *refreshing* interlude outside.

"Talk?"

Now who was toying with whom, Gavin wondered.
The lilting lift of her voice as she rose to stand not a
finger's distance from him, and the way her lips pursed in
their struggle to contain a smile, was sheer temptation to
put off discussion until later. She learned quickly.

"Shall I undress for this talk or do you wish to remove my gown for me?"

Too quickly, Gavin conceded, abandoning his dreaded discussion until later and reaching for the fastens of her bodice. His bride not only nearly matched him in height, but in passion as well. Standing perfectly still, she stared at his face until his fingers became awkward and clumsy. Deep in the sapphire depths of her gaze, Gavin saw the kindling of a flame that beckoned to be fed and satiated.

It was a mating call as ancient as time, issued from female to male without a word. The intensity of its demand left no time for talk. Only touch would soothe it, only complete possession would serve to quell it.

Once open, Krista's dress fell away to her ankles, revealing smooth white shoulders and the inviting swell of her feminine figure beneath the thin layer of her shift. As if the desire surging through his increasingly aroused body was on the verge of breaking, Gavin tugged at the hem, which she'd pulled through her legs and tucked into her waist. Then, running his hands beneath it, along the shapely length of her graceful limbs and body, he raised it over her head.

Although the light was dim through the hide-covered window, the golden tuft exposed at the juncture of her flat stomach and thighs worked a seduction the likes of which he'd never before experienced. The girl eased back on the mattress and lay still, not curling and smiling with moistened lips like a practiced vixen, but watching him with decidedly keen interest as he fumbled to unfasten his trousers. To his irritation, the leggings he'd forgotten to untie bound them as he tried to strip them down.

His face colored like that of a bumbling schoolboy in a whore's parlor. "Sorry, I . . ."

His apology was shattered by the curious touch of warm fingers that encircled the eager manhood which escaped the entanglement. Gavin held his breath, praying that the same self-control might be attained elsewhere. His throat went dry as she raised her somber, simmering gaze to his.

"To think I was afraid of this," she murmured. A smile toyed with her lips, revealing her amusement at her folly. "Now I think I shall never have enough."

Again the statement was directed to herself, but, combined with the firm but gentle coaxing as she pulled him onto her, clothes and all, it was nearly his undoing. "I canna wait, hinny," he whispered hoarsely, "so help me . . ."

As he positioned himself against the golden haven he'd but imagined the night before, Krista ran her hands over the gooseflesh that rose on his buttocks.

"Nor can I, husband."

Her breathed confession struck his neck as he gave into the wildfire coursing through his veins and the hands that suddenly pulled him downward. To his delight, she was as ready as he for the urgent union, continuing to guide his frantic thrusts with her hands, as if she had been starved for this moment. The bed creaked furiously with their impassioned dance, playing a high pitched and desperate music that could not be ignored by the pagans within.

The sight of Krista—her normally placid features enrapt, her lips parted so that just the tip of her tongue could be seen, her eyes half lidded, blinded by the flames that welded their writhing, damp bodies together—sent a bolt of desire streaking through him, only to explode upon reaching the intimate contact. His body shuddering with the violence of its erupting fire, Gavin was unaware that his partner reeled beneath him with the same quaking waves of the tempest.

When he no longer possessed the strength to support himself, he rolled to the side and closed his eyes, trousers still hanging about his thighs in a tangle with the leather leggings, and awaited the return of his breath.

"Gavin?"

Gavin grunted drowsily. Half the night and again today was more than one man could stand, even if it had been months since he'd been with a woman.

"Does . . . does it always stay like this?"

He chuckled and squirmed beneath the strong fingers that once again claimed possession of him. "Nay, lassie. Like the man, it needs rest. I'm nay bull. 'Twill wither soon enough."

"Right good thing," she giggled. "Or it wouldn't fit right in your pants."

Gavin opened one eye to see the girl sitting up beside him, her long golden braid hanging between breasts still taut and dark in the aftermath of their lovemaking. She was grinning wickedly. "Since you're so full of energy, how about untying those blasted thongs and helpin' me off with these trousers."

With far more success than he had had, Krista had the leggings off in little time at all, but not before her braid had played havoc with the spent manhood exposed to it. The tingling sensations that shot through his body were pleasantly arousing, rather than unbearable as before. Yet all Gavin wanted was to escape the chill and burrow under the covers with Krista in his arms. This was time to treasure, for after tonight, it was hard to tell when they'd have a chance to be together again.

"Gavin?"

"Aye, lassie?"

"Since it hasn't withered yet, would you mind if I . . . well, what I mean is . . ."

Again, Gavin shook with gentle amusement. It was the least he could do, considering the hasty satisfaction he'd just taken without regard to her need. "Climb aboard, hinny, though I'll warn ye, this stallion is fit only for pasture at the moment."

He watched through the dark slits of his lashes as the girl cautiously advanced on him. Her thighs, lean and strong from years of traveling on horseback, brushed silkily against the sides of his hips as she settled on the fascinating instrument of his passion.

The natural heat of the love-moist connection began to spread through his loins with a startling effect, which increased with the experimental movements of the golden goddess atop him. His breath caught as she grasped him, tugging without fingers, and his eyes flew open with the shocking impact of the slamming, pulsating response of his hot highlander blood. Who would have dreamed that the same blood ran beneath that cool collected exterior of his lovely wife?

When he found himself rising to meet the tentative plunge of her hips, he heard—and felt—her throaty giggle. "I did not think it was ready to wither at all!"

"Vixen!"

Krista laughed again, delighted with her discovery. "We must get your money's worth of this privacy while we can, husband. The march to Vincennes will not afford us the chance and I think I will miss it right much." Stopping the gyrations which were making it impossible for Gavin to think of anything but the moment, she leaned forward and kissed him soundly on the mouth. "I love you right good, Gavin Duncan, and I promise, not this war, nor savages, nor legions from hell will ever make me leave your side again."

"I'm not sure I want you to go on the march to Vincennes, Krista."

"Don't be silly, husband! I can ride, shoot, and hunt as well, if not better, than you. Soon," she snickered mischievously, "I will be able to do this better too."

There was no point in arguing now, Gavin reasoned with what little wit the wild impulses stampeding to his fevered brain would permit. He'd wait until later. Later, when he was able to contemplate being without this beguiling and resourceful creature, he decided, slipping his fingers up her inner thighs to titillate the sensitive skin there. For now, there was a challenge to be met . . . and one sweet torture deserved another.

Chapter Fourteen

The whipping of the north wind around the corner of the house awakened Krista the next morning, its icy blasts requiring her to force herself out of the cozy bed. It had been even warmer earlier, when her husband had risen to go with the men to fetch the weapons they'd agreed to purchase. Although she'd made an effort to get up then, Gavin insisted she sleep a while longer, since she'd entertained the men with harp and song well into the night, and tucked her in with a parting kiss that sent her off to a land of sweet dreams.

After reluctantly donning her buckskins and leggings, it was with even more regret that the girl packed away her plain blue dress and shift, as well as the nightgown she'd never needed. As long as her husband warmed her bed, she didn't suppose she would ever need one again. Caught up in the intimate memories of the time they'd spent there, Krista made up the bed and abandoned the last privacy she and Gavin would share for what was likely going to be a good while.

"Good morning, Madame DeMotte!" The upbeat tone of her voice was forced, as if it and the bright smile she put on would take away the melancholy that had claimed her as she'd prepared to leave.

"Krista," Marie De Motte acknowledged tersely. She pointed to a plate on the table. "Your breakfast is over there. I tried to keep it warm by the fire."

The familiar use of her name and the not so subtle chastisement passing her by, Krista accepted the plate of cold biscuits and the gruel that had simmered all night over the hearth and took a seat in the main room. There would be other nights, she consoled herself. Perhaps they would not be as soon as she would like, but they would come. She and Gavin had a whole lifetime to share together.

As she concentrated on the food, a friendly bark called her attention to the only other occupant of the inn at that hour. The little white dog sat wagging its tail at her feet.

"And good morning to you, Armand!" She broke off a bit of biscuit and started to hand it to the dog, when Madame DeMotte appeared in the doorway.

"Do not feed the dog in the main room!" she snapped imperiously. "It will teach him bad manners around our guests."

"Oh, I am sorry. I did not think."

Wondering what had put the proprietess in such a foul mood, Krista took a healthy bite of the biscuit. She was ravenous, even if the food was cold. Perhaps lovemaking increased the need for food, she mused idly, for she'd been starved when she and Gavin had stirred in time for supper the previous day. And then last night . . .

She snickered in private amusement. He kept swearing that she would be the death of him, yet Krista vowed she'd never seen a man so much alive as her husband. Whoever would have dreamed that what happened between a man and a woman could be so wonderful, that her stepfather's attempts at the act were as twisted as his greedy and lascivious mind. She owed so much to Gavin

for his patience . . . and his impatience, she thought
wickedly.

Was this love? A wistful smile settled on her lips. Did
feeling as if she were overflowing with warmth and affection, as if her heart would literally burst with happiness,
merit that label? Krista sighed dreamily, unaware that she
was being watched until Madame DeMotte entered the
room and took the seat opposite her.

"Now here is what I will be expecting from now on,
until your husband returns for you," she announced
stiffly. "First, you will wear a dress at all times. It never
hurts to have a pretty tavern maid."

Krista chuckled. "I wish I could, madame, but a dress
is hardly fit for travel in this weather. It will take us a week
to reach Kaskaskia with the new snowstorm."

Marie DeMotte rolled her eyes heavenward and swore
in French. "Always, the men, they leave the unpleasant to
us! You, ma fille, will not be going to Kaskaskia. You will
be staying here at Le Renard Rouge as my helper. Our
husbands made the arrangements yesterday."

Disbelief washed over Krista's face. "I am sorry, madame, but there must be some mistake. Gavin said only
this morning that he would return after they fetched the
guns. Surely he would not have made such a promise if it
were not true."

Marie DeMotte smiled unpleasantly. "You do not
know much of men, do you, ma fille? For the services you
provided him in *there*," she said, pointing to the back wall
adjoining the bedroom, "he would promise you *anything*.
That is why I always make certain my agreements with
men are in writing, backed by law, so that I have recourse
if they do not keep their word."

Krista sat motionless as her companion drew a paper
out of her shallow bosom and unfolded it for Krista to
read. "There it is in writing! Your husband's agreement

to indenture you for the period of seven years, or until the war's end, whichever is first. In exchange, he and his men received one hundred barrels of gunpowder. It is all there, notarized by my husband who is appointed magistrate for Petit Lyon."

It was a hastily written document, but it bore a seal of authority. Yet Krista would not accept what she was hearing until she studied the large signature scrawled across the bottom—the same as on her wedding certificate. She recalled admiring his large, well-formed letters. But was it the same man who had made love to her and spoken of the life they would build together?

"Men are all alike, Krista," Madame DeMotte informed her brusquely. "They pursue their own pleasure and the devil with the woman who must keep their house and raise their children. My Jean escapes his responsibility by playing soldier and stealing guns and ammunition from the British. He swears that it is for me that he does this, but do I have more than I had when this war started? Non!"

Upon realizing that her audience had gone deaf to her complaints, the mistress narrowed her gaze at the white-faced girl. "You are not going to swoon, are you? I've no time for hysterics."

The insult, small in comparison to the mortal wound of Gavin Duncan's betrayal, pricked at Krista's already suffering pride. The blue of her gaze frosted over, as cold as the wind blowing outside. Rebelliously, she shoved the papers away from her and rose from the table.

"I will not get hysterical, madame, nor will I honor this agreement!" Krista paced across the floor to the corner where she'd dropped her pack. "Did my *husband* leave me a horse?" From this day on, that term she had only learned to cherish these last two days would forever be a curse in her mind, to be spoken only in contempt. *How could he do this?*

"Non. But you will not need a horse to work here."

"With all due respect, madame, I will not work here. I am going to catch up with the Big Knives."

Marie rose from the table with a cryptic laugh. "I did not picture you the type who would go running after a man who had handed you off like used merchandise. You do not appear the clinging vine type."

"Some vines choke and kill, madame. My means may not be the same," Krista averred, searching through her pack for her knife, "but my purpose will be."

Perhaps she would drive her blade through his lying heart, she pondered, if he ever really had one. Her movement became more frantic when she did not find the leather sheath containing the gift Gavin had given her at the start of their journey. She knew she'd put it in the bottom of her haversack. Her nostrils flared with the growing fury that bounded through her veins.

"Bastard!" she swore under her breath, slinging the sack across the floor angrily. Had he left her nothing to survive with?

Her eyes ached with tears, yet she refused to give her companion the satisfaction of seeing them. She stared at the floor until her vision cleared, hardened with sheer resolve.

"I can not let you leave, Krista. You have a value to me and my husband."

Bitterness rose in the back of Krista's throat, intensifying her disdain. "And you think you will stop me?" She swung around, towering half again the size of the woman who stepped between her and the door.

Unintimidated by her companion's size, Marie stood with her scrawny black stockinged legs braced. "Non, ma fille," she answered, as if tired of the matter, "but this will."

Krista stiffened at the sight of the pistol the woman produced from inside her short jacket.

"I do not wish to use this, nor the chain Jean insisted I would need, but you leave me no choice." She waved the gun over toward the large woodbox. "In there. Get it out and put it on your ankle."

For a long moment, Krista considered the gun and the woman wielding it. Marie DeMotte was a bitter soul, hardened by a bleak life of poverty, judging from the looks of the inn and her threadbare French-Canadian dress. Aged beyond her years, there was a certain desperation about her that instinctively warned Krista, more so than the click of the pistol hammer, that here was a female to be seriously reckoned with.

"Do not be a fool, Krista, and force me to act the same. You will soon see that I am all that stands between you and my men. Do as I say and I will protect you. Fight me or run away, and I will turn them loose like hounds after the prize."

Krista lifted the heavy ball with a length of chain and a pair of leg irons attached to it. Some poor slave had no doubt worn them at one time. As she closed one of the anklets around her leg and locked it, the fate of the previous wearer briefly staggered her mind.

"One is enough. There is no need to shackle both your legs. It will hamper your work. Unfasten the other and leave it in the box."

"And *this* won't?" Krista scoffed, snatching grudgingly at the heavy ball.

"Only until you see that what I have said is true. I own your bond and I will keep it. Your fate here, ma fille, will not be so bad as that which you will tempt if you try to escape." Marie DeMotte's gaze was as brittle as the laugh that escaped her drawn mouth. "And it is surely better than remaining with a man who would trade you off like cattle."

The barbed remark struck its target right through the heart. Stung by the pain into angry motion, Krista reached down and dragged the chain toward the kitchen. Stopping only long enough to pull on her buffalo robe.

"Where are you going?" Marie called after her.

"The woodbox is nearly empty. If you'd keep any travelers warm tonight, it had best be filled."

"Alas, my back keeps me from filling it to the top. It is all I can do to keep things going here. You might as well fill the one in the kitchen too."

"Ja."

The bite of the cold air across Krista's face failed to penetrate the numb acceptance of her fate. She drew her scarf over it, so that only her eyes were pelted by the driving snow, and loaded as much wood as she could carry in her arms. The ball dragging a path through the freshly fallen white carpet, she made her way back and forth until both boxes were piled high.

"I did not expect you to fill the boxes all at one time," Marie chided as the girl stomped to shake off the snow clinging to her boots. "Come warm yourself by the fire, Krista. To take a chill and die of pneumonia will not do."

"May I use this peg to hang up my coat?"

"But of course! Such silly things you do not have to ask. This is your home too."

Home? The word echoed dully in Krista's mind. She had not had a home since she was twelve and it was beginning to appear that she would never have one, not of her own. "And where will I sleep? I would put away my belongings."

"In the bedroom with me, unless Jean is home. Then we will make your bed by the fire here in the kitchen."

"I mean nothing by this, but I would rather sleep in the kitchen at *all* times."

Inadvertently, Krista's gaze gravitated toward the small plank door that separated the two rooms, but she refused to respond to the resulting anguish. She would remain with Marie DeMotte for now. She would do the work she was asked to do, more if necessary—anything to keep her mind occupied with less disturbing thoughts.

She would not, however, lie in the same bed in which she'd been so cruelly led to believe she had found love for the first time. When she'd left it that morning, it was a haven. Now in the light of truth, it was a den of deceitful seduction and betrayal.

As if reading her thoughts, Marie DeMotte shrugged. "It will pass. A woman's first lover is always the hardest to forget."

"But I thought you said Gavin was coming back for me."

Where had those imploring words come from, Krista wondered in confusion. If there was one hopeful part of her that wanted such a thing to happen, she would banish it, blot it out. Gavin Duncan deserved nothing but contempt.

"Seven years is a long time, Krista, and the war . . . who knows how long it will last? He may even get himself killed by the British," Marie speculated dispassionately. "Any day, I expect the men to return to me with the news that Jean has been shot down during a raid."

"Well, I hope he is!" Krista ground out. "My husband, that is," she corrected upon seeing her mistress's disconcerted look. "I hope a British ball drills him through his lying black heart."

"To save you the trouble?"

"Ja, because I do not think he is worth even that much good!"

The vehemence of her declaration was designed as much to convince herself as it was her companion, to thaw that sudden chill of concern that had tripped her heart. It had taken her a while to fall in love, Krista reasoned, searching the cluttered kitchen for a broom to brush out the snow and dirt she'd tracked in, and it would take time to kill it.

"Have you a broom?"

"Behind the flour barrel in the corner."

Krista tugged it out by its wooden handle to find the bristles worn almost to the point of ineffectiveness. It seemed as though she was going to have ample time and work to put her misplaced love out of its misery. But it was going to be a long and tortured death from which she would never quite recover, she thought morosely. *Could one even survive without a heart?*

The bad weather continued through the remainder of the month and into February, making travelers as scarce as the news of the war. With little to do on that account, Krista devoted her attention to the filthy state of the inn. If she was going to live there, it would be clean, the way her mother and Widow Ames had kept Schuyler Crossing. Taking one section at a time, she scraped away the layers of dirt and dried tobacco spittle, layers which had been sprinkled with water in lieu of sweeping to keep the dust down during the summer. Then, with a mixture of strong lye and water, she'd scoured the planking down, a task requiring many repetitions before the natural pale gray patina of the aged wood was revealed.

The horizontally paneled walls received the same treatment and lastly, the kitchen and bedroom got their long overdue attention. Although her mistress expressed disdain at her industry, calling it folly, she sometimes slipped and admitted that the entire place seemed brighter and fresher. When Jean DeMotte and his men returned from yet another successful endeavor, the proprietess even backed the broom-wielding Krista, who, looking down at most of them, dared the men to rid themselves of their chewed tobacco spittle anywhere but in the crudely hammered brass spittoons she had polished to a shine.

Krista also learned that the strong-willed woman had meant what she said about protecting her. One night, after a particularly rowdy celebration over Hamilton's surrender at Vincennes, one of the marauders, by the name of Gaston, tried to drag Krista, ball and chain, to his bedroll. Marie appeared, her small bent figure lost in a nightshift, brandishing the pistol she usually kept tucked inside her waist.

From that moment on, the iron restraints were put in the bottom of the woodbox and Krista was allowed her freedom to move about. Not that the girl deluded herself into thinking Marie had done it out of concern for her. The woman was merely protecting her investment. Besides, even if Krista had contemplated escape, the harsh winter made it impossible.

Imprisoned for three months with Marie DeMotte, the girl had come to know her mistress quite well. She was greedy to a fault, often cheating the uneducated men who relied on her to work out their share of the booty. At first, Krista thought her addition errors were just that, but upon correcting her once, she was silenced by an almost murderous look and an order to go to the kitchen. The reward from Marie's calculated deceit was kept in bags hidden under a floorboard beneath her chest. To Krista, it was a miracle the men did not kill them all and make off with it, except that they had no idea it was there.

Indeed, no one would have gathered from their meager surroundings and the tattered clothing they wore that the

DeMottes had a haypenny to spare. Krista even wondered if Jean DeMotte had any idea of the wealth stored under his bedroom floor.

Only Krista's thorough scouring had led her to its discovery. She'd noticed a loose board upon moving the chest to clean under it. The plank had evidently been cut or patched. Since there was a knot in the up side of the board, she flipped it to see if the other side was clearer, and there it was—the accumulation of countless raids, enough to make life easy for Marie DeMotte for the rest of her days.

For all her greed, however, the woman insisted Krista eat well and take care of herself, particularly when her usual vigor faded into a lethargy with the approaching spring. One afternoon, while preparing a meal for a young couple who had stopped at the inn on their way to Cahokia, Marie came upon Krista staring out the window, lost in a netherworld that more and more frequently claimed her, instead of peeling the hot yams she'd taken from the oven earlier.

"Do not tell me that you still pine for that man!" *That man* applied to either Jean DeMotte or Gavin Duncan, depending on which had incurred her ire.

Usually Krista concurred with her mistress. She had even picked up her term for the errant Gavin Duncan. This time, however, she surprised Marie by bursting into tears. So taken back was the woman, who normally scoffed at hysterical females, that she was instantly at Krista's side.

"Qu'est que c'est? This is not my *Viking* helper. Are you ill?"

In all the time since Gavin had abandoned her, Krista had not shed one tear. That was one degradation she would not succumb to. Instead, she'd held all her pain inside and taken out her anger and frustration in her work. Until lately, she had begun to think she was actually becoming immune to the recollections of what they had shared and the heartwrenching aftermath. Now, however, she knew she would never be free of the man.

"W . . . worse," she sobbed brokenly. "I'm with child."

She had never been regular with womanly concerns. Hence, when she had not suffered the inconvenience of the curse for the first two months, she was not particularly alarmed. The third month she missed, she became a little suspicious, but noticed none of the other symptoms of pregnancy which she'd often heard women discuss in closed circles. She'd not been ill. Her appetite had been hearty as ever. She had no fainting spells, nor noticed any particular soreness of her breasts. Then, for what she at first thought was no reason at all, she began to dread rising in the morning and anxiously awaiting the moment at night when she might retire to the cot Jean DeMotte had brought in for her at his wife's request.

"Ah, I was afraid that this was the case," Marie consoled her, adding with rare brightness, "but that is not the end of the world. At least the father married you."

Married and sold her, Krista brooded bitterly. She had thought Gavin Duncan could hurt her no more, but she'd been wrong. His seed was growing in her belly, draining her strength, and she wanted no part of it! The world did not deserve a child of his blood. One of his kind was enough.

"Enough, Krista. We have guests who are hungry for their supper. We'll speak of this later." Marie patted Krista on the back. "Now go wash your face. The food is ready to go on the table."

Sleep was what Krista longed to do, but that was impossible, especially with customers present. She stepped outside where the tin washbowl and pitcher were kept and made hasty work of applying wet cloths to her tear-red-dened eyes.

If only Gavin had written or made some attempt to explain all this, she might have found it in her heart to forgive him—after she'd calmed down and accepted what she could not for the moment change. She supposed she'd secretly clung to the hope that he'd even return for her after Vincennes had been taken, but it was not the case. When no word from him came then, she'd made up her mind to leave in the spring.

Now that idea was foiled. She was too tired to walk to the trading post in the settlement, let alone make the journey to the mountains where DeMotte's bloodhounds could not possibly find her. Damn Gavin Duncan! she cursed, fortified with enough irritation to proceed with her chore of serving supper.

Although she was never rude, not even to Marie De-Motte in one of her sourest moods, Krista was not her usual cheery self as she placed the boiled meat and its accompanying yams and winter greens on the table for the couple. In fact, the way they smiled at each other, like she and Gavin had once done, almost made her blurt out a warning to the slim brown-haired woman. Instead, she bit her tongue and chided herself sternly. She'd been around Marie so long that she was beginning to think like her. Perhaps this young farmer was a decent man. Perhaps he would continue to fawn over his wife and cater to her every whim.

"Oh, Andre, I left my medicine in my bag and I must take it with the meal. Would you fetch it for me?"

Krista stepped aside from serving the meat so that their guest could do his wife's bidding. However, the moment he stepped outside, where the remainder of their belongings rested on a wagon under a large tarp, the woman looked up at Krista and smiled brightly. She was not a particularly beautiful woman, but there was something about her wholesome, well-scrubbed appearance that was almost saintly.

"I am sorry, madame, but I could not help but over-hear that you are . . . *enciente*," she finished awkwardly in pink embarrassment. "I know that you are upset now, but I must tell you that, no matter what the father of your child is, the baby is half of you as well. If I am any judge of character, I would say that you are strong enough to overcome any bad blood it may have inherited from its father."

"Perhaps I will lose it and then I will not have to be punished for having allowed a man to deceive me so good."

Krista clenched her teeth to keep the rest of the bitter-ness which rose like bile to the back of her throat from spilling out. This woman had a man who loves her. From the radiance on her face, it was doubtful she'd ever known what it was like to hurt like this.

"You must never say that!" To Krista's surprise, tears welled in the young woman's eyes. "Andre and I have lost three children," she explained, her voice taut with emo-tion. "It is so unfair! We would give all we owned for a baby and you do not want yours."

Shaken by the woman's genuine distress, Krista placed a comforting hand on her shoulder. "I am truly sorry, madame. I suppose I am acting foolish."

"A baby is a gift from God, dear woman. Cherish it with all your heart. Promise me you will."

Krista was not good at lying, but she managed to nod somberly as the woman's husband reentered with the bottle of medication she'd requested. "Will there be any-thing else?"

The woman smiled and quickly covered the fact that

she'd been on the verge of tears. "Just don't forget what I have told you."

Krista tried to smile back in acknowledgment, but her heart was not in it. She wasn't certain she could love the child growing within her. It was a stranger with poor testimony to its character, at least from its father's side. Nonetheless, the woman's words had made their impact, whether Krista received them willingly or not. The baby was also half hers, which was something to think about.

Chapter Fifteen

Krista knew there were certain combinations of herbs which women used to rid themselves of unwanted children, but no matter how she anguished over the child she carried, she could not bring herself to follow Marie De-Motte's suggestion to end the pregnancy. It may have been the plea from the young woman headed for Cahokia, for Krista had certainly felt more than her share of guilt for wishing the child away each time she recalled their conversation. Or perhaps it was because she'd waited so long to come to a decision that the rambunctious character growing within her womb had begun to take on a personality.

The first fluttering movements had startled the girl so, she'd spilled a pan full of fresh baked bread out on the floor and incurred her mistress' wrath, as well as Armand's gratitude. *He*, she mused on more than one occasion, was worse than his father—disconcerting her, distracting her, and sometimes making her laugh when there was little to laugh about. The baby was deemed a boy, by both Krista and her mistress, because of the worrisome symptoms that eventually came with it.

As spring blossomed into summer, so blossomed her body, until Krista felt as if she carried a barrel half in front of her. Unable to let out her cornflower dress to accommodate her expanding middle, Krista was forced to make a new dress from some material Marie purchased for her at the trading post. It was a bright green calico which, Krista thought, made her look like the Christmas tree that had always stood in the big window in their Vienna home during the holiday season—narrow at the head and growing progressively larger as it fell from the wide spread of her abdomen.

At least, as time progressed, she was no longer tired and her appetite had returned with her renewed energy. She kept the inn spotlessly clean—the only building in the small settlement that could boast that claim. Even when she felt like a cow, crawling about on her hands and knees as she scoured the floor, she refused to take Marie's advice to simply water down the dirt.

For people who took such pains with their appearance, it was beyond the girl how they could keep their homes so neat and tidy on the surface, pride themselves on kitchen fare prepared with filthy utensils, and live on layers of packed dirt, which was sprinkled several times a day and cleaned but twice a year! Those who did not have floors in their cabins at all were as well off.

Still, the tiny community intrigued the girl. On days when Marie sent her to the trading post, she could hear young girls singing love songs, the words *couer* and *amour* frequent among the lyrics. They wore narrow high-heeled shoes which left Krista to wonder how they remained upright.

Contrary to those on the other side of the Alleghanies, the French women were partial to skirts which revealed stockinged calves and, ofttimes, knees as well. It was much the length Indian women preferred. The advantage, of course, was that they were freer to work in the fields, meadows, and stables of the settlement without their long

Wish You Were Here?

You can be, every month, with Zebra
Historical Romance Novels.

AND TO GET YOU STARTED, ALLOW US TO SEND YOU

4 Historical Romances Free

AN $18.00 VALUE!
With absolutely no obligation to buy anything.

YOU ARE CORDIALLY INVITED TO GET SWEPT AWAY INTO NEW WORLDS OF PASSION AND ADVENTURE.

AND IT WON'T COST YOU A PENNY!

Receive 4 Zebra Historical Romances, Absolutely _Free!_

(An $18.00 value)

Now you can have your pick of handsome, noble adventurers with romance in their hearts and you on their minds. Zebra publishes Historical Romances That Burn With The Fire Of History by the world's finest romance authors.

This very special FREE offer entitles you to 4 Zebra novels at absolutely no cost, with no obligation to buy anything, ever. It's an offer designed to excite your most vivid dreams and desires...and save you $18!

And that's not all you get...

Your Home Subscription Saves You Money Every Month.

After you've enjoyed your initial FREE package of 4 books, you'll begin to receive monthly shipments of new Zebra titles. These novels are delivered direct to your home as soon as they are published...sometimes even before the bookstores get them! Each monthly shipment of 4 books will be yours to examine for 10 days. Then if you decide to keep the books, you'll pay the preferred subscriber's price of just $3.75 per title. That's $15 for all 4 books...a savings of $3 off the publisher's price! (A nominal shipping and handling charge of $1.50 per shipment will be added.)

There Is No Minimum Purchase. And Your Continued Satisfaction Is Guaranteed

We're so sure that you'll appreciate the money-saving convenience of home delivery that we guarantee your complete satisfaction. You may return any shipment...for any reason...within 10 days and pay nothing that month. And if you want us to stop sending books, just say the word. There is no minimum number of books you must buy.

It's a no-lose proposition, so send for your 4 FREE books today!

TREAT YOURSELF TO 4 FREE BOOKS.

AFFIX
STAMP
HERE

ZEBRA HOME SUBSCRIPTION SERVICE, INC.

120 BRIGHTON ROAD

P.O. BOX 5214

CLIFTON, NEW JERSEY 07015-5214

hems getting in their way—places they evidently preferred to devote their labors to in lieu of their cottages. Half jackets, which reached their waist and no more, took the place of the Dutch and English's cumbersome shawls and the little caps which topped their powdered and, sometimes, gaudily adorned hair, afforded a much better view of their efforts than the Easterners' hood or scarf.

Those whose clothes were tattered at best found long cloaks of gray, brown, or blue, which covered all from head to toe, convenient to make a proper appearance. Even the men wore these in inclement weather. Upon meeting acquaintances on the narrow dirt street which separated the small cluster of buildings, they would often salute each other with kisses, something Krista found amusing, particularly between men.

The natural hunger for news, especially of the war, became more and more satiated with the extraordinary influx of people headed west, precipitated by the arrival of fairer weather. Word was, flatboats carrying the settlers were thick on the river, despite occasional raids by Indians who had returned from their winter hunting to the war. The successes of Vincennes and other western engagements with the British and Indians appeared to ease the minds of the travelers as to the dangers of the wilderness. Even Colonel Clark was turning his attentions to building a new fort at the falls of the Ohio.

Once again that hope that refused to die in Krista's heart flared briefly. Certainly her husband would have time to, if not return for her, at least make some attempt to contact her. It was quickly dashed, however by the report that the British were launching an attack on the French and Spanish posts on the Mississippi in order to gain control of the river. Banding with the Spanish and French troops, Clark and his men once again marched off to repulse the enemy, but this time the result was more catastrophic for the settlers in the path of their retreat. The tales of the bitter retaliation on undefended towns and homesteads replaced Krista's entertainment at Le Renard Rouge almost every night.

By September, Clark's forces had spent the better part of the summer waging war against the various tribes that inhabited the Kentucky and Ohio valleys. Many tribes sought peace, although the Mingo, Wyandot, and some Delaware and Shawnee continued to burn and pillage, in spite of the Big Knives' presence.

Though she had vowed not to listen to any more talk of the war, especially about Colonel Clark's militia, Krista was just as attentive as the others in the room. She rested against the wall, the pressure soothing to her aching back.

The last few days had been unbearable. The inn was busy, forcing her and Marie up hours before daybreak to begin preparing the meals for their guests and keeping them occupied until their customers' thirst for news and drink was quenched at night. The strain showed on the mother-to-be's face as she kept a watchful eye on the tables, ever prepared to fill a noggin or tankard at the slightest indication that it was needed.

Tonight would be a later night than usual, for Jean DeMotte and his men had arrived that afternoon and had been drinking ever since, ignoring the food the women had worked so hard to prepare in the Indian summer heat. They had pulled the wagonload of supplies up to the back of the cabin, although Krista knew it was to keep an eye on it until they saw fit to unload it, rather than for the benefit of the women who needed them.

At least they had come in time. Earlier that summer, the inn had been packed with travelers passing through and supplies had run out. Water had had to serve as drink and no bread could be had with the game furnished by the local hunters of the settlement. Tonight, the last keg

of light wine, for which the French had a particular taste,
was nearly empty and, from the look of things, Krista
would have to fetch a new barrel herself from the wagon.
She'd rather go alone anyway. She did not like the
Frenchmen who rode with DeMotte, nor trust them—
especially after that night with Gaston.

The kegs were tied on the wagon in a pyramid fashion
and covered with a tarp. Holding the kitchen knife she'd
brought along in her teeth, she climbed up on the wagon
bed as agilely as her condition would allow. She dared not
cut the barrels loose and let them fall, for if they were to
break open, not even Marie could save her from the wrath
of the men. Somehow, she needed to work one loose and
. . .

A low ominous scraping noise warned Krista that
something was wrong, even before she felt the barrels
under her starting to roll. The knife fell from her teeth
with her cry of alarm and suddenly she was swept away
with the landslide of the cargo. A terrible pain erupted in
her head as it struck something hard, sending the stars
twinkling in the sky above her into a swirling motion. A
burn of jute on her arm alerted her to the presence of one
of the cords. In desperation, she grabbed for it and held
on as the barrels behind her rolled over her tucked head
and shoulders. And then the rope gave way, spilling her
into the midst of the fallen cargo where she landed awkwardly.

Stunned, she neither heard Marie's scream for help nor
felt the abrasions and bruises that covered her body. She
simply lay there, trying to determine if she was even alive
in the sudden stillness. It was only when the spinning
heavens above her were replaced by the heavy smoke-
blackened beams of the kitchen ceiling that she realized
she was being moved.

"Sacre bleu, it is her water! It is broken!" Marie De-

Motte exclaimed in alarm before breaking into a torrent of French which sent one of the men running to fetch a midwife.

Although the mattress on which she was deposited was far more comfortable than the scattered supplies she'd landed on, a terrible pain ripped through Krista's abdomen forcing her upright, arms clasping her middle. Her mind was instantly cleared of the daze which had claimed her with the realization that this was her time—hers and her baby's.

"Marie, the baby!" she gasped, as the woman shooed the men out of the room. *"The baby!"* Krista could not remember being so frightened of anything in her life than the labor that seemed to crush the very breath from her. Surely it was hurting the baby too! *"We have to get it out!"*

"He will do that on his own, ma fille," Marie retorted sharply. "Now lie down and calm yourself. I have sent for the midwife."

After what seemed an eternity, the pain gradually subsided and Krista fell back against the pillows in compliance. "How many does it take?"

The woman smiled patiently. "Many more than this, I am told. Now let me see to your head. You are bleeding there."

"Someone already cut the rope holding the barrels," Krista muttered irritably. "Those damned *men!*"

As Marie methodically cleaned the large bleeding swelling that stained Krista's golden hair a rusty scarlet, her body, thawing from its initial shock, began to report back to her the injuries sustained in her tumble from the wagon. Where the skin had come off both elbows and knees, a hot stinging sensation throbbed, and numerous bruises began to ache. The next contraction, however, wiped out all recognition of those minor complaints.

The night began to tick away in increments Krista

marked by her labor. Eyes wide with fear and stark with pain, she clenched her teeth on the rag the midwife had handed her upon arrival and thrust herself against the mattress, as if she could get away from the terrible agony tearing her apart.

She had been told it was bad, but she was not prepared for this. She wanted to cry, but that would take away the energy she needed to curse Gavin Duncan and everything about him. If he were to walk in at that very moment and fall on his knees, begging her forgiveness, she would have taken the knife the midwife had laid aside and stabbed him a hundred times for each pain she was bearing.

How anything could survive the terrible pressure that overtook her was beyond Krista. It robbed her of breath and reason and soaked her in perspiration until her hair was wet and clung to her neck and face. And when it finally released her, to what had become a dull, constant ache across her lower back, she was nearly faint from the exertion.

The women tried to force some whiskey down her throat in an attempt to ease her discomfort, or at least make it more tolerable, but the effort only resulted in violent retching which provoked another contraction and increased the pressure in Krista's head to the point where she became disoriented and lost track of time.

In the background, she heard the women speaking in low, concerned tones, but their words meant nothing to her anymore. She had, however, heard people speak in the same manner at a deathbed, where they did not want their patient to hear. It only confirmed her growing dread that there was only one escape from this excruciating ordeal for both her and her baby. Clinging to her last bit of conscious thought, Krista began to pray as her mother had taught her, her dry cracked lips moving silently.

"What is it she is saying?" the midwife inquired. Her

patient was a big girl, but it was also a big baby. Even worse for the mother, it appeared that it was coming feet first.

"She is praying." Marie wet another cloth and replaced the one on Krista's forehead. "How long has it been since Jean left to find the doctor?"

"Two hours." And if the doctor did not come soon, the girl would likely bleed to death, and die with the child. Although she was tall, her hips were narrow and simply would not open any further. The midwife shook her head ruefully. Such a pretty girl, so healthy and young. "Perhaps the fall has already killed the baby and that is why she is having such a difficult time. Poor—"

Krista's scream startled the woman, who turned to see the young mother struggling to sit up. "Non, non, you must not . . ."

"Let me up! I can not stand this!"

"Madame," the midwife shouted at Marie, trying to force the girl back down on the bed, "you must help me keep her down. She will—"

"No!" With a frantic sling, born of desperation, the hysterical girl sent the heavyset woman staggering backward.

"What is this, ma fille?" Marie chided, running around the bed to support Krista as her legs started to buckle beneath her.

"I . . . I don't want to die!" Krista panted. She clung to the thick round bed post to keep from collapsing totally. "The baby has to come . . . *now!*"

"She must lie down!"

Krista shook her head wildly. "Indian women do not lie down! They have it . . ."

"Let her be!" Marie warned the midwife. "Get a blanket and put it under her to catch the baby when it comes."

The proprietess shoved a towel over the post where the

expectant mother beat her forehead, trembling violently. Left with no alternative, the midwife did as she was told. Never in all her years had she seen such a spectacle. Whatever would be was in the hands of Providence now.

And it was to Providence that the suffering young woman pleaded until she was silenced by the tearing, burning agony of the child bursting from her womb. Snatching the bloodstained infant up as its mother fell to her knees, the midwife watched as Marie turned the unconscious girl so that she slumped against the wall on the blanket.

The baby was blue and surely dead, she thought, glancing down at it. However, a slight movement caused the older woman's breath to catch. "Sacre bleu, it is alive!" she exclaimed as the infant began to squirm and make an attempt to cry. She hurriedly cleared its mouth with her finger and gave it a sharp smack on the buttocks. Its loud protest filled the room with the happiest sound the French woman had ever heard. This was truly an act of Providence. "What a beautiful baby boy!"

"Quick, cut the cord and give it to me!"

"But the girl . . ."

"The cord, *now!*" Marie DeMotte demanded imperiously. She moved to hover over the midwife as she went about her directed task. "As far as you are concerned, this baby was born dead. Is that understood?"

The other woman looked up at her companion in disbelief.

"The girl did not want the baby. I know someone who does . . . someone who will pay dearly for it. Now hurry up, before she regains consciousness!"

"Then why tell her her baby is dead?"

"Because, you bumbling cow, it will be easier on her this way." Marie reached into her pocket and took out the purse she intended to pay the woman with. "*This* is your share." It was just a pittance compared to what Jean would collect from the young couple in Cahokia, but it was enough to still further objection from her wary cohort.

Money had that effect on people. Money meant power and Marie liked power she could sift through her fingers or use to exact her will. Besides, if the girl died, the sale of her child would make up for the inconvenience of having to run the inn alone again.

In the blend of feverish days that followed, Krista thought she was dying. She had seen her mother and father and longed to remain with them, but strangers kept intruding on their joyous reunion—strangers who, she was later told, were the doctor and midwife. When she finally emerged from the sweltering limbo where day and night were no more discernible than her company, she had no recollection of the labor which had nearly drained her of her life's blood, or of the stillborn baby boy who was buried near the garden in the backyard.

He had been the image of his father, Marie told her in a rare consoling tone, with reddish-brown hair and a gargantuan proportion which had made his normal birth impossible and nearly killed her in the process. Even if the child's father returned for her, however, Krista was assured that she need never fear the risk of childbirth again. The doctor had told them she would never bear another.

The news should have pleased her, but it didn't. Instead, the young woman plunged into a deep depression from which there appeared no escape. She had wished her baby would go away and it had. *He* had—that ornery little bundle of life who had worked his way into her heart without her ever knowing what he looked like or what it felt like to hold him kicking and squirming in her arms, rather than in her belly. As the woman going to Cahokia had said, God had given her a gift. Because of her ingratitude, He had taken it back and left her alive to suffer her remorse.

Her health gradually returned. Her body was rapidly restored to its slender proportion and, in time, Krista had once again taken over her responsibilities to her mistress. Her spirit, however, lay in the backyard, buried in a small grave. The only hint of life in her dull gaze showed when she played the harp at night and drifted back to another time—a happier time when she had been but a child herself. Marie let her keep the instrument in the kitchen by her cot, where she could wile away those evening hours when sleep would not come without disturbing the overnight guests spread out on the tavern floor.

One winter's night, after she'd built up the fire in the main room where two travelers continued to amuse themselves with dice and cards while other guests slept, she took up the instrument and cradled it against her shoulder lovingly. As she closed her eyes, her fingers took to the strings, plucking of their own accord a composition her father had been writing when he died.

When she came to the last of the notes embedded in her memory, she stopped abruptly, pained by morose thoughts—cut off, ending like his life, like her baby's, like her own.

"That music, fraulein, where does it come from? I am certain I know it."

Startled by the intrusion on her melancholy, Krista looked up to see one of the German men who had drifted into the inn that afternoon, paying in His Majesty's coin for their board and floor space out of the weather. Marie had whispered to her the two were deserters, but they hadn't acted the least uncomfortable when Jean DeMotte's men came in.

"It is nothing but a piece written by my father . . . many years ago," Krista added, equally certain the young man could not possibly be familiar with the tune.

"Ja, it was written many years ago by my Uncle Joseph. My father, his brother-in-law, finished it after his death."

Krista stared at the tall blond-haired man warily. "And *your* name, sir?"

"Klaus . . . Klaus Bruener."

Could it be a coincidence, Krista wondered. She strained to contain the spark of excitement that stirred a hope long dead. "My mother was a Bruener."

Klaus Bruener laughed, his eyes twinkling in the firelight as he studied her closer. "Then we are *cousins!* You must be one of Joseph and Mary Lindstrom's daughters! We were but children when we last met. Krista, your mistress called you. Ja, I think I recall a girl named Krista who could play the harp like an angel. I hated you! Papa was always telling me that if I studied very hard, I might learn to play as well. We moved to Vienna after your father's death."

"Your father was Rolf?"

It couldn't be, Krista cautioned herself, unconvinced by the young man's eager nod. She recalled Uncle Rolf and Aunt Gerta attending the funeral with their small children—one boy and four girls. The boy had been particularly troublesome, having come with the sole intent of making his sisters miserable. Krista recalled Uncle Rolf removing his son from the room and the howling that followed, pronouncing just punishment had been dealt.

Klaus ambled over to her cot and sat down beside her. "What are you doing in this godforsaken land? I thought your mother married a wealthy merchant."

Mama had never written to her family in Vienna again. She'd had her pride and didn't want them to know the real Herr Schuyler. "She married a poor merchant who pretended to be wealthy in order to marry a prosperous widow. They were both fooled."

"Well, it is common knowledge that even the most prosperous of musicians and composers are only as rich as their patrons choose to make them."

"Not to a greedy snake like my stepfather," Krista countered bitterly. "He married me off to a man who sold me into indenture for a wagonload of powder . . . a British deserter turned colonial."

"Indenture!" Klaus echoed incredulously. "What manner of man could do such a thing? The very idea makes me furious!"

"A silver-tongued Scot who I do not even know now is alive or dead. All he ever wanted was a guide and, when I'd served that purpose, he traded me off like a cow for something he needed more." Krista blinked away the haze that formed in her vision. She'd thought herself immune to Gavin's betrayal now, but it still hurt.

She felt Klaus's arm come to rest on her shoulder and looked up to see the compassion burning in his eyes. He was so young, she thought, and she felt so old. Yet, if she recalled properly, he was but four years her junior.

"Tell me, cousin. Purge this terrible grief I see in your eyes and let me share it. You see," he confessed earnestly, "we are both stranded, it seems, in a strange land. Yet, in my heart, I now know the reason. Together, we can rise above our misfortune and return to our homeland." He cupped his finger under her chin and lifted it. "You *would* like that, wouldn't you, Krista?"

Krista couldn't answer. The proposal was too absurd to consider seriously. Enemy armies and savages surrounded them, not to mention the Frenchmen Marie DeMotte would put on her trail if she were to run away. Her mother had once said never look back, but what did one do when there was nothing to look forward to? Life had become a mere existence for her. She had been simply waiting for her punishment to end, not by the fulfillment of a childhood dream, but by death.

Could this be the end fate intended instead? Was her beloved Vienna and all its glory now in her future, rather than her past? The stranger, her *cousin*, seemed genuine enough. His clean, handsome face was a mirror of compassion, sympathy, and something else. Pain? she wondered. He'd said he was stranded here, just like herself. Perhaps they both suffered from broken hearts—hearts betrayed and tormented by memories that would not leave them be.

There was no conclusion Krista could come to but this, generated not by logic, but by her soul. They were family, united by blood. That they had been reunited by her music, the one element in her life which had never let her down, could only mean one thing. Once again, there was reason to hope and live, if not for love, for her other passion—her harp and song.

Part Three

The battle's done, the storm is past
And freedom is hard won
Yet, still a flame within me lasts
For love that is undone

I will na let it flash and die
This hope which tortures me
Till we are one, my love and I
In love and liberty.

Chapter Sixteen

London 1784

The trumpet blasts heralding the circus parade that monopolized Bond Street on its way to Vauxhall carried up to the fashionable apartment where Krista Lindstrom ceased practicing her harp to listen. She would never forget the first time she heard such a commotion and remarked to her cousin that the king was surely coming their way. What a laugh she'd stirred among Klaus's upper-class friends! Gentlemen to the bone, they'd sworn they weren't laughing at her, but enjoying her freshness to the *ton*. Her naivete was charming. It was like showing the world to a child for the first time.

Krista smiled wistfully as she watched the equestrians ride across the intersection down the cobbled street, brightly costumed and waving to the shoppers and merchants. She supposed she had acted the child upon their arrival in London. So different from the primitive land she and her cousin had just barely escaped with their lives, it was even more exciting than Vienna. At least it had been at first.

There was so much to see and do, if one had the money and knew the right people. Her enterprising and engaging cousin, though lacking in an abundance of funds, certainly met the latter requirement. He had turned their capture by a British patrol in Natchez into their subscription to success in one of the grandest cities in the world!

She had been certain when they were brought before Brigadier General Bickham that a hangman's noose or firing squad was the only future that awaited them. Klaus, however, recognized the man's name and, with the same charm he'd used to cajole Marie DeMotte into selling Krista's indenture to him, proceeded to greet the man like a long-lost friend—one who had enjoyed a symphony as Herr Bruener's guest in Vienna before the war. While her cousin had recalled the wrong Bickham, the startled general turned out to be a brother to the man.

With that one common thread, her cousin wove an incredible tale of his serving with His Majesty's forces in the north and narrowly escaping capture by the crude frontiersmen in the Ohio Valley. He explained how, unknown to him, his own cousin, a gifted musician from the same family, came to be at an inn in a French village, held against her will. The two of them had managed to slip away, determined to return to their life of music and leave the wilderness to the savages, both white and red.

To prove their story, the general ordered a harp be brought in and insisted Krista play for them and the master of the small orchestra at the post. Her hands shook so that her captors might as well have swung a noose before her or put her a gun to her head. Instead, they sat back, leering at her buckskins skeptically, as if they doubted she was even female, let alone capable of making music on the instrument. It was only when Klaus took her callused hand to his lips and told her to play what was in her heart, that she found the courage to put her fingers to the strings.

The pure sweet music cast its spell on the men so that,

when she finished, they leapt to their feet, erupting in applause. So began the first of many concerts at that remote outpost until a supply ship arrived to carry them back to England. Krista had hoped to sail on to her homeland afterward, but there had been no money except that which her cousin had won with cards from some of the crew—just enough to purchase themselves clothing suitable to their new profession.

The sound of footsteps on the stairs outside drew Krista from her reverie. That would be Klaus! she thought excitedly, putting the harp aside. Five years they'd played in London's concert halls and finest parlors, but *this* season Herr Weis's little orchestra would have to perform without "The Golden Girl and Her Harp," as Krista was so frequently featured in the theatre and newspaper advertisements. They were going home at last to Vienna!

Krista threw open the door as her cousin reached the top steps, her face aglow. "Did you book our passage?"

"In a manner of speaking, liebchen. The captain will return with the spring thaw and . . ."

"Spring!" Krista gasped in dismay. "But Klaus, I gave you enough money for both passages to go *now,* before we must pay another month's rent. What did you do with it?"

Klaus turned away to hang his cloak on the ornate brass rack by the door. "I will pay you back, cousin, I promise."

The cold dawning of what had transpired washed over Krista, causing her to draw her shawl closer about her shoulders. One would think she would become accustomed to the bitter taste of disappointment. She knew her cousin's weakness for gambling. That very morning, when he took the money, stammering with astonishment and delight that she had managed to save so much out of her share of their earnings, she should have known it wasn't at the prospect of going home. Klaus thought London was heaven.

"I should have gone myself," she remonstrated stiffly. "Is there any of *my* money left?"

"Krista," Klaus slipped a placating arm about her shoulders, but this time, she wouldn't be taken in by his excuses.

"No! Don't touch me!"

Pulling away, Krista crossed the room to the stove which never seemed to afford enough heat to the apartment she shared with her cousin. She'd slept in log cabins far warmer, but then, wood was more plentiful in Pennsylvania than in London. Coal burned longer, but cost more.

She'd wanted to move into a smaller place in a cheaper district, but they had an image to maintain, Klaus insisted. So, the good money they made with their music was quickly consumed by the accompanying lifestyle. If one was to be the favorite of the elite, one must patronize them, her cousin philosophized.

That took money, which Krista seemed to manage thriftily. Yet, it seemed for every pound she put aside, Klaus spent two. She could not recall the last time he'd paid his share of the expenses. His passion for gambling kept him in debt to this lord or that earl, which was why she'd saved enough for both their fares. She'd long given up hope of Klaus ever purchasing his own, so that they could journey on to Vienna as he'd promised each year since they'd arrived in London.

"Is there any money left?" Krista repeated in a sharp tone.

Klaus's heavy sigh warned her of the answer before he worded it. "I gave the last to Maggie for her children. They were hungry, Krista!"

"So am I, Klaus! And disappointed and cold and . . ."

Krista bit her bottom lip. She hated to complain. God only knew, she didn't begrudge Maggie Higgins a pence. The widow who kept Krista's gowns in passable shape and sometimes worked as her maid when they were forced to entertain had all she could do to support her family. Her husband had been an actor, she a costumer, a dear sweet soul who had relied on a man—one killed in a duel over another woman's honor.

Marie DeMotte's parting advice to Krista had been wise. Never trust a man; and marry one only if he is wealthy. The money would make life with him tolerable after his attentions switched to other women or vices.

"I'm sorry, Krista. I was desperate."

"And now we *both* are!"

Krista turned away from the desolate countenance on her cousin's face before she weakened and forgave him. Klaus was a good soul with a kind heart. If she were to ask for the moon, her cousin would try to get it for her . . . with dice or a deck of cards. She owed her deliverance from the colonies to him and his generosity. He hadn't had to purchase her indenture, to spend most of the money he'd won from his mercenary friends before deciding to leave the adventure of war behind for a musical one.

Somehow, she'd thought that, at last, here was a man she could rely on. He was family. While it was true that he provided the money and the means of passage to England, it was she who saw the greenhorn safely down the heavily patrolled Mississippi and, by managing their money, kept him from debtor's prison.

Gambling was his only fault, not greed, lust, or deceit— vices of the other men in her life. When he had lost a handsome sum, he never lied about it. If anything, Klaus was the opposite of greedy. He was too kindhearted for his own good, always giving whatever change he had in his pockets to the street beggars.

As for Maggie Higgins, Krista suspected more than a charitable heart was involved. Klaus seemed to have developed a particular affection for Maggie Higgins and her children. He'd even passed up a weekend of chance at the Hunt Club to help nurse the littlest one through a fever while her mother worked at the theatre.

"What are we going to do?" Krista repeated, her tone softening as it, eventually, always did for her younger cousin. "We haven't the money for another month's rent."

"I have taken care of that, dear cousin."

Krista arched a skeptical brow at the suddenly bright face. "Might I ask how?"

"We have been engaged for the season to entertain at Lord Bickham's Athens Hall. Room and board is included in our agreement, as well as maid service. By spring, we should have ample funds for passage to Vienna, though why you would ever wish to leave our prominence in London still eludes me."

Krista moved closer to the stove. *"This* is hardly prominence, Klaus."

"All you have are childhood memories of Vienna, Krista! What must I do to convince you that opportunities in London far surpass what you could expect there. The population here is starved for culture. You have an adoring following. It will not be so easy in Austria. Can you honestly say you do not enjoy being the darling of the concert circuit, being pursued by gentlemen of means, not to mention a certain baron who is enamored with you."

"Foppish bores for the most part," Krista retorted disdainfully, "and Von Baden is an old man."

"Who could take you to his Austrian palace and treat

you like a queen. Now *that* would be the way to get there."

"What are you trying to say, Klaus?"

They had frequently debated the issue of leaving London, but this was the first hint that her cousin might wish her to go without him. As he had said, it was *she*, not he, who was the darling of the concert circuit. Klaus's talent was ordinary, sufficient to accompany her, but not sought after as hers was. What would he do without her to attract the jobs that afforded the luxury he enjoyed?

"I am saying that I have a life to live and so do you. I am going to save my money this year so that in the spring, I can ask Maggie to marry me. I could do so with a freer conscience if I knew that you had someone to look after you, a man who would love you as a woman should be loved."

Krista stared at the young man in shock. She'd known he'd developed an affection for Maggie, but a commitment like marriage was something she didn't think Klaus would ever make. Perhaps he was beginning to grow up after all.

"They call you the Ice Queen, Krista, unmoved by your admirers' attentions, incapable of feeling anything more than her music. But I know different!" Her cousin put an affectionate arm around Krista's shoulder. "You are a warm, loving individual who has buried her heart in her music for fear of being hurt again. You must free it, liebchen."

"My heart lies in a little grave in Petit Lyon, buried with another life I hope to forget," Krista responded at last. Klaus had a way of seeing into her soul where her darkest secrets dwelled. Sometimes, he was too perceptive for her liking. "And if being an Ice Queen keeps those dandies at a distance, then I'm glad they think of me that way."

"You can not contain forever this passion that burns in

your music. It is sin itself to deny the equally lovely woman inside you."

"Then I won't!" Krista announced. "My heart will soar in Vienna. I think I can sell enough of my things to earn my own fare, if you are certain that you will not go with me." A spark of excitement lighted in Krista's gaze as the idea took root. She hadn't considered going without Klaus, only because she thought he needed her.

"But I need you, Krista!"

"You just said . . ."

"Just for the season. I can earn enough to purchase a small house for Maggie and the children, if the 'Golden Girl With the Harp' is with me. Without you, the best I could do would be to work with one of the lower class subscription theatres. You know that. Just one more season," he pleaded earnestly, adding at her hesitation, "which would give me time to write a few letters of introduction to the right people in Austria. It would be much easier on you that way."

Krista nodded reluctantly. So close, she thought in dismay. "Well, at least I have already started packing. When are we to go to Athens Hall?"

"That's my girl!" Klaus planted a loud kiss on Krista's cheek. "We'll live the high life for one more season!" he exclaimed, almost skipping over to the window. "Did you see it? The circus parade?"

So like a child, Krista fretted silently. How would Klaus make out without her? Could Maggie Higgins and her family make the impetuous young man sober to a life of responsibilities?

"Would you like to go to the circus tonight? Baron Von Baden was at the club today and has seats right on the front row."

"I have much to do to prepare for our journey to Athens Hall. Perhaps we might leave some of our things with Maggie for the house you are going to buy when I leave."

"And miss the spectacle of a horse making tea and dancing to a hornpipe?"

Klaus's face was such a picture of comical indignation that Krista could not help but laugh. Of course she would go. She loved her cousin as much as she was capable of loving anyone. He was full of life, enough for the two of them. She supposed that was what had kept her going until now—Klaus and her music. And when spring came, all she would have would be her music.

Athens Hall was a sixty-room brick manor situated on the Thames, within convenient coach travel of London, yet far enough removed that Lord and Lady Bickham did not have to flee the city heat and stench in summer. It had originally been Bickham Place, built and named by the lord's great-grandfather, but upon returning from a trip to Greece, the current Lord Bickham painted the hand-made bricks white and built a classical portico on the front of the three-story mansion. Considering himself quite an authority on architecture, he was forever engaged in re-modeling the stately mansion after the classical structures he'd visited on his educational sojourn.

Lord and Lady Bickham were noted for their hospitality and an invitation from them was treated with almost as much regard as a royal one. In fact, the king himself was frequently on the invitation list, particularly for musical entertainment, of which he was a devoted fan. However, the embarrassment of the Prince Regent's recent escapades, and the king's dedication to duty, more often than not required polite decline.

The war with the colonies behind them, London's society literally boiled with the gossip of the regent's latest diversion, dividing its sympathies between the charming and extravagant Prince of Wales and the devoted, but dull, George III. Lord Bickham, no one's fool, managed to stay in the grace of both. He represented the conservative bent of the father and sought princely advice on renovating English buildings to the mode of the times.

Krista did not like her host, for he, like the grand facades he built on his investments, was not genuine. The fact that he was willing to pay the exorbitant retainer Klaus had negotiated, however, was solid proof that he was as avid a fan of hers as he professed to be.

"Fraulein Lindstrom, how lovely you are!"

Krista dipped graciously as her host lifted her hand to his lips, the tiered layers of her garlanded skirt billowing from the tiny vee of her waistline. "Thank you, my lord. I hope that our playing will not disappoint your guests."

Hat tucked under one arm for show only, for his powdered hedgehog wig would not indulge it, Lord Bickham threw his head back and laughed. "My dear woman, they could not be disappointed by you if you never even touched the strings of your harp. It is enough to drink in your beauty. Prune de Monsieur is a becoming shade. It matches the violet of your eyes. Your accommodations are suitable?"

"Your wife has made us feel quite at home, sir." Unlike her forward husband, Lady Bickham seemed to lack substance either to like or dislike, reminding Krista of a painted puppet dancing on her lordship's strings.

"She is far more accomplished than the first Lady Bickham," the lord conceded, turning to speak to Herr Weis. "You and your ensemble may begin your music at any time now, but save the lady's solo performance until later when everyone is present."

"As you wish, my lord."

Krista unconsciously tugged at the lace-bedecked neckline of the low-cut bodice which had commanded so much of her employer's attention. No matter how fashionable her clothing was, she still felt conspicuous. Other women were at ease with their breasts mounding as if to peek over the rim of their bodices, but Krista burned with the additional humiliation of looking down on most of her admirers. The consequential view of her bosom afforded by her uncommon height was something she would never become accustomed to.

"You've dazzled him completely, liebchen! But then, I expected no less."

Clad in a moss-green velvet coat and breeches trimmed in brocade ribbons, Klaus deserved equal admiration. Krista knew that before the evening was out, her cousin would have more than one invitation to a rendezvous somewhere in the massive home, rumored to be the seat of scandal away from London. His fair hair, powdered in vogue, and flirting blue eyes were as irresistible to women as the fine figure he cut in the latest fashion from Bond Street. Somehow, his admirers reasoned that accomplishment in the arts of music and the arts of love went hand in hand, and often seemed scandalously bent on finding out the truth of the matter, regardless of marital status.

Herr Weis tapped his wand on the table in front of his ensemble and waited for Krista to situate herself and her gown in their midst. She would play with the group for the most part of the evening, but popular request demanded a half hour solo performance of song accompanied by her harp. Resting the cool gilded frame of the instrument against her bared shoulders, Krista lifted her chin proudly and awaited the maestro's signal.

As they played Handel, guests began to arrive at the ballroom, where they were announced as they descended the steps to the receiving line. There they were greeted by

Lord and Lady Bickham, who reminded Krista of a pair of matched dolls in scarlet.

Lord Bickham's silk frock coat—lined, cuffed, and collared in rich black velvet—looked festive over a pale tricot vest which was piped in gold filigree. With matching calamanco trousers and ribbed silk stockings, he was the epitome of a gentleman of means. While he bellowed his welcome to the gay assembly of people passing them by, his wife remained poised at his elbow, smiling and acknowledging them in a less gregarious fashion, all the while struggling to avoid the silver scabbard of his ribboned ceremonial sword, which kept swinging about as he turned to greet the next in line.

Her fair hair was artistically piled atop her head and undoubtedly supplemented with horsehair and wool to attain its bouffant appearance. Adorned with black and scarlet ribbons and plumes to match her French gown, it had the look of a gargantuan hat or wig, too big for her small build. Unlike her husband, who appeared robust and full of vigor, she was pale and quiet, as if intimidated by his boisterous presence.

Until their arrival, Krista didn't think she'd ever heard Lady Bickham utter a single word without a prompt from her lord and master. Away from the man, however, she chattered gaily about this and that as she showed Krista and Klaus around the main floors of the manor and introduced them to the staff. While she presented a gay front, there was something missing—that certain spark of life in her pale violet gaze that would profess genuine happiness in her regal surroundings.

Oddly, Krista had felt a kindred spirit with the woman, as if they both were imprisoned by unseen bars and suffered from unspoken torment. Here was another woman going through the motions of life without really living it—a soul with secrets which would not allow her to enjoy the bounty life had to offer.

The ensemble took respite when the reception line dwindled and most of the guests were engaged in conversation over their glittering glasses of wines and liqueurs of every hue and taste. Choosing a light, fruity one from the tray on one of the buffets, Krista turned to plot her way through the milling crowd when she spied the monnacled Baron Von Baden making his way toward her. Her impulse to look away and pretend she had not seen him was thwarted when he raised his hand, demanding her attention.

"Ach, mein fraulein, how wonderful good it is to see you again. I was surprised to hear that you and your cousin decided to spend another winter in England. I'd so hoped to travel on the same ship."

In an attempt to make conversation at her last interview with her senior admirer, Krista had mentioned her hopes to book passage to Austria. Never did it cross her mind that the man would cut short his European tour to return to his homeland with them.

"There has been a change of plans, Herr Baron. It seems my Klaus has fallen in love with an English woman."

"With *many* English women," the baron corrected, nodding to where Klaus stood, surrounded by feathers, lace, and ribbons of all description. "And you, mein fraulein . . . is your heart also a flutter over some young swain, or do you still profess your music to be your only passion?"

Krista dabbed an embroidered handkerchief to her brow in an effort to recover from the heat put off by the large pot-bellied stove on a tiled platform to one side of the room and lightly sidestepped the leading question.

"It's very warm, so close to this heat. I think I shall walk over to the courtyard foyer to take some air."

To her dismay, the baron claimed her arm promptly. "Allow me to escort you, mein fraulein. I should hate to have you swoon without someone there to catch you."

"I have only swooned once in my life, mein herr . . ." Krista broke off, startled by the memory that had so unexpectedly materialized in her mind—Gavin in all his natural splendor, his beautiful body aching for her own as he approached her.

She banished it before it carried her further to the passion of their lovemaking, dreams of which in the wee hours of the morning would awaken her in a hot, breathless, and unfulfilled anguish.

She was grateful, her companion did not notice her discomfiture, but carried on the conversation. "So you are not one of those silly females who take a holiday climb to the top of a mountain, only to faint dead away and have to be carried back down?" The baron laughed at the idea. "Nonsense, is it not?"

"Yes, it is," Krista answered automatically. She shook the sudden dread that swept over her. God forbid tonight be a repeat of so many others, tormented by dreams. "And wearing such frills and frocks as this makes it all the more so. I think it is a trick to entice some young gentleman into coming to their rescue."

"I did not think you were of that nature. I would venture to guess that you would find the view of a snow-capped mountain exhilarating." The baron's eyes twinkled and his smile faded. "I only wish I were twenty years younger, so that I could climb up there with you and see the color flush your cheeks and the sun dancing on your hair. I like it, that you don't powder it or wear it piled in some ridiculous nature and dress it like a fruit cart." His palsied hand brushed a strand of pearls woven into

Krista's braid. "Like these pearls. They do not need a fancy gold setting, only a tiny thread to hold them together. A natural beauty has no need for adornment."

"Thank you, mein herr."

"I have a confession to make, fraulein."

Krista knew instinctively what her admirer was going to say.

"I am a foolish old man who has fallen in love with an angel."

"There are many things you may be, Herr Baron, but foolish is not one that I will believe."

"I have no heirs, fraulein. I thought the Von Baden line would die with me, but—"

"Herr Baron—"

"You are young and healthy, strong enough to run my estate until my son is of age."

"Herr Baron—"

"And you are Austrian."

"You don't under—"

"I could buy you anything you desire . . . *anything*, if you will return with me to Austria as my wife."

Krista finished her wine, waiting until the earnest proposal was done. She liked the old man. He was kind and born to a wealth that needed no pretense or show. Perhaps he reminded her of her father, who needed no fawning patron to perform at his best. But she could never serve as the baron's wife or mother of his child.

"I am more flattered that you can guess, mein herr. You are a true gentleman and a man worthy of respect, but I cannot marry you." Krista put her finger to the older man's lips to silence his protest. "I do not love you and, even if I did, I am barren, mein herr. I am told that I can never have children. Your line would die with you, regardless. There are many women who would gladly take you as husband and bear you an heir."

The baron's lips twisted sadly. "But none so honest as you, fraulein."

"I do not mean to hurt you, sir. I know that you are a kind and gentle person who does not deserve deceit."

"As you are, mein Krista." He cleared his throat. "And so, if you still wish to go to Vienna, I will see to your passage and introduce you to the right people."

"But Baron Von Baden . . ." Krista exclaimed, awe-struck by her companion's generosity. "How could I . . . ?"

"It is for selfish reasons!" he protested, waving aside her wonder with a gnarled hand. "I will be your discoverer, not to mention having the pleasure of attending all your concerts. You will have the cream of Vienna eating out of your lovely hand."

"I couldn't!"

Even as Krista issued her denial, she questioned it. It was what she wanted, wasn't it? It was all she'd dreamed of, returning to her homeland to play music. But there was Klaus. He needed her, at least through the winter. There was always someone, a voice ringing with self-pity reminded her. This was a golden opportunity!

"I demand to see Lady Bickham!"

Startled from her quandary by a bellow that filled the ballroom, Krista pressed her hand to her chest, as if to prod her frozen heart into beating again.

"What the devil is that?" Baron Von Baden sputtered irritably above the voices that rose in alarm and incredulity. Yet not even they failed to drown out the repeated thunderous demand to see Lady Bickham.

The two crowded into the enclosed courtyard foyer, but, even with her added height, Krista was unable to see what was going on through the sea of plumes and out-landish hairstyles. There was the noise of a scuffle, accen-tuated with the gasping of the crowd as the intruder refused to be subdued by the uniformed servants. A woman screamed and there was a rush to her aid.

"This has gone far enough, sir! What right have you to barge into my home uninvited, looking like a highwayman of the worst sort and demanding to see my wife?" Coming down the steps on the other side of the room, Lord Bickham drew his ribboned sword and raised it threateningly. "I'll have your head for this!"

"Put that toy away, or by the saints, ye'll ne'er play gallant with it again!"

That voice! Krista tried to rise up on her tiptoes to catch sight of the man who bullied the pompous lord of Athens Hall into submission, but the Scottish burr with which he spoke weakened her knees so that she staggered sideways into the baron.

"Fraulein!"

Krista managed a trembling smile. "Blasted heels! I wonder how I can stay on my feet sometimes. Perhaps we should go inside and see what the commotion is about."

By the time Krista and her companion worked their way to the small platform where the ensemble had been set up, the crowd had broken into scattered clusters, their voices blending in a loud hush from which little could be understood. Klaus, however, spying his cousin, broke away from the refreshment table where he had been speaking to one of the servants and walked purposefully toward them.

"Lord Bickham wishes for us to resume playing immediately to restore order to his affair."

"What happened?" the baron insisted, as Krista started for her seat.

"Some big burly highlander, smelling of horse and much in need of a bath, came swaggering in here, demanding to see Lady Bickham. As fierce looking a brute as I've ever had the misfortune to cross! The lady, upon seeing him, fainted dead away, and no wonder. She was carried into the other room and the two men, Bickham and the Scot, followed."

"Did he have a name?" Krista's voice was so small, the men barely heard her.

"He wasn't exactly in the mood for amenities, cousin. I thought he was going to snatch the bow off Bickham's sword and strangle him with it!"

The sharp tap of Her Weis's stick on the music stand ended any further hope of identifying the intruder. Krista inhaled and let out her breath slowly in an attempt to concentrate on the notes spread before her. She was being silly, of course. Gavin Duncan couldn't possibly be in London. He'd vowed and declared he'd never return to his Duncan Brae, and London was even more far-fetched. Besides, this wasn't the first time a boisterous Scottish accent had turned her heart to a quivering mass of apprehension.

The horns began the first notes of the minuet and Krista's harp blended melodiously. The music beckoned, soothing to the soul and commanding her whole attention. If he was even alive, Gavin Duncan was living in the wilds of America; and if he was dead, he was surely in hell.

Chapter Seventeen

Smoke from Lord Bickham's pipe drifted toward the ceiling as suspiciously he watched his lady regain her composure on the leather upholstered divan with the help of one of the maids and smelling salts. Although she appeared to be quite taken by surprise with the furious arrival of her one-time lover and brother to her late husband, his lordship wasn't quite convinced her swoon was genuine. She had mourned the younger Duncan's *alleged* death more than that of Robert Duncan.

By the diamond-paned window, the travel-battered Scot who had invaded their party stared out at the freezing rain that had begun to pelt it loudly. He was anything but dead, the lord of Athens Hall swore silently—a damnable inconvenience, if there ever was one. In an attempt to stifle the annoyance the brigand instigated in him, Bickham clenched his teeth on the stem of his pipe until they hurt. The audacity of the man, barging into his house, smelling like a stablehand and bellowing like a heathen! Yet the worse was that he would not speak with the lord of the manor, but awaited the disposal of Lady Bickham.

"Gavin, is that really you?"

Distracted from the window by the voice that had once

made his youthful heart dance at its slightest command, the Scot strode across the thick carpet which cushioned the seating arrangement around Lord Bickham's desk and knelt respectfully before the pale woman, now sitting upright against a pile of brocade cushions.

"And who did ye think it was, lassie?" Gone was the wrath in his voice and in its place was a deceiving gentleness, for his dark russet eyes still smoldered like the coals on the hearth. "I dinna mean to make ye swoon, but 'tis been a savage trip ye've called me on and I'm in nay better humor."

The fair-haired woman glanced nervously at her husband. "I?" she repeated, confusion returning to her overwide gaze. "I have called you to no journey, sir. I . . . I was told you were dead, murdered by savages."

"And who made ye think that, milady?"

"Why, your cousin Derek! He saw the ruffians make off with you as their prisoner, the same who blew up the King's powder and left him with a limp and a valorous decoration. He barely got his troops back to Detroit himself." Lips painted the same scarlet as the gown spread in silken splendor about the lady's small form made a perfect moue of disappointment. "And since Robert and I received no word from you, I . . . *we,*" she corrected primly, "had no cause to doubt it. Your brother said you'd get yourself killed with that surveying nonsense of yours."

Gavin Duncan almost smiled at Claire's attempt to fill him with guilt. It was a gift she had. But even the master of the art could not put additional weight on the burden he'd carried with him since that godforsaken war had ended. The mental picture of his wife's poorly marked grave in the back of the inn at Petit Lyon, the one lying next to that of the child who had taken her life, would allow nothing else to infringe upon it, nor lighten it.

"It was'na for lack of tryin'," Gavin answered flatly.

Aye, he'd tried to get himself killed after Marie De-Motte had told him the fate of his wife and stillborn son. Instead, his recklessness was rewarded with a four hundred acre tract in Illinois country. He'd set about working, all day and into the lantern lit night, thinking to wear out his body, yet he had only grown harder and stronger. Instead of four hundred acres of forest, he now owned a prosperous eight hundred acre estate overlooking the Ohio, manned by some of the very men he'd fought with. His punishment was to live and prosper, not die—to anguish over what was lost, not gained. Then DeMotte's nephew, who had fought with the volunteers during the war, contacted him.

"What exactly did happen to you, Duncan?" Lord Bickham interrupted sharply. "Where have you been?"

"Captive of the Indians for a while," Gavin lied smoothly. "They dinna care that the peace was made between the whites."

"My God!" Claire gasped, her horror betraying her knowledge of the atrocities reported to have taken place in the colonies.

"And upon escaping, I settled on some acreage with other survivors caught in the midst of that cursed war. We've done well enough in the new land. But then, the lady must know that. Otherwise, how could she have sent me the news of Robert's death?"

"I fear you have been misled, sir," Claire protested. "I would not have sent such news to a man I thought dead."

"I would rather think," Lord Bickham chimed in with his lady's denial, "that it is more likely, you discovered your brother's demise and thought to improve your circumstances by claiming Duncan Brae for yourself."

"The letter was in a *lady's* hand," Gavin insisted, ignoring the man who rose from his plush chair to fly to his wife's side. He leveled his stubborn gaze upon Claire.

"Besides, there is nothing in all of the isles to keep me here now. I'd nay have Duncan Brae now. *Someone* has seen fit to turn the hall of the Duncan into a *health spa.*" The word was spoken like curse. "A damnable summer retreat to the highlands! I would wager," the Scot issued lowly, the outrage that had sent him flying on horseback across the mountains and moors to London gaining ground again, "the old Robert himself is sputterin' in his grave with pure disgust."

"Gavin, the spas and baths are all the rage now," Claire informed him smugly. "The wealthy flock to Duncan Brae to bathe in the pure water of the loch and the coffers are running over with the result of Edwin's genius."

Gavin turned to his host, temples pounding with wrath. "So *you* are the culprit! What manner of man would whitewash the walls of a stone fortress, place useless Grecian columns and mother-naked statues in every corridor, and put a bathing pool in the center of the great hall? 'Tis the most fiendish sight these eyes have seen! Where once warriors boasted of their feats, simpletons strip themselves of their dignity and wallow in mineral water!"

"It would do you well to take advantage of such commodities, sir," Lord Bickham remarked dourly. "Your stench is as offensive as your manners. I fear you've tarried too long with the savages."

"Gavin!" Claire flew from her queenly position on the sofa to place herself between her indignant husband and equally volatile guest. "You must be exhausted from your journey. Let me show you to a room and, when you've calmed yourself, perhaps you'd care to join the festivities. Ours is the opening party of the season!" Her brightness faltered under the unmoved scrutiny fixed on her. "Please . . ."

Gavin exhaled heavily, letting off some of the steam

that flushed his face with anger. Perhaps there was a reason Claire did not want her husband to know she'd sent for him, he thought belatedly. She was as pale as death, not the glowing cultured rose basking in the glory of her social world.

Damnation, he didn't know what to think! All he knew was that someone had sent him a letter informing him of Robert's death and imploring him to come home. When, against his better judgment, he did just that, he found the halls of his ancestors mutilated with poorly imitated Grecian architecture and empty, but for the sparsest of staff. The *grieving* widow had remarried and was spending the season in London.

"The lady always winters with her new husband in their London home," he'd been informed by one of the older servants, indicating even the news the mysterious letter had carried was old. Robert had been dead three years.

Lady Claire had been so devastated by Laird Robert's death that her widow's dresses were hardly wrinkled before being cast aside for the courtship of Lord Bickham. Robert was barely laid to rest in the family vault when the rolling fields were planted in thorn hedges to challenge the hunters on holiday and a large pool cut into the stone floor where he and his lady had been wed. Not content to have London's creme of society at her disposal in the winter, the lady now had them in summer as well.

Gavin could have strangled the very life from Claire's beguiling lips when he'd charged into the ballroom, wet, cold, and furious. The sight of her, frail and genuinely frightened, however, had undermined his anger. He knew the difference between his former sweetheart's feigned swoons and a real one. When she pretended to faint, her breasts rose and fell rapidly with the excitement of her success in gaining her suitor's undivided attention. This time, her corseted bosom had been alarmingly still.

"I'll impose on your hospitality only long enough to arrange my passage back to Philadelphia," he answered tersely. "It seems I've been led astray for naught, as ye said, milady."

"You must have done well in your new life."

Ah, she was recovered enough for her curiosity to show itself. Whether from annoyance or survival instinct, Gavin was not about to give satisfaction. "Well enough, milady."

Lord Bickham stepped forward, assuming rightful control of the situation with a sniff of disdain. Determined not to reduce himself to the low level of his uninvited guest and toss him out in the night, he called a servant with the sharp ring of a bell situated on the corner of his polished walnut desk.

"Mr. Duncan will be staying the night, Jerome. Show him to a room and see that he has the rudiments for a bath and fresh clothing."

Gavin didn't miss the apprehensive glance the servant gave him, assessing and fretting at the same time. "I have clothing, sir. All I need is a place to wash and change."

"The lady and I must return to our guests. I wouldn't want to miss the soloist, would you, dearest?"

"Of course not, Edwin," Claire answered, too hastily and obliging for the woman who had once made men scrape and bow for her favor. "She is divine . . . one of the most popular artists in London, and Edwin was able to retain her and her group for the entire season."

"Then I look forward to it," Gavin lied once more.

A hot bath and a warm bed was more enticing than the idea of spending a boring evening listening to some prima donna, no doubt imported from Italy, trill notes that would shatter glass and do untold damage to the hearing of those sitting too close. But, he had committed enough social outrages for one night and further justified the English aristocracy's contempt for their Highland counterparts.

Not that he really cared. He only wished he hadn't been so blinding mad that he'd missed the expressions on the faces of the gaudily garbed guests who gasped and swayed in horror. The English were quite taken with pretense. It might prove amusing to play the game once more, at least until he discovered why Claire had sent for him.

That she'd denied it in front of her husband became more and more understandable as the man recovered from Gavin's bullish affront. Lady Claire, it appeared, had finally met a man who was as adept at manipulating people as she. She was actually afraid of him, judging from the nervous glances she kept sending his way during their discussion, not to mention her fervent denial of the letter. No other female in the whole of the British Isles would have been resourceful enough to find Gavin in his obscure retreat from the world and flush him out.

"Excuse me, sir," the servant interrupted Gavin's thoughts as they emerged on a second floor balcony which circled the ballroom below. "I must find out from the upstairs staff which of the rooms are not at present occupied."

Gavin stood patiently as an impromptu meeting was called by the servants' steps. Even the staff made evident their disapproval of him. And well they might, he thought, catching a glimpse of himself in the massive gilded mirror mounted at the end of the hall. He hadn't shaved in four days, nor, he admitted ruefully to himself, bathed.

The last time he'd let himself go like this was during the building of Duncan Brae . . . his American Duncan Brae. The house, nay, manor, was too fine to be inhabited by a man who looked as if he'd seen neither razor nor soap since his mother had weaned him. He'd even talked Tull Crockett, now his overseer, into trimming his beard and wearing clean clothing to meals. Although, Gavin had to agree with Tull, the food tasted no better, regardless of what they wore or if they were clean shaven or not.

Americans had a simple philosophy born of common sense. Even the wealthy were cautious with their money and not prone to the frivolity so flagrantly flaunted here. They had a country to build, a purpose to life besides trying to fill one's time with new adventures in leisure.

"Well, I suppose ye can put 'im in the wing with the musicians. 'E 'll have to share a parlor with the woman, but it's the only empty room aside from Lady Claire's inconvenience parlor. Half of London's 'ere tonight!"

Lips twitching with wry humor at the pomp with which he was being grudgingly served, Gavin straightened as his guide returned.

"This way, sir."

The two wings of the manor branched off from the ballroom through arched doorways supported by classical columns. Cherubs frolicked merrily in the shadows of the frescoes engraved in the ceiling of the long narrow hall. At regular intervals silver sconces provided light, but, instead of proceeding to the far end, where yet another staircase accessed the lower rooms and corridors, Gavin was shown to one of the first rooms.

The music, which had stopped briefly to polite clapping, started again, this time with the soft strains of a country ballad rather than the formality of the popular composers of the day. Its melody wafted through the open doors of the corridor, teasing Gavin's mind with its familiarity and drowning out the servant's instructions.

"The adjoining room is a parlor, sir, for the use of Lord

Bickham's lady musician. For obvious reasons, it is requested that you use this door to exit, rather than . . ."

The servant broke off as Gavin backtracked to the balcony above the splendid scene below. Gentlemen of means and their lady companions stood motionless in their silks and plush costumes, their attention fixed on a singular young woman in the midst of her colleagues.

Like a delicate violet flower blossoming among lesser vines, she sat on heaps of silk garlanded with flowers of inferior beauty, her music unfolding with each graceful stroke of the harp. Then, with a voice sweet and beckoning to the ear, she began to sing. Transfixed, Gavin stared down at the willowy creature with pearls the color of her bared shoulders woven in hair of spun gold.

The anguish within him, stirred by the girl's performance, was numbed with disbelief. Tall, straight, graceful, she was an exotic image of the wildflower who had captured his heart, an orchid in violet silk to his wild rose in blue wool flannel. Her voice was as pure, her talent as flawless. Gavin moved slowly around the rail of the balcony, hoping to catch a glimpse of her face, but she kept it turned toward the audience.

Hers was a poise and grace born of years on the stage, not one harbored in some remote wilderness where it could never be fully appreciated. She was a queen holding court, regal and proud, not a shy country girl who preferred to remain inconspicuous. Her white skin and tapered fingers had only known the labor of her music, not the hard survival that had left calluses on the gentle, capable hands of the woman who had saved and then renewed his life.

But he would know her before the night was out, Gavin decided resolutely. He would bask in the soothing spell of her harp and song and join the throng of admirers who, as she brought her song to an end, exploded in enthusiastic applause.

"The maid has put fresh water in your room, sir. If there won't be anything else . . ."

Reluctantly, Gavin pulled himself away from the rail. "That girl, who is she?"

"The Golden Girl With the Harp, I believe she's called."

"Her name, man!"

Flustered by Gavin's impatience, the servant stammered. "It's Austrian . . . Kristine Lindsay, Lin . . ."

"Krista Lindstrom?"

"There you go, sir! Everyone has heard of her."

Jaw clenched, Gavin nodded and stepped inside his room where his staggered emotions might right themselves without observation. Was this yet another cruel reminder of what he'd lost? There seemed no end to them at times. First Duncan Brae and now this.

He would see for himself what he could not bring himself to accept on the servant's word. She resembled his late wife in coloring and manner, indeed shared the same name. But he would look into the sapphire depths of eyes that had haunted his waking and sleeping hours—wide, curious eyes capable of a myriad of emotions to stir the blood. And if he discovered the girl he had married, the one who was supposed to be in that lonely grave in the wilderness village, he'd . . .

Gavin's hand shook as he opened the satchel containing his belongings. Take one step at a time, he cautioned himself. There was much amiss—much he did not understand, but would before this night was out.

When the elegant gentleman in the dark topaz suit of king's cloth approached him, Klaus Bruener was as intrigued as the his lady companions. That this was the heathen Scot who had forced his way in earlier, clad in the tartan of his clan, was difficult to believe. But for his accent, he appeared English to the bone. His manners were as courtly as the Prince Regent himself and his mischievous eyes, the color of a fine bourbon, were enough to send the dourest of the ladies into a pinkened fluster.

Yet, he seemed oblivious to his casual conquests, as if another purpose occupied his mind. Perhaps that was why he sought Klaus out, for that much they had in common. They were acting the gallant swains, but their hearts belonged to one woman. Klaus's was Maggie Higgins. Whom the Scot fancied was of no consequence. It was enough to find a gentleman with whom to converse, one not bent on conquering some gentlewoman's virtue before the night was out.

"I've heard that your harpist is also from the colonies," Gavin remarked casually. "But I find that hard to believe."

With the same finesse he used to evoke sympathy for his cousin before her talent earned her the adoration of the *ton*, Klaus Bruener launched into the sad story of Krista's past—how her husband had abandoned her to indenture and how he, Klaus, had rescued the girl from her desolate circumstances and brought her to London and a happier life.

"And ye say the blackguard sold her into indenture for a shipment of gunpowder?" Gavin remarked with conjured disgust. "And he dinna leave a letter or write to such a lovely creature?"

"Not a word!" Klaus affirmed fervently. He'd actually become quite good with his rendition of Krista's misfortune and the excess of fine wine he'd consumed only added to his theatrics. "He as much as killed her. Look for yourself at the admirers who would offer her a life of wealth and ease, and yet, all she yearns for is her music and homeland."

Gavin followed the young man's gaze across the room where the vision in violet could hardly be seen for dandy swains of every description.

"Those fools try in vain to win her heart. She vows it is dead, buried in the wilds of Illinois. Only one man stands a chance of winning my cousin."

The odd satisfaction Gavin felt that Krista was not taken in by her adoring following faded. "Oh, and who might that lucky soul be?"

"The old man at her elbow . . . Baron Von Baden. He wishes to take her to Austria, which is her dream."

"Well, I should like to at least speak to the bonnie lassie before she's swept away by nobility."

Klaus laughed out loud. Now he knew who had captured the giant Highlander's heart. "Why didn't you say so, sir? I should have known my cousin had caught that wicked eye of yours."

Instinct alone made Krista look over the heads of her admirers as she stepped up on the small platform where the orchestra was assembling for the last set of dances that evening, for she was in no way prepared for the introduction that followed. Indeed, she didn't recognize the man accompanying her cousin until it was too late . . . too late to flee, too late to bolster her undone composure. The moment her gaze locked with the hard accusing one of dark amber glass, her worst fear came to life.

"Krista, liebchen, I wish to introduce you to yet another of your admirers. We have much in common, as . . ." Klaus hesitated in embarrassment over the failure of his wine-blunted memory. "What was it you said your name was again?"

"Duncan," Gavin answered flatly. "Gavin Duncan."

He looked so young without the beard, Krista thought

in the midst of her bewilderment. His noble features were smooth and proud, yet hardened as his gaze. He stood like a statue swathed in the plush of the most fashionable of her admirers, from his laced shirt and black tie to the black stockings that were the envy of the most flamboyant macaroni of the *ton*. Yet, for all his lace and gold ornamentation, the impeccable cut of his coat and breeches left little doubt that here was a man to be reckoned with. No amount of frippery could daunt the masculinity he fairly exuded.

"I am pleased to make your acquaintance . . . *again.*"

Her cold hand hung limp in his warm one as he raised it to his lips and brushed it politely. The touch seemed to drain the last of her stilled blood, leaving her heart beating in her chest like a hollow drum.

"Krista?" Klaus whispered, alarmed at the lack of color in his cousin's naturally rose-hued cheeks.

"Herr Weis is ready." Her words came out slowly, mechanically. She withdrew her hand and held it to her chest, as though it had been contaminated. "I must play."

"Who *are* you, sir?" her cousin demanded of the man who still held Krista's blank, lifeless gaze.

"I am the husband, come to collect his runaway wife, man, and no concern of yours." The threat was gloved in a velvet tone, dealt like a sharp blade eased between the ribs, gently, but no less dangerous.

"God's death!" Klaus cursed, staggering back in astonishment. "Krista, I . . . the name, it meant nothing until now. How dare you, sir!"

In one fluid motion, Krista was between them, the sweet scent of her perfume, a decided contrast to the repugnant oil she had once doused her body in, drifted up to Gavin's nose, as if flaunting the fact that he could only look, not touch. Enticement, however, was far from her mind. It seemed to require all her concentration to speak.

"Take your seat, Klaus. We must play."

Once satisfied the young man was going to obey, she climbed up on the platform and assumed her seat without so much as a backward glance at the Scot who had assisted her. Eyes blue as midnight stared blankly at the disconcerted maestro, awaiting his signal. At the sharp tap of the wand upon the music stand, her hands poised gracefully, a breath from the strings of the harp cradled against her shoulder.

It was the instrument, not the woman playing it, who came alive. She moved without emotion, her face solemn, her demeanor cold as the marble angels gracing the corners of the ballroom. Guests took to the dancing, failing to notice the change which her fellow musicians found alarming. Her notes were precise in time and tone, but for all the feeling involved, they might have come from a music box.

Chapter Eighteen

"I shall sleep on the floor at your door!" Klaus declared nobly, pacing back and forth at the foot of Krista's bed. "If he even tries to see you I'll run—"

"Klaus!" Krista's voice cracked with irritation as she looked up from rummaging through her trunk. "You will go to your room and leave me in peace. I cannot worry with your theatrics. One hotheaded fool at a time is enough!"

"But if he attempts to come to your room . . ."

"I shall tell him I am done with him."

"But *can* you, cousin? Even now your hands are trembling."

"Only because I fear you might force Gavin into doing something rash. Thor's thunder, Klaus! Didn't you see the size of him? He could break you in half if he were of a mind."

"And not you?"

"He would not lay a hand on me to harm me. I know him well enough not to fear physical harm. His specialty is mental abuse," Krista denounced bitterly. "Except that he cannot hurt me any more. I feel nothing for him but hatred. Nothing he can say or do will change that."

There it was! She couldn't explain why she'd kept the

hunting knife Madame DeMotte had returned to her after Gavin's desertion. It couldn't be because of sentimental attachment, but it was exceedingly appropriate for the occasion.

"And if he remains in England, what will you do? I cannot let you run away with no place to go because of him."

"I have a place to go, Klaus . . . Vienna."

Krista's calm demeanor was unsettling to her cousin. Indeed, she hardly understood it herself. That moment in time when she recognized Gavin Duncan lasted an eternity. Their glittering surroundings faded until there was only unspoken animosity between them. Then a strange, chilling calm had come over her and she gained a perspective which stripped the inevitable confrontation of its threat. He couldn't hurt her any more than she had already been hurt. It was that simple.

He figured no more in her life than she did in his. He had made his place somewhere, whether in the highlands or the wilderness was of no concern to her, and she had made hers. If he knew what was best for him, he would not interfere with her plans, for she would not have it. Never again would a man dictate to her. *Never*, she thought vehemently.

"Krista?"

Unaware of a feral light glowing in her gaze, Krista turned to the worried young man she had momentarily forgotten. "I am expecting someone, Klaus, but I will tell you before I leave of my plans."

"You are going to Vienna with the baron," Klaus guessed in a tone flattened with disappointment.

"Herr Weis is perfectly capable of finding another harpist to replace me, and you," Krista cut her cousin's protest off by raising her voice, "will be happy with Maggie. It is time, cousin."

"You won't *marry* him!"

"I shall travel in his company only." Krista stepped behind a dressing screen to shed her gown and cumbersome accessories. "Tomorrow I'll sell my jewels for passage and be gone by the week's end."

She would need to be rid of her corsets and hoops, if she were to move about freely. Her negligee, ruffled so that it fell from her modestly scooped neckline to the floor in a flowing sequence of linen, would serve well enough, although she found herself, longing, for the first time since she'd left the colonies, for her more practical buckskins.

"You never told me you kept the jewels your adoring admirers lavish upon you! I thought you'd returned them."

"Some of them refused to take them back. I see no harm in using them now."

"No, not at all!" Klaus agreed hastily.

She'd wounded him, Krista mused. It was hard enough for Klaus to live in the shadow of her success, but harder still to think she'd held something back from him after so long a time. She hesitated with only the slightest pang of remorse, before her emotions returned to that numb level which would not allow her to feel at all.

When she emerged, Klaus rose and stood motionless as she approached him and dismissed him with a hug. This was a matter of survival. As she had once withdrawn her protective wing from her sister Marta, so she would do with her cousin.

"We'll speak more tomorrow, cousin."

Klaus shifted awkwardly under her cool assessment, as if he wanted to protest and yet, knew it would do no good. "I don't know what to say."

"*That,* I cannot believe!" Krista smiled, a tolerant smile she frequently bestowed upon her younger relative. "Gute nacht, Klaus."

It was like sending away a child, she thought, closing the door to the corridor behind him and leaning there for a moment. But Klaus had made the decision to remain in London and she needed to move on. There would be no second thoughts this time, nothing to hold her back. Perhaps returning to the city of her birth would be what she needed to be born again. God knew she wanted to live, and live again she would—once she'd dealt with Gavin Duncan.

The first floor was vacant, save the few servants who cleared away the remains of food and dishes from the buffet tables set up along the wall. The guests had retired to the upper chambers of the manor, which was exactly what Gavin Duncan wanted to do, although his purpose was not necessarily the same. His hostess, however, had pressed a hastily scribbled note in his hand, imploring him to meet her in the library. Consequently, Krista had been able to deftly avoid him, disappearing into a convenient corridor behind the musician's platform before he could make his way through the milling dancers to catch her.

The large clock in the main hall rang the hour of midnight, challenging those who remained awake to hasten to slumber before the morning hours rolled around. Damnation, where was she? Gavin paced over to the window restlessly, his mind wandering to another woman, rather than the one who kept him waiting.

He still was incredulous that Krista was alive . . . alive and more beautiful than he'd ever dreamed she could be! God, what she must think of him, if anything her cousin had told him was true and not conjecture calculated with the purpose of escaping her alleged bondage.

He *had* written her and then cursed her for her stubbornness in refusing to answer. He was coming back for her as soon as Vincennes was won. She was all that kept him warm as he'd plunged breast deep into icy waters and marched through a hell, as cold as it was reputed to be hot, to reach the outpost. As he and the men celebrated their astonishing victory, he'd ignored the French tavern wench who wished to make the night all the more victorious and toasted his new wife, who had done as much as they toward the winning of the battle by providing the powder they'd needed so desperately.

God help him, he'd also signed the indenture papers . . . but only because that deceitful old hag would have it no other way. He'd made certain to add a clause stating the agreement would end with his return or with the seven years the woman insisted on, whichever came first. Then Tucker Hardy received a fatal wound in a skirmish with Indians and the men elected their newest recruit as their second-in-command to Tull Crockett. They'd needed him, and his wife was safe, if somewhat miffed, in Petit Lyon. "Give 'er the bounce of the winter to cool off," Tull had advised wryly.

But summer found them pursuing Shawnee and every other Indian the British had managed to stir against them, just to make certain Krista and the other innocent women and children in the wilderness settlements did remain safe. Before Gavin had a chance to think, he found himself marching to join Von Steuben's regulars to fight Benedict Arnold in Virginia. Patriotic fever, he called it, that startling dedication with which he took the colonials' cause.

What good would life be for the family he planned if it were not free of the tyranny his ancestors had battled futilely to throw off for ages? Besides, he'd been promised land, land where he could build a new life with his frontier wildflower. It had kept him going during the worst of times, when hunger gnawed at his insides and frost chewed at his toes through the holes in his boots. He never dreamed that it was all for naught.

The cursed witch, Gavin swore silently. It was all so clear now, what she'd done. He'd kill the shriveled crone himself with his bare hands if she weren't already dead and called to hell by Satan himself for like company. "Such a pity," she'd lamented as she showed him Krista's grave. "She suffered so bringing your son into this world."

He'd barely registered the second, smaller grave beside Krista's. All he could feel was the guilt Marie DeMotte heaped on his conscience with a deceit that bent her shoulders with its terrible weight and twisted her demented mind all the more. Yet, if not for that and her insatiable greed, he would never have known about . . .

"Gavin?"

Gavin spun about at the sound of Lady Claire Bickham's voice. "Is that why ye sent for me, woman? Did ye think to make me the fool twice spurned?"

Startled by the angry burst of words, Claire stepped backward, her hand clutched to her breast. "*Twice* spurned? I don't know what you're talking about. God in heaven, Gavin, the world all around me is going mad, don't tell me you are too! I couldn't bear . . ." A sob choked off the rest of her attempt to speak.

Detached, Gavin watched as she collapsed to the floor in a heap of scarlet silk and tears. "Spare me your theatrics, Claire. Why did ye send for me?"

"I didn't send for you, you thick-brained Scot!" the lady challenged brokenly, "but I am for . . . forever indebted to whoever did. Oh, Gavin, I need you so!"

There was a time when he would have run to take the arms extended to him and gladly kissed away all those large crocodile tears streaming down Claire's flawless cheeks. But that was past. Instead, Gavin marched stiffly

to her side and drew her to her feet without further word
or favor.

"I have a confession to make," she sniffed as he seated
her on the leather divan where she'd recovered from her
swoon earlier.

"You're dreadfully unhappy. Lord Bickham is a tyrant
who will not let you have your way."

Claire's eyes widened in amazement, spilling more
tears in the process. "That too, but . . . but what I have
to say is of far more consequence." She inhaled deeply
and let out a trembling breath. "I . . . I fear I killed
Robert."

This time it was Gavin's turn to stare in astonishment.
Could this be the same Claire who delighted over two
young men dueling to death over her?

"I loved London so much that I . . . I left him at
Duncan Brae to rot in those damp, cold highland winters." Her lower lip slipped out beyond the upper in a
manner which used to set Gavin's heart back a beat.

"Don't be ridiculous! If Robert had wanted you there,
he'd have fetched you back."

"*You* would have, Gavin, not your brother."

Gavin felt his patience rapidly waning. "Is this why
you've arranged this liaison . . . to tell me you broke my
brother's heart and was not the dutiful wife?"

"Gavin, what has made you so cruel? You used to—"

"I *used* to love you, Claire. Now, if that is all, I shall—"

"Gavin, for the love of God, listen to me! You are in
danger. I feel it in my bones, just as I did before Robert
died. Don't you think it odd, even for Robert, that he
would waste away to a skeleton of what he was?"

"Especially if the highlands are so regenerative to one's
health," Gavin remarked cryptically.

Claire closed her eyes and turned away. "I'm paying

dearly for my folly, Gavin. Believe me, death would be a welcome friend to me."

More theatrics? Gavin wondered.

"I led Lord Bickham on the merriest of chases. He was so charming, so exciting compared to your brother. I fear that was what led to Robert's death."

"Are you suggesting Bickham had something to do with it?"

Claire sighed, as if the burdens of the world pressed her breath from her chest. "God help me, yes. I fear Robert was slowly poisoned. You know how he loved to eat and yet, on his deathbed, he was but a skeleton of his old figure."

"Why are ye tellin' me this, Claire? Do ye wish me to call him out and set ye free to marry another soul who has caught your fancy?"

"You are a bastard," the lady responded harshly, like one wounded and eager to inflict her suffering on another. "I am telling you this to warn you for your life, you arrogant fool! Edwin has invested much in Duncan Brae, thinking you dead. I would not put it past him to . . ."

"To hell with Duncan Brae! I would'na ha' it now, if 'twere bequeathed to me by the old laird himself! Ye can tell him that."

His back to the room lined with expensive leatherbound volumes, Gavin looked out into the darkness, his words surprising even himself. He'd wanted to see it one more time, as it was when he was a lad, learning to hunt and seeking the adventures of his ancestors among the lochs and braes.

"I only wanted to warn you. My husband is a powerful man."

The hand against his back left him. In the reflection of the lamplight on the window, Gavin watched as Claire moved away and turned to leave—a pale ghost of a soul, not the proud beauty she'd once been. He knew well the feeling. Until tonight, he thought he'd bear it forever. It was pity that softened his heart as he called out to her.

"Milady?" Never had Gavin seen a more pitiful countenance than that which met him as he caught up with her. "I'll take care," he promised gently. "Dinna worry your pretty head about the likes of me. I'm not my brother Robert."

"No, my heart, you never were. I know that now, for all the good it does."

He brushed a stray strand of hair from her face and smiled down at her. "There are some things, lassie, that are written in the stars, things we canna change. 'Tis only fit to work on what we can control and leave the rest to Providence. Now get ye to bed, lest telltale lines beneath your eyes start scandal waggin' on the tongues of those fan-wavin' hens I met tonight."

Claire laughed, partly from relief and in genuine amusement. "You haven't changed, Gavin. You're as wickedly delightful as you ever were."

The mischievous quirk of his lips fading, Gavin put his hand to his hostess's back and ushered her toward the door. "Aye, but I have. We all have, milady."

His mind bedeviled even more by the interview with Claire, Gavin climbed the steps to the west wing of the manor where his room and yet another interview awaited him, one he'd anticipated all evening. However, as he neared the arched entrance of the corridor, the sound of an opening door and suppressed voices made him press against the wall.

Cautiously peeking through the crack where the arched doors were hinged to the gilded frame, he was intrigued to see the elderly baron who had dominated Krista's side earlier, bending over a slender hand extended from a lace-edged sleeve. He couldn't make out the conversation, but easily ascertained that it suited the older gentleman most agreeably. Gavin doubted the old codger had walked that spryly in years as he made his retreat down the length of the hall and disappeared into a stairwell.

Caught up in his own intrigue, the Scot failed to notice the scarlet-attired figure who had watched him leave the library. All that occupied Gavin's thoughts as he ducked into his room was what his wife was up to, entertaining at this hour. He mustn't lose his temper, he cautioned himself, against the insane rush of anger that filled his veins. Whatever nonsense she was about could be stopped with a firm but gentle hand. But first, he would hear from her own lips her reasons for leaving Petit Lyon. Then she would have his.

His coat and cravat discarded, Gavin tried the door to the adjoining chamber. It came open, but not without difficulty. Upon sticking his hand through the crack, he discovered a chair there and wondered if Krista or the indignant servant who had shown him to his quarters had put it there. Did she even know his room adjoined her private parlor?

The chair slid across the carpeted floor noiselessly. A harp sat on a stand near the window. By a highbacked chair near the hearth, a book rested on a table, open to the page where she had left it. But for the sudden urgency that pressed upon him to end the separation and settle their differences, he would have taken time to see what manner of literature fascinated his ever surprising lady, for, after seeing her in her element tonight, he had no doubt that she was every inch one. His hardy wild rose had become as cultured and lovely as its garden counterpart.

"Krista?"

Gavin cleared his throat nervously and repeated the name that had been strangled by taut emotions. Every muscle in his body coiled with the same. When no answer came he knocked, faintly, so as not to disturb the other guests, particularly that gamecock cousin of hers. Try as he might he could hear no sound in the room. Lips thinning in irritation, for surely she could not be abed so soon, he lifted the latch.

He expected another chair, or like obstacle, but the door swung open without resistance. In the dim light put off from the shallow hearth, he could make out a single figure in the bed. Gavin's breath caught in his throat as his gaze roamed over the ruffles of her negligee, rising and falling slowly in slumber.

He leaned over the resting figure and ventured to caress the smooth taper of her chin with his fingers.

"Wake up, hinny. We've much to make up—"

"Get away from me or I'll cut off all that makes you a man!"

The stinging prick of a blade, dangerously close to accomplishing her threat, made Gavin rise slowly, so as not to provoke the seething angel further. "Ye made that threat once before, lassie, and as I recall, ye were glad ye dinna carry it through."

Gone was the cold blank stare she'd possessed earlier and in its place was a mad burning rage. "That was before I knew how deceitful you could be." She came up from the bed, following him with the lethal knife she'd hidden in the folds of her gown, yet holding back, as if she were still undecided about seeing her threat through. "You are right good at lying."

"So was Marie DeMotte."

The knife pressed deeper, this time breaking the skin of his abdomen. "Your signature was no lie! You sold me like . . . like a cow when I was of no use to you any more!"

Gavin winced, his back to the door he'd closed behind

him. "Damnation, lassie, take care wi' that blade, lest ye . . ."

"I have dreamed of this," she went on, oblivious to his warning. "I wanted to feel your lying flesh give with the force of my knife and see your life's blood draining from you like it did me when your son ripped my body apart to be born . . . while you were off playing soldier!"

" 'Twas nay game we played, lassie. Many good man died, Captain Hardy one of 'em. I thought ye'd be safe . . ."

"So safe you didn't need to write me?" The girl snapped pitilessly.

"I swore my love to ye, lassie. I've done that for nay woman and I'll not . . ." The blade moved away instead of pressing in for the kill. Gavin stared at it as she backed far enough away for him to see it.

"It's the one you gave me," she told him. "I kept it all these years, even though I never thought I'd see you again." Her chin quivered as she struggled with the rage and hurt that boiled in her mind and filled her eyes with tears that would not spill.

"I went back for ye, hinny."

Krista swung the blade in an arch, driving him back against the wall as he reached for her. "Stay back, or God help me, I will cut you right good!"

"And all I found was a lyin' witch and two empty graves."

"One!" Krista averred, her lips curled into a snarl. "I told Marie to tell you what she wanted if you came back . . . that I had died with . . . with my . . ."

She couldn't speak, let alone see the desperate lunge for the knife in her hand until it was too late. All she could do was cry out in agony, not from the hands that twisted it from her wrist or the arms that wrestled her down to the floral carpet, but from the raw memory that had never healed.

"I might as well have died with him!" she accused, trying futilely to reach Gavin's face with her clawed fists. "You killed us! *You killed us!*"

Fearing to hurt her and yet trying to keep her from taking her outrage out on him, Gavin pinned the writhing, sobbing woman to the floor with his body, but she would not be quieted. With a strength equal to that of some men, she fought him, kicking, biting, and spitting until he was left with no alternative but to strike back. He cursed himself even as he slapped the hysterical woman and wished it was Marie DeMotte he had in his hands, so that his own fury might be vented. Was there no bounds to the woman's poison?

"I h . . . hate you!" Her voice rising to a bloodcurdling shriek, she spat at him again. "I hate . . ."

Gavin lifted her, shaking her in a desperate attempt to restore some semblance of reason to her. No longer was he spurred by the initial rush of anger and retaliation, but by compassion born of the truth that had surfaced. He knew now that his wife was not party to the deceit, but a victim. They both were. "Hush, lassie! I know, I know . . ."

The loud explosion of the door bursting open behind them was followed by the sudden choking pressure of an arm across his throat and the furious, "Take your hands off her!"

To keep the girl from bearing their weight, Gavin fell to the side and rolled on top of the young man in the nightshirt with such force that his breath was crushed from his chest. Throwing off the arms that went limp with the impact, the Scot twisted and cuffed the smaller man on the temple with the side of his fist. His victim reeled against the cushioned floor and struggled through an unfocused gaze to get up.

"Don't force me to hurt ye, lad. I'm beholden to ye for takin' care of my wife, but this is between her and me!"

"Haven't you done enough to her?"

Gavin followed Klaus's attention to where Krista gathered the voluminous folds of her negligee in an attempt to rise, a dazed look on her face. Swearing, he turned away from his adversary to assist her. "I'd nae harm ye for the world, lass. Ye must know that."

"What is the meaning of this!"

"Gavin, you're bleeding!"

His hand going to his abdomen, as if to doubt Claire Bickham's alarmed cry, Gavin shook his head tiredly. " 'Tis only a scratch."

"Take this man into custody until the sheriff can be sent for!" Lord Bickham ordered the two servants flanking him.

Gavin sensed more than felt Krista sway next to him and caught her in his arms. Seemingly disoriented, she accepted his strength, as if drawing on it, as he helped her to the edge of the bed.

"This is a matter between my wife and me and none of your concern!"

"Your wife?" his host and hostess sputtered simultaneously.

"The wife he abandoned in the wilderness," Klaus accused tersely. "And then saw fit to wrestle her to the floor and beat her only moments earlier."

"I was trying to slap some sense into her. She was hysterical . . . hysterical enough to cut me with her knife."

"Good God, look at the size of that blade!" Bickham picked up the knife where Gavin had slung it and studied it in awe. "Is this yours, madame?"

Krista looked at the weapon, stained with the blood she

had drawn and shivered. God help her, what had she almost done? What was she doing now, clinging to Gavin as if her very life was at stake? She straightened, an effort to her weary spirit.

"It is," she answered. "I am sorry if I . . . if I disturbed you. I was not prepared to see a man I thought dead and I . . . I became hysterical, like he said." She lifted her gaze from the shining blade. "Please leave us . . . *all* of you," she reiterated for Klaus's benefit. "I am in no danger."

"A *wife*, Gavin? How could you not tell me?"

" 'Twas none of your concern, Claire. Now if you all will leave us."

"Claire?" Krista echoed numbly. *"Your* Lady Claire?"

Had she not been so exhausted, she might have given the woman more assessment than a cursory glance. But now, it was all too much for her. If she could only sleep, maybe she would wake up and this would all be one horrible nightmare. Accusing blue eyes shifted to the man at her side, glazed with anguish and defeat. Through the haze which became more and more obscure, she heard her own voice, a childlike whisper.

"You can't hurt me any more."

Chapter Nineteen

A swoon would have been most welcome to Krista, but her innate immunity to such frivolity prevented total darkness from taking over. Instead, she was all too aware of the man who settled her back against the pillows of her bed, demanding the others keep their distance.

"I am all right!" she insisted, throwing his arms away from her.

Yet Krista made no attempt to rise from the bed. Truth was, she didn't think her legs would support her. Nonetheless, she was determined not to serve as further spectacle for the gaping assembly who had gathered in her room. What she had to say to Gavin Duncan, she needed to voice in private. The five years of brooding hatred had boiled over in her mind, but once again, she had gained control. She could not afford further hysterics so close to leaving her unhappy past behind and returning to the only life which promised fulfillment.

"I am tired and distraught, but there is much which my . . . *husband* and I need to discuss."

Summoning a reserve she was unaware of, Krista gathered the folds of her dressing gown about her and swung her legs off the mattress. She tolerated Gavin's assistance, refusing to let the concern on his face undermine her intent to dismiss him once and for all from her life.

"Ye heard the lady. 'Tis between us and none other."

Upon moving to the highbacked chair near the hearth, Krista seated herself like a queen about to preside over court, her cool demeanor hiding the anxiety that made every nerve ending scream for reassurance. Gavin, no less in command, ushered the last of the spectators out of the room, his barely suppressed hostility sending a clear message to Klaus as her cousin made one last lame attempt to intervene on Krista's behalf.

" 'Tis between us, lad. Dinna force me to give her further cause to hate me."

Hate? Krista almost laughed at the inadequate description of what she was feeling. There was no word to her knowledge to describe this torment from which she had sought relief for five long years. She looked dispassionately at the knife Gavin laid on the table. God help her, she'd almost killed him, adding guilt to the quagmire of emotions he'd bequeathed to her with his brutal deceit.

There was only one answer, one she'd tried to run away from when the opportunity finally presented itself. She would have to face him, tell him—the man and not some conjured image her tormented mind had cursed and denounced in lonely hours when sleep would not come— that he was no longer a part of her life.

"This will not take long . . ." Krista stumbled over his name. "Gavin."

"Are ye certain ye wish to deal with this now, lassie?"

"This is long overdue, Gavin Duncan." Grateful for the support of the chair, Krista forced herself to go on. "I once loved you. I now only feel contempt in my heart for you."

"Contempt fed by a spiteful old woman, lassie. Things were not as they seemed and, by thunder, ye'll hear me out before I leave this room."

"Nothing you can say, no lie you can invent, will change my mind," she warned him.

"Then take this once more in your hand, lassie," Gavin challenged in return. He seized the knife from the table and folded her cold fingers around it. "And if ye would still use it, when I'm finished, I'll offer nay resistance, na' blame."

Here was a far more dangerous adversary than she'd counted on. A ranting, raving Gavin Duncan, she could deal with, but this new, civilized side of him was beyond her experience. She waited in silence broken only by the sound of his footsteps as he approached the hearth and stared into the glowing coals.

The firelight highlighted his grim, chiseled features. Like a warrior of old, he began a tale designed to tug at the strings of a heart. It was a beautiful story, too beautiful to represent the bitter past. Naturally, it involved a noble prince and respected warrior among his peers. But this young man was caught in a war in which he did not believe. He was wounded and lost, not only in body, but in spirit. Betrayed by love and bleeding from a wound inflicted by his comrades, he fled through the wilds of a savage foreign land until a vision gave him hope to go on.

Krista listened, detached, as Gavin described how, blinded by bitterness, he'd failed to recognize his salvation at first. Reluctantly, memory began to substantiate parts of the engaging saga with common feelings of fear, distrust, and then the gradual evolution of respect and affection. They had been through a lot together, fighting for their very survival and leaning on each other's strengths to see them through. But this story had an unhappy ending, she reminded herself sternly. It was all for nothing.

It continued to unfold and not in the way she recalled it. It was she who had been lied to, not him. It was she who had been traded off like cattle, not he who had been deserted while he risked life and limb for a new beginning with the woman he loved. Yes, Marie had technically lied about the graves, but theoretically she had told the truth. Krista was dead and buried along with her son, as far as spirit was concerned. She had not lived since, not truly. What she experienced now was existence, treated to a breath of freshness on occasion by her music.

Gavin spoke as if he had been the one wronged, as if his unselfish love and concern for her had been rewarded by heartless abandonment. It wasn't that way at all, part of her argued against the sympathy stirred by the spell-binding account. Dear heaven, but that soul-rousing burr of his could still work its easy way with a woman's heart.

If the said woman was alive, that is, Krista mused. Moving and breathing did not constitute life. He'd been devastated by the sight of the graves, he said. He had no reason to go on living and yet, neither war nor hard back-breaking labor would reward him with death.

"Because death was too good for you, perhaps," Krista suggested icily when the tale was done.

She turned the knife in her hand, studying it as if she'd never seen one before. She recalled the day Marie had returned it to her for her own protection, and the mixed emotions she'd felt. Gavin had been absolved of taking back his gift, but Krista knew only more anguish.

"I only wish I could believe you suffered as you said."

Gavin turned from the hearth, his face stricken with the pain he'd relived a thousand times. "Believe it, woman!" he sneered bitterly. "We've both had our share of fiendish devilment and all because of Marie DeMotte."

"Don't blame your deceit on her!" Krista chastised scornfully. *"You . . . left . . . me."*

"You still believe that?"

"Yes!"

A sob caught in Krista's throat. Not now, she prayed.

She couldn't break in front of him. The sound of renting material brought her clenched eyes open to see her companion kneeling before her, his muscled and scarred chest bared to her scrutiny.

"Then be done with it, hinny!"

Earlier she could have buried the weapon in his heart without second thought, but now, she could only look with confusion into his challenging gaze. She didn't believe him. She wouldn't be taken in by his emotion-riddled confession. Lies came too easily from his silver tongue and, once burned, she would not risk its scorch again.

"Do it!" Krista winced at the thunderous outburst and pulled back as the Scot tugged the hand with the knife toward him until the blade indented the skin over his heart. "This is what ye want, isn't it?"

Krista shook her head. "No, I . . ." She bit her bottom lip in a frantic attempt to stop the tortured whimper gaining momentum in her chest.

Gavin took the knife from her trembling fingers and tossed it aside, expelling his breath in a rush with it. "Then what is it ye want, hinny?" he inquired tenderly, raising her captured hand to his clean-shaven cheek.

"I want you to go back," Krista pleaded, no longer able to control the tears streaming down her cheeks. "Go back and leave me alone."

"I dinna think you're tellin' the truth, lassie."

Krista turned away and buried her face in the wing of the chair, crying softly. "Even if I did believe you, Gavin Duncan, I could not be your wife again. I cannot love you. I can never forget your betrayal. I *can't!* I have worked so hard to build a new life and you have built yours, apart, not together! We have no place in our lives much less our hearts for each other now. I am dead, Gavin! I can't feel love, I c . . . can't feel anything, but this awful terrible hurt!"

Five years of heartache, five years of tears, erupted in the sobs that shook Krista's shoulders. The truth, regardless of what it was, could not remedy that. If Gavin's confession was in earnest, it could not bring back their baby son or make her forget the pain of his loss. Her hatred of the child's father had killed her baby, but avenging it with the father's death would only cause more agony.

"I hated you so much, it killed our baby! I'm tired of hating. I do not wish to be like Marie, consumed with it." Krista turned her tear-swollen face up at Gavin. "Just leave me what little peace and happiness I can find in my music. Let me go home to Vienna with Baron Von Baden and try to forget. Please, Gavin, let me go!"

Gavin regarded the distraught woman, emotions no less fierce playing havoc with his mind. Never in his life had a woman brought him to his knees. Never had one twisted his heart and mind in a wringer of sentiments he could not begin to fathom, much less deal with. It left him with a sense of helplessness and rage that was difficult to separate.

"I canna do that, lassie."

"I don't love you."

"That may be," Gavin conceded, choking on the frustration that coiled his body into aching knots. "But ye'll return with me to the home I promised."

"I won't!"

"And be mother to the son ye thought was in the other empty grave."

Krista wondered that she had any strength left to drain from her beleaguered body, yet she felt as if she were losing it. "He's dead, Gavin, killed by your deceit and my hatred of it."

"Nay, hinny, the lad's alive and livin' at Duncan Brae."

"You're lying!" Krista averred passionately. "I cannot believe even you would say such a thing to hurt me so! I did not think you could hurt me more, but I was wrong!"

There was no doubt in Gavin's mind that Krista's shock was any less real than her pain. Again he swallowed the rage he felt for Marie DeMotte, for his tortured wife deserved none of it. "Did ye ever see the child, lassie?"

"I was unconscious for days, nearly dead myself!" the girl murmured suspiciously. "But Marie said—"

"Lies, lassie, all lies," Gavin cut in. "She sold the baby to a young French couple in Cahokia. None would ever have been the wiser, had the wife not taken ill and died. The husband brought the baby back to Petit Lyon to its natural mother . . . a mother who had gone away by then. But for my corporal being there at the time, the old witch might have sold the child again."

"Your corporal?" Krista repeated mechanically, not daring to believe this even more incredible story.

"Jean-Luc DeMotte, the innkeeper's nephew. We fought together on the Indian campaigns and he later accompanied me on the surveying missions commissioned by the government," Gavin informed her shortly. "Jean-Luc confronted his aunt, who, after all that time still lied about your death. But she admitted to selling the baby so she would not have to raise it. He, of course, brought Joshua to Duncan Brae on the Ohio. He's been there ever since, Jean-Luc *and* Joshua," Gavin clarified. The young man would not hear of hiring a nanny, but appointed himself the child's guardian.

"And Marie?"

"Dead . . . of pneumonia, I heard."

"The inn?"

"Jean-Luc sold it, since his uncle had been killed before the war ended."

"*Joshua.*" Krista repeated the name over and over in her mind.

" 'Tis been a cruel fate and a vicious woman that's kept us apart, hinny, nay lyin' on either of our parts."

Krista avoided Gavin's pressing gaze. She wanted to believe him, but his story was so . . . so unbelievable. Marie DeMotte had been a greedy soul, but Krista never dreamed she would stoop so low as to sell a child . . . her child. God in heaven, had all this suffering been for nothing?

"So much," she cried softly, looking up through her tears at the somber man before her. "So much lost, Gavin!"

Gavin drew her to him. Her wet tears dampened his chest and her scalded cheeks were not against his skin. He brushed the stray wisps of golden silk which had escaped her braid away from her face and kissed each one, as if to keep it in its new place.

"Nay, lassie," he whispered at last, when her grief was spent and she lay against him, drawing ragged breaths. " 'Tis so much found . . . and look there through the window." He drew back so that she might see the first rays of the morning sun tying to force its way into the room through the heavy drawn drapes. " 'Tis an omen, hinny, and ye know what it says?"

Krista shook her head and looked up hopefully at the reassuring face above hers. She wanted so much to believe in him.

"It says, 'tis time to go home, nay to Vienna, nor the highlands, but to the Duncan Brae on the Ohio."

But she couldn't, no matter how wonderful he could make things sound. "I will think about it," she conceded slowly. "I would like to see your Joshua."

"*Our* Joshua, lassie. He has your eyes, big and blue and full of mischief."

"The mischief is all yours!" Could the boy really be her son? *Their* son? Her brief smile faded and died. "I do not love you, husband. If I return to America with you, it will be as the boy's mother, not as your wife."

" 'Tis a bit late for courtin', don't you think?"

Krista failed to rise to the beguiling attempt to lighten her humor. "I don't want courting, Gavin Duncan. All I want is peace."

Chapter Twenty

"How do you know he isn't lying to you?"

Klaus Bruener stepped out of the way as Krista proceeded to the dressing table to finish her hair before accompanying him downstairs for the noon day meal. They would naturally take their meal in the kitchen as hired musicians and she hated to think that she was holding up the others, who had sent Klaus to check on her when she did not appear for the morning practice.

Like the ladies of leisure, she'd slept fashionably late, although her reasons were entirely different. When Gavin finally left her to make her decision, instead of dwelling on it, she'd succumbed to exhaustion. The night had produced too much for her weary mind to digest. Now, in the light of the mid day sun, she was somewhat refreshed and the same doubts her cousin voiced troubled her as well.

"Why would he lie now, Klaus? What purpose would it serve? Gavin does nothing without a purpose."

"Look at you, cousin!"

Klaus came up to the mirror and tucked in a stray wisp of the golden hair which had escaped Krista's simple coiffure. She disdained the high piles of false hair and the use of flour paste to stiffen one's own hair into unnatural shapes. Instead, she kept ribbons and silk flowers woven in her braid, which she wrapped in a demure knot at the back of her neck.

"You are a beautiful, desirable woman," he pronounced proudly. "He no doubt has seen his error in judgment and is determined to set it straight."

"So you think he could want me . . . for myself?" Krista inquired, the idea not so distasteful as it should be.

"Or a mother for the child, whosoever it is. My God, Krista, how could you even contemplate going back to that heathen land?"

"Because that child may be mine!"

"And if he isn't?"

Krista met her cousin's challenging gaze in the mirror, her face contorting in dismay. "I do not know!"

"You will go back, find out it's another woman's brat and then what? Those colonials surely can not appreciate your talent. You'd have to earn your way back."

Krista got up and brushed the goldenrod-striped taffeta of her dress into place over the wide hoops that flared from her narrow waist. She hadn't thought of that. Gavin had insisted on taking her to the Ohio, but he'd said nothing about helping her leave. But Philadelphia was civilized enough for a harpist to survive and earn enough for a passage back. Or she could demand that Gavin give her the money in advance for a return passage. As proof of the validity that she would not need it, she thought, for if the boy was her son, she would not leave him.

"I shall insist on return passage in advance," she agreed, extending her arm to Klaus. "Shall we join the others? I am famished."

Keeping to the back stairwells, Krista made her way down to the grand kitchen which boasted not one, but two fireplaces as large as some rooms she'd slept in in her time. Staff in starched white aprons were scurrying about to set out the meal for the hostess and her guests in the main dining room, leaving Krista and Klaus to make up their own platters and retreat to the pantry where a long trestle table was set up for the use of the staff. After explaining the episode of the night before as an unexpected and shocking reunion, she was about to announce to the others that she would be quitting the ensemble, when one of the servants came in to fetch her.

"Miss Lindstrom . . . I mean, Lady Duncan, the Lady Claire is asking that you join her guests."

"I am not nobility," Krista insisted in an attempt to ease the maid's embarrassment as well as her own.

"But you are married to the new Lord Duncan, are you not?"

"Well yes, but . . ."

"For no longer than it takes to get a divorce," Klaus finished for her.

"Oh, Herr Bruener," the maid exclaimed, as if suddenly remembering something important. "A young boy came by and asked me to tell you that his mother is not well . . . a Mrs. Higgins."

"Did he say what was wrong?"

Krista put a comforting hand on her cousin's arm. "Perhaps you should go see, instead of practicing. We do not play until this evening after supper."

"You'll be all right?"

"I will be fine!" Krista assured him, touched by his stalwart support.

Ironically, it was she who provided stability for Klaus, but not because the young man intended it that way. He really believed he had saved her from a life of misery and he had. He had provided her with hope and purchased her freedom. The rest had been up to her survival skills and solid wit.

Krista wasn't intimidated by the ladies and gentlemen eyeing her curiously as she entered the long dining room, made to look twice its size with massive gilded mirrors. There was only one who could make her feel unsure of herself and he was not present. Besides, she had grown accustomed to speculation from fans and admirers who were not content to accept the story that she had come with her cousin from the colonies to escape the war. Perhaps the mystery surrounding her was part of her appeal to them.

"Lady Krista, do come sit next to me! I promised Gavin I would take personal care of you."

"You do me honor, Lady Claire."

The mistress of Athens Hall had traded her scarlet silk of the previous evening for a deep blue day dress of a polynaise fashion with a matching diamond print on the white ruffled underskirt. Foregoing her massive wigs, she had arranged her powdered hair in three large curls, each held in place with jeweled combs. As she motioned to the chair next to her with regal grace, her pale blue eyes were no less assessing than Krista's darker ones.

"Nonsense, dear! Our husbands are off on whatever missions and I am dying to hear how the brother of my late Robert came to marry London's most celebrated harpist."

"We *all* are!" one of the other women tittered, her china tea cup clattering against its matching saucer as she replaced it. "Although, I must say, the baron has taken this news quite hard."

"Baron Von Baden has left?" Krista's concern lifted the woman's brow in disdain.

"What man in his right mind would challenge that devilishly handsome Scot?"

"Gavin made it quite clear last night that no one would come between the two of you. I've never seen him so . . . intrigued," Claire finished tactfully.

"Where exactly is . . . Gavin?" Krista folded the linen napkin in her lap and awaited her hostess's answer.

"Gone to book passage for two to Philadelphia. If you need one of my maid's to pack your trunk . . ."

Krista shook her head in denial, not only of the offer, but of her husband's presumption. She'd not told him that she'd go. She'd said she would think about it. Damn his impudence!

"I have music to play tonight, milady. I'm afraid he'll have to make other plans or I can follow on another, later ship."

"Then *you* tell him," Claire averred with a shiver. "But then, you surely know what a bullish creature he can be."

"I will . . . and right good too!"

"Just listen to her accent. She even sings when she talks!"

Krista smiled graciously at her gentleman admirer and proceeded to butter one of the fresh scones the servant had placed on her plate. She was not the shy frontier girl Gavin Duncan had charmed with his brawny build and devilish tongue. She had learned to accept attention as her due. She was confident in her music and her ability to please the cultured ear.

If anything, she needed him even less than before, a most pleasing thought to her independent nature. In fact, she would definitely take another ship, she thought, hardly aware that she'd just made up her mind. She'd use the money she received from pawning her jewels and demand he foot the cost for her return . . . in advance.

The rules would be set from the start . . . by her, not the laird or squire of the Duncan Brae on the Ohio. Her life was her own for the first time in her twenty-odd years and she was not going to relinquish her independence to a man ever again.

"Excuse me, Lady Duncan, but a young lad from town

delivered this package for you. Should I have the maid put it in your room?"

Before Krista could answer, her hostess waved the servant in. "Of course she'll take it here," she said enthusiastically. "It's undoubtedly a present from Gavin. He was always the thoughtful one."

"Is there a card with it?" Krista asked as she took the package into her lap and examined it.

She wasn't expecting anything . . . unless this was her husband's way of earning his way back into her good graces. Her lips thinned. If that was the case, he'd wasted his time right good, for she was not the sort to be won with silly gifts and empty promises.

"I'll bet it's flowers!" one of the other ladies at the table ventured, waiting expectantly as Krista untied the string.

"It does have the shape of a flower box," Claire agreed.

It was a flower box, not the first she'd ever received. Her apartment was frequently filled with them after an opening night or performance. Feeling on display, Krista pulled off the lid and moved the paper aside to reveal exactly what the women had guessed.

It was flowers . . . dead roses to be exact, tied together with a black ribbon. Uncertain if she was the target of some aristocratic jest beyond her understanding, she glanced around the table suspiciously, only to discover the same bewilderment perplexing the faces of her companions.

"If Gavin sent them, he sent them from the colonies!" she remarked with a nervous laugh, breaking the strained silence.

Or was this Gavin's idea? Was he trying to tell her something? Dead flowers for a dead love, she reasoned, as Lady Bickham fingered the dried petals with a noticeable shudder. The idea that her hostess might have sent them died at the sight of her stricken face.

"Perhaps you might tell me more of this, milady," Krista suggested coolly.

Claire drew back her hand, as if she'd been scalded. Her cheeks paled beneath the artificial blush she'd applied to them. "No! I . . . I think someone very perverse had made you the object of a jest."

"A poor jest!" Krista's admirer snorted indignantly.

Lady Claire rang the small silver bell at her side sharply. "Jerome, take these away!" Krista could not help but notice the way the lady's hands shook as she gathered her skirts up to rise. "Ladies and gentlemen, the parlors are awaiting your disposal, since I'm certain you men are literally craving a good smoke and perhaps some billiards. As for us females . . ." She sighed dramatically. "We'll just find something to do to pass our time without your company."

Although she went through the motions of joining the titter of amusement resulting from her charming theatrics, Claire's laughter was as shallow as her smile. As the others divided in the hall to pursue their own interests, Krista was ushered toward the parlor, as if it were preordained that she remain among the company of her new peer group. However, at the entrance, she held back.

"I am sorry, ladies, but I must practice if I am to play for you tonight."

"But Krista," Claire objected, "You don't mind if I call you Krista, do you dear?" Before Krista could answer, she went on, "You are no longer just a *hired* musician. You're family and the wife of the new Lord of Duncan Brae. Your place is with us now."

Left with little alternative short of being rude, Krista followed Claire into the room and took a seat at a small game table while the other ladies took up the needlepoint and handiwork they'd brought along to pass the time between entertainment and meals. Each one felt obligated to comment on another's work, affording the girl some respite, but when that initial politeness was done, attention once again shifted to her.

"So tell us how you and Lord Duncan met," the lady next to her encouraged brightly. "I'd wager it was most romantic."

Krista twisted the silky material of her dress in her hands under the table. Although most of the English population seemed indifferent to the outcome of the American war, she couldn't imagine telling these people that Gavin Duncan was a traitor to his country, let alone that she had rescued him from death. In fact, the truth was so bizarre, she doubted they'd believe her if she told it.

"My stepfather had a tavern and Gavin met me there."

"You must have sung him one of those sweet love songs and entrapped his heart!"

"No," Krista evaded uneasily. "We were bundled off and got married right good after that."

"Bundled?" Lady Claire inquired, snapping from the troubled silence that had claimed her.

"In Pennsylvania, we have a custom where . . . where the father with many daughters to marry off will invite a suitable young man for supper and offer to bundle him up for the night with one of them."

Her outlandish gift of dead roses had shocked her companions into a state of confusion, but this left them utterly speechless. Forgetting their manners, they stared at the young woman as if they did not believe what they'd heard.

"Do you mean to say, dear," Claire recovered awkwardly, "that . . . that your stepfather permitted you and Gavin to . . ."

"Ja," Krista affirmed self-consciously. Her skin burned scarlet from her toes to the top of her head. "We shared a bed with a board between us." The gasps of horror that echoed around Krista were enough to draw the luxurious draped away from the walls. "And a knife!" she added hastily. "Fully with clothes . . ."

"I never heard of such a barbaric thing!"

"Many women find a husband in such a way," the girl attempted to explain. "It is good sometimes."

"Aye, that it is, lassie."

"Gavin!" Krista heard her own voice blend in with Lady Claire's as the grinning Scot stepped into the parlor with a gallant bow.

"Ladies, if ye'll excuse . . ."

"Gavin, I must speak with you!" Claire rushed from the table she shared with Krista, her gathered ruffles leaving a trail of sweet perfume in her wake. *"Now."*

"And I must practice," Krista announced, grateful for the excuse to take her leave of both her company and her husband. If the Lady Claire wanted him, she was welcome to him. It appeared she was accustomed to having him at her beck and call as it was. She met Gavin's scowl innocently. "We play tonight."

Watching as his wife swept out of the room, tall and slender in the burnished stripe of her dress, Gavin Duncan barely restrained himself from throwing off Claire's hand to follow her. The business of the morning had vexed him and it appeared that Krista was bent on doing the same, something he did not need.

As he had made his way to the stables that morning to fetch his horse, he'd nearly run into the lord of the house, who was intent on taking his leave in a most urgent manner. Suspicious, Gavin remained in the back of the stables until the coach pulled away and then followed it along the highway into London. At their destination he'd felt foolish, unable to imagine what threat the business Lord Bickham had at the St. James coffee house could possibly be to him. Yet, something in the back of his mind refused to let the matter be dismissed so easily—something about the painted sign hanging above the door through which Bickham had disappeared . . . masked, no less!

The Black Rose. Gavin studied the name until it came to him. The night before he'd left Detroit with Captain Messick and his men, he'd been engaged in a game of cards with some of the regulars from his former brigade, as well as the militia. They were talking about a masquerade ball given by a club called *The Black Rose,* a society with counterparts in some of the major cities in the colonies.

The description of this particular affair which followed was so depraved, that Gavin had thought it a jest of some sort contrived to put him on. At least, what he recalled of it. The rum had been better than the company at the time to a man who had just received word that his sweetheart had married his brother. But he did remember that Messick, initially distrustful of the strangers in his camp, had from that point on treated the regulars like long-lost friends.

Upon considering what he'd seen of Lord Bickham, Gavin hardly found his association surprising. Rather, it was the hour of his appointment and his urgency which still plagued him after he abandoned his quarry to make his way to the docks. He had little trouble acquiring a space for two, for few travelers were anxious to undertake the journey with the coming of winter almost upon them. His worst task lay ahead in convincing his wife to share the cabin with him.

Absorbed in the exact way he might approach the subject, he paused with the rest of the crowds to allow a gruesome procession headed toward Tyburn to pass by. The execution wagon preceding the hearses and mourning wagons generated as much excitement as the King's birthday parade. Gradually the conversation of the crowd penetrated his thoughts, and he realized the prisoners were being executed for treason to the Crown.

Made more uneasy, for although the war was over, sentiments ran high among some on both sides of the sea against turncoats, Gavin tugged the letter he'd received out of his coat to study it once more. The elegant lines implored him to return to Duncan Brae, for, not only was his brother dead, but the writer feared for her very life. Instead of a signature at the bottom, it was ended with one of the frivolous scribblings Claire had always marked her notes with. Hearts and flowers were favorites. For this missive, it had been a rose with a curled stem and a ribbon colored black, like the flower.

"Gavin, there's something I must tell you!" Claire confided, backing against the door to the now empty ballroom. It clicked shut, assuring their conversation would remain private. Nonetheless, Claire looked about the room frantically, as if expecting to find someone watching them.

"At the risk of such scandal?" Gavin quipped wryly.

He leisurely followed the woman to the center of the room where she glanced up at the balcony surrounding its upper perimeter. The way she twisted her hands in front of her, one would think she was physically wrestling for words. She was genuinely distraught and instinctively Gavin knew it had to do with Lord Bickham's visit to the coffee house. "Would it have anything to do with the Black Rose?"

Claire spun on the heels of her delicate slippers, her hand clutched to her chest as she stared at him. "You knew?"

"I know that your husband made an urgent trip this morning to a certain coffee house on St. James."

"Oh my God!"

"And that all of this is somehow tied in with the mysterious letter I received."

"I never sent it! I swear by all that is holy, I never sent it!"

"You dinna draw the little black rose in lieu of your signature on it? I thought that was one of your . . . peculiarities."

"Gavin!" Claire seized his arm and peered up at him with wild frightened eyes. "You must leave and take Krista with you!"

"That is just what I've been tryin' to do all mornin', lassie."

"No, I mean now! Right away!" Trembling on the border of hysteria, the woman looked over her shoulder again, as if she feared the devil himself might appear. "They'll kill you and take her if you don't." Her last words trailed off, choked in her throat so that she had to force them out in a terrified whisper. "And they'll make her a slave . . . like they did m . . . me!"

Gavin caught the swaying woman in his arms and pulled her to him as she began to sob hysterically against his chest. "Who, lassie?"

"The roses! S . . . she got the roses, j . . . just like m . . . me!"

"Who, Claire? What roses?"

"That w . . . woman!" she wailed pitifully. "I deserved it. I let them kill Robert, b . . . but I w . . . won't let them kill you."

Barely able to make out the words which came in stuttering bursts of emotion, Gavin swept his distraught companion up in his arms and carried her to a staircase which led to the second floor balcony. "Hush now, Clary, hush!" he whispered, trying to calm her so that he might make some sense of her babbling. "What is it you're tryin' to tell me, lassie?"

She was still beautiful, he thought as he brushed away the tears from her scalded cheeks, and frail, more frail and docile than he remembered. She moved him, not with the passion he'd once felt, but with sympathy. There was no doubt she had paid for whatever game she'd played. Bickham had snuffed out her spirit and left her a lovely, hollow shell of the woman she'd been.

"They want Duncan Brae, Gavin," she said, her face contorted with misery.

"Who?"

"Edwin and that awful woman . . . the one who runs the den of debauchery! You've never seen anyone so grotesque in all that make-up and china silk. She . . . she must have sent you the letter." Claire's eyes widened in protest at the skeptical arch of Gavin's brow. "I swear, it wasn't me! Do you think I'd want you to know what happened . . . to see me like this? And they're going to do the same thing to Krista!"

"What, Claire? Do *what?*"

Once again, his companion looked about the room wildly. "Walk into the garden with me. I fear being overheard."

Gavin took off his coat and placed it over Claire's shoulders as they passed through the terrace doors leading to the beautiful symmetrical gardens beyond. The afternoon sun beat warm on his shirt and waistcoat, easing the bite of the cold air. His arm about her, he walked at her side through the paved pathways until they reached a large rose arbor where winter brown and leafless vines formed a canopy over the benches on each side of the path. She dropped down on one and pulled his coat about her with a shiver.

"They will make her a widow and then give her a new

husband, only . . ." Claire inhaled deeply to fortify herself. "Only he will be a master and she his slave."

"How do ye know this?"

"Because Krista received the roses today . . . the *black* roses. I . . . I received them just before Robert was poisoned."

"Poisoned? Are ye certain?"

"It's a devil's club, run by a . . . a demon woman! They're going to make Duncan Brae their summer retreat. Gavin, you have no idea how depraved these men are!"

Gavin frowned as Claire threw herself into his arms again in another fit of hysterical sobbing. He had no use for Duncan Brae, though the sight of what had been done to his ancestral home had fired his highlander temper to its limit. He'd built his own. Why would this woman send for him? How did she find him? Everyone had thought him dead, thanks to his cousin's testimony.

"I would d . . . die if I could, but I can't," Claire sobbed, drawing away to stare up at him. "It's all my fault for flirting with Edwin and flaunting Robert's money before the *ton*. Robert was so boring! Not like you. If you'd been the Duncan, I'd have never left the highlands or been seduced by the glamour of London."

"The glamour or Lord Bickham, Claire?" Gavin asked perceptively.

"Both. He was so delightfully wicked, like you," she told him, adding dispassionately, *"Or so I thought*. In the Black Rose everyone was masked and it didn't matter what one did with whom. I'd stayed cooped up in that drafty castle so long, Gavin! I wanted to live again and be desired."

His face a mask of stone in spite of the bitter memories Claire's confession stirred, Gavin listened to the tale of how Lady Duncan came to be courted by Lord Edwin

Bickham of Athens Hall. The courtship was wildly romantic, the sort that would appeal to the frivolous Claire Eaton Duncan and sustain her over the summer she spent with the husband who suddenly began to fail in health and appetite.

The black roses arrived as Lord Duncan lay on his deathbed. She'd cast them off, thinking some loyal servant to the laird had played a cruel joke to make her feel guiltier than she already did and made haste to London in hopes of forgetting her troubled thoughts. She was still bedecked in black silk when she was abducted on the Promenade and spirited off to a night of lunacy and sheer terror.

The story rang familiar to a rum-sodden memory as Gavin listened to the tearful confession, dismayed that anyone could be subjected to such a nefarious deed, much less the girl he had once loved. The men around the campfire had laughed that they'd made women their slaves, but Gavin had only thought them to be bragging about their prowess with the fairer sex, as soldiers were prone to do with a belly full of rum and an attentive audience of fellow men.

"And now it's Krista and you. They've named her the Queen of Sin, the Black Widow."

" 'Tis a fearsome tale you've told, lassie."

"And all true, God help me," Claire whispered fervently. "So get your bride and go, before it's too late. Edwin's already been to that witch!"

"Aye, I've been made the fool, well enough," Gavin ground out ominously. "And one too many times." He glanced down at the devastated woman wrapped in his coat and leaned forward to buss her on the forehead. "You've paid a harsh price for your fickle ways, lassie, but ye dinna deserve this."

"So you'll go?"

Gavin drew her against him. "Aye, I'll go, but I'll pay a visit to my lady friend first."

Claire pulled away with a gasp. "For the love of God, Gavin, you mustn't. Just leave and forget you ever heard of me or Duncan Brae."

"I canna do that, lassie. But I would ask a favor of ye. Get my wife to the *Fair Wind* at Bingham dock. The captain is expectin' two."

"How?"

"Damnation, woman, think!" Gavin exclaimed impatiently. "Tell her anything, but get her there."

"But her trunk . . ."

"Damn the trunk, it's her I'm after."

Claire tried to force a smile through her pain as she looked at the handsome features she used to trace idly with playful fingers. "You really love her, don't you?"

"I've much to make up for, if that's what ye mean."

So did she, Claire mused wearily. "And what if you don't make it to the ship?"

"There's a cabin for two, whether I come along or nay."

Uncertainty clouded her face. Surely he didn't mean what he implied, not after all she'd done.

"Take nay more than ye need and get on the ship. I've a fine place for startin' over and 'tis plain that's just what ye need."

"Oh, I couldn't! I've made so many mistakes . . ."

"Haven't we all, lassie?"

Gavin's laugh was a bitter sound. Claire knew pain when she heard it. It was an emotion she'd grown accustomed to since Robert's death. She also knew that stubborn streak of Highland fierceness which now glittered in whiskey dark eyes and it frightened her, not just for Gavin, but for them all.

Chapter Twenty-One

"No!" Krista declared stubbornly to the very nervous hostess who had summoned her from her practice with an unlikely tale of intrigue. "This is another of Gavin Duncan's tricks to get his way."

"Milady, I vow on all that is sacred, it is not! Those roses mean certain death to him and untold horror for you. Believe me, I *know!* We must gather whatever clothes we can make do with and flee to the docks."

Although Claire's distress seemed real enough, Krista had her doubts. Her harp stand placed next to the window, she couldn't help but see the couple in the garden, walking arm in arm like reunited lovers while she practiced. Gavin had kissed Lady Bickham and comforted her, his coat wrapped about her shoulders to protect her from the weather. It was a timely reminder for Krista that he had come to England to his lost love, not to find her. She was an accidental discovery.

"Why do you care whether I go or not, milady?" the girl challenged coolly. If Lady Claire was going, there was no need to find a mother for his son. The woman was jumping at the chance to run away with her highlander.

"Because I love Gavin too much to face his death again . . . and I would not wish my fate on the worst of my enemies." Claire cleared her throat, her fingers clutched about it nervously. "He loves you, Krista. I've never seen him in such a turmoil over a woman before."

"If I might say so, milady, it's you who seems in a turmoil. You go with him on the *Fair Wind,* if you wish. I will make my own arrangements."

The man hadn't even had the decency to try to convince her to go himself, although if he had, Krista was uncertain that she'd have been able to hold back the punch she longed to deliver to that arrogant jaw of his. The nerve of him to expect her to travel, not just at his beck and call, but to accompany him and his lady fair! It didn't make sense, even for Gavin.

"Don't be a fool!" Claire stomped her slippered foot angrily on the carpet, startling Krista from her confusion. It was the first show of spine she'd seen in the woman. "Gavin may not even make it to the ship! His last words to me were to see you to safety! It's the least I owe him after betraying his love."

"Hasn't he already gone to the ship?" Krista asked, taken back by Claire's insinuation that the Scot was in danger. Actually, it wasn't like him to let someone else do battle for him. He loved the fight too much.

"He's gone after the ones who killed his brother!"

Alarm began to prick along the nape of Krista's neck. Yes, that would be more in keeping with that Duncan pride of his. God in heaven, could this incredible story be true? She looked at Claire suspiciously. At least the part about the danger, she mused, for she would be hard pressed to believe there was nothing between the man and woman she'd witnessed clinging to each other in the garden.

Her bravado failing, Claire's shoulders fell and the fire in her gaze faded from one of annoyance to a plea. "Will you go with me or not?"

Krista tried to dispel the jealousy which had given rise

once more to unrequited bitterness and pondered the possibilities to this bizarre play in which she was involuntarily involved. Gavin was her link to her son, if the child did exist as he said. His explanation of how the baby had been taken from her was reasonable, more so than the story Claire had just told her.

"Well, *I'm* not staying. I have a chance to escape this hell I brought on myself and, if you have one ounce of the sense you were born with, you'll do the same. I'll be in my room, packing. Jerome should have the carriage around back of the house in half an hour as I instructed."

The slamming door made Krista flinch. If there was merit to any of this, she did not have time to think about it. Perhaps if she packed a spare dress and a few things in a satchel, she might accompany the Lady Claire to the docks and hear the explanation of this travesty from Gavin himself.

Resolved at least to that point, Krista snatched down one of her day dresses from the back of the door and shoved it into the bag she usually reserved for her music. She didn't believe a sea voyage lay ahead of her any more than she believed in the danger Claire had come to warn her of. She had not, however, survived all those years in the wilderness by not being prepared.

Lifting her hem, she tied the thongs of the sheath of her hunting knife around her stockinged calf resolutely. Even the threat of danger aside, she would not leave to chance that any woman aside from herself might be left to raise her son. She would have the truth, if she had to swim the Atlantic to find it.

With the jewels which would afford her passage packed in the bottom of her case, Krista started across the main gallery on the second floor to the opposite wing reserved for family members and guests. It seemed she'd only reached the double doors leading to the master suite when

Claire stepped through, bag in hand. The women stared at each other for a moment before coming to life.

"I have decided to at least accompany you to the ship."

Relief flooded Claire's face. "Thank God! I did not want to face Gavin without you! We'll take the servants' staircase."

"What have you told the servants?" It wasn't ordinary for a hostess to abandon her guests to afternoon naps to gallivant about the country.

"I told Jerome I need to see my physician . . . that my headaches have returned and I've misplaced my medication."

It sounded contrived to Krista and she was certain that the servant was not wholly convinced of the validity of his mistress's tale himself. He had the look of a man torn between two loyalties, distraught and ill at ease.

"Shall we expect you to return before tea?"

"I shall do my best, Jerome. If I do not, ask Lady Huntingdon to take my place and explain this dreadful malady."

"Yes, milady."

The vehicle shook as the coachman helped the Lady Claire into it. Cloaked in a fur-lined pelisse of burnished gold wool, Krista followed, struggling with the lace layers of her hem to keep them from catching on the steps. Many times she envied men their simpler and more practical attire.

It wasn't until she turned away from the closing door behind her that she realized there was something amiss. Lady Claire sat spine stiff against the corner of the tufted velvet seat, her eyes round with fear. Following the woman's startled gaze, Krista discovered herself looking into the polished barrel of a cocked pistol.

"And where are you ladies off to in such a rush?" Lord Edwin Bickham asked, his mustached smile fixed without hint of amusement. At his sharp tap on the side of the coach, the vehicle pulled forward.

Krista eased down on the seat beside Claire and glanced at her expectantly, but the woman was rendered mute with sheer terror. "Your wife is ill. We are going to a physician."

"Which one, *Lady* Duncan?"

"Halsworth," the girl ventured boldly. She'd seen a physician's shingle with that name somewhere along the walk from Chelsea to Whitecastle while window shopping. "Dr. Oliver Halsworth. I've recommended him to your wife, since her own physician has not helped her headaches."

"Are you planning to stay with this doctor overnight?"

Leaning forward, Bickham flipped open the lock on Krista's case to reveal her hastily packed belongings. Pistol still trained too close for any attempt to disarm him, he rummaged through it with his free hand with a look of satisfaction.

"Couldn't have you brandishing that hideous knife of yours, could we, milady?" When no answer came, he repeated his initial inquiry. "Exactly where were you ladies going? To meet Duncan, perhaps? I'm told he left here a short while ago."

With a calm she was far from feeling, Krista looked out the window at the passing hedgerow which opened onto the main thoroughfare to the city. "It appears, milord, that we are going where you are taking us."

"No matter, the authorities will find him, I would think. Did you know he was a traitor to the Crown when you married him, Lady Duncan?"

"A traitor, a liar, a thief of hearts, but how can it matter now that the war is over?" Krista asked innocently.

"It matters to some, milady, some who would see your

husband and all like him dead . . . not just in this country, I might add."

"Then I hope they will wait until I am done with him first! I meant to use that knife and I still do. I will find a replacement for the one he took from me and run it through his lying black heart!" Seeing the interest spark in their captor's gaze, she went on. "I would put nothing past a man who would sell his wife into indenture for money and then leave her carrying his child to fight for the King's enemy. If my cousin had not found me, I would still be enslaved to that rebel innkeeper!"

"A child?" Bickham prompted, stiffening at the mention of the baby.

"A son," Krista informed him, adding hastily, "Born dead."

People who would kill and manipulate the way Claire had described would think nothing of harming an innocent lad. If she and Gavin did not survive, at least the child would be safe, she thought, somewhat assuaged by the relief she saw wash over Bickham's face.

"No wonder you kept your past so secret, my dear." The man glanced over at his wife, who appeared on the verge of a sickened swoon. "Speaking of secrets, Claire, what have you told Lady Duncan about . . . her *roses?*"

Claire literally trembled under her husband's inquiring scrutiny. "N . . . nothing."

Too fast for Krista to realize what he was about, Bickham brought the pistol across the woman's face with a vicious backhand. Claire cried out sharply, covering the glowering red mark left by the gun with her fingers. "Dear God, Edwin, I beg you, please! I only told her Gavin was marked for death!"

Krista cringed inwardly at the way the female shriveled into hysterics in the corner of the coach, babbling incoherent apologies. From far and away in the recesses of her

mind, another scene came to the front. It was Mama
crying and begging for reason and Herr Schuyler ranting
and raving, his nostrils flaring even as Lord Bickham's
were at the moment. Herr Schuyler had not hit her
mother, but Mary Lindstrom Schuyler was no less badgered than Claire.

"Wait!" Krista put out her arm to block the blow that
streaked across the small space between them. "She was
going to take me to him." She shrugged in feigned disgust.
"I saw them together in the garden, sneaking kisses beneath the trellis. So I agreed to run away with her and my
husband!"

"I wasn't going to run away, Edwin, I swear it!" Claire
denied frantically. "She's lying! I was taking *her* to *him.*"

"She is the one who lies. What reason did she have to
bring clothes? I, on the other hand, as the murderer of
Lord Duncan, was prepared to flee for my life."

"You bitch!" Claire lunged out of the corner at Krista,
but before her clawlike nails reached their intended target, the pistol whipped again across the woman's face,
knocking her senseless to the floor.

"Did you really think I cared about Gavin Duncan?"
Krista taunted scornfully as Claire attempted to crawl up
on the seat. "I want him dead, but now, how will we find
him?" She cast an accusing gaze at Lord Bickham. "Unless," she went on thoughtfully, "we use your wife as bait."

"That will be up to the madame," Bickham countered
nervously. "I don't trust either of you. Madame Rose will
decide which course to take."

"Ohhh . . . nooo!"

Krista drew back her legs as Lady Claire fainted dead
away, sprawling on the floor between her and the man
with the gun. The only satisfaction she could feel was over
the fact that the woman was no longer conscious and able
to provoke her husband into further abuse. Sympathy for

what Claire had lived these last years welled in her bosom. Lord Edwin Bickham was no more than a fanciful version of Gunter Schuyler—a bully of a man who delighted in humiliating women.

"I'm surprised Gavin had anything to do with a feather-brained weakling like her!" she scoffed, turning away from the still figure to watch the buildings marking the spreading outskirts of London.

"Oh, Madame Rose will like you, milady, indeed she will."

There were still a large number of men present in the game room behind the false back wall of the coffee house on St. James. All of them masked, they'd met in Madame Rose's private parlor, called by an urgent message inscribed with her unique signature—the black rose. The very idea of the "Golden Girl with the Harp" submitted to their perverse brand of slavery had left some literally drooling. It would be as the madame had said, "An angel brought to hell." But that was the fate of an angel who married a turncoat. Governments might forgive, the society would not.

For once, Derrick Duncan was the source of society envy, rather than scorn as the eccentric who hung in the shadows of the club and took vicarious pleasure in viewing, rather than participating, in the wicked revelry—revelry which was as likely to occur before those gathered as it was behind the closed doors of the upstairs apartments. Of course, even though the madame had chosen him to be the official "husband" of the lady harpist, she would become society property. Even now, arrangements were being made so that the lady could be made a widow proper.

"I'd wager those long legs of hers will wrap about a

man twice!" one of the elegantly attired patrons speculated with a lascivious grin.

"It all depends on the man, love," the equally well-
dressed woman in his lap retorted. "You are starting to
resemble my late husband," she teased, playfully poking
her finger into a paunch that stretched the buttons of his
waistcoat. "The poor soul would require a wench with the
limbs of an ostrich!"

"Damn a woman with a spiteful tongue!"

The lady in question leapt from her disgruntled companion's lap and darted around the table, laughing as he
gave pursuit. The indignant gentleman captured the lady
by the waist and pulled her against him, grinding his hips
against her silk-swathed buttocks suggestively.

"I say, shall we count you in this hand or not?"

"Not!"

"Not!"

Staring at each other in surprise, the two broke into
laughter at their unanimous chorus and, arm in arm,
started for the grand staircase leading to the second floor.

Gavin Duncan pressed himself against the wall, hidden
behind the drapes which fell to either side of a statue of
some oriental god. He needed a distraction in order to
reach the second floor where the garish Madame Rose
had disappeared after the clandestine meeting he'd witnessed. These people spoke of murder with the same
nonchalance as a change in the weather. The morbid
details of this lord's or that earl's untimely demise rolled
off their tongues like water off a tiled roof.

Not only had he heard his own hanging planned, to be
executed with some well-placed bribes, but he'd heard
confirmation of how his brother died. Derrick Duncan,
freshly returned from the colonies and recovering from a
poorly healed leg wound, had spent the winter with his
cousin at Duncan Brae and administered a poison the

madame herself had made of special herbs and roots. Robert had literally wasted away while Claire lived the high life in London . . . just as she'd said.

Except, the lady had not killed Robert, Gavin thought grimly. She was simply a victim of her own foolishness. His brother had been murdered by his cousin and as compassionless and degenerate a group of individuals as he'd ever crossed. Even the savages had the excuse that they did not know better than to commit atrocities. It was part of their culture. These deviates, however, were obviously well-educated men of means and quite often title. No better than the Tories and British who used the Indians to fight a wicked war against defenseless men, women, and children.

He was half tempted to burn the den of iniquity down around them and be done with them all, except that Derrick was on his way there. Gavin had heard the madame issue orders to fetch him so that he might be appraised of his impending increase in fortune. Then he would have the two he wanted and Krista would be safe. He might even get out alive, Gavin thought wryly.

A ringing of the bell over the door of the club alerted the members to the entrance of someone in the front of the coffee house. Their general rowdiness quieted until it could be determined if the visitor was a member or not.

Gavin peeked through the cracks in the heavy drapes as the double doors to the game room below opened to admit three newcomers. There was a woman and a man, holding between them a half-conscious female.

A cold dread crept up Gavin's spine as he recognized the dress Claire had worn earlier and the tall proud carriage of his wife. Why had Bickham brought them here? The plan was to see him hang first. Damnation, what had gone wrong?

"Move aside, gents. My wife is not herself," Bickham

announced, prompting the men to clear the table of the cards and playing tokens so that the moaning Lady Claire might be placed upon it.

"Someone fetch some cold cloths, please!" the other woman ordered crisply, her lilting accent shocking the gathering into stillness, rather than spurring them into motion.

"It's her!" One of the men exclaimed in horror. "Bickham, have you lost your mind?"

"This is unheard of, bringing in the uninitiated!"

"They were on their way to flee the country with Gavin Duncan!" Lord Bickham answered the charges belligerently. "What would you have me do, kiss them goodbye?"

"Madame will . . ."

The loud ring of a gong silenced all protest. At the top of the steps a stocky figure in painted silk stood imperiously. Gavin pulled back as the woman referred to as Madame Rose limped down the steps and past him, leaving the overpowering scent of strong jasmine in her wake. His nose, unaccustomed to such an assault, began to tickle threateningly and he grabbed it with his fingers before the sneeze he felt building could materialize. His heart beating loudly in his ears, he gradually released his breath and attempted to see what was going on.

"This does indeed change things, Lord Bickham. Might I ask why the dears were fleeing?"

Krista lifted her chin defiantly as she answered. "*She* fled to run away with my husband. She told me he wanted me to go with him, but I knew better. No doubt, they planned to get rid of me, so I accompanied her for one purpose only . . . to kill him."

Madame Rose snickered skeptically. "The angel with the harp came to kill the devil from the highlands?"

"Believe what you wish, madame! I know my reason for coming here," Krista spoke up defiantly. "As long as we have her, my husband will come. All I ask is the privilege to draw first blood. Then I don't care what you do with him."

Gavin's lips thinned at the unadulterated anger in his wife's voice. Was that what this was all about? Was Krista a part of this?

"You surprise me, dear. There is such passion in your heart for the one they call the Ice Queen." Madame Rose drew the scarlet plume under Krista's rebellious chin. Small beady eyes peered curiously at the aloof young woman from painted hollows which were tapered to black points on each cheek. "But I wonder just how much hate you are capable of?"

"Enough to cut Gavin Duncan's heart out with my own hands, that is, if you can fetch him to me."

"My word!"

"Strike me blue!"

"I never dreamed!"

The shock that echoed around the room did not leave the man in hiding unaffected. How could he have been wrong about her? Gavin was certain the boy would soften her heart, if he could not.

"Then show us exactly what you intend to do, pet." The madame withdrew a small jeweled dagger from the wide sash at her waist and handed it, handle first, to Krista. "On Lady Bickham."

"Nooo!" Claire struggled to sit up dizzily, but one wave of the madame's hand brought the three men who had been playing cards to the woman's side to subdue her. Staring in horror at the gleaming blade pressed into Krista's hand, Claire started screaming to her husband for mercy.

Krista met the glittering gaze of the madame with tight-jawed determination. "I have no love lost for this woman who steals into the garden with my husband to plot against me."

"Damn you, you bitch! I tried to warn you . . . to tell you," Claire shrieked hysterically. "This will be you some day, I swear it!"

So that was what had changed. Krista had seen them in the garden. Gavin reached for the loaded pistols in his belt in disbelief. He'd brought them to use against his brother's murderers, not his wife, but she was as irrational now as she was last night when she'd turned her blade against him. Throwing the curtain aside with one hand, he leveled the pistol at the gold-cloaked figure hovering over Claire.

"Dinna move, hinny, or I'll be forced to use this! All of ye, stay still as the dead, or dead you'll be!"

As if in a trance, Krista turned slowly away from the table to face him, the jeweled dagger glittering in her hand. "Right good!" she complimented him in a glacial tone. "Yours is the only blood I really want."

"Stay where ye are, hinny," Gavin warned, "And you laddies let the lady free."

Krista hesitated, staring at the barrel of the pistol aimed at her while Claire staggered away from the table toward Gavin, her tortured whimpers the only sound in the room as she stepped behind him to safety.

"Now I've two shots and I mean them for my brother's murderers, so if you laddies would like to turn out your pockets and roll down your hose so I might see you intend no harm, I'd suggest ye do it now . . . lest I be forced to dispose of you first."

Sobered by the deadly pistols no one wished to tempt, the men did as they were ordered. In the periphery of her vision, Krista saw them back away against the wall, their hands raised above their heads, so that only Madame Rose and Lord Bickham flanked her—Bickham, who was easing back the cock of the gun he was withdrawing from the folds of his coat. Fearing to move, for she could tell by Gavin's wary gaze that her act had gone a little too well, she motioned toward the gunman urgently with her eyes.

Yet her silent warning only added confusion to her husband's face, confusion for which there was no time. "He's got a gun!" Krista swung the blade around, slashing at the arm that pointed toward the Scot as two shots exploded simultaneously. Her nostrils filling with the sulfur stench of gunpowder and the smoke from Bickham's gun assailing her eyes, she lunged forward and tried to make good her aim. Her victim, however, collapsed beneath her and the blade was buried in his thigh between them.

Suddenly, she felt herself being yanked into the air by two wiry arms and pulled against the fleshy middle of the madame. Pressed to her temple was a small ladies' pistol, the hammer drawn.

"Now we are even, you devil! Even if you hate her, you won't want to see a hole blown into this fair brow, now would you?"

Wiping a bloodied hand on her gown in despair, Krista closed her eyes and swallowed dryly. Not even her heart would beat in the loud silence that followed as Gavin considered the stand-off. But her mind refused to stop working or be rattled. Adrenaline cleared her thoughts instantly, bringing to the forefront the image of her hunting knife strapped to the calf of her leg. If she could just bend down.

She'd only swooned once before, but she'd witnessed enough genuine, as well as contrived, faintings to risk provoking the madame's trigger finger. With a low moan, growing in volume, she relaxed, her head falling forward limply and tugging at the one arm which held her. The gun seemed to follow her down, its metal barrel cold against her sweat-dampened brow, and then her ears split with the thunder of pistol fire.

The floor splintered just beyond Krista's feet. She didn't know how the madame had missed, nor was there time to find out. With one thought in mind, to get her knife before the pain bursting in her temple from the recoiling blow of the pistol blackened out all hope, Krista crumbled in a heap of taffeta and lace. Then she felt it, the carved bone handle, smooth to her fingers' touch.

Blood roaring in her ears—or was it the battle cry of the giant of a man who leapt over her—she drew out the blade and tried to focus on the fray in which she seemed to be directly involved. There was another scream and Gavin was hurled away from Krista and the fallen madame by some unseen force. Through a blur, Krista saw the reason . . . another pistol had appeared from the folds of the black satin of the madame's robe.

Grasping the knife firmly, she drove it backward and in, just below the sash. The pistol tipped in the spasming hand that held it. Rolling away, Krista cringed as it struck the floor and went off. Scrambling, crawling, she made it to her feet.

Gavin! She turned to look back, afraid that she'd see the giant highlander clasping his chest in spite of her attempt to save him, when a powerful blow struck her in the back propelling her forward.

"Go, lassie, keep goin'!" Gavin Duncan bellowed.

He caught her by the back of her pelisse before she sprawled outright from the overzealous aid and helped her regain her feet. But for the black-looped fastenings, she'd have fallen out of it. As it was, she righted herself and kept on going, through the back corridor which, she discovered, led to an alley. Slamming into the wall of the next building, she turned to see Gavin bringing Claire out, half carrying her like a sack through his arm.

"Murder! Murder!" The accusing cries followed them like bloodthirsty hounds after their prey.

Chapter Twenty-Two

The bilge of the *Fair Wind* was musty and wet. But for the faint light that filtered through the grate above them, they would be left to pitch darkness, which would be the undoing of the woman quivering in Gavin's arms. It was bad enough that they lay between the ribbing of the ship in the stagnant sea water that inevitably gathered there, but each time they heard the scratching and scurrying of their rodent companions, Claire buried her face deeper into his chest and smothered her frightened whimpers there. It would be ironic, after their miraculous escape, if something as simple as a bilge rat were to give them away to the authorities searching the decks above them.

Next to him, Gavin could just make out Krista's stoic features. Her face was smeared with dirt, her gown soaked and in tatters. Like Claire's, her hair had come unraveled in the jarring race toward the dock and hung in tangles about her shoulders. With no one to hold her or cushion her from the filth from which the more fragile Claire was spared, she endured the discomfort in necessary silence.

He wondered if he could have pulled the trigger, had she continued to play the macabre scene he'd interrupted, instead of warning him of Bickham's threat and going on to save his life instead. Gavin closed his eyes. Thank God, he'd not been put to the test. To her talents at wilderness survival and accomplishments in the music world, Krista would have to add acting to her repetoire.

The footsteps above them were coming closer and closer. Gavin pulled Claire to him tightly, as the shadows of the search party cut through the light above them. Krista's only reaction was to glance upward and lean her head against the bulwark behind her. If she was afraid, she didn't show it. She simply waited, as if having turned her fate over to her Maker. The only sign that she was bothered at all was the way she kept rubbing her hands on the front of her dress, as if trying to wipe away the blood stains from the wounds she inflicted on Madame Rose and Lord Bickham.

"Shall I look down here, sir?" one of the guards asked his commander. Light from above was cut off completely as he stood over them and peered through the grate into the darkness of the bilge.

"Not unless you wish to soak your uniform and frighten the bilge rats. Not even cold-blooded murderers would stoop to that, particularly those of feminine gender. You'd hear them screaming in Whitecastle."

"As I told you, neither I, nor any of my men have seen the fugitives you described. So, if you've no further business aboard my ship, sir, I should like to get underway with the tide."

"Of course, Captain Miers. Again, you have my apologies for the inconvenience, but it is a matter of necessity. Having found the stolen farm wagon near the market, we know the scoundrels are in this area . . . and since Lord Duncan has land holdings in America, it's only natural to check those ships bound in that direction."

"Jamaica is my destination, sir. Sustaining British appetites for sugar, molasses, and rice is my livelihood. I've no wish to cross the Crown by harboring its enemies.

By the by, if you stop by my cabin, I've an excellent case of Jamaican rum from which I'll be glad to share a bottle with our protectors. 'Twill come in good with the cold winter nights ahead on the waterfront."

The senior officer chuckled in delight. "We'll not turn down a remedy such as that! Show us the way, sir!"

As their retreating footsteps faded, Gavin saw Krista exhale in relief. The hands that had clutched the front of her dress released it and started once again to rub at the bloodstains. He found himself wishing with all his heart that he might crawl over to her and take her into his arms with reassuring kisses, rather than be forced to focus his attentions on the distraught Lady Claire Bickham.

They would remain below until they were underway, lest any of the crew be tempted to collect on the reward being offered for their capture. It was what the captain and Gavin had decided on, after Gavin swam out to the ship to tell him of their misadventure, while Krista and Claire hid in the back room of one of the dockside taverns which was known along the riverfront to deal in black-market trade on occasion.

The ladies were smuggled aboard in large wooden barrels right in front of the port authorities and then forced down into the bilge below the hold of the ship. Claire had rebelled hysterically, but by going in first and inviting her into his lap, Gavin was able to convince her that this was a better fate than a Tyburn tippet.

The commands echoing from above deck could not be given fast enough, it seemed to Gavin. The ship groaned and creaked as she was set free of cleats on the loading dock, her thick lines drawn aboard with a scraping sound that seemed to vibrate the very skeleton of the ship in which they lay.

"T'is only the lines scrapin' the sides and deck, lassie," Gavin consoled the wide-eyed woman in his arms.

"It sounds so old as to break apart," Claire whispered shakily. "Will we be safe?"

Gavin's chest shook in mild amusement. "Safe as can be," he assured her. "The *Fair Wind*'s a Virginia built craft, swift and sound. Although we wouldn't want the gentlemen who just left to know it, she was a privateer not so long ago, by the name of *Liberty Rose*. She's now outfitted for trade . . . of sorts."

He didn't miss the skeptical lift of Krista's golden brow. Yes, it was a blackmarket ship, but an honest captain of His Majesties' protectorate would have turned them in. He'd suspected something was amiss, even as he'd made the arrangements that morning. If Claire had not sent the summoning letter, then someone wanted him back in the British Isles for a reason.

Had they wanted to ensure he wouldn't return to Duncan Brae, or was it simply a vendetta of bad blood because he'd turned to the patriot cause? From what he'd been able to gather, it was both. At least the first matter had been successful. As a wanted murderer, Gavin would be a fool to try to claim his ancestral title and land, not that he'd wanted it in the first place. As for the second reason, any group of villains might unite under the guise of a noble political cause. If anything, lingering hatred between former Loyalists and patriots simmered hotter in the United States than in London. But in the states, no one knew who he was, aside from those few close friends he'd made and fought with. He was simply Gavin Duncan, volunteer in the Virginia militia, surveyor, Scottish immigrant.

The sun was going down when the captain sent his first officer to fetch their stowaways and restore them to passenger status in the aft stateroom Gavin had purchased. With a porthole on the starboard side and a gallery window, only the captain's cabin could measure up to its wainscoted mahogany paneling and spaciousness. Yet, spaciousness was a matter of opinion, Gavin realized quickly as, cold and wet, the women stood in the middle of the small space and stared in confusion at the two narrow berths afforded them. He had not planned on bringing Claire.

"This is for you ladies, of course," he explained quickly. "I shall make my own arrangements with the captain, once you are comfortable."

"Comfortable?" Claire echoed shrilly. "Look at us, Gavin! We have no clothes, no belongings, no . . ."

Krista wanted no part of Claire's hysterics, but when the woman threw herself into her arms, sobbing, she tried to think of something kind. After all, this was a lady who had been spoiled and coddled all her life. Even if she weren't, the last twenty-four hours was enough to drive anyone mad. She had lost everything—a husband, a life of wealth and influence—but she wasn't the only one who suffered at the moment.

"Don't look back, milady," Krista heard herself saying. "What's done is done. It can't be changed. We must deal with the present for now."

She looked up at Gavin, struggling to follow the counsel her mother had often handed out. Her harp could be replaced. Vienna was not going to disappear from the face of the earth. She could earn her way back there with her talent someday, since the jewels were still in her bag in the Bickham coach. But only Gavin Duncan could help her find her son.

"If you will leave us, sir, I think we should get out of these wet clothes as soon as possible. We can wrap in blankets while our dresses dry," she clarified to her startled roommate. "Will you ask the captain to send a boy with some water and hot tea or coffee?"

"What are we going to do?" Claire wailed, shaking Krista bodily with her vocal and physical distress.

"And if there is a doctor, something for the lady's nerves would be right good. The captain's rum, if nothing else, will do . . . and some ointment for her cheek."

Gavin shook himself from the sight of the two bedraggled women clinging to each other like lost friends, when he knew the only thing they had in common was something that sent most at each other's throats with unsheathed claws. Except that Krista was no ordinary woman and Claire was certainly not herself at the moment. The understatement almost put a smile on his thinned lips.

"Aye, and I'll see if some clothing might be found for ye."

By the time Gavin returned with a couple of night shirts donated by the officers, Claire was lying in one of the berths, covered to her neck. She still trembled, but her tears spilled silently from puffy red eyes. Krista, still dressed, had made use of the water the cabin boy had brought earlier and scrubbed the worst of the smudges from her face, as well as the Lady Claire's. A wet cloth now lay over the bluish swelling Gavin had noticed earlier on her patient's cheek.

"Ye'd best change into this," he told her, handing her the oversized shirt. "The back of your dress is soaked and ye'll take a chill."

"Is there a doctor?"

"Of a sort. He's on his way. The captain thinks he can find some other clothes, but this is the handiest for now," the Scot added upon seeing Krista's confounded expression.

"Gavin?"

Gavin edged around Krista to where Claire reached for him. "Aye, lassie?"

"I'm so sorry. I'm going to try to be brave . . . but where will you sleep?"

"I've a bunk in steerage across the companionway."

Claire closed her eyes with a satisfied sigh, but continued to hold the strong hand she'd clutched to her breast.

Krista glanced from one to the other in a mixture of anger and pity, neither of which could gain supremacy. "I think I had best change before the doctor arrives."

"Then do it, lassie."

"In private."

Gavin expelled an exasperated breath. "What would ye have done, if we were but two, sharin' this room?"

Krista tilted her chin at a defiant angle. "Asked you for privacy." She'd warned him that if she returned to the colonies with him, she would not go as his wife. Why was he acting the injured husband and at the same time fawning over another woman? Did he think her a blind simpleton, not to notice?

"Aye," Gavin answered wryly, "Nay doubt ye would . . . and for all ye've been through, I'll see that ye'll have it, at least for now."

Chapter Twenty-Three

The first full day of their journey at sea was calm and uneventful. Claire had spent a restful night, thanks to the sedative the doctor gave her. For Krista, on the other hand, sleep was fraught with an emotion-riddled debate between her heart and her mind. Instinct told her to let the past remain in the past. She was with Gavin now. They were on their way to the grand home he'd spoken so dreamily of as they'd lain in each others arms in the quiet of that small bedroom tucked behind the tavern— their home and their son.

She longed to hear more of the boy, but to do so would mean allowing herself to be in the commanding presence of the Scot and, no matter how scarred she was from his betrayal, there was a part of her that trembled, no, looked forward to his touch. For years she thought Gavin had killed any longings she might feel for a man, but she was wrong. She was more vulnerable than she'd been as a novice in his masterful hands, for she'd tasted the exquisite and danced to the music of his fiery seduction. She trusted neither her body nor her mental defenses to stand up to such compelling temptation.

Not even the doubt which blackened the waiting horizon of their love, not even the wounds, still raw in spite of time's healing touch, could stop the warm memories of those precious two days from disarming her without warning. And if that were not enough, Gavin Duncan in the flesh, going out of his way to charm her made her tremble at the thought of weeks at sea with no escape from him.

It was difficult to resist the grin that accompanied his presentation of the ladies' wear he and the captain had managed to find among the ship's stores. Claire, no more immune than Krista to that devilish appeal, fairly squealed over the few dresses and accessories the captain just *happened* to have aboard.

That the fickle woman didn't question their good fortune was a wonder to Krista. The clothes were stolen and God only knew the fate of their previous owners. Nonetheless, with her gown in tatters, she had little choice but to accept the presents gracefully, for neither of them could continue to go about the ship in men's nightshirts.

"You have put us in the hands of brigands!" Krista muttered heatedly as Gavin escorted them down the steps to the captain's dining room for their first meal with the officer.

Captain Jeremy Miers was a charismatic man, Krista learned, with a good sense of humor. He was proud of his ship, a large Virginia built schooner, rigged fore and aft. Its main purpose was to haul cargo, dry goods, and sundries from England to Jamaica and rice, tobacco, and rum back. He owned plantations on the Caribbean island, as well as one in the Carolinas, where the second pride of his life was situated—the mother and sister for whom the gowns Krista and Claire wore had been purchased.

The man completely won over the desolate Claire with his charm and his stories of plantation life, so that by the end of the meal, she was toasting the future with the rest.

Krista was certain the fine liquor had a lot to do with her roommate's fickle change of heart, but the handsome master of the *Fair Wind* had made a decidedly good impression on his guest as well.

For all his rakishness, however, he made good his word. The captain promised a smooth voyage and the following days proved him out. The sun favored them with warmth to offset the chill of the blustery winds which played havoc with the sails overhead. Claire's enthusiasm for her new life, however, changed drastically the first day of ocean travel. No longer in the protection of the river and channel, the ship began an endless series of rolls.

By the end of the third week at sea, however, the mal de mer vanished as quickly as it had taken her. Keeping busy, the two women aired out the stuffy cabin in the more temperate climate into which they were sailing and scrubbed it top to bottom with lime and water. With that done and the dresses repaired, there was little else to do except walk the decks and read from the captain's impressive library of books—something else he'd acquired in London for his mother and sister.

The *Fair Wind* reminded Krista of a small self-sufficient village on water, so avoiding a private audience with Gavin Duncan did not prove as difficult as she had at first feared. Eventually she began to relax. There was rarely a corridor or hatchway that did not have someone coming or going, nor was there a rail where the seamen were not close by seeing to one chore or another.

Unlike her first voyage, when she and Klaus were confined with the other passengers in small interior cabins, Krista had her run of the ship, aside from the men's quarters in the forecastle. Mornings, while Claire pretended to understand the charts over which the captain and his navigator pondered, she found her way to the sail and cordage room where she watched the sailmaker ply his craft, while other seamen repaired cord and rope for assorted uses on the ship. There were interesting exercises on the gun deck in the afternoon, which the captain laughingly justified as necessary for protection against the real pirates that plagued the seven seas.

The kitchen, however, became her favorite stop, for the cook was always anxious to get her opinion of one dish or another, or treat her to something fresh from the stone oven built into the forward main deck. Better yet, he possessed a fiddle with which he'd sometimes entertain the crew at night. When Krista told him of her interest in music, he insisted that she try her hand at the instrument. While he and his young helpers worked to make the best of the salted provisions to which they were now reduced, Krista sat on a nearby skylight and tried to sound out some of the tunes he was teaching her.

It was a glorious way to spend an afternoon, especially since the green waters of the Atlantic had given way to the intense blue ones of the Caribbean. The warmer weather no longer required her pelisse on deck, the sleeves of her dress more than sufficient to keep her warm. She'd have been tempted to roll them up, but for propriety's sake. It was bad enough that the length was a good eight inches too short. The shapely portion of her exposed leg drew more than one sly look from the men whom she found to be friendly and respectful, a result of the captain's strict discipline.

"Now that's soundin' more like it, missus," the cook called out to her as she finished a lively reel. "You got a knack for strings."

Krista beamed in delight of the approval and the applause of those seamen within earshot. She knew she'd played it too slow and stumbled here and there like any other beginner, but she loved the camaraderie she'd come to know in the last weeks. The sailors weren't much different from the trappers and hunters she'd worked with. They were down to earth folks who had learned to live in harmony and respect with nature. Oddly, she was more at ease with them than at the captain's table, where Claire decidedly reigned.

"Especially heart strings," a softly burred voice complimented, stepping around the barrels strapped to the forward mast. "Ye never cease to amaze me, lassie. Is there nothin' ye canna do?"

"Play the fiddle," Krista retorted in kind, her eyes as bright as the sky overhead. "But I'm learning right good, I suppose."

"I didn't think ye could get more lovely than that first night I saw ye in London, but with the breeze blowin' those golden curls about your face and the sun turnin' it pink as a bairn's behind, you're a sight to behold."

Krista turned to look out at the sun-bright ocean. Gavin's words were as enchanting as the day. But for their audience, it would be so easy to step into his arms and bask in a wholly different kind of warmth than that beating down on the deck of the ship. She could handle the charming Scot like this, indeed, even enjoy his company. In public she felt no threat.

"Did the captain say it was only another day before we reached Kingston?" she asked, a wistful note infecting her voice as she studied the horizon, blue on blue.

"Ye sound as though ye'd be disappointed, lassie."

Gavin leaned on the rail and studied Krista's profile—an oval face with high cheek bones which tapered to an impertinent chin. He'd studied it dozens of times without her knowing, sometimes when she wasn't even there. It haunted his mind at night and robbed him of sleep to think she was only a few yards away, warm and full of life.

At least she wasn't making a point of avoiding him now. She was becoming more at ease with him. They'd even shared conversations from time to time as they watched the endless waves roll past to an undermined destination. He'd told her about Joshua, although that subject often put her on guard. He knew she needed time to accept him, to learn to trust him again, but the waiting was sheer torment and the acceptance of her sudden withdrawals almost impossible.

Instinct told him she longed to be in his arms as much as he longed to hold her. He'd felt it, as if the male in him was somehow communicating with the female in her. It was a magnetic attraction far removed from logic, invisible, but nonetheless quite real. He'd seen it in captured stolen glances or outright contemplation from across a deck, too far away for him to press it and too many witnesses to his liking.

It beckoned even now. He moved closer and put his arm about her waist, entrapping her and the fiddle between him and the rail. Damnation, he was her husband. Surely there was no harm in such a small gesture of affection.

Krista stiffened instantly at the close contact.

" 'Tis nay harm to enjoy the beauty of this God's earth close to a friend, lassie," he chided gently.

At that moment, one of the watches shouted from his lookout to the poop deck, where the captain sat listening to his fair lady companion reading from a book of poetry they had been enjoying.

"Sail ahead!"

Krista made no effort to escape the confines of Gavin's arms. Instead she pointed at a speck on the horizon. "There, Gavin, look!"

It was not the first sail they'd spotted since leaving England. Sometimes, to idle away hours, he and the ladies would take up the crew's game of watching to see who might spot another ship first and guess how long it would take to come abreast of them.

"What colors?" the captain questioned in return.

"I would say two hours or so, ja?" Krista guessed.

Gavin squinted in the sunlight and leaned closer, until Krista's back rested against his chest. "Less," he observed matter-of-factly. "She's under full sail."

"She bears none, sir!"

"Course?"

"Straight for us!"

"Men to your stations! Set all sail for Jamaica!"

The order seemed to break the easy atmosphere that was common on the top deck into a scramble of activity. From the forward hatch, one man after another popped up while others made their way below to the gun deck forward of the officers' cabins. The riggings were literally crawling with them, each running up the ropes with a specific purpose as their captain escorted his lady companion down from the upper deck and approached the rail where Krista and Gavin observed the commotion.

"Trouble?" Gavin asked tersely.

Miers shook his head. "I have my doubts, but a cautious captain is a wise one. These are the home waters of some of the worst cutthroats on the sea and I'll not be caught unawares by any of them."

"You mean *pirates?*" Claire gasped in alarm.

"She's not flying her colors. Could be a coincidence or not. I'm just preparing in case there's a filibuster waiting at the bottom of her flag staff to shoot to the top just before she blows."

"Oh my God!" Claire swayed unsteadily against the captain, who caught her gallantly in his arms.

"There's no need to worry, madam," he assured her. "If they are pirates, they're in for a rude awakening. The *Fair Wind*'s crew is not just an ordinary group of sailors.

These men are battle-hardened and more than capable of repelling any attack. But first, we are going to try to outrun them. If they give chase, we'll know the cut of their cloth."

"In that case," Gavin told Krista, returning to their speculation, "I'll amend my guess to tomorrow morning, if at all."

Like everything else on the sea, the impending confrontation dragged out. Once his men were prepared, the captain abandoned the deck for supper in the dining room, leaving the first officer in charge, for the approaching ship was still far behind in the wake of the *Fair Wind,* even at sundown. Conversation centered on their pursuer and previous conflicts which the captain and his crew had survived.

As colorful and successful a picture as the captain and his officers painted, Krista was still ill at ease when she at last retired from the upper deck to her cabin. Claire, full of the good wine that accompanied the meal each night, fell asleep instantly upon striking her pillow, in spite of her earlier fretfulness. Krista, however, bolted upright in her bed and held her breath each time she heard a noise from the deck above, expecting the roar of a cannon at any moment.

Once, she was brought out of her bed by a loud commotion on the deck, followed by shouting. As she scrambled toward the companionway, her heart in her throat, she was relieved to meet Gavin Duncan on his way below.

"What was that?"

"I was on my way to tell ye, lassie," Gavin admitted, " 'Twas nothin' more than a pulley come loose from the riggin' and crashed to the deck. I thought to find Claire hysterical by now." He looked beyond Krista to the door she'd left ajar in her haste.

Feeling foolish, Krista returned to close it before it

swung against the bulkhead and awakened her peacefully sleeping friend. "Is the ship any closer?" she asked, turning back to Gavin in concern.

"Aye, a bit. She's smaller and faster, but, like the captain said at supper, she'll be in no hurry to overtake us till mornin'."

"So she is a pirate's vessel?" Krista shuddered involuntarily. A battle was frightening, no matter where it was fought, but at least on land, one could escape or run away. Here in the water, there was nowhere to retreat if the ship were sunk.

Gavin was tempted to lie, to tell her they weren't certain, but didn't. "Aye, lassie." He took her by the shoulders and pulled her to him, surrounding her with a comforting embrace in the dimly lit corridor. "But I'm certain Captain Miers and his men will surprise the lot, if they do catch up with us. The *Fair Wind* packs twelve three pounders from the war . . . kept them for protection, since American ships are on their own now against the likes of corsairs and such. The Royal Navy was a mighty protection our ships have learned to live without."

Krista rested her head against Gavin's chest, listening to the strong, reassuring beating of his heart. Standing in the middle of a companionway in his arms was far preferable to the lonely bunk she'd just abandoned. She wished that the moment might go on forever, just where it was. One man could not stop a shipload of cutthroats, but she had never felt safer.

"If they do attack," she murmured, "I'd like a gun. I'll fight them or do whatever I have to do to get home."

Gavin could hardly believe he was holding the woman, much less that she'd referred to Duncan Brae as home. "Ye needn't fret over that, lassie. There's not a man aboard who wouldn't fight to his last breath for ye. Ye've that effect on us."

Krista drew away and looked up into the shadows surrounding his face. "Even you?"

His lips brushed hers before she had a chance to consider drawing away, yet she remained close, waiting for his answer. Gavin pressed his forehead to hers, afraid of frightening her off and yet desperate to make some other contact. "I'd lay me doon and die for ye, lassie, this very minute."

He wanted to cry out, "For the love of God, believe me, Krista!" He ached to make her see the truth of his declaration. He wanted to make her forget everything wrong and make it all right for her. He wanted to love her, to worship her, to wipe away that fearful look that sometimes entered her eyes, all too quickly followed by distrust. Instead, he prepared, but did not want, to let her go.

To his astonishment, the girl didn't pull away at all. She leaned into him again, her arms returning the embrace that enfolded her. "Hold me, Gavin . . . until morning."

A floodtide of joy swept through him as he picked her up in his arms and stepped to the door of what he had begun to think was the loneliest place in the world. Pausing to try the worrisome latch, he was suddenly abashed as Krista said, "I only wish you to hold me. You can do that here."

Gavin's voice was taut as he answered. "Ye have to learn to trust me, hinny. Ye have my word, I'll hold ye to your heart's content, and nay more."

Instead of answering, Krista reached down and opened the latch for him. Without the small inside lamp lit, the cabin was pitch dark, yet Gavin eased the woman down on the bottom bunk with unerring accuracy. Over the weeks, he'd memorized every inch of the cubicle, fantasizing of this moment when Krista would finally let down that icy wall of distrust she'd built around her heart and, now that she was here in the flesh, he thought his own would give out.

Much as he longed to plunder her lips with the passion now churning in his loins, he only ventured a tender buss on her forehead and drew her to him. He forced himself to dwell on what he had, rather than what was yet denied him. Her scars were deep and he wanted to heal them, something that could not be done with passion, but with tenderness. Tenderness was what she was hungry for, what she craved. He'd given his word, no matter how his body screamed to throw fate to the wind and seek fulfillment in the soft one cautiously curling against him. And by all the gods, he would keep it . . . at least for the night.

Chapter Twenty-Four

The door to Gavin's cabin burst open, slamming against the bulkhead. "Gavin, Krista's gone! I've looked . . ." Claire blinked in the semi-darkness of the cabin as two figures bolted upright on the bottom bunk. "Oh my! I . . . I'll wait back in my cabin."

Gavin eased his hand off the hammer of the pistol he kept on the washstand beside his bed. For a moment he'd thought the pirates were upon them. He exhaled in relief as the girl who had slept peacefully in his arms climbed to her feet. In the small shaft of light coming in from the door Claire had left ajar in her hasty retreat, Krista was brushing down her gown self-consciously.

"I canna think why she's so shocked. Ye are my wife!"

"I wonder if the pirates are still giving us chase?"

Refusing to rise to his bait, Krista opened the door the rest of the way and peered up at the skylight overhead where the sun flooded in in its morning splendor. Her arms raised, one over her eyes, she was a sight to behold, enough to take his breath away. Her gown skimmed over her corseted figure, lace accentuating the swell of her breasts, presenting a fetching sillouette. Sunlight seemed to play in the wisps of hair that had come loose from her braid during the restless night she'd spent, creating the aura of a bedraggled halo.

Much as he longed to drag her back into the cabin and seize a taste of heaven, he leaned over and pulled on the boots he'd kicked off earlier. "I think I'll go topside and see what the situation is. Shall I have the cook send ye somethin' in the cabin, or will ye take your meal in the dining room?"

"I'll get something later." Instead of going on into the cabin she shared with Claire, Krista rested against the door frame, watching as Gavin ducked out of his own quarters. "I . . . thank you for last night."

Gavin took her hand to his lips. " 'Twas my pleasure, hinny."

Yet that was not enough for a man so long starved for the lady's attention. Taking her hand to his waist behind him, he bent down and kissed her tenderly on the lips. Krista neither moved toward or away from him as he dared to linger a bit longer than chastity permitted. When he drew away, he saw the corners of her mouth twitching in the beginnings of an embarrassed smile and his insides curled with renewed longing.

"I will be topside soon," she promised, opening the door beside her and stepping sideways into the aft cabin, the blue eyes he'd come to adore never leaving his face until she disappeared behind it.

"Well, it's about time!"

Krista shook herself from the afterglow of Gavin's kiss and looked at her roommate blankly.

"That you went to him, silly!" Claire rolled her eyes heavenward, that she had to explain.

"Ja," Krista recovered, her cheeks growing warm under her companion's wicked scrutiny. "It is foolish that we cannot at least be friends."

"Friends? I don't think that is what Gavin has in mind."

"But that is how it must be," Krista insisted stubbornly, starting to unbraid her hair to restore it to order. She couldn't let her heart or body overrule her mind. This time she would not simply go to Gavin, eager to be his wife because it was what was expected. Whether Claire agreed or not, didn't matter. Gavin knew her feelings and, after last night, appeared for the first time to be respecting them.

"Well, I hope that Jeremy will stop being the gentleman! Nearly five weeks at sea and he'd only kissed me six times!" the woman complained. "Although," she added, a sly smile spreading on her lips as she handed Krista a silver-handled hairbrush the captain had given them, "he did say he wanted to take me to his parents' plantation while the ship resupplies in Jamaica. I shouldn't mind a planter husband."

"What about Gavin?" Krista asked, shocked at Claire's admission.

"Oh, I owe so much to Gavin and you for taking me away from that horrible life. I suppose Gavin's always looked out for me. I used to call him my big brother."

Krista cut skeptical eyes at her companion.

"When I was little," Claire admitted peevishly. "And now he loves you and I do hate being a third party."

"You are really serious about the captain?" Krista inquired, wondering how such a fickle heart knew what it wanted as she brushed out the tangles in the silken cloak of hair hanging about her shoulders.

Women like Claire and Marta were beyond her comprehension. She was only capable of loving one man, not skipping from one to the next, changing husbands like changing dresses. The one she had given her heart to had betrayed her love and she wanted none other.

The question was, did she want him? For the sake of
the child, if for no other, their friendship was preferable.
So involved in her thoughts was she, that only when a
nearby explosion heralded the beginning of the impending battle, was she reminded of the pirates who had given
them chase. But Gavin had that effect on her, making her
feel uncommonly safe from the rest of the world. It was
only him that troubled her.

"Oh dear God, they're attacking," Claire whispered, as
if afraid the rogues might overhear her. She sprang from
the berth to the stern window seat and threw open the
casements. "I hope Jeremy gives them the royal devil!
Look!"

Just as she pointed to the starboard side of the ship, the
Fair Wind bellowed and shuddered, returning the fire.
Krista dropped her brush and grabbed her excited companion by the waist as the woman nearly lost her balance
and pitched into the sea.

"Dear God!" Claire wailed, staring at the floor as if
expecting it to suddenly sprout water. "They've hit us!"

"That was *our* fire!" Krista reprimanded impatiently.
However the sight of the other ship ship sheering off
infected her with equal fervor. "We've frightened them
away, I think!"

Without waiting for Claire to recover, Krista bounded
out of the cabin to the top deck. As she burst through the
hatchway, she charged into the broad chest of Gavin
Duncan, who was on his way down to see to the women.
The impact nearly sent the two of them sprawling, but for
Gavin's quick reflexes. Instead, he grasped the rail and
caught the startled woman by the arm, holding her tightly
until they were both stabilized.

" 'Tis naught to be afraid of yet, lassie," he assured her,
as she peeked around him at the retreating ship. "I was on
my way to put your mind to rest."

"Have we scared them right good?"

"We've just exchanged shot," Captain Miers explained from the poop where he watched the ship through a spyglass. "They'll be back."

The captain's prediction came from experience. Krista watched from the rail of the quarter deck, too fascinated by the disciplined frenzy of reloading the deck guns and fitting the riggings of the sails to worry with the tea and beaten biscuits the cabin steward brought up for Claire. While the pace seemed frantic, it was only in preparation for the next confrontation, which took place after the dishes were cleared and the women were sent to the cabin below for safety.

"She'll likely swing by and grapple us this time," the captain explained to them, his eyes dancing at the prospect of the fight and confirming Krista's original suspicion. While a gentleman on the outside, Captain Jeremy Miers was a bit of a pirate at heart, as were the men watching in anticipation from the gun ports, riggings, and rails.

From inside their cabin, Krista heard the thump of the hooks as the privateer laid claim to the schooner. In her lap was the blunderbuss the captain had given her, an ancient gun that had belonged to his grandfather. While she was only afforded one shot, he guaranteed she would clear a wide sweep with it. Not that he thought she'd need it.

Claire, while wanting no part of a gun, sat on her own berth armed with a pewter pitcher. Her delicate features were contorted in the worst way in an attempt to keep from becoming hysterical again. "Jeremy says we mustn't leave the cabin under any circumsta—"

Her companion's repetition of their instructions ended in a scream as the entire ship seemed to explode. It sounded and felt as if the freeboard of the ship had been

ripped away with the cannon fire, leaving the cabin alone
intact. Almost simultaneously, the vessel shuddered, expelling its own fire. Thor's thunder, they would both be
sunk. A lump of fear welled in Krista's throat as she too
began to repeat the captain's instructions in her mind.
Stay below. His men would be distracted with worry and
unable to fight wholeheartedly if the women were on the
deck.

Wholeheartedly was an understatement from the
shouts and yells echoing from the upper deck. Occasionally she caught a bit of Gavin's bellowing brogue and then
the resounding clash of steel. The pirates had undoubtedly boarded the ship and Claire was now at her side,
trembling hands around her paltry pewter defense.

"We're going to die."

Gone was the bravado she'd put on for the captain.
The woman was as white as death, as Krista didn't doubt
that she was as well. At least, it felt as if all the blood in
her body had abandoned her skin to rush her pounding
heart.

"That is not what the captain said," Krista repeated
with less conviction than she'd wanted to project.

A thud and scraping noise distracted her from the fray
above to the stained-glass window in the stern. Across its
sunlit pattern, she made out the shadow of a rope swinging precariously. Realizing instantly what was amiss, she
bolted to the window and flung it open. Just below her
were three men working their way up from the water's
surface, dripping wet with cutlasses in their yellowed
teeth. Finding only women defending the stern cabin, the
first to reach the level of the window removed the blade
and tipped it against his scarfed forehead in salute.

"Well, well, bonjour, ma bonne fille!"

Without hesitating, Krista brought the butt of the gun
down across the pirate's broken smile, sending him ca-

reening into the water below and taking the man below
him in the process. The third man, however, drew a pistol
from his belt and fired it. Krista ducked inside, shriveling
to the floor as the wood of the window casing splintered.
The man was up the rope before Krista could position her
gun, but as he swung into the room, Claire laid him out
cold with a loud clang of the pitcher. Between the two of
them, they heaved the unconscious pirate, who hung halfway across the sill, outside and into the swirling blue
water.

"Right good!" she complimented, turning with an encouraging smile to Claire, only to see the woman faint
dead away.

A second glance outside confirmed that some of the
Fair Wind's men were addressing the attempt to board at
the stern by cutting the ropes. With that threat seen to,
Krista hauled Claire into the corner of the window seat.
Stay below, she told herself again, as she contemplated
the door leading to the companionway.

Suddenly the door burst open and Gavin Duncan
charged in, face blackened with smoke and powder. His
lawn shirt was ripped and stained here and there with
blood—whose, it was impossible to tell—and his dark hair
had come unbound from his queue and fell wildly about
his face and neck.

"Are ye alright, hinny?" he shouted, taking up as he
saw the trumpet-shaped barrel of the gun Krista brandished at him.

Krista lowered it, nodding. The stench of the battle was
now permeating their room. "Claire fainted. How goes
the battle?"

"We've driven the blackguards back!" The ship shook
again with the thunder of its guns, forcing Gavin to brace
himself against the bulkhead. "But I heard some were
tryin' to enter the stern and . . ."

"We took care of them," Krista informed him smugly. A smile of relief lighted on her lips. "Are we badly damaged?"

"Some to the freeboards." Gavin glanced upward anxiously. "I'd best get back up."

Without waiting for Krista to acknowledge him, the big Scot sprang out of the cabin with an agility and speed uncommon to his build. Glancing at her still companion, Krista took up her gun and followed in his wake. The battle was over and Claire was safe and far from worried at the moment.

She emerged on deck and was shocked at the destruction, in spite of all she'd imagined below. The planking was splintered in many places and littered with the bodies of those who had not fared well in the fight. Ignoring the chaos around her, Krista grabbed a bucket of water from the barrel next to the aft pump and started seeing to the wounded.

One of the gunners who had taken time to explain the workings of his profession lay nearby, groaning and bleeding from a head wound. She immediately ripped the remains of his shirt off and started to wash away the blood with part of it. The other part, she used to bandage the wound, which had looked more serious at first. The man was just dazed, she realized gratefully.

Smoke still hung thick, so thick that Krista could barely make out the other ship. She could, however, feel the heat of the fire which was commanding the pirates' attention. Recalling the captain's reason for not wanting a woman on deck, she kept a low profile and continued with her self-appointed task, all the while keeping an eye on the poop deck where Gavin and Captain Miers stood by, oblivious to her presence. The number of bodies around them, clad in tattered rags, bloodied and filthy, were evidence that the battle had waged fierce on the quarter-deck as well as the top and main.

"They're making away, sir!" one of the mates shouted, drawing Krista's attention to where the pirates were frantically cutting the lines holding the two ships together.

"Lash her, lads!" the captain commanded.

Krista didn't realize what the captain was about until she saw the men spring to the riggings. Like monkeys, they leapt from one set of sails to the other, half hidden in the fog of smoke, and lashed the square sail yard of the pirate ship to the *Fair Wind*'s fore shrouds.

"Fire gundeck!"

Krista staggered as the guns on the lower level belched fiercely, shaking the deck out from under her feet. Her waterbucket rolled away from her as she grasped one of the skylights for support and looked up at the poop as though Captain Miers had lost his mind, tying the two vessels together! She'd thought the point was to get away, to outrun them!

With a loud shout, the crew of the *Fair Wind* poured over the side, joining those mates who had driven the pirates onto their own deck and nearly been stranded. Through the choking black fog that filled the air, Krista crawled toward the aft pump where she'd left her gun, fearful of the retaliation of the dread scourge of the sea. Her uncharacteristic height allowed her to peek over the roof of the deck house at the poop where the aggressive commander barked orders—orders which echoed from one end of the ship to the other and onto the privateer as well.

Suddenly the captain waved his spyglass over his head and pointed up in the air. "They've surrendered!" he shouted triumphantly.

A bloodied cutlass in hand, no doubt relieved from some unfortunate rogue who crossed him, Gavin Duncan whooped and danced a little jig over to the rail to get a better look at the white flag being hoisted on the burning ship, but yards from them. Krista might have chuckled, had she not been so disconcerted by all that was happening.

She started to look back to the pirate ship, where both pirates and seamen now fought a common enemy of fire, when she caught sight of one of the bodies behind Miers and Gavin, moving. To her horror, the bloodsoaked cutthroat eased a pistol out of the wide yellow sash at his waist and aimed it. Krista couldn't tell which of the men standing at the rail was in his sights, but it didn't matter. Lifting the blunderbuss to her shoulder, she rested it on the poop itself and fired.

The gun thundered, scattering shot, but Krista did not see whether or not she'd hit him. She thought the piece had backfired, the way it slammed into her shoulder with an impact that sent her reeling backward across the deck. As she stumbled frantically for footing, she heard a loud crack, like the splitting of a tree struck by lightning. She had no idea where it came from. All she knew was that Gavin was shouting at her and pointing overhead, his face blanched as he broke into a dead run and leapt off the poop to the top deck.

Her foot caught on something, or someone, and then she was falling backward. It was only then that she saw the reason for the Scot's sudden panic. The very sky itself was falling down around her—wood, canvas, and smoke. She had no time to feel any of the fear on Gavin's face, or anticipate the horror of her fate. For instead of the crushing weight of the tumbling mast, another pain assaulted her from behind, as if splitting her skull. Through its agonizing haze, she saw the sail floating down over her like a white blanket, but the result was a black and blissful numbness which neither pain, nor Gavin's anguished pleas to respond to him could penetrate.

The time it took to reach Kingston with the pirate ship in tow seemed an eternity to Gavin. With the pirates as prisoners, the crew of the *Fair Wind* was divided between the two ships. Holes of great proportion, where broadsides had been fired, gaped in the freeboards of both. To slow their progress even further, the foremast of the pirate vessel had been sheared off, as well as the topsails of the *Fair Wind,* which had fallen on his wife.

That she was alive at all was a miracle. The skylight and the rail had taken the brunt of the mast, so that, after tearing through sheets of canvas, he'd found Krista spared the crushing weight of the mast itself.

The ship's doctor sewed the small cut in the back of her head, pronounced her free of any broken limbs, and then informed them that there was little they could do, except to wait. Day and night, Gavin remained at her side, trying not to notice the deathlike pallor of her cheeks. He forced her to swallow broth and water, fearful that she'd die from lack of nourishment. As she had once done for him, he bathed her and lay at her side, although no fever accompanied her coma.

The moment the ship sailed into Kingston harbor four days later, he carried her off the gangway to a carriage which transported them to Lluidas Vale, home of the island's most prominent doctor. Doctor John, as John Quier was known to the islanders, insisted Gavin and Krista remain at his home, rather than have the lady suffer at the slave hospital of mortared field stone which he operated to keep the negro property of the plantation owners in good health. While the accommodations were much improved over the ship, Gavin was dismayed to find the doctor could do no more than the ship's physician had done.

"Time will tell," he advised the distraught Scot after examining Krista. "She's a healthy girl, but head wounds are unpredictable. It's doubtful we can sustain her nutrition levels indefinitely."

Instead of taking advantage of the doctor's hospitality, Gavin sat by the large bed upon which his wife slept and fed her a spoonful at a time of the jellied broth prepared by the cook, followed by spoons of water. He neither bathed nor shaved, not wanting to spare a moment from Krista, lest she regain consciousness only briefly and he miss the opportunity to tell her once again how much he loved her.

He did take meals at the bedside, although his appetite was far from adequate, and sent Claire into Kingston to find a seamstress for the clothing Krista and she would need for the trip home. Captain Miers gladly accompanied the woman at Gavin's request, but Gavin did not miss the grim exchange of glances between the two. It appeared that he was the only one who believed Krista would need them.

He refused to let their unspoken thoughts enter his head, not after they'd come through so many trials. He couldn't believe fate would play such a cruel trick on them after going out of its way to reunite them. The mast might have crushed her, but it didn't. Gavin took that as an omen. This was a test, a test he would not fail by giving up hope.

Nor would Krista. The strange limbo in which she drifted lightened from pain to a vague awareness of the presence of the man at her bedside. He spoke to her in terms of endearment, with an emotion that tore at her heartstrings and yet she could not respond. She heard the doctor tell this man that she might not live, that her darkness might claim her forever, but she would not have it. She had to live. The will was strong in her, although she could not fathom its reasoning. All she knew was that it was a necessity.

"For the love of God, Krista, come back to me," the man was saying. "I need ye, lassie."

She wanted to see him, this man with the resonant voice. He obviously cared a great deal for her, but she didn't know why. His hands were warm, sandwiching hers between them. His touch was gentle. Yet, he was in such pain . . . pain she somehow knew.

She longed to tell him that she heard him, that she was all right and would not leave. Sometimes the frustration was unbearable. If she could only squeeze his hand, ease his mind. She issued a mental command to her fingers, reaching for him.

"Krista?"

There! she thought, encouraged by the burst of hope in his voice, an excitement that had not been there before. A tiny twitch at the corners of her lips reflected her own joy. Concentrating, she tried again.

"My God, Krista, wake up, lassie! Doctor!"

His hands were gone and Krista knew a terrible disappointment. He shouldn't have let her go! She might sink back into that feelingless oblivion. "No!"

Gavin froze at the door of the bedroom and turned back toward the bed, Doctor Quier's name on the tip of his tongue. To his amazement, the hand he'd left was lifted, fingers stretching toward him. "Doctor, come hither quickly!"

He sent a rug flying across the polished mahogany floor of the plantation house as he bounded back to the bed and claimed it. "I'll nae leave ye, lassie. Just speak to me. Can ye squeeze my hand again? Come along, now, do it!" he encouraged gently before shouting in a bellow over his shoulder, "Doctor, where the devil are ye?"

The outburst so startled Krista that she opened her eyes and stared for the first time at the man who had not let her go. His size alone was enough to account for the intimidation she felt, but his roaring voice was unnerving. Instinctively, she tried to pull her hand away, as if fearing he might take his frustration out on her.

"Praise God, you're back, hinny! I . . . I . . ."

To her wonder, the man seemed to collapse. His broad shoulders folded inward and one giant hand covered his face, a stricken face. Such a strange reaction for a man as strong and stalwart as he. Krista touched his trouser leg lightly, no longer afraid, but before she could reassure him, another man burst into the room.

This man was not as bedraggled as the first, nor was he any more familiar. Older, with graying hair, he rushed up to the bed, a smile beaming on his face.

"Well, well! How are you feeling, Krista?"

Krista shrunk away from his touch when he reached for her head, her fingers somehow finding the hand of the one who had beckoned her from her netherworld. *Krista* . . . that was what her rescuer called her.

"Easy, lassie. This is your doctor. Ye took a nasty crack on the head," Gavin reassured her softly.

Such eyes, Krista thought. They kindled with a warmth she could feel. It was regenerative to one who had been without emotion for so long. This man wouldn't let anyone harm her, of this she was certain. What she didn't know was his identity.

"Your name . . ." she whispered, pausing to clear her throat. "Who are you?"

"Dinna jest, lassie." Even as he spoke, Gavin knew from the blank look she gave him that she made no jest. He sought out the doctor across from him in alarm.

"This is not unusual for such a blow as she took," the man announced matter-of-factly. "She's only just regained consciousness. Give the rest of her memory a chance to come back."

Krista remained still as the doctor unwrapped the bandage, which formed a gauze cap at the back of her head. It was tender to his touch, this blow she had evidently received. The odd thing was, she couldn't for the life of her recall how it happened. She could only recall the man on her right refusing to let her fade away. From what was even more of a mystery.

"Do you remember your name, girl?"

"Krista," Krista answered after some thought. "It's what you called me," she told Gavin, venturing a shy smile. He was a sight with his unshaven face and disheveled appearance, but even so, he was handsome—handsome and quite grave at the moment.

"What is your full name, hinny?"

Krista stared at him, her mind groping into a void she could not explain. "I asked you first."

"I'm called Gavin Duncan, hinny." Gavin took her hand to his lips and brushed her knuckles affectionately. "I'm your husband."

Krista caught her breath. *Her husband?* The shock registered with a numbing disbelief that showed on her face.

" 'Tis true, lassie, and I very nearly lost ye. Dinna ye ken naught of the pirates?"

Her husband, Krista's mind echoed again when the mention of pirates brought no recollection. The wonderful things he'd said to her were the sort a loving husband might say. It made sense. What didn't make sense was why she couldn't remember anything about him beyond that wonderful lifeline of a voice.

"Then I must be Krista Duncan?" It was more of a question than a statement, reflecting her confusion. Her eyes became glazed with frustration. "Why can't I remember?" she demanded of the doctor, as if he possessed some magic potion which would restore what she'd lost. It was unnerving to only recall a dream world and a voice. It was frightening. She struggled to sit up. "Why?"

She looked around the room for the first time. Nothing was familiar, including the nightdress she wore. Across the room, a dressing table with a large oval mirror revealed a wide-eyed ghost of a girl with hallowed cheeks and trembling lips. She put her hand to the high buttoned collar of her garment. Who was that girl?

"No," she cried out, shaking her head as Gavin tried to ease her back against the pillows. This wouldn't do at all. She wanted to go back. "I'm lost! I've lost myself!"

"Hush, lassie, you're not lost. You're here in Jamaica at the doctor's house with your husband."

"But I don't remember!"

"Here, Krista, drink this."

Krista froze as the doctor handed her a small cup containing a bitter smelling medication. She leaned into Gavin, tight-lipped. He was the only one she trusted. He was the only one who cared. Somehow she knew that.

It was only after Gavin took the cup and offered it to her that she accepted it. Tears spilling over her cheeks, she rested in the cradle of his arm and shuddered at the taste.

"Here, young lady. Chase it with a good canary."

Again she accepted the offering only when Gavin presented it to her. This time it was much more pleasant to the taste. Wine, she registered, not medication. Gavin eased her against her pillow and, still holding her hand, took a seat in the chair beside the bed.

"I'd suggest you get some rest yourself, Mr. Duncan," the doctor recommended. "Your wife might recall you better if you shaved and bathed."

Gavin never took his eyes from Krista's anxious gaze. "Aye, that I will, if ye'll send a servant up with some warm water."

"Perhaps if I might speak to you outside . . ." the doctor suggested when Gavin failed to rise to his hint to leave.

The Scot kissed Krista's hand again. "I'll be right back, hinny, I promise."

Reluctantly, Krista let go of the fingers she'd managed to clasp. She had no reason to believe otherwise. It was just that, of all her memories, he was the only tangible one from a vague and intangible world.

Gavin walked stiffly out of the room, closing the door behind him. "How long will this last?" he asked in exasperation.

The doctor shrugged. "Sometimes a few days, sometimes a few weeks . . . sometimes a lifetime."

Swearing under his breath, Gavin ran his fingers through perspiration damp hair, forcing it off his face.

"At least she's accepted you as her husband. I've seen women deny their spouses, actually fearing them. Right now, you're her only link with the past . . . the only one she trusts."

The irony of his predicament struck Gavin with a bitterness which gathered in the back of his throat. "Aye, *for now*," he agreed tersely. Life was indeed full of twists, twists beyond his ability to comprehend.

Chapter Twenty-Five

"You look simply lovely!" Claire Eaton complimented Krista as the girl turned in front of the mirror to admire the new dress her husband had bought her.

It was beautiful, Krista thought, and cool, considering the warm climate. Its caraco jacket was a deep rose taffeta picking up the tint of the roses on the lawn apron which covered the matching underskirt. It too sported a pleated linen ruffle, much like those which adorned the three quarter sleeves in layers and graced the neckline and jacket trim. A large bow accented the front at her bodice, which dipped low in the fashion of the day. Around her neck, she wore a simple ribbon choker.

"Now, let's try the hat."

Krista sat down at the dressing table obediently, leaving the placement to the friend who had so graciously outfitted her at Gavin's request. She had yet to become accustomed to the girl in the mirror. It was certainly she, whoever that was, which made it difficult to know how to act. Was she a merry person, a pensive one? She pursed her lips in thought as Claire placed the wide tambourine hat, likewise ruffled and adorned with pink and white plumes, on her head.

"Of course, it would look better if you'd let me do your coiffure properly.

Properly meant powder and the addition of someone else's hair to her own, which Krista refused. Stylish or not, it looked ridiculous to one, who, in view of the heat, chose to braid and loop it up off her neck.

"Gavin has chosen the loveliest room at the Devonshire for you. There's a balcony overlooking the street and harbor and its only a block or so away from the market! My word, I've never seen such a conglomeration of colors! There's not a column or rail without clusters of flowers and bright ribbons for the dancers. Can you imagine, dancing in the streets?"

Krista shook her head. She couldn't imagine dancing at all. She wasn't certain she knew how.

"Of course, Jeremy and his parents are coming in from their plantation to join us! You should see a sugar plantation! My word, I never dreamed it took so much work to make one lump of sugar . . . and the blacks. . . . Have you ever seen one before this trip?" Claire caught herself and grimaced as a familiar, painfully lost look met hers in the mirror. "Oh, I'm sorry, dear!" She hugged Krista apologetically. "The way I keep forgetting, one would think I was the one with amnesia!"

Claire was sweet, but often short of good sense or logical thought. Throughout the week, she'd flitted in and out with boxes upon boxes of clothing and accessories for both herself and Krista. Her captain, as she referred to Captain Miers, had much influence over the local seamstresses and was able to get them to drop everything in order to accommodate his passengers. Every woman who could wield a needle had been working on the orders.

It was all overwhelming for Krista. Everyone had been so kind to her over the last week, since she'd regained consciousness, especially her husband. He rarely left her side, unless she was with Claire. While she was entertaining, and sometimes made Krista laugh at the outrageous things she did to attain a look of perfection for her captain, Krista was glad when Gavin returned again. There was a certain peace in his presence she needed, at least until she felt more certain of herself.

When he'd announced that he'd made arrangements for them to spend the holiday in town, rather than impose on the doctor's hospitality further, she'd been disconcerted. A thousand doubts assaulted her. What if there was someone there who knew her and she didn't realize it? Was there something horrible in her past which had blocked out her memory, as the doctor's book suggested as a possible cause for her amnesia? With so many loving and considerate people surrounding her, she couldn't believe that was possible, yet it still troubled her.

"I want to get ye to myself, lassie," Gavin had told her one night as he tucked her in the large bed.

Krista wondered if that meant that from this point on he would share her bed, for, until now, he'd been sleeping on a small cot in their room. After all, he was her husband and she did so love to be held by him. The very thought made her warm and brought color to her pale cheeks.

Later, in spite of a canopy, it was the sun that warmed them as she rode next to Gavin Duncan in the open carriage he'd secured to transport them to the town. Krista hardly knew whether to admire the man, attractively clad in snug fawn trousers and a dark brown coat which set off the width of his shoulders and narrowness of his waist, or the fresh greenery that passed endlessly by them. After being caught in her curious scrutiny by her husband, however, she concentrated on the scenery, unaware of the deep blush which inflamed her neck and face and endeared her all the more to him.

Jamaica's rolling hills and winding roads were a panorama of nature, dotted here and there with wattle and daub shacks as well as elegant manors. Smoke rose from the sugar factories while black slaves peppered the fields of cane and loaded it on wagons to haul to the mills. Insects were as abundant as the greenery, which made the fan Krista fluttered in front of her face all the more useful in swatting the pests. It was all so strange, but nonetheless enchanting.

The sloping fields down to Kingston were divided into symmetrical squares by hedgerows. Beyond it lay the town itself, a spreading cluster of pastel brick and wood buildings at the deep blue water's edge. Streets ran parallel to the docks and warehouses. A random scatter of masts appeared painted on the sun-glazed water against a backdrop of blue hills across the protected cay.

"Duncan Brae slopes down to the Ohio like this, lassie, but I'll wager that at this very moment, instead of the sun glaring off green slopes, it's blinding bright on snow."

Yes, Krista thought. Perhaps that was why everything looked so odd. She was used to cold weather and snow. That would not have appeared so foreign to her at this time of year. "Tell me what it would look like."

Gavin chuckled and slipped his arm behind her casually. "What, the house?"

"All of it," Krista encouraged. He'd told her about their home, about their son, yet she never tired of hearing about them. Perhaps, if she heard it all enough times, she'd remember.

"Well now, the house needs a woman's touch. It's sparsely furnished and decorated, for all its size and grandeur."

"Why haven't I done that?"

"Because it's just been finished, so to speak . . . while you were away visiting your relatives in England."

Krista couldn't imagine leaving a child of hers alone or

abandoning her new home to visit Austrian relatives in England. It was all so bewildering, in spite of Gavin's logical explanations. Her cousin was a musician in England, but they'd gone there to visit Claire, the late wife of Gavin's brother and ward of the Duncan family, to settle the estate. Of course the death of a brother would merit such travel, but to leave their son! And why Claire had dropped her married name for her maiden name had no explanation except to verify the woman's inconsistency.

As they entered the settlement by the bay, they passed townhouses with inverted tray roofs and gaily clad balconies, exactly as Claire had described. Perhaps it was her sister-in-law's own excitement that began to infect her or the bustle of the streets themselves, but Krista began to feel the life of the city in her blood as she looked from side to side, not wanting to miss anything. She found herself pointing to this and that in a wonder, much like a child's, and squeezing the large hand which was entwined with her own with each thrill.

To give her an extra show, Gavin instructed the driver to take High Street. Although the docks were usually busy with the loading of cargo and the marketing of the street vendors, today there were costumed dancers frolicking about in bare feet on the sandy street. Small sloops loaded with produce anchored close to shore, obviously a main source of the fare on the stands and trays of singing vendors.

"Can we look?" Krista asked, turning bright eyes toward the man at her side.

"Ye mean get out and walk?"

"Ja, that would be right good!"

"Are ye up to it?"

The girl nodded eagerly and started to help herself out of the carriage before the driver even brought it to halt.

Gavin caught her arm and settled her back on the seat, a chiding expression on his face. However, after jumping down and turning to assist the ladies, it was replaced with a cock-eyed grin which instantly sparked a smile on Krista's lips.

She didn't wish to displease him. After all, he went out of his way to please her and she was grateful. But she did want to prove to him that a memory loss did not make an invalid. The last two days at the doctor's house, she had been eager to walk around and escape the bed in which she seemed to have been born—as long as it was with Gavin.

There were several stalls among which to browse when one wasn't caught up in watching the gaiety of the costumed dancers. One of the men closest to them was called Jaw Bone. Wearing a white painted mask and wig with long curls, he paraded around in a troupe of dancers, all of whom balanced small replicas of houses on their heads. The bright reds, yellows, blues, and greens of their clothing were as festive as their mood.

"Buy me pretty lady hat!" a mulatto woman called out, spotting Krista's fascination with a wide-brimmed hat woven of banana leaves. "Me putta on bootiful flowers, yes? Keep mal de soleil from soff cheek."

"Silkee pretty for lady, mastah!" another called out, vying for Gavin's attention.

"You're not going to buy that ridiculous hat, are you?" Claire exclaimed in horror upon seeing Krista removing the ruffled and plumed tambourine to try it on. "Why, you'd look like one of those field slaves!"

"But it keeps the sun out of my eyes," Krista pointed out practically. "We all need one!" She turned suddenly to her husband. "That is, if you agree, husband."

The sight of his wife staring up at him, eyes bluer than sapphire and cheeks a hot pink across the ridges from the sun-baked ride, was enough to make Gavin want to buy her the entire stock. He leaned down, unable to resist planting a kiss on the tip of her upturned nose, which also had suffered from the morning sun's exposure.

"We'll each take one," he announced to the woman. "You choose mine, lassie."

Krista chose one much like her own, but without the adornment of flowers. As she reached up and placed it on his head, she returned the small affection and then stepped back, as if she'd committed some crime. The truth was, she wanted more than just the affectionate busses he gave her. At first they were sweet and reassuring. Now they seemed to tease her, to make her wish for more. She may have lost her memory, but she had not lost her ability to long for the passionate attentions of the man she loved.

Gavin, however, disarmed her alarm. "Would I get another kiss, if I purchased you two hats?"

"You two look ridiculous!" Claire averred, turning away as if she didn't know them. "Next thing you know, she'll want to put one of those trays over her head and carry fruit!"

"Ye should talk, woman!" Gavin teased, pointing to the tall bouffant puff of silk Claire boasted, heaped with clusters of grapes, plumes and ribbons in violet to match her dress.

"You never had a civilized bone in your body!"

"That may be so, lassie, but . . ." Gavin's train of thought faded as he noticed Krista studying the bare black feet of the rotund saleswoman. Beneath the soft kid of her slippers, he could see her wriggling her toes in quiet speculation. "But a man only goes through life once and it doesn't pay to overlook the simplest pleasures."

Krista drew back, startled as her husband dropped to

his knees and gently lifted her hem. "What are you doing?"

"Treating you to the feel of warm sand between your toes."

"That settles it! I'm going on to the inn before I'm seen with the two of you!" With a sniff of disdain, Claire turned in a circle of chintz skirts and stomped back to the coach. "Shall I send the carriage back for you?"

"Oh, I dinna think so," Gavin decided, his face a picture of mischief which reminded Krista of a boy, rather than the man he was. She wondered if their son was a smaller version. Heavens, how could a mother forget her son?

"Now the stockings," her husband reminded her, banishing the brief melancholy that threatened so unexpectedly.

Krista sat on the edge of the cart loaded with baskets, hats, and trays woven from the leaves of the trees which grew along the beach further down from the docks and lifted her skirts so that Gavin might remove the gartered stockings she'd donned earlier. Although she was already warm, the touch of his fingers as they slid along the taper of her legs, baring them as he did so, made her grow even warmer. Without thinking, she snapped open her fan and waved it under her chin.

"You are cheating a stir, husband," she chided timidly.

Gavin looked around to see that the two of them had attracted considerable attention, not only from the vendors, but the patrons as well. " 'Tis you causin' the stir, hinny, and none other." And not only in the onlookers, Gavin thought with a surge of frustration over the sudden longing that leapt to life in his loins. It was becoming a familiar torture, but no less one. He tucked the stockings in the shoes and shoved them into his jacket pocket.

"Then you should too," Krista rebounded lightly.

"Take off that hot coat of yours and leave it here with the lady for safe keeping."

Gavin wondered at the wisdom of the enchanting waif swinging her bare feet back and forth playfully, but the invitation was more than he could resist in the tropical heat. If the shoes and jacket were gone when they returned for them, so be it.

"Here's a sum for your trouble," he told the grinning woman, "and there'll be an equal amount waiting for you at the Devonshire House if you'll take them back there for us this evening."

"You betcha, mastah. Me be dere 'bout sun'nown, plenty time for supper."

Looking the odd couple, Gavin and Krista started hand in hand for the edge of the settlement where the line of shacks gave way to beach. It was madness, but there was little sanity in his thoughts where Krista was concerned. He'd already arranged to have a special celebration supper later that evening for the Miers family in appreciation of their graciousness to Claire during Krista's recovery. The last thing he needed to do was overtire his wife. Yet, she looked anything but tired as she walked by his side, matching his stride with little effort.

In no time at all, they'd rounded the natural bend of the beach, beyond the fishermen's huts where nets were strewn for mending, and entered a private world of their own. The noise of the town and the playing children behind them, only the gentle lapping of the water on the sand broke the contented quiet of the spot.

"I wish I had trousers instead of these blasted petticoats and skirts," Krista sighed, breaking the prolonged silence. She lifted her dress to avoid wetting the hems and stepped into the shallow water. "It's so warm! Why, it's like a bath!"

"Aye, women's dress is not the most practical," Gavin

admitted, "but it is fetchin'." He leaned down to follow suit and roll up his trouser legs.

"Am I *fetchin'*, husband?" she mimicked.

"The most fetchin' woman I've ever laid eyes on . . . so bloody fetchin' I'm sorely tempted to ravish ye right here in the sand!"

Krista wasn't certain why she bolted, skirts lifted high, and splashed through the ankle deep water ahead of her husband. It was an instinctive reaction, as inexplicable as the laughter that sang from her lips. She sped past the forest of spindly pine that grew along the sandy beach and hopped over slabs of black rock jutting up from the white bed.

Although she didn't realize it, Gavin wrestled with the same quandary. He knew why he pursued her, but it confounded him that he held back, his hands a breath from her waist to catch her lest she fall. What he did not anticipate was the rock that caught the big toe of his right foot and sent him hurling forward with a pained yelp. Much as he intended to assist his tiring wife, it was he that was her undoing, for unwittingly he brought her down in the shallow water with him.

Squealing in astonishment, Krista struck the water face first, landing on her knees with Gavin's arms wrapped solidly about her waist. All around her, her skirts and petticoats billowed, clouds of lace and linen filled with air.

"Are you hurt?" she gasped, turning on her knees to see Gavin sitting back holding his foot, a terrible grimace contorting his handsome features into a comical mask. He looked so ridiculous, Krista heard herself giggle.

"There's nay blood, but it feels as if I've busted my blasted toe on this damnable rock-infested beach!"

"Let me see." Krista hauled her skirts out of her way and crawled toward him on her hands and knees, unknowingly presenting a scandalous view of the bosom to which her taffeta bodice now clung.

Gavin swallowed, forgetting the toe she pried out of his grasp to examine carefully. She rubbed it this way and that, until he thought his body would scream with the intensity of her innocent ministration. When she leaned down, however, to treat it to a medicinal kiss, he could no longer deny the urge to seize her in his arms and return it most heartily upon her lips.

If he expected resistance, he was disappointed, for instead of pulling away, Krista welcomed his attention with equal fervor. Her arms slipped around him, fingers spread on his back, kneading and edging him closer. Her lips were salty with the ocean water, but warm and yielding to the tongue with which he engaged in sensuous plunder. Her own was weakly defensive at first, but under his tutelage, became more aggressive, as did the hands that worked their way up his back to play havoc with his neck and ears.

He'd vowed not to take advantage of Krista's trust to satisfy his lust, but his willpower was not sufficient to stand up to the warm and willing body that pressed against him, as if suffering from the same feverish malady. When he forced himself away, to give reason a chance to deal with each of them, however, he was hardly prepared for the heartrending words that tore from Krista's chest.

"I feared you did not want me, husband. Had I done something wrong in the past?"

Gavin pulled her to him tightly. "Nay, hinny, nay," he whispered raggedly. "I feared I might cause ye hurt . . ."

"I am hurting now, husband. I feel only half a woman, half a wife, the way you treat me."

Krista pulled her head away from his chest and raised her uncertain gaze to his. She didn't want him thinking her wanton, yet that was exactly what his searing kiss had made her. She wondered, even as he rose, that she might find enough strength in her jellied knees to do the same.

Gavin saved her from finding the answer, for, bending over, he swept her up in his arms and carried her to the dry beach where he gently set her on her feet against the slope of a waving palm. Unable to speak for fear of breaking this magic spell that suddenly enveloped them, she watched as Gavin stripped off his wet shirt and spread it on the dry bladed grass.

The mere sight of his rippling sinew and lightly furred chest increased the already frantic pace of her blood. So strong, so manly, and yet, so gentle, she thought as he took her up in his arms and tenderly laid her down on the sand.

"Never think you're half a woman, lassie," he reprimanded gravely, lifting her skirts to find the fasten to the bulky petticoats she'd complained of earlier.

The bows gave way with a simple tug. The garments came down over her lips with ease, taking with them the drawers which had clung skinlike to her wet body. She did not see the hand that closed possessively over the golden tuft at the apex of her legs, but she felt its searching fingers and shivered when it found the sensitive bud of her femininity. Her eyes grew wider with the gasp of pleasure which was promptly sealed within by the demanding mouth that claimed her lips once more. And then they closed, so that she might savor this insane hunger that consumed them both until breath was taken in short gasping intakes, between the frantic exchange of kisses and caresses.

And when she thought she could bear no more of this delicious torment, the devilish fingers offered reprieve. They worked their way to her shoulders and under her dress, skimming the garment off to expose the satiny smoothness beneath to hot marauding lips. On they charged until her breasts, now taut and aching, were exposed to their heady mischief.

Krista writhed in the fiery throes of pleasure Gavin inflicted so masterfully, hardly able to keep her head sufficiently to return his favor. Each time she touched him, felt the coiled desire straining for release, her insides curled with the same, until she found herself tearing at the fastens of his trousers between them, her hand brushing the hard evidence of his anticipation, now swollen beneath the wet material.

Upon realizing her intent through the fog of passion that infected him as well, he raised himself sufficiently to allow her easier access. Her fingers shook as the flap came loose and she glanced up apprehensively, only to be assured by the fiery coals of longing burning in his gaze.

"Go on, lassie," he encouraged breathlessly.

Hands on either side of him, Krista shoved the pants down, unveiling his manhood in all its glory. As she tentatively touched it, Gavin fell against her, catching her hand between them.

"Mercy, hinny, I canna stand much of that."

Krista held his gaze as she withdrew her hand and slipped her legs around him in frank invitation. "Then love me, husband."

Needing no more prompting, Gavin claimed the warm, welcoming body beneath his. In spite of himself, he managed to be gentle at first, fearing she might not be as ready as she claimed. But as her limbs tightened about him and her hips thrust upward to receive him, he lost everything, but his ability to feel and respond. The volcanic fulfillment that shook them both and left them clinging to each other in the damp, breathless aftermath eventually led to a sweep of guilt for taking his pleasure so selfishly. He rolled to his back, drawing the half-clad woman on top of him.

If he had disappointed her, however, her smiling face did not betray it. "I love you, husband!" she sighed softly, planting elbows on his chest to look down at him. "That is the only thing I am sure of."

Gavin opened his mouth to reply, but she silenced him with a finger.

"Thank you for loving me."

Krista, real and beautiful, looking down at him, was more than Gavin could deal with. Astride his body, her legs entwined with his and her passion-ripe breasts grazing his chest, he could only mumble a lame, " 'Twas my pleasure, hinny."

Joy was something Gavin had learned to do without for so long, that he was overwhelmed. He wanted to laugh and cry at the same time. Krista . . . his Krista. This would surely be the most memorable Christmas he'd ever spent. The only thing that would improve it would be sharing it with Joshua, the little boy who had been as timid as his mother at first . . . until he learned to trust Gavin. But there was time for them, he told himself, pulling Krista down to kiss her again, to show how much he cherished her . . . a lifetime to be filled with love.

Carolers out in the streets heralded the Christmas season with song which drifted up to the second floor of the Black Rose. The night before, a more raucous revelry had shaken the panes in the windows as its masked members drew tokens, matched female to male, and meandered up to the upstairs rooms to finish their celebration in carnal delight. Those who did not participate watched through the peepholes strategically located in each room. The Christmas Queen, chosen by the male membership, walked about clad in evergreen ribbons, a halo of mistletoe inviting pleasure from any and all.

Above it all, Madame Rose reigned from her gilded chair on the balcony overlooking the gaming room. She neither smiled nor scowled, but looked on with indifference, as if she were tired of the wicked games of her invention. It was difficult to tell if her painted eyes were open or closed at times, but no one was overly concerned. Self-indulgence was the rule of the day, or night, as it were.

She had not been herself since being stabbed by the female companion of Lord Gavin Duncan. The knife had missed her vitals, but left her with a burning hatred that had manifested itself throughout London, which was why most of the members were relieved to hear that she was leaving the Black Rose to the society and retiring.

Daylight found her ready, bag and baggage for the coach headed for Billingsgate where a packet bound for Nova Scotia was anchored. The uniformed servant who accompanied her did not know her mission, but after depositing her at the gangway, he was much relieved to see his ex-mistress shuffle with her cane up the gangway. Whatever it was, it bode ill for someone, for in all the years he'd known the madame, he'd never seen her so obsessed that the society's amusements no longer interested her.

Chapter Twenty-Six

Their time in Jamaica was precious to Krista. Each new day brought sunshine and love, equally warm and intense. Her relationship with her husband was at last as it should have been, though she not only understood his reasons for withholding his desire, but loved him all the more for his thoughtfulness. The market, the new clothes and experiences, and the hours spent on isolated beaches made her feel giddy with childlike delight.

How she ever knew how to swim eluded her, but the water was so inviting, as was the man who coaxed her into it. At first she was mortified when her wet underclothing became translucent, showing all nature had given her to those whiskey-burning eyes of her husband. Then Gavin had stripped naked as the day he was born to reassure her there was no danger of being discovered in the isolated cay and she'd abandoned herself to the sun, the sea, and the man.

Then there were the nights, cooled by gentle trade-winds that blew in from the vine-covered balcony overlooking the harbor. Krista was beginning to think herself an obsessed woman, for even the slightest of Gavin's attentions—a wink, or an innocent touch of his hand—made her blush inside and out and sent her thoughts drifting wickedly to a later hour when they would once again be alone in their quaint room on the second floor. She often wondered how she could have forgotten such wild and rapturous loving between them, much less the man himself with his sinewy body—lean, eager, and hard to the touch. All she did know for certain was that she could not have loved him more than she did now.

It was entirely too soon that the *Fair Wind* was made fit from the battle damage and ready to proceed with her voyage to Philadelphia. A melancholy look on her face, Krista stood on the deck with Gavin at her back and basked in his closeness as they silently bade the blue-green island goodbye. Once they cleared the harbor, leaving behind ships of every description and origin, she focused on the sea ahead.

She mustn't look back. The advice that came to her uninvited made her wonder at its origin. Had someone once told her that? It wasn't Gavin, for he'd denied it upon being asked, but agreed that it was a sound counsel. It was advice they shared with the distraught Claire, who was devastated to hear on their last night in Kingston that her Jeremy was not going on to Philadelphia with them, but taking the pirate craft, refitted and renamed the *Dauntless*, to Charles Town where his wife and family abided.

"I shall never so much as look at another man again!" she sobbed, so often that her companions were growing immune to her outbursts. "Men are deceitful brigands who toy with a girl's heart and then pierce it with their treachery! Except Gavin," she admitted with a grudging look at Krista. "And *you* have him."

"I'll give her less than a week ashore and she'll find a replacement for Miers like that!" Gavin teased, snapping his finger in emphasis.

"Never!" Claire averred with a shudder. "Don't think

I haven't heard how uncultured and crude American men are. Perhaps a previous Loyalist," she speculated, the idea appealing to her fickle nature. "One still of means, of course," she added hastily. After all, she'd heard of the many Loyalists who remained behind being stripped of everything they owned.

"Dinna even think of it, lassie!" The sternness in Gavin's tone startled Krista into looking at her husband's face. "There's hard feelin's and bitterness that would not go well for ye, do ye ken? Even now, there are raids from the north led by displaced Tories and their heathen allies . . . as cruel, senseless, and bloody a works ye canna imagine."

"But what of Duncan Brae?" Krista asked in alarm, wondering that Gavin had left their son there.

"Dinna fear there, lassie. My men are fighters to a one, most of them served with me in the war. Besides, there's not been a local attack since year before last, so it's been dyin' doon. The cowards are sticking closer to their northern borders and camps."

"I should simply die if I saw a savage," Claire exclaimed, "I just know it!"

"Well now, there's friendly ones, lassie."

"How can you tell if their friendly?"

"They don't shoot at us."

Krista nearly choked, for Gavin was at his worst again and poor Claire was clearly being had. "You can tell by the make of their clothes, the beadwork and trim, their arrows . . ." She broke off and glanced at Gavin in surprise. Her fingers flew to her lips, as if she were checking to see that they were the ones who had spoken so authoritatively. Another part of her past coming back? she wondered, bemused.

"You were fluent in the Lenape language and knew them well. In fact, you were our guide."

"Her?" Claire stared at Krista as if she'd grown horns. "How could you associate with savages?" Pale blue eyes narrowed at the man beside Krista. "You're teasing us both now, aren't you?"

"Nay, lassie. Krista was . . . is quite a lady," Gavin complimented, tugging his wife closer so that she fit into the cradle formed by his back and arms.

Krista's gaze sparkled brightly as she looked up at him over her shoulder. "Perhaps if I see this land again, I'll remember."

"Aye," Gavin agreed, hoping his reluctance didn't show. If she never remembered it would be all right with him. She was everything and all he wanted and the prospect of her memory returning was threatening to the relationship they had built between them. "But I will warn ye, ye'd best enjoy the luxury of the trip and Philadelphia, for the travel west is nae as comfortable as that which we've experienced thus far."

Claire blanched with incredulity. "Not as comfortable? My word, Gavin, I've been deathly seasick, assaulted by murderous pirates, led the merry way by a smooth-talking lothario, and now you tell me it's going to get worse?"

Gavin patted the distraught woman on the shoulder. "I shall do my best to see you both as comfortable as my means will allow," he promised somberly, although, from the mischievous twinkle in his eye, Krista could only guess at what was in store.

Her husband's means, Krista found out upon arrival in Philadelphia, were considerable, at least where luxury could be had. For three days, they occupied a room in one of the city's finest inns and dined at others recommended to them. A dance commemorating Valentine's Day gave her the chance to wear the only ballgown her husband had ordered. A beautiful shade of turquoise with pink flowered garlands draped from a sashed waist around the skirt and over both shoulders, the gown made her the belle of the ball, although Krista vowed the attention she received was because of her uncommon height and due to neither her latest fashion, nor the beauty he declared she possessed.

As much as she enjoyed being with Gavin, however, and moving around the dance floor to his slightest touch, she was relieved when the night was done and they retired to their room. It was hard to explain the fear growing in her chest, when she couldn't fathom it herself. But the closer they came to returning to their home and son, the more uneasy she grew.

By day, her husband managed to distract her with the purchase and ordering of furniture for their new home. Here Claire was in her glory, as she offered her expertise. Until then it had never occurred to Krista that she would be running a manor house, something which she had no idea how to do.

"I shall teach you, dear," her companion offered magnanimously, after spending what Krista thought a fortune.

As they prepared to leave, the new items were crated and placed on wagons lined up to go to Pittsburgh. There were two hundred pack horses in the train with gay collars and stuffed bells proclaiming their individual personalities. It amazed Krista that only two men were required for every fifteen animals. According to the pack master, they were loaded with salt, nails, tea, pewter plates, and any other provision which might fill the needs of the families on the western frontier.

Behind them was a line of Conestoga wagons, part of the group with which Gavin had arranged for their travel. Their bright blue bodies, which reminded her of a canoe on wheels, were curved to keep the freight from shifting too far as it crossed the mountains between Philadelphia and Pittsburgh. The bright red sideboards she likened to a circus wagon, although, again, she was at a loss to recall where she had seen either a canoe or a such a wagon. Covered with a white hempen cloth tied down at the sides and end, it was said they could carry four to six tons in weight.

"I can not believe he expects us to crawl up into that thing and ride over hill and dale!" Claire complained, drawing Krista's attention from the beautiful matched team of dapple grays, which was no less adorned with gay color and ribbons than their counterparts ahead. "Where is Gavin anyway?"

Krista glanced around the mass of confusion as the drivers checked the lines and harnesses of their teams. Toward the rear of the train, she spied Gavin monitoring the loading of their trunks and furniture. He'd asked them to remain at the line office where crude benches would afford them seats until it was time to board their wagon. A smile instantly flashed on Krista's lips. The very sight of her husband made it happen every time, especially when he . . .

Her intimate train of thought vanished at the appearance of a little boy who came barreling around a wagon, shouting and waving at Gavin. Surprised, Gavin turned in time to catch the youngster as he leapt into the Scot's arms. A weak feeling washed over Krista as she took in the child's reddish brown hair peeking out from under a fur cap much like some of the drivers wore pulled down over their ears to keep the winter air from biting too harshly. Trailing behind, a man wearing buckskins and a buffalo vest stepped up to Gavin and hugged him as enthusiastically as the youngster before stepping back and gesturing wildly toward the west.

Then Gavin's gaze found hers and she knew for certain the identity of the boy in his arms. It was her son. A hundred questions all raced to Krista's mind, creating naught but confusion in the midst of her shock. Her son! In her private moments she'd wondered what she would say to him, how she might explain why she didn't remember him, but none of those words were retrievable as the distance closed between them and she glimpsed for the first time those wide blue eyes Gavin swore were hers.

The child wasn't smiling by the time they reached the plank walk surrounding the freight office. Instead, he looked at Krista curiously, as if expecting her to do something. What that was was beyond her. It was all she could do to remain standing.

Her child. God in heaven, why didn't he look familiar? Her chin shook, the only sign of the anguish that surged in her heart. Helpless, she shifted her gaze to the only source of assurance she could depend upon . . . Gavin.

"Lassie, I've a fine surprise for ye, as 'twas for me. *This,*" he said, poking the child playfully in the stomach, "is our son, Joshua. Joshua, say hello to your mother." Gavin put the boy down and straightened his coat.

"Heavens, he's Gavin's image, but for the eyes!" Claire exclaimed beside her.

"Pleased to meet you, Mother."

Krista took the small gloved hand extended to her. "And I you, Joshua," she managed nervously. "You are such a pretty child!"

"I'm handsome like my papa, not pretty," the boy corrected indignantly. "You're pretty."

"Ah, the boy has his father's taste in women," Gavin teased, enveloping both Krista and the boy in his arms. "I'm so happy I could shout clear to Pittsburgh!" To Krista's astonishment, her husband did whoop, her son chiming in. Her ears were still ringing when she was released. "This busybody Frenchman saw fit to travel cross mountain and valley to meet us. They arrived yesterday and only found us this morning."

"We camped, Papa, and hunted our food! I even made biscuits over the fire!"

"It is not for you to brag so," the young man who accompanied the child chided sternly. "Although the presence of such lovely ladies is an inspiration to the heart."

Reminded of his manners, Gavin spoke up hastily. "Excuse me, ladies. This is Jean Luc DeMotte, Joshua's . . . er . . ."

"Nanny," the young man finished with an unabashed smile.

"Jean Luc, this is my wife, Krista . . ."

"I have most looked forward to a . . . to meeting you, madame. The captain's letter was a joy to my heart to read. Imagine him finding you across the sea after fate had so cruelly separated you. It is the meat of which romances are written."

"Meat, indeed! It is the *stuff* of which romances are written," Claire informed him, a singular brow raised in disapproval of his buckskin-clad figure. "They do have clothing made from something other than animal fur in Pittsburgh, don't they?" Her pale eyes raked up and down the tall slender figure. "And razors?"

"To be certain, madame, but I shall fare warmer than you, I reckon, before this journey is out. Being the gentleman I am, however, I shall be honored to lend you my coat."

Were it not for her own quandary, Krista might have laughed at the mixture of indignation and bemusement on Claire's face. It was clear the woman was not certain whether she had been complimented or insulted.

"I would not presume to accept such an offer. The

stench of its previous owner has not yet left it. My word, I do hope *you've* not been teaching this child English!"

"Jean Luc, this is my . . . ward," Gavin announced wryly. "And wife of my late brother. She has a lot to learn about the frontier, having been raised among London's elite."

"They do not teach manners there?" Jean Luc asked, his dark brown eyes widening in feigned innocence.

"We are taught not to mingle with the . . . the hired labor." Claire turned to Krista. "You must hire another nurse, a real one with some degree of culture and education."

"No!" Joshua objected. "Jean Luc is my best friend, isn't he, Papa? He taught me to hunt and fish and I can swear in three languages!"

"Three?" Gavin inquired.

The boy nodded proudly. "English, French, and Lenape. I've been listening real hard to Red Deer an' Tucker says I'm sharp as Miss Tuck's tongue!"

"The housekeeper," Gavin provided, upon catching the question in Krista's glance. "My overseer's wife."

"You taught the child to swear?" Claire demanded, appalled.

"Non, madame, that he learned for himself. He is as smart as the overseer does say." With a perfectly mischievous wink, Jean Luc turned away from the gaping woman. "It looks as if we are ready to leave. I brought your horse as well . . . unless you wish to ride in the wagon with the ladies."

Gavin grinned. "I hope you've brought liniment too. I've not been astride a horse in months!"

"Joshua!" Krista bit her lip as the child, who had started to race toward their wagon, halted and turned back to her. "You must talk to me in the Indian language. Perhaps it will help me remember."

Krista's heart seemed to swell with relief at the wide snaggletoothed smile that blossomed on the boy's lips. "Sure!" As if he'd had second thoughts, Joshua ran back to Krista and threw his small arms around her in a tight hug. "I reckon I got the prettiest mama in the whole country!" he exclaimed. "An' if you're half as smart as me, you'll pick it up in no time a'tall!"

"Oh my word, his English is atrocious!"

"It sounds right good to me," Krista vowed, turning into Gavin's arms as Joshua bolted off again. His expression told her what she already felt in her heart. It was going to be all right.

The ride across the mountains was rough and the inns that were interspersed at timely intervals afforded them sparse shelter for the cold nights compared to that which they'd become accustomed to. Yet, the ordinaries, often without a separate accommodation for the ladies and boasting dirt flooring rather than plank, were a great relief from the jostling, bruising ride inside the Conestoga. No amount of blankets purchased along the way could provide sufficient cushion or warmth to stifle Claire's chronic complaints.

Krista felt sympathy for the woman. She had seen the luxury to which Claire was accustomed. Indeed, she knew it herself and frequently wished for a coach, rather than the heavy wheeled wagon. Krista, however, was the sort who was happy anywhere, as long as she was with the man she loved and the son she was coming to know. Her bruises were carefully examined and tenderly treated by Gavin whenever there was a private moment to be had, although those times were scarce.

Claire did not have that advantage. She'd been hurt and seemed bent on taking it out on the unwary Frenchman who continually asked for her comfort and usually was blamed for her lack of it—as if he represented this new hell she'd been sentenced to. After several days of this, Krista began to suspect that Jean Luc's provocations were not so innocent as they seemed, especially when she caught Gavin and her son exchanging grins as Claire launched into a tirade denouncing them all as heathens, while the Frenchman simultaneously admired with equal fervor the wild and untamed beauty of her angry expressions.

While Joshua seemed amused at his Aunt Claire's adversity, he was equally concerned for Krista's. His English was not all it should have been, Krista knew, but neither was her own. His manners, however, were as gallant as the most noble of men. He outdid his father in seeing to her welfare. Did she need to stretch her legs? Was she warm enough?

One afternoon, he'd even given up riding his spotted horse to cuddle up in a blanket with her and tell her about Duncan Brae until his eyelids became heavy with sleep. At that moment, with Joshua in her arms, that empty void that had caused her untold worry vanished, replaced by a fulfillment that, while decidedly different, was as ancient and natural as the one his father had introduced her to. She was a mother, holding her sleeping and contented child.

Some nights Joshua slept on a tavern floor between her and Gavin on the coarse mattresses and blankets provided by the Regulars or teamsters, although sleep was hardly possible, surrounded by the burly and rugged men who snored above Claire's sighs of exasperation and disdain. Other nights, the boy favored Jean Luc with his company, so as not to hurt his friend's feelings.

Krista imagined Jean Luc was glad to lie down, regardless of who slept next to him. Gallant to a fault, in spite of the hard time he gave Claire, the young man did, however, take pains to plant himself between the woman and the other guests, just as Gavin did with Krista on the opposite side of their small entourage.

It was always late when they arrived at the taverns and inns, spaced in eighteen to twenty mile stretches along rutted roads. There, they mechanically ate a frugal supper before retiring. Then, a scant five hours later, they had to be up and moving again, usually by the light of a horn lantern or a farthing candle. It was no wonder her son sought Krista's comfortable lap more and more as they neared Pittsburgh.

The frontier settlement was a welcome respite from the journey, although it could not compare to Philadelphia. Nonetheless, Gavin was able to secure private rooms for them, heated with shallow hearths which cast glorious heat into the winter chilled rooms. That, as well as the hot meals and good beer and wine managed to restore even Claire's humor. Invited to the wedding of the innkeeper's daughter, she insisted on unpacking one of her gowns for the occasion, shining like a twinkling jewel against the homespun dresses of the other guests.

"Mon dieu, I can not believe my eyes!" Jean Luc sputtered, hurrying to brush away the droplets of beer spattered on his worn coat as the women descended from the upstairs room in their finery.

Gavin Duncan said nothing, but his sentiments were no less impassioned. Lovely beyond words, his wife shyly walked behind her more glamorously attired companion on Joshua's arm. Instead of silk and lace, Krista had chosen a vermilion dress, its overskirt and bodice fashionably trimmed with piping which matched its contrasting underskirt. Her braid crowned her head in a plain, practical, and unfashionable style, but its effect was as regal as her carriage.

In spite of the intimate afternoon they'd spent together while Joshua napped in Jean Luc's room next door, it was tempting to spirit her back up the steps to the first real privacy they'd shared since leaving Philadelphia. If not for Joshua's excitement over escorting his mother to the affair, he wouldn't hesitate. As it was, Gavin couldn't bring himself to disappoint the child who stared up at Krista with adoring eyes. Like himself, the boy had fallen in love with her. Something about her quiet, shy manner and vulnerability aroused a protective instinct in the best and least of men, gently commanding adoration and respect.

Jean Luc recovered first, seizing the hand Claire extended to accept her due. "Mesdames, you are both robbing me of my breath, such is your beauty!"

"You!"

Gavin nearly choked with amusement at Claire's shock as she realized the identity of the freshly washed and attired, not to mention clean shaven, man who claimed her hand.

"I can't believe it! She's actually going to dance with him!" Krista remarked in surprise at Gavin's elbow.

"Only because she has na recovered from the shock. Somewhere between a *do si do* and a swing, he's likely to ken the sting of her palm, if not that sharp tongue of hers."

"Gavin Duncan! How unkind!" Krista glanced back at the couple as they took their places at the end of a group lined up for a reel. "I think he's right handsome and charming."

Gavin slipped his arm around Krista's waist. "Are ye tellin' me I've cause to be jealous, hinny?" If every lamp and candle was extinguished in the room, Krista's eyes would deny the darkness itself.

"Not of Jean Luc, husband," she replied, her lashes dipping in a fashion that tripped his pulses and sent them staggering forward at an increased pace. Gavin's gaze dropped to her cherry lips, now pursed, half teasing, half smiling.

"Mama, would you like to dance? I know that one."

"Here is your competition, husband." Now a full smile blossomed on them and Krista's face deepened to a similar coloring as she turned to the little gallant awaiting her answer. "I would be right delighted, Joshua, but I am not sure that I know . . ."

"I'll teach you!" the lad offered eagerly. "It's *right* easy."

Joshua's inadvertent use of her expression brought a startled look to the wide blue eyes that sought Gavin out. Suddenly they both laughed and fell into each other's arms, dragging in the boy with them.

"Papa, if we don't hurry, the song'll be over!"

Gavin bussed Krista on the lips, in spite of his son's protest and the curious looks cast their way. "I'll deal with you later, woman!" he threatened facetiously, turning her over to his son.

As she was dragged off, Krista looked over her shoulder and chuckled. "I can't wait, husband!"

Gavin grinned, so full of happiness that all the liquor in the keg against the wall couldn't make him higher. Hers were his sentiments exactly.

Chapter Twenty-Seven

The snow falling noiselessly on the landscape gave the two-story brick home on the knoll above the river a majestic cloak of ermine ice. Footprints, which were beginning to be filled, led from the house to the large Swiss barn built into yet another hill in the back. At first glance, they were the only sign of life about Duncan Brae, those and a few discernible tracks which led south along the river toward Fort Massac.

From the master bedroom window, Krista stared out at the serene morning, hurriedly braiding her hair. Gavin always wanted it down. Sometimes, like last night, he tugged off the ribbon when she was asleep and spread her hair on the pillow, just so he could look at it. He enjoyed watching her sleep, he told her when she awakened to his tender, teasing kisses, but he took even greater pleasure waking her up.

Krista sighed dreamily. It was a lovely way to greet the day, she had to admit, even if it had taken more time than she had to spare to brush the tangles out of her hair and restore it to order. Now, however, she had company coming and could not leave the preparations for their belated holiday celebration completely to Gavin's housekeeper.

After all, she'd had two weeks to adjust to the new

home and recover from the bone-chilling trip down the
Ohio by keelboat. Poor Claire had sneezed and sniffled
for the first two days on the water before relenting to don
the buckskins Gavin had purchased at Pittsburgh. Crossing the mountains had been cold, but the wind fairly
carried them down river, biting fiercely through their
cloaks and wearing down her resistance. The only advantage to the weather was that it had speeded their trip.

Dressed like men, Krista and Claire had huddled inside
the long narrow cabin of the keelboat, seated on the crates
and sacks being carried down river, and waited anxiously
for nightfall, all the while peeking hopefully through the
hide-covered windows for sign of a settlement where they
might lay over for the night and enjoy a hearthfire and
warm food. Such accommodations, when available, made
them appreciate their cross country travel in Conestoga
comfort even more. At least taverns and inns could be
counted on with more regularity.

Then they'd rounded a bend on a frosty bright morning, two hours away from the last river town, only to be
hauled out on the cold windy deck by Gavin Duncan and
his son. Following his pointed arm with her gaze, Krista
saw Duncan Brae for the first time—a piece of civilization
cut out in the wild, surrounded by nature's landscape and
glittering with its snow-capped roof like a fairy castle
against the sky.

Indeed, she felt like a princess. As the boat was brought
up to a small landing at the foot of the sloping hill, a
carriage burst over the crest and headed for them, its
prancing chestnuts heralding their approach with brass
harness bells. By the time Gavin lifted Krista onto land,
the spry coachman pulled up the horses and leapt to the
ground before the vehicle came to a complete stop.

"By thunder, Mary's been watchin' that river bend
every mornin' for the last week for you folks."

"Tull," Gavin greeted the man, shaking his hand first and then suffering a bearlike hug from his overseer.

"An' where's that half grown scamp o' yours?"

"Over here, Tull!"

Joshua waved from the back of the keelboat where he'd helped the oarsman bring in the boat. The man called Tull returned the gesture, but his sharp gray eyes shifted even as he did so to Krista.

"Well, I be hornswaggled and dipped in tar, if it ain't Miss Krista herself! Couldn't believe my ears when Frenchie read that letter sayin' you'd found her."

Krista's ribs still ached from the enthusiastic hug the hardy frontiersman had given her and her ears still rang with the stories he began to tell Joshua, who had by then joined them, about what a top notch guide and frontier-woman his mother was. If Gavin hadn't stopped him, Tull Crockett would have joined them inside the coach and kept right on talking. As it was, Claire, who had gone unnoticed until that point, was ushered inside and Gavin escorted them to the house while his son and men saw to the unloading of the supplies and furniture.

He'd carried her into the great hall, empty but for the winding staircase which climbed to a landing over a shorter back door, and set her down before Duncan Brae's sturdy housekeeper, who came charging at them with equally hearty hugs of welcome and was later introduced as Mrs. Tùll Crockett.

"There's no denying that boy with those blue eyes of yours," she declared upon releasing Krista.

"Why would I deny my child?"

Krista never received her answer to the peculiar statement, for Gavin immediately put Claire under the housekeeper's care and proceeded to tend to his wife personally.

"My wife's taken a chill on this trip and I'll be seein' to her comfort before I resume office as laird of the house," he announced over his shoulder as he took the steps two at a time with her gathered in his arms. "We're not to be disturbed."

Krista's cheeks grew warm at the memory. Naturally, she'd protested when Gavin kicked shut the door to the bedroom behind him, cutting off Mrs. Crockett's amused snicker, and dropped her unceremoniously on the bed with an ominous, "Alone at last!"

His grin was like a boy's but the smoldering look in his eyes was anything but. While he built a fire in the hearth, she'd watched contentedly from her perch on the large pencil post bed close by, a plain piece which matched the only other furniture in the room—a washstand with bowl and pitcher. What had she done to deserve such a man as this?

Gavin soon stood before her as nature intended, eager to kindle quite a different fire as he began to relieve her of her garments.

Krista ran her hand over the quilts of the freshly made bed dreamily, her body remembering the fiery touch of his devilish work. Then and there, he'd taken her. Cradled by the featherbed beneath her and covered with the hard male body of her lover, she'd been oblivious to the cold. The frenzy to strip and burrow beneath the quilts, flesh against flesh, had ignited the volatile desire which had been denied them for so long, so that she found herself as eager as he for fulfillment.

As she had been more than once on the river journey, she was again caught up in a wild current, but this time, it was the bed that was jolting and thrashing like the boat speeding through the rapids. The clashing of their bodies, the rushing sound of their blood coursing through their veins, the dampness that slickened their skin with heat rather than cold water spray made it impossible for her to think of anything but the pleasure which rocked her in a giddy state of consciousness.

It wasn't until she heard Gavin whispering raggedly against her neck, "Welcome home, Mrs. Duncan," that she knew he too had spent his passion. The slur of his accent betrayed the fact that the same druglike lethargy assaulted them both. What started out as just a moment to close her eyes, evolved into awakening hours later, alone in the cozy featherbed, which only added to her homecoming embarrassment.

Just as she had overslept that morning, she thought, coming back to the present in a contented mood tinged with melancholy. She slipped off the bed and tossed her hairbrush on the washstand. But this time her husband was not downstairs. He'd been summoned the day before to Massac by a tall and wiry mountainman who claimed to be her uncle. Gavin had, however, promised to return by nightfall today for the belated Christmas dinner Mrs. Crockett was preparing. Once again, before her uncle could say much about the circumstances of their marriage, much less her family, Gavin changed the subject and hurried away with the man.

Well, she would have answers when the men returned, she decided, a frown creasing her smooth brow. Wonderful as he was, there was something Gavin was hiding from her. All she could hope was that it was not something terrible she had done. Yet, the way it was being kept secret, she could not help but fret.

Krista brushed her woolen day dress down over her petticoats and abandoned the sparsely furnished master bedroom for the walnut staircase leading to the first floor. The smell of frying bacon grew stronger as she made her way to the kitchen in the back, through rooms mostly furnished with the still crated pieces they'd brought from Philadelphia. While Mary Crockett worked at the large

hearth, Joshua and Jean Luc attacked a stack of buck-
wheat cakes with equal vigor. Tull had accompanied
Gavin and Kurt Waltari to Massac, leaving Duncan Brae
to the two at the table.

At the sight of his mother, the boy leapt to his feet and
ran over to hug her. "We were extra quiet this morning,
so we wouldn't wake you and Aunt Claire!" he announced in a voice loud enough to jolt the other woman
out of a sound sleep, if she was still in bed. "Ma Mary said
you'd best get your sleep while Papa's away."

"Joshua!" Jean Luc reprimanded, shoving a jar of molasses at the boy. "You need more molasses."

"You said I used too much awhile ago!" the boy objected crossly.

"Well, I was wrong. Now *eat!*"

It seemed that the scarlet flushed Jean Luc and Krista
were the only two chagrined at the boy's slip, for Mary
Crockett's wide shoulders were quivering with amusement. "How many cakes for you, missus?"

"One will be right good," Krista answered, not wanting even that after seeing Joshua's plate swimming with
thick molasses over a diminishing island of hotcakes.

"Bacon?"

"No . . . thank you," Krista added, walking over to the
coffee pot sitting on a trivet near the glowing coals of the
hearth. She poured herself a cup and carried it back to the
table.

Her husband had no shame when it came to spiriting
her off to their bedroom. It was his right and he saw no
reason for her embarrassment that they shared the natural relationship afforded a husband and wife. Nonetheless, Krista could not help it. In fact, she wasn't sure that
Gavin wasn't indiscreet on purpose. He admitted that he
delighted in seeing her blush.

"I've got my own hammer and bar," Joshua informed

her proudly, "so I can help Papa take the crates off the furniture this afternoon. It'll be just like Christmas."

Krista spread a little honey and butter on the hotcake Mary put before her. "It will be fun to see what the furniture will look like. The rooms are so empty."

"Hah, those rugs you brought has made a world of difference," Mary piped up from the hearth. "At least a body can walk through a room now without it echoin' all through the house."

"Gavin says the house wasn't finished when we were separated. Why don't we have furnishings from our other home?" Krista thought aloud.

"You didn't have one."

"Indians burned it."

Jean Luc and Mary Crockett exchanged an awkward look before the Frenchman took the lead. "That is to say, the Indians burned it down, so you did not have one."

This wasn't the first time her questions had been parried. "Where was Joshua?"

"With you and the master in town, so I heard. I wasn't here then," Mary informed her. "Me 'n the mister come when the big house was started."

"I thought I was with my other mama," Joshua piped up, as confused as his mother.

Jean Luc pushed away from the table and clapped the child on the back. "Are you going to the barn with me, or will you stay here with the women and chit the chat."

"That is chit chat, Monsieur DeMotte."

"Ah," the Frenchman exclaimed with a mocking bow toward the woman entering the room, "the queen arises from the beauty sleep. How sad it has not improved her humor." Claire's appearance was impeccable, as always, but it was clear that she had not yet shaken the night's sleep.

"Don't you have something to do?" she grumbled,

taking the cup of tea Mary had ready for her and starting through the small pantry separating the kitchen from the dining room. "Like socialize with your peers in the barn?"

Their guest never ate a meal at the crude board table in the kitchen if Jean Luc was present. Instead, she chose to sit on the one chair in the dining room and take her meals from the crate that contained the new table. While their verbal enmity provided more than a little amusement for the onlookers, Krista had seen the speculative looks they gave one another when they thought no one was watching.

"Bah," Jean Luc shrugged, turning to Joshua and raising his voice. "We might as well go, mon ami. One grouchy cow is as good as another, I suppose."

The clatter of china, cup against saucer, followed by an indignant sniff revealed the retort had not missed its mark, but Jean Luc had pulled on his coat and was out of earshot with Joshua in tow by the time the woman recovered sufficiently to address it.

Mary Crockett turned and pointed a spatula at Claire as she charged back into the room in time to see the back door slam shut. "Sit!" she ordered, silencing the protest on the younger woman's lips. "I got enough to do without the two of you startin' up first thing."

"What did Joshua mean by his *other* mother?" Krista inquired, taking up the subject that had been washed away in the tide of Claire and Jean Luc's ongoing battle.

Ordinarily, Mary Crockett was not one to mince words or hold back an opinion. Instead of answering with her usual candor, however, she shrugged, keeping her back to the table. "Oh, you know how younguns are. Never know what they're goin' to come out with."

Shut out again, Krista mused, glancing knowingly at Claire. Caught in speculation, her companion busied herself with cutting a small piece of sugar for her tea. They were all in Gavin's camp, whatever this dastardly secret was. The only weak link was Joshua, who knew almost as little as she did.

"I imagine she was one of the women Gavin paid to take care of the child after you were separated from him by the war. I mean, it's only natural," Claire explained hastily at Krista's troubled expression. "He thought you were dead and you thought he was dead. You're probably just as well off you can't remember, dear." With a heavy sigh, she lifted the tea to her lips for a sip. "I only wish I could forget *my* past."

Krista glanced over at the kitchen window where something had caught Mrs. Crockett's eye. "Is it our men?" she asked.

"Don't think so." Mary Crockett squinted and wiped away the condensation from the narrow panes so all that blurred her vision now was the irregularities in the glass.

There were two dozen or so riders, too many to be Gavin's party, and they were riding hard toward the homestead, as if the devil himself was chasing them. They were wearing furs over their clothing, like Krista had seen several of the men do, and left a trail of smoke behind them, as if carrying torches. In the back yard, Joshua was flushed out of the barn by the commotion and started yelling and pointing in their direction. Her son, if he was her son, a troublesome inner voice interjected, was excited, but something in his manner told Krista it was not favorably.

"Jehosophat, it's Injuns!" Mary Crockett swore, tearing away from the window for the rifle kept loaded and ready over the door.

"Oh dear God," Claire gasped, her usual pallor fading to an even whiter hue. "What will we do?"

Krista did not hear a thing beyond the word *Injuns*, for instantly she was on her way out the door to where her

son had become transfixed by the approaching spectacle.
It seemed natural to grab up the hatchet kept near the
woodpile for the splitting of kindling. Her skirts swirled
about her long legs as she ignored Mary's call to get back
into the house and raced toward Joshua. A rifle shot split
the air, making way for the hellish shrieks that followed.

"Get in the barn!" Krista shouted to her son.

Even as she did so, she saw Jean Luc dash out and grab
the child. Unarmed and unable to shoot back, he dragged
the boy into the barn, yelling for her to follow him. Krista
had every intention of doing so, but her feet became
tangled in her petticoats and skirts and the next thing she
knew, she was sprawling in the snow, halfway toward her
goal. Jean Luc's and Mary Crockett's urgent shouts that
she take cover were drowned out by the hideous yells and
thunder of gunfire and hooves which were bearing down
upon her.

Suddenly Jean Luc was at her side, lifting her to her feet
as she clasped the handle of the hatchet she was reaching
for. "Madame, quick . . ."

The arm that had lifted her to her feet suddenly jerked
away. As Krista found her footing, she saw Jean Luc
reach down and break off an arrow that had lodged in his
thigh.

"Jean Luc!"

"To the barn!" he gasped, trying once more to usher
her into cover before the Indians, who had cleared the
zigzagged fence surrounding the yard of the estate, could
reach them.

"Bastard Wyandots!"

A rusty horseshoe flew past Krista as she gathered her
wits and reversed roles with Jean Luc, helping the limping
man with her free arm past the cursing child in the doorway and into the cover of the barn. Behind her, a horse
shrieked and reared, unseating the savage who had nearly

overtaken them. There was no time nor inclination to correct the child's startling vocabulary, for two more red-skinned marauders were already on the ground and chasing him.

"Joshua!"

Krista left Jean Luc and charged at them, swinging her hatchet wildly. The first, she clipped across the forehead, leaving a bloody gash as he fell in her wake. The second, who had grabbed the kicking and cursing boy, let him go as Krista leapt on his back, her momentum carrying them both to the ground. Having dropped her hatchet upon impact, she locked her arms about his neck and clung like a ferocious tigress as he tried to throw her off.

"Madame . . . !"

"Go for help!" Krista shouted above the din of the screeching heathens who surrounded her.

She waited, expecting like retaliation, but for some reason the savages seemed intent on subduing her, rather than taking her life as she heard about in the horror stories told in the taverns and inns along the way from Philadelphia.

"Let me go, you gut-lovin' puppy eater!"

As her arms were pried from around her victim's neck by bruising fingers, she saw Joshua being hauled up onto the back of a horse. More hands wrestled her to the ground and lashed her wrists and ankles together.

"Joshua!" she cried out as she was hauled painfully to her feet and thrown like a sack of wheat over the back of one of the wiry horses.

Frantically, she looked back at the barn where she'd last seen Jean Luc in time to see a torch flying through the air toward the large stack of hay in the back corner. The stables were opened by painted Indians who drove out the team horses Gavin had left behind. Smoke assaulted her nostrils as her captor turned his horse away from the burning barn and kicked its sides to ride to the edge of the fray to watch as his comrades took the house and the women inside.

It didn't take long. Mary Crockett was no match for their numbers and Claire was utterly useless. While Joshua cursed to his captor's amusement in all three of the languages he had learned, Krista watched in horror as the attackers smashed every window, leaving a blazing fire in their wake, while their comrades struggled to get the hefty housekeeper and an unconscious Claire onto horses.

"See what happens when ya get fat and lazy?"

The use of English, crude as it was, startled Krista. She twisted from her precarious position to look up into an unwashed and unshaven face with a tobacco-stained grin spread wide across its gauntness. Although garbed like the others, this man was not one of them. He was white beneath his filth and paint.

"You've come quite a looker, gal. Who'd 'a thought it?" Eyes, red and jaundiced from years of drink, seemed to bug out of hollow sockets, wild and crazy.

"Girty!"

The name was spat, as if it put a bad taste in her mouth. Indeed, it did. She'd never liked the man who had fought with the Indians against the colonials. He was a viper who had betrayed his country, a traitor and murderer of the worst sort. His deeds were so hideous, they were spoken of in whispers around the tavern fire at Petit Lyon. She had not liked the idea that he'd known their mission to transport powder to Clark. He had sent that raiding party to intercept them and kill the Mingo peace messenger. She knew it as sure as she knew her own name—Krista Lindstrom Duncan.

* * *

"It ain't normal, Wyandots bein' this far south," Tull Crockett swore riding next to Gavin and Kurt Waltari as they studied the evergreens spotting the thick forest, the smaller ones in particular.

"They may have come down to the licks," Waltari remarked, expressing his own doubt in his tone, rather than words. "It's early and they're too far from home to have plunder in mind. Must be a hunt."

Gavin tightened the tie on one of the bags filled with the presents he'd purchased his family at the post general store. "The general just wanted to put us on our guard, laddies." A corner of his lips twisted wryly. "And line us up for another surveying expedition this spring."

Gavin told the man to find another surveyor this time. Before, he hadn't had many ties to keep him at Duncan Brae. Tull and Mary were fully capable of running the place and keeping the young Joshua in line. He'd promised his son that this year he'd take him, but was certain the boy could be made to understand his change of plans. They needed to spend the spring and summer at home with Krista, to help her adjust to this new life as wife, mother, and mistress of Duncan Brae.

"The look on the old man's face when ya told him ya needed to see to some shoppin'!" Tull snorted in amusement.

"Ja!" Kurt chimed in. "Bad enough that you said no, but to spend the rest of the afternoon at the trading post instead of finishing off the general's private bottle of bourbon was more than the old feller could comprehend."

"A married man has other responsibilities. Besides, you two stood fair enough in my stead."

"Christmas in March!" Tull derided under his breath. "Sounds to me like marriage has made ya daft."

"We missed the holiday with Joshua, man, and . . ." Gavin broke off upon seeing the impish grin on his overseer's whiskered face. "The devil take ye, ye fur-faced old codger!"

"What about that one?" Kurt Waltari reined in his horse and pointed to a plump evergreen to their left, its branches beginning to sag with the snow which had been falling since they'd left Massac. It was just narrow enough at its widest point to squeeze through the front door of the manor.

"I never thought I'd be out huntin' a tree to bring inside the house, 'ceptin' for firewood!"

"I'd bring her the whole damned forest for one pretty smile." Gavin turned from his overseer to the Finn. "You're the one who said her family practiced the custom. What do ye think?"

"Perfect!" Waltari pronounced, reaching into one of his saddlebags to withdraw a hatchet. "I'll cut it and we'll have it in tow in no time at all. Krista used to love to decorate the tree. It was the only time her mother could get her to pick up a needle without big fussin' just to make the garland. Her sister Marta did all the holiday baking."

The Finn still could not believe that the gentlewoman who had met him at the door the morning before, needlework in hand, was his lost niece. She did resemble the gangly buckskin-clad girl he and Eva had taken under their wing, but the difference had been startling.

Krista had become a lady in a graceful way, not haughty like the other woman who had refused to join them at the breakfast Mary Crockett provided. At first appearance, she seemed to have at last found her niche. However, as his visit progressed, Kurt had not missed that brief flash of melancholy clouding the gaze that searched him out from time to time. Poor child still had not found the real Krista.

"How is that plump little haus frau?" Gavin inquired politely, breaking the long silence which threatened another lecture on his wife's right to know the whole truth. Dealing with Kurt Waltari was like dealing with a father-in-law, although the two of them had come to be good friends on their surveying trips. The Finn cared more for the girl than her stepfather ever had.

"Marta had her fifth child last fall. Eva is staying with them this winter with our two. We're a productive lot." The wiry mountain man cut his pale blue eyes sideways at Gavin. "But you'll find that out right soon, I think."

Most of the time, Waltari's observations could be taken as gold, but Gavin knew this prediction was not to be. Not that it bothered him. He was so grateful for Joshua, he needed no other child, he assuaged himself. Never one to dwell on what he didn't have, he changed the subject deftly. "And Many Husbands?"

"Married a Hessian deserter."

Gavin dismounted and fetched a rope while Kurt Waltari cut down the tree for the house. He didn't particularly care for the widow of Gunter Schuyler, but Krista would want to know as much about her family as possible and the time had come to tell her everything. He'd come to the decision last night, not because of the advice his two companions gave him over a bottle of horrendous liquor, but because the charade could not go on forever.

Her questions were becoming more and more frequent and the lost expression she got from his evasive answers was enough to shred his heart. He had drawn them all in on his selfish scheme, enlarging the web of deceit spun years before when he'd left her at Petit Lyon. If he had not won her trust and love by now, then it was beyond his ability to do so.

Chapter Twenty-Eight

Krista tried to catch the edge of the blanket wrapped around her with her teeth and draw it up to block the stinging wind from her cheeks. Her hands bound in front of her, it was all she could do to maintain her balance on the galloping horse trailing on a line behind her captor. Joshua rode ahead, accompanied by one of the warriors, as was Claire, who had fallen off her horse so many times that she'd been hauled up in front of one of the Indians. Mary Crockett, like Krista, had been allocated her own horse, one of Duncan Brae's, and rode stoically at her side on a similar lead line.

The storm that had been raging had stopped, but it seemed it was only to catch its breath. They rode directly into it, pausing only long enough to pick Claire up twice. The second time, Krista had thought they were going to kill the sobbing woman then and there. Speaking to the Indians in the broken language which had come back to her, she managed to explain that the Saggenash woman could not ride and needed a warrior to help her stay on. She didn't know whether it was from rare pity, or shock that she spoke their tongue, that encouraged them to listen.

She'd also warned Claire to cease her hysterics, explaining the contempt their captors held for such a show.

Not that Krista thought the English woman was faking her terror. She was certain Claire was frightened senseless and it grieved her to use fear against fear to shock her companion into silence. However, had the woman kept up her sobbing and wailing, Krista knew the Indians would kill her and move on without a backward glance.

They would have no patience with anyone for holding up from their escape to the north. Since they'd ridden away from the flaming manor and outbuildings of Duncan Brae, they had stopped only for Claire. There was no respite for food, nor drink, nor rest for their horses. Night, however, would be upon them soon, prematurely, due to the thickness of the dark clouds sprinkling the earth with their crystalline white powder.

They would be forced to stop, Krista thought, burying her face as deeply in the blanket cocoon as she could. Or they'd freeze. Ever since they'd left Duncan Brae, she kept a motherly eye on Joshua. The brave riding behind him, however, had him bundled up tightly within the confines of a buffalo robe. With that and the body heat of his companion, Joshua appeared comfortable. Too comfortable and sure of himself, Krista mused, as if he were undaunted by their abduction. Oddly enough, her son's stalwart manner infected her, reassuring her when her imagination strained at its limit to stir panic.

"Papa will come for us," he'd told her confidently when the Indian tore him from her grasp at the burning plantation. "Jean Luc will fetch help."

The words kept echoing over and over in her mind, undermining her efforts to remain calm as she considered Jean Luc's fate and the possible end that awaited the rest of them. She wanted to believe with Joshua's childish faith, but could not. She doubted Jean Luc could help them at all. As far as she knew, the marauders had not found him, for there was no evidence of a freshly taken scalp. But all she could think of when the roof had caved in was that Jean Luc had been burned alive in his hiding place. It came to her for the first time that she was glad Gavin and the other men had not been there. The raid would have been much bloodier on both sides, resulting in the gruesome deaths of her husband and his companions in the end, for they were greatly outnumbered and outgunned by British supplied rifles and deadly arrows. The men would never have made it to the gun case and supplies kept in Gavin's office.

A shout ahead brought Krista back to the present. Peering through the slit in the snow-soaked blanket, she saw a small village in the distance, illuminated by cookfires. A few of the Indians rode ahead to be met by the men of the village at its outskirts. By the time Krista and the rest caught up, they had been ushered into the camp and the village women gathered to take their horses.

Upon hitting the ground, Krista thought her legs would go out from under her. Numb at first, they began to burn and sting as she willed them to carry her toward the Indian who was handing down her son to one of the women. The moment the woman set him down, he made straight for Krista.

"Are you okay, Mama?"

Krista forced a smile. "I'm right good, but I am worried about your aunts," she confessed, nodding to where Mary Crockett helped a tight-lipped Claire toward one of the fires.

Before they reached it, however, they were surrounded by some men of the tribe. Krista recognized them as Shawnee, not Wyandot. The two tribes had fought together during the war, mostly for the British.

Claire screamed as the blanket in which she was wrapped was yanked off her and her hair was grabbed and examined in the firelight by one of the braves. "Dear God, don't scalp me!" she sobbed pitifully.

The Indian shouted at her, freezing her pleas in her throat as she recalled Krista's advice.

Mary suffered the same exposure and scrutiny, although her graying brown hair did not present the novelty Claire's fairer locks did.

From the edge of the circle, Krista held Joshua in front of her and watched, expecting at any moment to be hauled before the Indians for inspection. The discussion going on, unintelligible at the distance she was from the others, ended abruptly and all four prisoners were reunited and escorted to one of the bark long houses where a decided warmth from the many small fires inside made them welcome. They were directed to a small cubicle and left under guard while the Indian women served them something to eat and provided dry blankets.

Conversation between them was practically nil. They were exhausted, both physically and mentally, and it took all their strength to change into dry clothing. Krista made certain Joshua was dry, much to his disdain, before taking a seat by him close to the smoldering embers and luxuriating in the heat herself.

Her toes and fingers ached as the blood began to circulate more freely in the moccasin boots she'd been given to replace her soaked leather slippers. Even Claire had accepted the replacement clothes without complaint and was eagerly edging as close to the fire as she dared, her blonde hair in tangles about her face and neck. Dark circles under her eyes and the tears that hung there unshed indicated the weariness and hopelessness they all were beginning to feel.

"What will become of us?" she whispered, hugging her knees and rocking back and forth.

A crudely carved bowl of corn mush and some sort of

meat lay untouched beside her as she addressed her question to the dried stores and baskets hanging in the rafters of the structure, a sampling of the summer's bounty put away for winter by the hard-working women of the tribe. Blended with the scent of the woodfire, it was not unpleasant. In fact, the woodsy, spicy smell offered a misleading sense of security, particularly after their trying cross country journey.

"Nothin', so long as we keep our heads," Mary Crockett answered, slipping her bandaged arm around the girl. "If they was set on killin' us, it'd 'a been done afore now. Like as not, we'll be took into the tribe, this 'un or that 'un, I reckon. All we got to do is hold on till our menfolk catch up with us. If I guessed right, the ones what captured us want to trade us off. I think we're holdin' 'em back and they want to git north with the horses."

"Which was right likely why they scattered Gavin's prize cattle," Krista agreed thoughtfully. She'd seen the herd run out of the barn. The savages had killed a few before gathering up their intended plunder and making their unhindered escape.

The fat, pasture-raised stock her husband was breeding could not have kept up with the horses at the rate the Indians had pushed. The matching team of chestnuts and breeding stock her husband had been accumulating was sweet enough prize. She and the other prisoners were an added bonus, especially she and Claire with their golden hair. Mary, while older, was strong and healthy, a good prospective slave, if not attractive to a young warrior as a wife.

"You'd best eat," Mary encouraged Claire gently.

Claire came out of her trance to stare at the meat the older woman held out to her. Like an obedient child, she took it and began to nibble at it with little interest.

"Besides," Mary went on philosophically, "if these are

the Injuns we're bein' left with, we got a decent chance of being found by our menfolk. This bunch ain't been as quarrelsome since the war ended as them that took us. They'd trade us back."

"Then you and Jean Luc can bury the hatchet, Aunt Claire," Joshua chimed in helpfully. "You can get married and maybe we'll get some peace around the house."

"Boy, you got more mouth than brains," Mary Crockett chastised, but a chuckle showed she was amused at Joshua's parroting of something he'd overheard.

Grateful for the distraction Krista found herself joining in the amusement. Even Claire managed a smile. Yet the brief relief from tension Krista enjoyed suddenly vanished. Why hadn't they inspected her and her son?

The answer came early the following morning, before the campfires had been built up for the day and the camp had fully awakened. Unlike Claire and Mary, they were not to be left with the Shawnee. Krista was shaken from a sound sleep born of sheer fatigue by two Wyandot warriors who dragged her from the cubicle along with Joshua. There was no chance to speak to Mary or Claire, who were awakened by the commotion, no time to even think about resisting. The rest of the raiding party was already mounted and waiting for them to be placed on the same horse, Joshua in front of Krista. After receiving a slice of pemmican to nibble on for breakfast, they were led off from the camp.

Simon Girty rode at the head of the group, making it impossible for Krista to ask any questions until a few hours later when they stopped for a brief parlay near a stream. Hugging Joshua in the hollow of her arms, Krista tried to make out what was going on. The group was evidently splitting up to confuse anyone who followed them. After the majority of the Indians rode off, shouting and yelping wildly, as if boasting of their fierceness, Girty took the line to her horse himself and led them into the stream, two remaining Wyandots bringing up the rear.

It was an old trick, hiding their tracks in the water so that it appeared that all of them had ridden off in the direction the rest of the Indians had taken. Old and effective, Krista mused in dismay.

"Where are you taking us? Why didn't you trade us with the Shawnee?"

Simon Girty looked over his shoulder, his wild gaze settling on Krista. "Because you are worth more than a few horses and cows, gal. There's someone offerin' a sack of gold coin for you. I reckon when they see I got the boy too, there'll be a nice bonus."

The revelation staggered Krista. It never occurred to her that this was anything more than a random Indian raid. "Who?"

Simon Girty grinned, his leathered skin crinkling on either side of his jaundiced smile. "I reckon you'll see soon enough. It ain't that far."

That was probably as close as Simon Girty ever came to uttering the truth. An hour later they emerged from the stream and started uphill along increasingly rugged terrain. Unaccustomed to the prolonged riding she'd done the past twenty-four hours, Krista's legs and arms ached relentlessly as she struggled to keep her seat and hold Joshua. Yet, she paid her discomfort little heed. Her mind worked in a feverish, futile attempt to ferret out the identity of the one who had paid to have them kidnapped. Who would have a reason to arrange this?

The question echoed over and over in her beleaguered mind as they approached an old blockhouse, a remnant of an earlier time when the brush and young trees now surrounding it had been a cleared field to keep an enemy at bay without cover. The roof sagged in one spot, but the ridge pole was as straight as the day it had been installed.

The second story was larger than the first, as in most of the earlier forts where the building itself was the shelter and haven from the enemy. Smoke rose from the stone chimney—smoke that smelled oddly of spice and perfume.

"Smells like they're burnin' dried flowers and rotten fruit, don't it, Mama?" Joshua remarked over his shoulder.

Krista barely nodded, for somewhere in the back of her mind, the scent registered as familiar. It was incense. But where had she been where incense was burned here in the wilderness? It was an experience that still escaped her returning memory. The only sickeningly sweet smell of incense she recalled was that permeating the drapes and furnishings of the Black Rose in London—that den of iniquity from which she, Gavin, and Claire had barely escaped with their lives.

A waterfall of dread splashed over her, washing away her strength. Had she not been seated, her legs would surely have given way with the sapping of her blood from her skin. The simple primitive setting grew more sinister by the moment as the bloody scene they left in their wake was re-enacted in her mind—Lord Stanton sprawled on the floor, Gavin's bullet and her knife wounds draining him of his life's blood, the spongy yield of flesh as she'd driven the same blade backward into the stomach of the hideous Madame Rose to save her husband's life, the shouts of "Murder!" that followed them, even in her dreams.

"Well, now, come on down off that horse and meet your official kidnapper, gal. I'll take the boy first."

Krista clung to Joshua instinctively. "No!" Was it one of the men who had witnessed the gruesome escape? In desperation, she kicked at Girty's face and dug her heels into the sides of her steed. The animal lunged forward, yanking the lead line from her captor's arm, where he'd draped it to help them down, and nearly unseated Krista and the boy, but for their prowess on the back of a horse. However, before the animal had reached the edge of the clearing, the flailing line was caught up by one of the fur-clad Wyandots. Instantly, the other Indian dropped a rope noose over its head from the opposite side and together, they brought the horse to a stop.

"Try somethin' like that again, gal, an' I'll slit that boy's throat from ear to ear, just to watch 'im bleed. He ain't been figgered on anyways."

Reluctantly Krista let the man take the grim Joshua down. One of the Indians took the boy and shoved him toward the door roughly. Intent on looking after her son, Krista was startled by the hand that locked painfully around her arm and yanked her unceremoniously from the saddle. She struck the hard frozen ground on her side, pain shooting from her hip down her leg and from the elbow which broke her fall. Before she could assess the damage, she was hauled to her feet and shoved toward the open door where Joshua had disappeared.

Since her legs seemed to work, in spite of her discomfort, she assumed nothing had broken. She was just badly bruised. The steps having long been decayed, she grabbed the jamb of the door and pulled herself up, wincing at the agonizing cost of her effort. The overwhelming aroma of incense in the room added to her dizzying pain nearly made her swoon.

But for Joshua's outraged cry, she might have. Instead, she swayed unsteadily on her feet and reached for the boy who hurled himself into her arms. "Mama, are you hurt? Mama, please don't get sick."

Of all those who lived at Duncan Brae, only Joshua had discovered the nausea which had caused her appetite to diminish of late. He had a habit of coming into the master bedroom after supper where Krista read to him before his bedtime. That seemed to be the time it was the worst. She assured him it was nothing to be concerned about and made him promise not to say a word because it might hurt Mary's feelings about her cooking.

"It's the smell," she assured him, taking him to her and drawing strength from him as she had his father.

For Joshua's sake, she mustn't show the weakness born of sheer terror she felt taking her over. She told herself that there was no such thing as ghosts, yet a fiendish apparition stood before her, painted eyes shifting from the boy to Krista and back again. The silk swathed figure stepped closer and caught Joshua's chin in her gnarled fingers.

"Well, well, what have we here, another Duncan?"

"My son!" Krista averred, trying to push Madame Rose's defiling hand away from Joshua's innocent face. Simon Girty, however, dragged her back. "Let him go and I will do whatever you wish. He has done nothing to you!"

"No, but his mother did." The madame clasped an arm to her side, as if to demonstrate her point. "It was a nasty wound." A sinister laugh rumbled in the woman's thick throat. "I've dreamed of nothing but meeting you again, my dear. The boy will be an unexpected addition to my *pleasure.*"

"Where's the gold you promised, lady?" Simon Girty interrupted.

Madame Rose sighed with feigned patience and untied the pouch the man had been eyeing at her waist. "Here, my man. There will be double that back in Detroit, if you and your friends see me safely returned there tomorrow."

Girty emptied the pouch on the table. The gold coins clattered as they struck the worn surface, glittering in the light of the candles. The same glitter lighted in the eyes of the two Indians watching silently from the door, arms folded in front of them and still as the statues Krista had seen gracing the halls and corridors of London's most prominent buildings.

"Twice that, did ya say?" Girty questioned suspiciously. It was clear from his expression that he did not know what to make of the woman. He did, however, know the value of the coin she paid.

"Twice, plus the opportunity to partake of tonight's ceremony."

"Why can't ya just be done with your *ceremony* and let us be on our way? I know danged well, these hills'll be crawling with Bluecoats and Big Knives by tomorrow."

The Madame raised a haughty brow. "You didn't cover your tracks?"

" 'Course I did! I ain't no fool, but neither is the Big Knives. They'll lead the soldiers after us like hungry wolves on a bloody trail." Girty's bulging eyes switched to Krista curiously. "What kind'a ceremony?"

Madame Rose adopted the smile of someone who had just won a generous prize. "Oh, you'll enjoy it, I can promise you that. But we must wait until midnight . . . not a moment before. You find her attractive, don't you?"

"She's a woman, ain't she?" Girty snickered before turning to translate the possibilities he saw developing to his companions.

"And if your taste is, shall we say, more diverse, there's always the boy."

"No!" Krista grabbed up the only weapon she could find, an empty trencher sitting on the table, and rushed the woman, swinging furiously.

The resounding crack as it struck Madame Rose's head, the split which already ran down its center breaking completely apart, echoed above the rushing feet of the man who tried to take it from her before she could strike his gold mine again. Krista, however, was like an angry tigress fighting to protect its child. Letting Girty have the remains of her weapon, she clawed at the woman's face, gathering up the make-up which gave the madame a waxy deathlike pallor under her nails as she did so.

Using her weapon against her, Simon Girty struck her across the back of the head as she renewed her attack. A pain-filled fog exploded in her mind. Krista made one last lunge, hands locking in the woman's hair as she was pulled away. Behind her, she could hear Joshua fighting and screaming, but it barely registered. What did register was the face hovering over her, still hideously painted, but without the wig she held in her hands.

The same shock that rendered her still exploded in a curse from the man holding her down. "What in the name of hell . . . you're a man!"

As if trying to regain his composure, the man called Madame Rose swung away and shuffled toward the hearth, shoulders as erect as his crippled gait would allow. From the thick mantle, he withdrew a small cloisonne box and opened it, snorting the powdery contents up the long angular nose that had made him a particularly ugly woman. After a few moments of contemplation of the fire, he pivoted abruptly, chin lifted in an imperious tilt.

"Man or woman, my gold is the same. Do you have a problem with that, my good man?"

Simon Girty repeated the challenge to the Indians. Krista did not see or hear their answer. All she heard was Girty's "Not a bit, friend, not a bit."

Gavin Duncan blew into his hands in an effort to warm them and looked around the Shawnee encampment for any sign of the women and child Kurt Waltari was asking about in their native tongue. There were many nods, suspicious looks directed both at the guide and at his companions, and an occasional waving of the hands. There had been no choice but to follow the mountain man there on his hunch that the retreating Wyandots might try to get rid of their hostages along the way. A hunch was all they had to go on. The snow had covered their tracks.

The man at Gavin's side coughed and shivered within the confines of his buffalo robes. His dark eyes expressed his impatience with the parley, but he held his tongue. Jean Luc could use that restraint with anyone but Claire. Something about the two seemed to bring out the worst in the other. The night before at the tavern, Tull had enraged the young man by insisting that it was love.

Jean Luc had been frantic when he intercepted them on their way home. They'd already known something was wrong. They'd seen the smoke rising in the distance and, having left the tree behind, were making haste toward Duncan Brae as fast as their horses could carry them. A thousand horrible images assailed Gavin's thoughts as he urged his stallion on. The sight of Jean Luc, limping, bleeding, and covered in soot confirmed the least of them.

Joshua and the women had been taken alive. The house and outbuildings were burning even as they'd spoken, too far gone to try to save. Jean Luc had managed to slip out the back in the cover of the fleeing cattle and hidden until the Indians rounded up the horses and made off with their plunder. As the young man spoke, breaking into torrents of French in exasperation, Gavin cursed himself over and over for his complacency in thinking the renegades would not venture this far south. Now he suffered the consequences. Duncan Brae was in ruins and his family was held hostage by the heathens.

It never crossed anyone's mind to go back to Massac for troops. By the time the soldiers organized a march, the

Wyandots would be too far away to even hope to catch. Instead, they'd forged ahead, following the tracks which were rapidly being covered by the snowfall. He'd barely paid heed to the smoldering ruins he'd left in his wake. His mind was on his wife and son, just as Tull's was on his Mary. Jean Luc's passionate insistence that he accompany them was all but an admission of his feelings for Claire.

"That sharp tongue of hers will be her death!" he exclaimed as he washed out his wound with whiskey and wrapped it with the linens provided by the people on the first homestead they'd come to.

Their neighbors had not only furnished them with additional ammunition and powder, but sent their eldest son to Fort Massac with the news of the attack. With a sack full of fresh-baked biscuits in their packs and heartfelt sympathy, the three men had been seen off on their grueling chase a costly hour later.

With the worsening of the storm, they were forced to stop at nightfall and take shelter in a thick cluster of trees. Huddled around a small fire, they'd tried to rest, but rest would not come. They were each imagining the terror their loved ones were experiencing at the hands of the savages. The night was the longest Gavin had ever spent and he was grateful when it started to lighten enough to see. The snow had stopped, but the wind left behind served to cover whatever clues might have been left.

"Duncan!"

Gavin shook himself from his misery and leapt from his horse to join Kurt Waltari and the small group of Indians in front of the great lodge. It was hard to tell from the Finn's impassive face whether they'd had any luck or not. Just as he reached the group, however, a shout distracted them all.

"Mr. Crockett!"

Breaking away from the Indians who escorted them out of another lodge, Mary Crockett ran toward her husband. Behind her, held firmly between two more braves, was Claire Eaton. Gavin's heart flipped within his chest as he stared at the opening where the two women had emerged, but the next one to step out was an Indian woman wrapped snugly in a fur robe. She might just as well have stabbed him with a knife instead of giving him a piercing look, for the pain that assaulted him was just as merciless. Refusing to give up hope, he looked around the encampment at the other lodges, thinking Krista and Joshua might have been separated from the women.

"The Wyandot took your wife and son with them. They left here first thing this morning. We're about four hours behind them," Kurt Waltari informed him grimly. "We'll have to bargain for the other women. The chief says he'll take six horses like the ones the Wyandot captured."

"What?" Gavin tried to think what the guide had said after telling him about Krista and Joshua, but the words had become unintelligible to his stricken mind.

"Six horses," Waltari repeated.

"But we have not got six horses!" Jean Luc called out in frustration, eyeing the braves who held Claire away from him.

"I have given the chief my word as a brother that they will be paid as soon as you can round them up and deliver them."

"Done!" Gavin agreed, turning to mount again. "Now let's get after the others."

"We need fresh mounts, Duncan. The chief is willing to trade them for the ones we have. He does not wish to anger the Big Knives or the Bluecoats as his Wyandot brothers have."

"Then let's be done with it, man!" Gavin averred in exasperation.

He started unfastening the girth on his saddle. Four hours, he thought feverishly. Four hours could be made up before the Indians got into their own territory. He'd stop for nothing until he did just that. Four hours stood between him and all that mattered to him. Four hours and two dozen bloodthirsty savages.

Chapter Twenty-Nine

Four hours, Krista speculated, searching the dark gray skies through the peep hole in the wall. Maybe six before night darkened the hills again. Then there would be the long wait until the evening reached the pinnacle of midnight. She refused to even think of the nature of the ceremony the men downstairs were planning over the East Indian rum being lavishly distributed. If she allowed her imagination to run wild, she would be of no use to herself or to her son.

She looked down at the sleeping child, who lay wrapped in a blanket next to the chimney of the fireplace that heated the first floor of the building. Such faith, she mused quietly. He was not the least worried, now that they were locked in the upstairs room. He believed Gavin Duncan was going to ride in on his prancing smoke-gray stallion and rescue them. Krista wanted to believe that herself, but she had learned long ago that the best person to depend on was oneself.

Not that she didn't think Gavin would try to rescue them. She was certain that he would. But it was hard to guess just when Gavin had discovered what had happened to them. If she and Joshua were to survive, she had to come up with a plan. Without thinking, she rested her cheek in her hand and caught her breath at the pain from where she'd been struck.

"I wish I'd had time to get my knife. I'd have cut that bastard to bits," Joshua murmured sleepily, peering up at her from under thick dark lashes.

Krista looked at her son, not daring to get her hopes up. "Did you say *knife*, Joshua?"

The little boy nodded and sat up. Krista watched as he dug into his miniature boots and pulled out a small dirk, much like the one his father owned. "I've been saving it for the right moment, Mama, but there's just been too many men to take on at once. Jean Luc said there was time and a place to fight, an' I just haven't seen it."

Krista almost chuckled. Such grown-up thinking for such a little man. Instead, she drew Joshua to her and squeezed him tightly—her son, her brave and smart little boy. Most children would have been reduced to tears, not. waiting calculatingly for the moment to fight off their captors. More determined than ever to escape, she finally pulled away and held out her hand.

"Mama has an idea, Joshua, but I have to have the knife."

Joshua looked up at her, somewhat skeptical. "You remember how to use it?"

This time, Krista did laugh. It helped relieve the tension and brought a grin to the boy's face. "Ja, I know right good how to use it."

"What'll I use?" he asked as he trustingly handed it over.

"I hope you will not need a weapon. All you will need is speed. Can you run fast and hide out in the woods over there until Mama escapes?"

"I'm not leaving you alone with those bastards!"

"Joshua!"

"That's what they are!"

Krista let her objection go. "I need you to slip out and

run off their horses. That way, when they go after them, I will be able to get away. I may need this knife if they leave a guard."

"Like that man-woman?"

Krista mastered a shudder. She still could not believe that Madame Rose was a man. "Ja, that is right."

Eyes taking on an excited glow at the prospect of his part in the escape, Joshua leaned forward and whispered in a conspiratory manner, "How'll I get out?"

"Come, I will show you." Krista took him by the hand and led him over to one of the patches nailed down over holes in the overhang of the upper floor, once used to shoot down at the enemy trying to hide against the outside wall of the first floor.

"Watch your step, little one," she cautioned, feeling the floor bowing under her weight.

That particular section had rotted, exposed from above by a hole in the sagging roof. Therefore, it was easy to pry up the shingle covering, although Krista worked slowly to avoid making any noise that would attract the men getting drunk below. The opening revealed was small, too small for her to squeeze through. Joshua, however, could manage, if he held his arms over his head and dropped to his feet into the snow bank below.

Krista went over the plan once more. After she lowered Joshua through the hole, he was to sneak around to the lean-to where the horses were stabled and turn them loose, then spook them with the small blanket he'd slept in and slip into the woods behind the structure and hide until his mother found him. Hopefully, the men would consider the horses a greater loss than the child and go after them first.

"Now, if Mama doesn't come out, don't come back. Run for help, along the creek bank we followed up here," she instructed calmly.

She didn't feel calm. She wanted to drag Joshua against her again and hug him tightly. She wanted to somehow tuck him in a pocket and keep him safe while she took the risk. Yet, she had confidence in the child to do what was necessary. He'd been reared by the Big Knives, born to the wilds. It was herself she doubted. She was the one too big to slip away and hide. She would have to fight her way out.

"But—"

"Your papa is surely on his way. He'll need you to lead him back here to rescue me, if I can't escape. Remember, our tracks were hidden in the creek for a while. He might not be able to find us." Not wanting to treat him the child, with such an adult mission ahead of him, she took his hand and pressed it to her lips. "It's the only thing we can do, ja?"

"Okay, Mama." As Krista struggled to her feet, the boy threw his arms around her lips and hugged her. "We'll outslick these varmints, Mama! Papa said you're a survivor and I know I am. Don't worry."

Krista's heart ceased to beat as she lowered the child down through the hole as far as she could before letting him go. It was the only thing they could do, she reiterated for her own sake. As the boy dropped into the snowbank, which engulfed him to his waist, he winked at her. She smiled. He was reassuring her and, somehow, she was beginning to believe they did have a chance.

Tiptoeing noiselessly across the room, she kept an ear on the commotion below. There was no indication that anything was amiss. Relieved, she cut away the hide cover over another window so that she could watch Josh's progress when he left the cover of the overhang and made for the lean-to. Her breath halted in her chest when she spied him forging ahead through drifts of snow, keeping low so that they provided him cover as well. At the same time, pride welled in her heart. He was his father's son, brave against all odds.

When she saw the first horses back out of the shelter, freed by the small fingers she'd reluctantly let go, she swallowed dryly. They showed no sign of even wanting to leave. The fourth and then the fifth and last emerged, followed by a small blanket-swinging figure. The loud voice that often earned reprimand when used in the house, burst the snowy silence and the scene erupted with the galloping hoofbeats of the startled animals.

"Run!" she whispered, urging the child to stop his chase and seek the cover of the trees as she'd instructed.

As if he'd heard her over the scraping of chairs and expletives resounding from the first floor, Joshua glanced briefly up at the second floor where he knew she watched and then darted into the woods. Not daring to linger at the window any longer, Krista rushed to the wall broken by the inside chimney and pressed against it, using the stone cover to hide from the sight of anyone coming up the narrow curving steps to check on them.

"The boy . . . over there!" she heard the man called Madame Rose shout from the door beneath her.

"The hell with 'im, he ain't worth shit without our horses!"

"Where's the woman?"

"Find her yourself!" Simon Girty hollered back, breaking into the Wyandot dialect as he spied one of the horses by the creek.

Krista remained motionless, listening to her captor swearing as he hastened from window to window below, no doubt hoping to spy her. If she was fortunate, he would go outside to continue his search, facilitating her escape.

But that was not to be, she realized, as footsteps neared the stairwell and stopped. "Madame Duncan, your child will not escape. You've sent him to his death. He'll freeze by nightfall."

Not if she could get to him, Krista vowed silently. Come on. Come up the steps. She balanced the knife deftly in her hand. She wouldn't miss. She couldn't afford to. Joshua's life depended on her.

"I only saw one set of prints leading from the blockhouse. I know you are up there."

A board creaked, betraying a tentative attempt to peek around the opening. Could he know she was armed or was he such a coward that he did not wish to confront her? She refrained from attempting to see how far the man had come. She would wait until she heard him reach a halfway point. Then she would . . .

Three steps in quick succession brought Krista out of her cover at once. She threw the knife the moment she glimpsed him and then flattened behind the chimney as a pistol shot exploded and echoed in the rafters. The ball ricocheted off the stone chimney, dangerously close.

"You . . . knife-wielding bitch!"

Something fell, striking each step until it came to rest at the curved opening. It wasn't the male madame. She could hear him breathing heavily, a gurgling throaty sound that told her he was gravely wounded. Praying that what she'd heard careening down the stairs was the pistol, she eased around the warm chimney to see the silk-clad figure sinking against the steps. Blood seeped through the fingers spread on his chest, scarlet against scarlet.

Gathering her courage, she started down. She wanted to retrieve the knife, but she couldn't bring herself to do so, any more than she could bear to look at the face of the man she'd mortally wounded. Joshua, she reminded herself stalwartly. She needed to get to Joshua before the boy did something foolish, like coming after her. Without a backward glance, she stepped around the rasping figure and ran outside.

Much as she wanted to see where Girty and the savages had gone, she waited until she was in the cover of the trees behind the lean-to. As far as she could tell from the tracks, all three men had taken off to the north after the horses. Which meant the route south was safe, at least until they caught up with them.

"Joshua!" she ventured in a loud whisper.

"Told you we'd do it!" a confident voice responded from what appeared to be a thicket of briars and holly. Part of the "bush" was thrown to the side and the little face she'd come to adore beamed at her, scratched and bloodstreaked, but beautiful.

"You sure did!" Krista acknowledged breathlessly. "Now we have to get away before them come back, ja?"

"Ja!"

Hand in hand, the two raced downhill toward the creek. There was no time for Krista to consider how cold the water would be to her feet. If she didn't use the same tactics as the Indians to hide their trail, they would surely be found in short order. Instead of going south though, Krista chose the northern route.

"They will expect to pick up our trail south," she explained to the boy, trying to ignore the icy water sweeping around her knees as she picked the child up and swung him on her back to keep his feet dry.

She and Uncle Kurt used to laugh at the reluctance of their trapper friends to cross streams and fords in the midst of winter. Uncle Kurt had sworn it was their Scandinavian blood that kept them from catching their death, that they were bred in ice water. But that was how many years ago, she wondered, shivering with each plodding step.

"Step and blow," she reflected aloud, repeating the

exercise she'd learned to take her mind off the chill and keep going. "Step and blow."

The phrase was not strange to her son. Hearing his voice echoing it in her ear gave her the encouragement she needed to keep on. Once they'd gone far enough, she would double back on the opposite bank. She'd noticed on the way to the old abandoned fort that the hills to the west looked oddly familiar. In fact, now that she thought of it, she recalled her uncle talking about a fort that had once been used in the French and Indian War. If those were the same hills she'd once trapped with the mountain man, Petit Lyon lay to the south of them. Better yet, she knew of shelter between them and the French settlement where Joshua had been born. All she needed to do was to get her bearings.

Leaving the creek behind after walking a half mile or so through its twists and turns, she made her way determinedly to the top of a snowy crest with Joshua clinging to her hand in an effort to keep up with her long stride. From time to time, she glanced down at him and gained courage from his smiling face. He trusted her completely, just as he trusted his father.

He hadn't questioned her at all since taking to the creek, except to ask if she'd buried his knife in the man-woman's heart. Krista's nod was all the answer he needed. From that point on, he'd done his best not to hold them back.

By the time they reached the ridge, perspiration dampened both their brows in spite of the cold. Krista's feet had ceased to ache, indeed to feel anything. But they were there and they continued to work. Even more encouraging, she thought she knew the way to the settlement. She recalled traveling occasionally with the DeMotte gang to the caves where they kept their stores to bring back more supplies to the inn.

"Mama!"

Krista froze at the alarm in Joshua's whisper. She looked down at the child expectantly.

"On the flag salutin' side," he told her. "I thought I saw something move."

Without actually turning, Krista cut her glance to low growing trees and brush to their right. Although she saw no indication that anything or anyone was hidden there, she tightened her grasp on Joshua's fingers and started forward at a gradually increasing pace. Time would soon tell and, if they were going to make a run for it, it might as well be in the right direction.

She wanted to break into a full gait, but to do so would require carrying Joshua or leaving him behind. Unable to execute the first, for her own steps were becoming increasingly unsteady, she could not choose the latter either. "Breathe, step, breathe step . . ."

A sharp pain stabbed at her ankle and suddenly she was falling, plummeting down the hill. Joshua's name hung on her lips, but she was too winded to call for him. She could hear him running after her, or was that the beating of her heart? No, it was too loud to be either. Struggling to hold on to consciousness, Krista lifted her head and stared at the feet that halted next to her—not those of a small child, but the moccasined ones of an Indian.

It was nearing dark when Gavin Duncan and Kurt Waltari, having left Jean Luc and Tull Crockett at the Shawnee village to see the women home, stealthily made their way up to the abandoned fort. Its smoking chimney had hailed them long after they'd lost the tracks of their quarry. They'd been fooled into following the Indians' trail for a mile or so, when they met a lone hunter who had seen them ride past his homestead. Two dozen, he swore, and there had been no woman among them and certainly no child, only warriors returning with some horses. "I figgered it was bad news for somebody. Only time an Injun's got an extra horse is if'n he's stolen it."

Kurt Waltari had sworn vehemently at himself for being taken in by the trick, vowing that he should have known when the tracks showed the travelers had stopped and milled about, that they were trying to cover a trail. They'd split at the stream, taking Krista and her son with them. Such was her uncle's distress, Gavin found himself offering him solace, rather than focusing on his own sense of utter helplessness.

They backtracked to the stream bed and followed it for several miles before they were rewarded with the sight of the smoking chimney. According to Waltari, the only chimney he knew of in the area was that of an abandoned French fort, a perfect place to hide out. It made sense to Gavin, at least the shelter part. What didn't make sense was why the group split up. Were some of them injured? He lost count of the times he'd prayed it was not his wife or son, that he and the trapper would not come upon their scalped bodies, half buried in the snow.

Kurt Waltari nudged Gavin, bringing his attention from the fresh tracks that went off in a bizarre pattern across a clearing to the building itself. The door was open. Gavin glanced at the man, finding no explanation in his pale blue gaze, only bewilderment. Nothing had been normal, not the raid itself, nor the retreat north. If Krista and Joshua weren't in the fort . . . Gavin refused to finish the thought. They had to be.

Exercising caution, the two men made their way to the building and tried looking inside, but it was too dark to see anything. It did, however, possess a strange smell, diluted by the draft created by the open door and inconsistent with the setting. With a growing feeling of dread, Gavin eased around the door jamb, his gun ready. The room was empty, although the dying fire and remnants of a bottle of rum on the table evidenced that it had not been abandoned for long. Squinting in the dim light, Gavin made out the dark opening of a stairwell climbing steeply to the second floor.

"Smells like somebody burned a French whore."

"Incense," Gavin whispered, the nature of the scent coming to him.

"Well, I'm goin' to look around out here before it gets too dark and see if I can make sense of those tracks. Don't seem to be anyone in here, but if there is, holler."

With an acknowledging nod, Gavin took up a candle and lit it in the embers before proceeding toward the stairs to investigate. A thick, slippered foot with silk stockings lay just beyond the curve in the steps. Pistol primed and cocked, Gavin stepped into the stairwell and stared in disbelief at the familiar silk robes.

His mind reeled with a barrage of recollections of all that had taken place since he'd been summoned so mysteriously to England. It had been a diabolical scheme that resulted in Robert's death and nearly destroyed his whole family. There was no doubt in his mind that the dead man was Madame Rose, but it was also his cousin, Derrick Duncan.

Why? The question bounced about in his head until the sight of the small dirk buried in his cousin's chest interrupted Gavin's confusion. It was the one he'd brought Joshua from Scotland. "Joshua!" Gavin shouted, sprinting past the still figure to the second floor of the building.

The light of the flickering candle danced on the rafters above. In the distance, another fainter light filtered in through the roof. Moonlight. The storm had passed unnoticed by him, clearing the skies for the first time in two days. But that was the only good news the empty room held for Gavin. Krista and Joshua had been there, but were now gone. Whether they'd escaped or been carried off by the ones who'd made those bizarre tracks outside remained to be seen.

Gavin's shoulders drooped in defeat as he turned to go back down the steps. Upon reaching Derrick Duncan, he grasped the handle of the dirk firmly and drew it out. To his shock, the man gasped, tensing and then falling back against the step. Gavin set the candle down and drew him up by the folds of his robe.

"Derrick!"

The man's eyelids fluttered and the painted lips, stained with a trickle of dried blood, moved. "Cousin . . ." He swallowed and strangled with a weak cough. "Duncan Brae was mine . . ."

"For the love of God, I never wanted the blasted place and Claire was glad to be free of it! You're a crazed, sick man."

Eyes that had closed flew open and hatred fairly leapt out at Gavin, so cold and bitter that he released his hold. "I wasn't always. I wanted to be a part of that damned family, but you and Robert . . . damned arrogant Scots . . ."

"Where's Krista and my son?"

It was difficult to tell if the dying man coughed or laughed. "Lost in this storm. I'm only sorry I didn't return the favor of the knife to her murderous heart. Twice, mind you, she . . . she . . ."

"Where did you last see her?" Gavin demanded, taking the man up again and shaking him roughly to bring him around.

Never had he felt such a sense of helpless rage. He wanted to finish the job his wife had started and yet, Derrick was the only hope he had of finding her. The night was clearing, but that made it no less cold.

"Thrice, she got me," Derrick murmured thickly. "She rendered me a cripple when she blew up the powder with a toss of that blasted torch. Then she made me useless as a man with that knife of hers." He coughed again. "Now . . . it seems, she's killed me."

"Derrick!" Gavin pleaded with the man whose eyes rolled up under closing lids. "Damn you, where are they?"

The waxy lips moved, gurgling breath easing through them. Frantic, Gavin lowered his ear to them in hopes of understanding his cousin's last words. It was all he'd have to go on.

"Dead . . . I hope."

Despair welled deep within Gavin's chest as he shoved away from the dead man, dropping him as if burned by the whispered words. There it boiled and simmered until it could not be contained. With a loud impassioned cry, the Scot vented it as he staggered through the empty room toward the door. He could not hear Kurt Waltari's concerned hail, nor could he see the tall Finn who ran toward him. All he knew was a terrible, tearing anguish which would not give him respite.

As if touching Derrick had contaminated his hands, he began to wash them in the snow, rubbing frantically until Kurt grabbed his shoulders and shook him. "Thor's thunder, man, what is it?"

"It was *him,*" Gavin managed in a choked voice. "It was that sniveling bastard all the while!"

"Pull yourself together, Duncan. I've found Krista's trail."

The mention of his wife's name worked like a balm to Gavin's emotional wounds. "Where?" Steeling himself, he climbed to his feet and ran his hands through his wild uncombed hair. She was alive, he told himself. Fate wouldn't take her from him now, not after all they'd been through. It hadn't taken her in Jamaica and it hadn't taken her now. "Where, man?"

"Leading off to the creek. From the way the other

tracks are spread out, it looks like the horses ran off and the Indians went after them. There's another set leading back, like they'd caught up with them, and then they shoot off again to the northwest."

"Are they givin' the lassie and the bairn chase?"

Kurt shook his head. "Not at the speed they left here. My guess is they're moving to join up with the others. I don't know how my girl did it, but she got away with the boy."

" 'Twas a mother protectin' her young." Gavin motioned for Kurt to precede him. "Show me the trail, man. We've a moon and I'll follow it to my dying breath before I'll stop this night."

While the moonlight and the snow made their task easier, in places that were shaded by the branches of the tall trees overhead, they still had to resort to using a lamp confiscated from the cabin and follow the trail on foot until it disappeared completely at the running creek. Once again, they relied on Kurt Waltari's instinct and headed north.

"I know my girl. We talked about this sort of trick many times," he'd explained, his pride coming through in his tone.

Gavin could only hope and pray. He wouldn't think of Krista and Joshua huddled in the cover of a fallen tree in this cold. Instead, he adapted her uncle's outlook, for his own sanity, if for no other reason. Twice she'd escaped death at Derrick's hand. Who was to say, except a bitter dying man, that she'd not done it a third time? She was a survivor. She'd always been. It was instinctive, even after her years of living in London's luxury, with a harp to replace her hunting knife and musket.

"Ah ha! Ja, they are here, just like I thought!"

Rushing to where Kurt Waltari squatted, Gavin peered down at the footprints emerging from the creek. They were a single set. "There's only one pair. How do you know it was Krista and the boy?"

"No mama would put her baby in the water. You just follow these and soon you will see two sets of footprints— hers and the boy's."

Gavin found it difficult to breathe normally as they followed the clear set of tracks which broke into two sets, exactly as the experienced trapper had predicted. He practically ran ahead of his companion, his sharp eyes picking up the trail easily where the forest thinned on the incline of the hill. At the crest, however, they stopped. It was evident the girl had taken a spill and rolled a good distance downhill.

Kurt Waltari came up behind Gavin as he examined the place where Krista had fallen. "Someone has found her. See there," he pointed off toward the southwest. "The moccasin prints are deeper, bearing the weight of two with the smaller ones beside them."

Gavin scanned the sight for any sign of blood, any reason for Krista's fall, but to no avail. Accepting whatever happened, he pressed on, catching up with Kurt Waltari, who now pursued the tracks with a determined vengeance. Although his companion did not voice his sudden concern over the latest discovery, Gavin sensed it. He too thought Krista was injured, as well as in the hands of an Indian. Whether friendly or nay, remained to be seen. What was heartening was that there was no sign that Joshua had struggled. His prints had fallen in beside the savage's, innocent as the snow that encrusted them.

There comes a point on a march when the body becomes numb to the discomforts as well as thought. It just keeps on going, eating on the run, stopping only when nature demanded. Cold and exhausted, the two men pressed on until the tracks circled around a bluff cut by nature out of the hill they were descending. Gavin flexed his booted feet back and forth in the stirrups of his saddle. Since the trees had thinned, they'd been able to follow the trail on horseback again, but when his companion dismounted, so did Gavin.

"Look down there," Waltari pointed out. "The tracks lead around and back toward the bluff. My guess is, there's a cave in there or some kinda sim'lar shelter."

Gavin nodded and sniffed, catching a whiff of woodsmoke. He willed his heart to remain calm. He wasn't sure he could stand any further torment. Just let his wife and son be safe, he fervently pleaded, his eyes closed momentarily.

"I'll slip around one side," he spoke up suddenly. "You take the other. I'll lure them out."

Gavin waited until his companion disappeared over what looked like the cave entrance. A fresh burst of adrenaline seeped through his sinewy body as he straightened to his full height and pulled back the hammer on his rifle. Taking a deep breath, he lifted his head to the star-studded sky and began to sing from deep within his chest. Half wail and half melody, his ancestral war song echoed through the trees as he marched around to the opening, which was faintly illuminated by firelight. Keeping close enough to cover, lest an enemy come charging out, he watched for any sign of reaction.

He'd begun to wonder if the people inside were deaf, when a childish version of the same chant answered him. A blade wedged in his throat, preventing any more notes from escaping, as the small singer charged out of the cave, making straight for him.

"Papa! I knew you'd come! Mama and I have had the greatest adventure—"

Gavin grabbed the child up in his arms and swung him around. "Have ye now? And where is your mama?"

"She remembers, Papa. She outsmarted ole Simon Girty and that man-woman and threw my knife right at him."

"Girty!" Kurt Waltari exclaimed, coming up behind them. "This has the looks of one of his tricks."

"She's told me all about how you and her . . . she," Joshua corrected before continuing with the same breath. "How you got married! You were a greenhorn, Papa," the boy chided, smug about his discovery. "But even after you tricked her into staying with the old woman who took me from her when I was born, she loved you anyway."

Gavin's heart ceased its plummeting descent at the mention of the return of Krista's memory. Perhaps he hadn't heard right. "She *what?*"

"She loved you right good anyway." Krista stood in the opening, swathed in blankets and leaning on the arm of a robed Indian. "Even if she didn't trust you, she never stopped loving you."

With Joshua balanced on one arm, Gavin closed the distance between him and the girl. She went willingly into the circle of the free one, accepting the kiss he planted tenderly, gratefully, and lovingly on her lips. "And I never stopped lovin' ye, lassie," he confessed, his voice taut with emotion. "I've regretted what happened since the day it was done, but I did it to protect ye. I didn't know . . ."

"I know that now, husband." Krista blinked the tears of joy from her eyes. Love had driven them apart and brought them back together . . . with the help of their Indian friend. "Thanks to Red Deer."

For a moment, Gavin had completely forgotten the Indian who now spoke to Kurt Waltari in low tones, affording the family their privacy. "Red Deer?" As the fur-robed man turned toward him, Gavin caught a glimpse of his familiar scarred face in the moonlight.

"Your woman once saved my life, Scot man. It is good that I am at last able to repay my debt to He Who Glides Over Mountains."

"How did you find them?"

"I was hunting when I saw the smoke of chimney. When I climb ridge beyond, I see He Who Glides Over Mountains stumble and roll to bottom. Little Scot man tell me how they escape Girty man, so I bring straight to my camp."

"My feet were nearly frozen," Krista told them. She shuddered. "If not for Red Deer rubbing them back to life . . ."

"Why don't we go inside where it's warm, instead of standing out here freezing in the cold?" Kurt Waltari suggested gruffly. "It's been a damned long twenty-four hours or so."

"Unbearable," Gavin agreed, leading Krista into the cave with his son balanced on his hip. "I could'na bear the thought of losin' ye again, lassie, nor could I bear to keep the truth from ye any longer. 'Tis been hell."

As Gavin settled down in the pile of furs that had served as beds for his wife and child before his arrival, he drew Krista into his lap. Joshua, not to be left out, started to pile into hers, but her Uncle Kurt caught his arm and pulled him aside.

"So tell me about this adventure of yours, boy. That's what braves and Big Knives do around a campfire."

Eyes wide and sparkling with excitement, Joshua plopped down between the Indian and the trapper and launched into his tale. While she tried to listen, Krista only had eyes for the man holding her possessively, as if he feared the world might take her away again. His gaze was fixed on Joshua, who was as adept as any of his Duncan ancestors at boasting, not only of his own feats, but those of his mother as well.

"An' when they set fire to the barn, I was ready to cut their heathen hearts right out, but Mama and the others needed me."

Krista gave a cry of dismay. She had been so caught up

in her own happiness that she'd all but forgotten Mary and Claire . . . and Jean Luc. But before she could tell Gavin what had happened, he covered her lips with his finger.

"Jean Luc and Tull are no doubt back at Duncan Brae with their women right now. 'Twouldn't surprise me at all if we didn't have a weddin' soon. Claire was surely glad to see Jean Luc, even more than he was to find her safe and alive."

Uncertain as to what part of Gavin's news she found hardest to believe, Krista merely stared openmouthed.

Her uncle picked up the story. "That boy was in a way when he caught up with us. We tried to get him to stay at the neighbors and take care of his leg, but he'd have nothing of the kind. *I could not rest until I am certain that the lovely lady from England ees safe from all harm!*" Kurt Waltari quoted in a Finnish imitation of Jean Luc's heavy French accent.

Krista shook with Gavin's laughter as well as her own. They'd all been through an ordeal and yet they had not lost their ability to see humor in even the gravest of circumstances.

"We'll have babies all about, swearing in French, Lenape, and English."

"Not *my* children," Krista corrected her husband, tongue in cheek.

" 'Tis too late, lassie. I fear Joshua has'na had much of a mother's upbringin'."

" 'Tis not Joshua I'm speakin' of," Krista mimicked softly. At Gavin's blank expression, she covered her belly with her hand. " 'Tis the little one I'm carrying."

"Didn't I tell you?" her uncle bellowed, ending with a loud whoop that was puny in comparison to the one that emerged from Gavin's chest.

"By all that's holy, lassie, are ye sure?" the Scot asked,

covering her hand with his own, as if seeking some sort of confirmation.

"Right sure."

"But ye said . . ."

"That's what I was told. It seems that was another lie, husband."

Somewhat perplexed by all that was happening, Joshua crawled over to where Krista and Gavin were talking softly. "Am I going to have a brother, Mama?"

"I don't know, Joshua. It might be a sister."

Gavin laughed at the boy's indignant expression. "Dinna wrinkle your nose at that, Joshua. If ye get a sister this time, we'll try again." He hugged Krista tightly. "By God, we'll fill Duncan Brae with bairns, American clansmen."

"But there's nothing left of Duncan Brae," Krista mused aloud, looking up, suddenly sober, at the man holding her. It was gone, burned to the ground. All her husband had worked so hard for.

Instead of dismay, Gavin's whiskey-hued gaze glowed with the frolicking flames of the campfire, undaunted.

"Ah, but there is, lassie," he contradicted her. "Ye see, Duncan Brae is'na a thing which can be destroyed. 'Tis neither on the bonnie braes of the highlands nor on the banks of the Ohio. Ye canna see it, but ye know it's there in the heart of every man, Scot or Finn, Indian or Englishman. It's light is as bright as the fire ye see there before ye. 'Tis the home of a man, warmed by the flames of his longin' for love and liberty."

Krista met his lips as they descended once more, sharing their warmth and basking in the love they conveyed. The words rang true, spoken from heart to heart. She could feel them, these flames of the soul which had brought them together against all odds, flames that neither war nor time had been able to extinguish. They were eternal, these flames of love and liberty.